The Packhorseman

Fire Ant Books

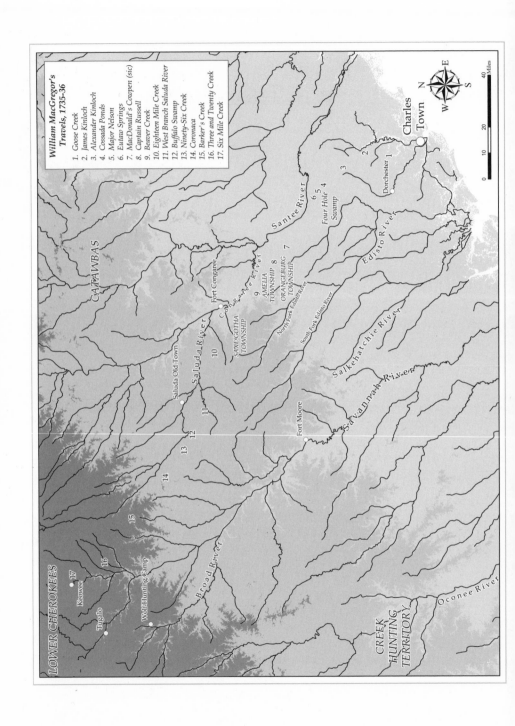

William MacGregor's
Travels, 1735-36

1. Goose Creek
2. James Kinloch
3. Alexander Kinloch
4. Cossada Ponds
5. Major Nelson
6. Eutaw Springs
7. MacDonald's Cowpen (sic)
8. Captain Russell
9. Beaver Creek
10. Eighteen Mile Creek
11. West Branch Saluda River
12. Buffalo Swamp
13. Ninety-Six Creek
14. Coronaca
15. Barker's Creek
16. Three and Twenty Creek
17. Six Mile Creek

The Packhorseman

CHARLES HUDSON

THE UNIVERSITY OF ALABAMA PRESS
Tuscaloosa

Copyright © 2009
The University of Alabama Press
Tuscaloosa, Alabama 35487-0380
All rights reserved
Manufactured in the United States of America

Typeface: ACaslon

∞

The paper on which this book is printed meets the minimum requirements of American
National Standard for Information Sciences-Permanence of Paper for Printed Library
Materials, ANSI Z39.48-1984.

Library of Congress Cataloging-in-Publication Data

Hudson, Charles M.
The packhorseman / Charles Hudson.
p.   cm.
"Fire ant books"
Includes bibliographical references.
ISBN 978-0-8173-5540-1 (pbk. : alk. paper) — ISBN 978-0-8173-8240-7 (electronic)
1. Scots—South Carolina—Fiction. 2. Fur trade—Fiction. 3. Cherokee Indians—Fiction.
4. Indian traders—Fiction. 5. South Carolina—History—Colonial period,
ca. 1600–1775—Fiction. I. Title.
PS3608.U343P33 2009
813'.6—dc22

2008041892

To Charlie and Ann Rebecca

Author's Note

In 1735 the principal town in the British colony of Carolina was Charles Town. Not until 1789, after the American Revolution, did the people of Charles Town change the spelling of its name to Charleston.

[Packhorsemen] are a Sett of bad People not to [be] depended on, a kind of Bandite, the very Refuse of all Provinces, who harbour themselves here from the Laws of the Land.

—Captain Raymond Demere, 1757

It is a hard case for [the Indians] that their first visitors [—packhorse-men—] were a debauched indolent dishonest set, without the fear of man or God and only afraid of labor.

—George Stiggins, c. 1844

Contents

Acknowledgments

This book is much the better for having been read in an early draft by friends and relatives who blessed me with encouragement and criticism: Kathryn Braund, Mary Jo Magee-Brown, Robbie Ethridge, Peggy Galis, Gene Hodges, Jim Hudson, Terry Kay, David Liden, Ron Rhody, and Leah Sullins. It was also read by members of the Folio Club of Athens, Georgia.

I am grateful to a long list of scholars and readers who generously gave me benefit of their specialist knowledge and judgement: Mike Cofer of the South Carolina Historical Society for assistance with early maps; Jenifer Stermer of the Kentucky Horse Park and Sam Getzner for advice on horses, and Heidi Simmonds for her horse Kalin; Theda Perdue for identifying the "Little Charmer" as an eighteenth-century social type on the Southern frontier; Mark Williams for his firsthand knowledge of the Keowee archaeological site and its setting, the troubles of Tugalo, the sound the water made in the ford at Keowee before it was impounded, why the Cherokee trail was situated where it was, and for several factual corrections; Scott Jones for his amazing understanding of primitive technology and the resources of Southern fields and forests, and most particularly for a helpful tutorial on the challenge of collecting bark in winter; and again to Mark and Scott for their fascinating research on the long-term role of the beaver in the ecology of the Southeast and its importance in the early Indian trade; Brett Riggs for his knowledge of Cherokee archaeology and early history and for his thoughts on music; William Jurgelski for giving me benefit of his knowledge of the environmental history of the Southeast as well as his literary insights on how some of the faults of an earlier draft of this novel could be improved; Marvin Smith for advice on the ammunition required by black powder guns; Michael Heitzler, mayor of Goose Creek, for a most informative tour of Goose Creek and vicinity; Nicholas Butler and Art Rosenbaum for advice on early American music; Bettina Somerville and Scott Sikes for a *Scotus americanus* perspective; and Carol Mason and Gregory Waselkov, readers for The University of Alabama Press.

I have had two teachers of fiction writing. One was Hollis Summers at the University of Kentucky in 1958–59, and the second has been Joyce Rockwood Hudson, my live-in chief editor and fiction coach.

I have not been able to take advantage of all the advice and information so freely given. Full responsibility for all that does appear here is mine.

This novel is as true as I could make it to the society, culture, economy, and natural environment of 1730s Carolina. But all of the characters and the events in which they participated are fictional.

The Packhorseman

I   Highland Born

William stood at the rail of the *Cecilia* as she sailed into Charles Town harbor on an April afternoon in 1735. The Carolina sky was as blue as the day God made it. Barely twenty years old, William was medium tall, thick through the neck, shoulders, and chest, with arresting blue eyes and a head of unruly blonde hair. In his boyhood imaginings he had Vikings in his ancestry, but the grimy, cramped quarters and bad food he had endured on the voyage from Glasgow had taught him that the sailor's life was not for him. He could scarcely wait to get his feet on solid ground.

As the vessel approached the wharf, William looked over the heart of Charles Town's commercial quarter as it faced the harbor. Though paltry compared to the city he had left behind, it was here by the wharves that the greatest wealth of the colony was made and lost. He recalled the stories he had heard of Charles Town in the taverns and coffeehouses back in Glasgow, especially the stories about Carolina's early struggles with Spaniards, pirates, and Indians. Squeezed in between two tidal marshes, the town bore the marks of her short history. A large bastion with heavy cannons lay alongside each of the marshes. The two bastions were connected by an imposing brick seawall facing the harbor, and a curtain wall ran inland from the bastion on the left. William guessed that it circled round the town, connecting to the other bastion on the right. Because the town was fortified, space was dear. He could see it in the way the buildings were crowded up close to each other. Most were two or three stories high. A tall steeple rose skyward on the northern side of the town. Church of England, no doubt.

As William leaned on the rail studying the new terrain, a pudgy, red-faced young man appeared at his elbow.

"Well then, William Campbell," said Edward Flowers in the spirit of familiarity that had grown up between them in the short time since Flowers had come aboard at Barbados. "We have reached our destination. I see you have packed your bag and are ready to go."

William did not entirely trust Edward Flowers. His comradery seemed to be based solely on the fact that William was the only other passenger on board who was near his own age. It was clear from Flowers's clothing and speech that he was from a much higher station of life than William's. And Flowers's character was unappealing. He was an inveterate gossip who loved to prattle about the inmost secrets of his friends and acquaintances in Barbados, as if all the foibles and stupidities of the world were theirs, not his. Until now William had been carefully reserved with him. But today the two were parting ways, going out into their separate worlds, and William decided to meet him squarely, lowering his guard.

"Aye, I am more than ready to set foot on this new land," he said, straightening up from the rail to his full height. "And I want ye to be the first to know that the minute I set my foot on Carolina soil I will no longer be William Campbell."

Flowers's eyes widened in surprise. "If you'll not be William Campbell, then who will you be?"

"William MacGregor," he said. "MacGregor is my true clan name and in Carolina I am free to take it back."

"Now this is interesting," Flowers said eagerly, sniffing a secret come to light. "I've heard of the MacGregor trouble in Scotland, but I confess I don't know much about it."

"I will tell ye then," said William, looking at him eye to eye, knowing that this puffball of a man had no awareness of the world he was about to describe. "Our tale goes back over a century, when King James I, of the House of Stuart, pronounced the MacGregors to be a renegade clan. And why was this done? Because we exacted just vengeance on a neighboring clan who had killed two of our men most blatantly and cruelly. For that the king outlawed and condemned us and decreed our very name illegal. Think of it. Our own name could now land us in prison or worse. So what could we do? Different MacGregor families took on whatever surnames they could. My family took on 'Campbell,' even though some of the Campbells were amongst the very ones who hunted down our men with dogs, branded our women with red-hot keys pressed to their cheeks, and confiscated our land, all in the name of the king."

"But that was long ago," said Flowers. "It's ancient history now."

"Not so," said William. "That was not the end of it. After a time things cooled off, to be sure. The proscription was lifted, and we MacGregors got our name back. But then came 1688 and the Glorious Revolution. The Scottish Protestants in the Lowlands joined in that uprising with Protestants in England and frightened King James II and his Catholic retainers into exile in France. So now the Protestants were able to put one of their own—William of Orange—on the throne of England and Scotland."

"And why would the MacGregors object to that?" asked Flowers. "It was the Catholic Stuarts who banned your name. Now they are exiled in France. What could be better?"

"Ah, but it is not so simple as that. Many MacGregors, like many other Highlanders, are Catholic in their sympathies. To them the Protestants were more of a threat to their Highland way of life than were the Catholic Stuarts, never mind their old troubles. So many a MacGregor clansman joined in with other Highlanders to bring a Stuart—James III—back from exile in France to the throne. The Protestants became desperately fearful and suspicious of these actions, and hardly a day went by that some Highlander was not dragged into prison. It became so dangerous to utter the word 'James' that the Catholics began to call their exiled king by his Latin name, 'Jacobus.' And from that came the rebels' present name—Jacobites—still greatly feared in our own day, which makes my tale not ancient history after all."

"That part of the story needs no explanation," said Flowers. "Are you a Jacobite, then? I ask as one whose family has always been solidly on the Protestant side."

"No, I am not a Jacobite, and I will thank ye not to imply that I am."

"Well pardon me, my dear fellow," said an exasperated Flowers. "If your diatribe is about nothing, I fail to see why you have aired it."

"It is not about nothing," William said cooly. "My father was a Jacobite, but that does not make me one. Indeed, it is the very reason I am not. He showed me by example the folly of taking that side. He got caught up in a botched uprising, and he and a great number of his fellows were killed in the battle at Sheriffmuir. That was in 1715, the year of my birth. Because of our clan's role in that uprising, we were yet again persecuted and our name was again proscribed. I was born, made fatherless, and outlawed all in the same year."

"And made a historian, too," Flowers laughed.

"It is no laughing matter," William said curtly. "The minute my foot touches Carolina soil, I intend to be rid of this baggage. I am taking back my own name and keeping it for good."

"Well enough," said Flowers, brushing the whole story aside. "And if that will be your first step on Carolina soil, what will be your second?"

"My second will be to take myself to my uncle Duncan MacGregor's tavern, and from there I will find a way to make a living in Carolina. It's what the Highland Scots have always done. To keep body and soul together, we have to leave kith and kin behind and go wherever opportunity exists in this ever larger world."

Flowers shrugged, and William could see plainly that he had no sympathy for the MacGregors' troubles, nor for the plight of the Highland Scots, nor perhaps for anyone. Along with the bad food and the rolling deck, he would be glad to be rid of Edward Flowers.

As the passengers disembarked from the *Cecilia* onto the wharf, an officious little man recorded their names on a list. Not a one looked back wistfully at the ship they left behind. The *Cecilia* would go on with her business, plying the Atlantic in the tobacco trade, hauling hogsheads of leaf from America to the newly prosperous tobacco lords in Glasgow. On this return voyage to America, she had carried them out of Glasgow on a cold winter's day in February. On her decks and in her bowels they had endured two months of the gray, restless Atlantic before enjoying a brief respite in tropical Barbados. There she had picked up a cargo of rum and a few more passengers, and then came the final sprint that had brought them here to set their feet at last on the sandy soil of coastal Carolina. The *Cecilia* would continue on to the tobacco ports of Virginia and Maryland before completing her round-trip back to Glasgow and the world they had left behind. But William, like the others, did not give her a backward glance.

He tested his sea legs, out of practice with solid ground, and tried not to walk tipsy as if from drinking too much rum. Once he had somewhat gained his footing, he looked around and tried to take in all that surrounded him. He could scarcely believe that he had truly come to live on the other side of the world—and that he had done it by paying his own way, without the necessity of taking on the burden of indenture. Had it not been for the death of his Aunt Callie, he would never have been able to afford the passage. Not only had the good soul taken him into her home during the final years of her life, but when she died, she left him the major portion of her meager estate. After her funeral, William had written a long letter to her brother, Duncan, who lived in Carolina, to tell him of her death. In reply Duncan beseeched his nephew to come to the colonies to seek his fortune. William, to his own surprise, had the means to consider it. His small inheritance was enough to book passage, though with precious little to spare. Now that he was finally here, he would have to find work right away.

First, however, he had to find his uncle's tavern. He looked around to get his bearings, all his senses alert. He watched a small flock of birds foraging near the water, rather like Scottish blackbirds, but larger and more iridescent, making the air ring with a loud *shreet, shreet, shreet.* The newness of the place washed over him. Breathing in deeply, he took in the complex smells of the town. Foremost were the pleasant, pungent odors of the naval stores in crude barrels on the wharves—pitch, tar, and gum from the inland pine forests. But there was a softer, sweeter smell mingled in the moving breeze. He sniffed it out and savored it—the scent of April flowers. Beneath it all was the dank odor of the mud flats that lined the shore, the smell of the sea as it merged with the land.

He watched a gang of black slaves amble by, dressed in worn, drab clothing, singing the same sad songs he had heard earlier in Barbados. They looked to be on their way to offload cargo from the ships or to load on cargo destined to other ports. As their song faded, he became aware of the cries of street vendors hawking food and small items to anyone who would buy. Their singsong cadence was not quite the same as that of the vendors in Glasgow. Then another sound intruded, a dim clatter of hoofbeats growing ever louder, and a jingle of bells becoming audible. He looked around and saw a train of packhorses coming down the street along the bay. It was not like any packtrain he had ever seen in Scotland. The horses, notably sweaty and worn down from a long journey, each carried three packs lashed onto their packsaddle: one to each side and one on top. The train was led by a hard-looking young man in rustic clothing. An Indian, tattooed on his face and upper chest, brought up the rear. He wore a breechcloth to cover his nakedness. A belt tied around his waist held up a pair of leather leggings as well as a hatchet and a knife. The words that were shouted between him and the packhorseman were in a language like nothing William had ever heard before. He had seen Indian slaves on his stopover in Barbados, but in dress and demeanor those were little different from the African slaves. This man was of another sort. There was something in his bearing that reminded William of clansmen from the remotest parts of the Highlands, men tempered hard in the forge of everyday life. He moved confidently as one who had no doubt that he could meet the physical challenges of his world, whatever came his way.

William was fascinated. He stood and watched as the packtrain pulled up in front of a large dry goods store. The two men got down, tethered the string of horses to a rail, stretched their limbs, and then commenced talking in their strange language until the merchant came out. The white packhorseman went inside with the merchant, while the Indian began untying the bundles and piling them up beside the street.

William tore himself away from this scene and hoisted to his shoulder the canvas bag that contained all the possessions he owned in this world. Still walking none too steadily, he began to make his way westward from the bay, the sun in his eyes as he proceeded along the street that ran through the heart of the town. In some ways this was like a town in Scotland, but in other ways not. The houses were built in the European manner, but the trees were different. One tree in particular caught his attention, tall, with large, leathery, oval leaves. And on the ground beneath it William was amused to see a bold, long-tailed bird, pale gray above with a whitish underbelly, dancing a gay little jig as it pranced forward and backward, opening and closing his wings. A gentleman of the town came passing by, making a slight tip of his hat.

"Sir," said William, bowing slightly, "can ye tell me what bird that is?"

"Why, son," said the man, coming to a halt, pushing back his hat, and looking William up and down, "you must be new to this country. That is a mockbird. He knows no song of his own, you see, but mocks the songs of all the other birds. Usually he is a day bird, but sometimes he sings in the dark of night, and when he does it sounds like you have a parliament of birds debating outside your window. This fellow can put a nightingale to shame."

"Thank ye, sir," said William, pleased with the man's genuine friendliness. "I hope to hear that song for myself before long. And now may I trouble ye to tell me where I might find the Packsaddle Tavern. I know it is on King Street, but I don't know which of these streets that might be."

"You are now on Broad Street," said the man. "Continue on and you will come to an old churchyard at the corner of Meeting House Street. Keep west on Broad through the old city gate and the next street will be King. Turn right—that will be to the north—and you will find the Packsaddle about halfway down the block. And good luck to you, young man."

"Thank ye again, sir," said William, making another bow.

As he continued on to Meeting House Street and the old churchyard, he saw what was left of the town wall and moat, which no longer marked the town boundary as it must once have done, for the town was spilling out to the west. William walked on, and before long he reached the corner of King Street and took a right turn. His heart beat a little faster. He noted that he was now walking north, and according to the man's instructions he was almost to his uncle's door. As he looked for the tavern, another packtrain passed by, heading into town with horse-bells clinking and the packhorsemen yelling commands and cracking their long whips, making a spectacle of themselves, happy, evidently, to have reached their destination safely. It appeared that this street was the main thoroughfare to and from the interior.

Turning his attention back from the packtrain, he saw the Packsaddle Tavern suddenly before him, the silhouette of a packhorse artfully painted on the sign that hung out over the sidewalk. William dropped his bag off his shoulder and stood for a moment to collect himself. The tavern was a three-story house, tall and narrow, faced with wide clapboards. It was situated next to the street on the northeastern corner of its lot. As with many houses in this town, its gable end, not its front, faced the street. With two rooms along the south-facing front side, it was only one room wide along the street side. A piazza on the front faced a narrow garden with flowers, herbs, and a few fruit trees, enclosed by a low wicker fence. Between the house and garden a carriage drive led through a work yard with several small outbuildings to the stable. Beyond the stable he could see a large vegetable garden.

William felt encouraged by the substance of the place. It was modest perhaps by Edward Flowers's measure, but rich compared to any of the houses of William's kin in Scotland. And yet, despite this encouragement, his heart was thumping harder than ever. What would it be like to meet Uncle Duncan? His mother had told him that just before Duncan had been arrested and transported to America, he had come to her house bearing a dirk—a memento of William's dead father. That was the last time she had seen him, and William himself was but an infant at the time. He knew Duncan only from the stories of others and from the letters that had come to Scotland from this faraway land. How would he recognize him?

Picking up his bag, William climbed the steps to the piazza. Now he could see a middle-aged, balding man sitting in a chair at the far end, reading a newspaper.

William hesitated a moment and then asked, "Would ye be Duncan MacGregor?"

The man cocked down a corner of his newspaper and peered over it. "I am he. And who might you be?"

"Yesterday I was William Campbell, but today I am William MacGregor."

"Billy Boy? By God!" Duncan rose quickly from his chair and strode over to his nephew, grabbing him hard by his shoulders. "Can this be you? It surely is!

You are a balm for my poor old eyes, the spitting image of your father David, God rest his soul. Mary!" he shouted. "Come see what the cat dragged in!"

William heard a commotion inside the house, and then a small, open-faced woman came out the front door, wiping her hands on a white work-apron. When she saw the young stranger, she hesitated, puzzled.

"It's Billy Boy—Davy's son!" said Duncan. "The bairn I held in my arms so long ago has grown into a young man, and a handsome one, I'll tell you."

A wide smile broke over Mary's face and she hurried forward to embrace him. "Oh Billy, I am so glad to see you. I have heard so much about you from Callie's letters that I feel I already know you." She stood back and looked at him, smiling and shaking her head in wonder. "You were such a joy and a comfort to your aunt. She used to write—more than once, I'll tell you—that Billy is a gentleman in whose breast beats a wild Highland heart. And what a stout mixture that is, she would say." Mary's smile faded. "How sad it was to hear of her passing. I never knew her but through her letters, and yet I felt she was my own sister."

"Yes, I too loved her well," said William. "It was a terrible shock, cut down like that by apoplexy, as if by a bolt of lightning. She fell ill one day and died the next. But her kindness to me continued on. She left me enough to pay my passage, and in a way I feel she is with me still, her hand on my shoulder."

Mary smiled again and nodded, tears sparkling in her eyes.

"Your voyage!" said Duncan. "Tell us about your voyage."

"Och, it was the longest two months I ever spent," said William. "I never realized how attached I am to having solid ground beneath my feet. I still walk as if I expect this very floor to rise up and meet my shoes. And yet our captain said it was a good voyage. And most days, it is true, the weather was fair enough. But there were storms. We ran afoul of one I thought would blow us out of the water." He laughed. "The sailors said it just a little wind and rain."

"Even the sailors prayed in a storm that hit us when I came over," said Duncan. "That entire voyage was like a journey through hell. But I had the added experience of being herded onto ship at gunpoint to be transported, and my accommodations were somewhat below that of a bilge rat."

"Ah, but you both got here safe and sound," said Mary. "And why are we out on the piazza gabbling like so many Guinea fowl? Come inside and have some tea."

She led the way into the house, entering a central hallway with a staircase that led to the upper floors. To the right of the entry was a sitting room, and to the left was a dining room with a long table and several small ones. Duncan guided them into the dining room, and he and William sat down at the end of the long table. Mary went out through another door to get coffee from the kitchen, which was in a separate building behind the house.

"And your mother," said Duncan, "how is Margaret?"

"Och, she was well enough when I went to say farewell to her. But she refuses to budge from the braes and glens of the Trossach Highlands. She still loves most in the world that place where she and my father tended their herd of shaggy cattle. She rents a smallholding where she raises most of her food, but she has to work long hours at a hand loom. Her rent keeps rising, and though I've tried to persuade her, she refuses to see that the clan lairds are ceasing to be protectors of their kinsmen and are ever more becoming money-grubbing landlords. She would die before she would come down to Glasgow, and she thinks little better of Edinburgh. It's a poor life she has there, but when she sets her jaw, it's like arguing with a stone."

"Aye, Margaret is a stubborn one, all right," said Duncan. "But David forgave her that. He himself had such a bold and ungovernable tongue, he could argue the hinges off a door. Your mother had to be stubborn to stand up to him. She was his true match. And after all, who can blame her for loving the Highlands?"

"I'll grant ye that. But the Highlands have no future," said William, "which is why I went down to Glasgow. But I have to admit that I do have great love for that land. I still get homesick for it. I loved the old family life of Clan Gregor. We were still a clan, no matter what names we had to use for ourselves. When the chief called a *chéilidh* for a christening or a wedding, it was true MacGregors that came from far and wide. For me there's ne're been anything like those gatherings since I left the Highlands."

"Well do I remember," said Duncan. "It was the same in my day. We feasted to our heart's content and drank the best whiskey ever made."

"And such talk there was," said William, "such stories of heroes and cattle raids. When the talk ended, we heard tales chanted in meter, and when the tales ended, we heard the music of fiddle, pipes, and drum—and such dancing we did!"

"Aye, I do remember so well," said Duncan. "Is there sweeter company in all God's world than kith and kin?"

They fell quiet, each lost in his memories. As if on cue, Aunt Mary returned with a steaming pot of coffee. She took a plate of freshly cooked rolls out of a pie safe that stood against the wall nearest the kitchen and smeared them with butter and preserves. After two months of ship's fare, William felt he had landed in heaven. He savored the coffee and ate more of the rolls and preserves than he should have done.

Uncle Duncan settled back with his cup of coffee. "The Highlands teach a boy more than hero tales and dancing," he said. "What about the manly arts, Billy? Were you in the hills long enough to learn them?"

"Aye, I am Highland born and Highland raised," William said proudly. "And I thank God for that. My mother boasts it was the Highlands that gave me the rough skills I need to meet life's trials, and I can't deny it. I learned to wrap myself in my plaid and sleep out on the ground in the mists and night frosts. I learned to jog for miles and miles through the high hills. Among my mates I learned how to wrestle a strong man to the ground and to fight with every kind of weapon from the ash singlestick to the sword and dirk. I even learned the bow and arrow. And then, hardest of all, I learned to govern my temper and be polite in my words, for every man around me was as armed to the teeth as I was."

Duncan smiled and nodded approvingly. "A man must be able to protect himself. But there's also a living to make. In the midst of all that fighting, did you learn cattle-droving? Now there's a man's work, if ever there was any."

"I did," said William. "All the ins and outs of it. After a hard winter, with many of our own cattle dead from starvation and cold, I learned how to raid and lift cattle from those whose herd the winter had spared. Such like was no crime in the Highlands."

"That's right," said Duncan. "Cattle are as native to Scotland as red deer are, and the pastures they graze are planted by no man. Lowland law does not agree, but a Highlander knows what's what."

William nodded. "And of course, I learned to protect our own cattle from being lifted. I heard stories told and retold of great cattle raids, and I learned that the greatest duty of a chief is to protect his people's cattle. I came to under-stand that a chief proves himself by leading raids on other herds to keep his own herd strong, while at the same time he makes sure his herd is never weakened by another man's hand. It's not enough to just take some and lose some. You've got to get them and keep them. Those were some of the lessons I learned before the age of sixteen. I grew to manhood there, true enough, and I would not trade anything for those Highland days."

"Nor would I," Duncan said quietly. William saw that his eyes were misty. Again they fell silent. Aunt Mary was sitting back, letting the two of them talk, and did not interrupt the silence.

Finally William reached down into his bag. "Let me show ye something, Uncle Duncan." He felt around for a moment and pulled out a long leather scabbard that held a dagger. He handed it to his uncle, who slowly unsheathed the twelve-inch, spear-point blade and inspected it.

"Do ye recognize it?" asked William.

"Oh God, yes," said Duncan. "It's your father's dirk. The same one I took off his body at Sheriffmuir and carried home to your mother. It brings back to me that terrible day as if it were yesterday. Poor David lying there a-bleeding on the cold ground."

"I have never been told exactly how he was killed," said William. "My mother refused to talk about it."

"She didn't know much about it," said Duncan. "I didn't tell her much. But I was right there when it happened. I saw your father die with my own eyes. I can tell it to you now, if you want to hear it. Twenty years has eased the pain for me."

"Aye, indeed I do," said William. "I've come across an ocean to hear this story."

"Here it is, then," said Duncan, settling back in his chair. "When we Highland Jacobites rose in 1715 against the reign of King George, we meant to claim the throne for our own King James III. That meant taking our fight to the Scottish lords who had thrown in with King George. We marched down from Perth under the command of the Earl of Mar. Bobbing John we called him, for he could never make up his mind. We camped a few miles north of Stirling, which we intended to assault in the first light of the coming morn. It was a bitter cold November night, and when we woke up at dawn our plaids and beards were covered with thick hoar frost. But the Duke of Argyll, who was defending Stirling, surprised us and got the jump on us. Even though we outnumbered him three to one, he did not wait for us to arrive as we expected him to. Instead he took to the field. So as we marched to Stirling that morning, we suddenly found Argyll and his men right there on our left, holding the high ground at Sheriffmuir. After his usual dithering, Bobbing John finally got us into a battle formation, but now we were taking the assault, not giving it. We MacGregors were on the left wing of the formation and were among those who took the worst of it. We stood our ground, though, until Argyll bore down on us with heavy cavalry. The bulk of those great horses was terrifying, I can tell you. It was all we could do to stand and fight. The horsemen would come charging in and we couldn't stop them a whit. They would break through our formation and take a toll on us, thin us down, but then we would form up again and press back. This went on for three hours. Toward the end of it, one of those horsemen came bearing down on Davy. I saw it with my own eyes. Your father did just as he should. He was a skilled fighter, I can tell you. The rider was right-handed, and so Davy darted to the horse's left side and slashed its nose with his broadsword. That made the horse turn away to its right and bear its rider and his sword out of range. But then a second horseman—I can see him still—came out of nowhere and blind-sided poor Davy with a saber cut to the neck. I ran to where he fell, but he was covered in blood and breathing his last. My God, there was so much blood I'll never forget it. Those horsemen were all around us and not enough of us left anymore to fight back. I took Davy's dirk and fled with the others to the River Allen and crossed its icy waters. I cannot tell you how terrible it was to leave my own brother's body behind.

"Once on the other side of the river, we formed up again, and we still outnumbered Argyll. But true to his name, Bobbing John could not make up his mind to give the command to counterattack. We could have done it. We were strong enough and all of us were in a fury from the losses we had suffered. But Bobbing John couldn't see it. He turned tail, and we had to slink back to Perth, burning Lowland villages as we went.

"That was it for me. I slipped away from the army and went home, as did many another Highlander. But we were hardly there any time before the law came after us. I was taken to Glasgow, tried as a traitor, and sentenced to be transported to Carolina. The next thing I knew they were taking me to the harbor and putting me on the *Susannah*. They packed us on that ship like so many slaves from Africa."

Duncan shook his head. "Your father dead and me transported. I tell you, we were fools to fall in with Bobbing John. Young and foolish. Young and foolish."

"Well, that is water under the bridge," said Mary, getting to her feet. "Life goes on, and here we are. Now, Duncan, let's give this boy a chance to settle in." She turned to William. "Did you bring more than that one bag? We can send a man to your ship if there's more."

"Everything I own is right here, Aunt Mary. My clothes, a few books, and some whiskey for me to sip now and then and remember the taste of the Old Country." He reached in and pulled out a tiny keg for her to see.

"I've never seen one so small," she laughed.

"A cooper friend made it for me as a farewell gift," said William. "And my mates filled it with the finest whiskey I've ever tasted."

"Well then, you're all set," said Mary. "Now take your bag and claim one of the beds in the room to your left at the top of the stairs on the next floor."

"I don't want to be beholden to ye," said William. "I do have enough to pay for my lodging, but it will have to be the cheapest bed you have."

"You'll not pay us a farthing, Billy MacGregor. This house is here for you. Blood is blood. You take any bed you want for right now. Though it may well be that when the traders and packhorsemen come here looking for lodging, we'll have to move you to higher and hotter quarters on the top floor."

William was pleased by the kindness, though a bit embarrassed. "I scarce know what to say," he said. "It seems I've crossed the wide ocean and found the same family I left back home. Aunt Mary, you are the dearest woman in the world. But I will only stay here until I can support myself."

He hefted his bag to his shoulder and made his way to the stairs and up to the second floor. The room to which he had been directed contained three beds, a couple of small tables, and a few chairs. Choosing a bed with a well-filled feather tick and clean bedding, he leaned his bag against the wall, loosened his clothing, and lay down to test it for comfort. When was the last time he was on a bed like this? He reached his arms back and rested his head on his hands. Looking up at the ceiling, he tried to imagine all that he had to do in the days ahead. And before he knew it, he was asleep.

William awoke to the ringing of a small bell and the sound of a woman's voice. "Billy! Billy Boy! It's time for supper." For a long moment he had no idea where he was. Then his mind cleared.

"Yes, thank ye, Aunt Mary, I'll be right down."

From the angle of fading sunlight coming in through the windows, he judged it to be about seven o'clock. He rose from his bed, tidied up his clothing, and went downstairs to the dining room. The tables were set, and a few candles were lit. Uncle Duncan sat at his end of the large table and three men sat near him on his right side. Duncan held up his hand. "Come here, Billy—I should say William—we've saved a place for you. Come sit here beside me." He motioned to the chair on his left hand.

As William approached the table, the men stood up.

"William MacGregor," said Duncan, "I'd like you to meet Dr. John Lining, Mr. Robert Allen, and Mr. Isaac Kinloch." Each man nodded to William in turn. "All of these fellows are neighbors. They take their meals with us more often than not."

From their dress William could see that they were middling men, neither rich nor poor. They wore knee-length coats of plain material, and under their coats, though the weather was warm, they wore sleeveless waistcoats, also cut long, embellished with colorful silk floral embroidery.

William put out his hand to each, and then they all sat down, with William across the table from the others. Though their clothing was similar, the men were as different from each other as could be. John Lining, the eldest of the three, was tall and lean. He wore a slightly bemused look that gave William the sense of a man who had thought hard about life and had come to terms with it. Robert Allen was rather fleshy and from his bright eyes and quick smile it was clear that he relished the good life and its pleasures. Isaac Kinloch, who wore a full beard, was the most reserved of the three. He seemed the sort of man who would coolly size up a situation with careful calculation.

Duncan took up a large pitcher and poured mugs of beer all around. The men toasted the King, then Governor Robert Johnson, and finally they toasted each other's health. They had an easy familiarity with each other, and they folded William right in amongst them.

He enjoyed the beer and forgot that he was hungry until Aunt Mary came through the door along with a young black woman and announced, "Supper is served."

The two women carried plates of food, which they placed on the table without ceremony. The fare was cold roast beef and a cold pilau made of cowpeas and Carolina rice—hoppin' John they called it. But what Billy found most pleasing was entirely new to him: thin cornmeal fritters with lacy, brown edges. Cornmeal fritters had not yet made their way to Scotland. Aunt Mary apologized to Billy for the spareness of the meal, explaining that their big meal was served at midday.

"This is all I could possibly eat," William assured her.

"William," said John Lining, as he served himself some beef, "Duncan has told us that you intend to make your fortune with us. How do you propose to do it?"

"I wish I knew the answer to that question," said William. "Tomorrow morning I'll be out on the streets to see if there's a place for me in Charles Town."

"We'll keep our ears open for opportunities," said Robert Allen.

"Thank ye kindly," said William.

For a few moments the men concentrated on their food and drink. Then they began to converse about recent occurrences in their lives, making light inquiries into each other's daily affairs. Clearly they were well acquainted, almost like family. When a lull came in this conversation, Robert Allen turned again to William and asked: "Now tell me, my boy, are you as chauvinistic a Highlander as your uncle is? To hear him tell it, he would be there yet had he not been so summarily dismissed."

"There's more than one way to be driven out of a place," said William. "I love the Highlands and the people there, but I would not advise anyone who wants to earn a living in this day and time to throw in his lot with the Highland way of life. The problem for us, you see, is that most clansmen hold their land not by written title but by *coir a' cleadhaimh.*"

"And what would that be that for those of us who don't speak Gaelic?" asked John Lining.

"It is land taken by the sword and held by right of conquest. In the old days the clansmen did their business by verbal agreement; there was no need for writing or reading. But then the Argyll Campbells got up some strength and began seizing their neighbors' land. At first they threatened simple murder and rape, against which we had some defense, but then they changed their tactics to seizure by means of written documents. They used charters that trumped traditional rights to land. They used piratical mortgages, rigged courts of justice, and, worst of all, government letters of fire and sword. That's how the MacGregors ended up under the heel of greedy overlords. We were slow to learn that in this new day it is only the written word that matters when it comes to land. And once landless, there was no choice but to devise a new way of life, and not one that has endeared them to the King. They have turned, in the main, to plunder and protection money from cattlemen who pay to keep their cattle from being lifted."

"And what lessons have you learned from this?" asked Isaac Kinloch, as he worked at slicing off a piece of beef from the roast. "That sounds to me like a hard school."

"What I have learned," said William, "is that the Highland life is doomed unless the people there learn the ways of the wider world that encroaches upon them. But that makes the Highland way of life twice doomed, because as they learn the ways of the world, they cease to be Highlanders. I came to realize that my only hope was to get some book learning and leave the place behind. It was that or be gobbled up by the Campbell dragon, as so many others around me had been."

"So you have some education?" asked John Lining, who had cleaned his plate and was now leaning back in his chair.

"I went as far in our little school as I could go. It was a high-thinking Pres-

byterian school—a mission school of the Society in Scotland for the Propaga-
tion of Christian Knowledge. They forbade us from speaking Gaelic, so I had
to learn English, and I learned it well. And with that, much that bound me to
the old ways began to fade. My Presbyterian schoolmaster went on about what
devils the Catholics and Church of Scotland men are, and the Catholics and
Church of Scotland men around me went on about what devils the Presbyte-
rians are. All of them could not be right, and I wasn't sure any of them bore
the truth for me. So I let them have their religion and turned elsewhere. I read
every scrap of print I could get my hands on. Newspapers made their way into
the Trossach hills, and I knew that the world was moving forward in Glasgow.
I longed to go there to be part of the new life. It seemed as enthralling to me as
the Highlands were stultifying."

"And what was it, then, that set you in motion?" asked Robert Allen.

"I had an aunt who lived there," said William.

"My sister Callie," said Duncan. "Callie was ten years my elder and was herself somewhat educated. An unusual woman she was, perhaps because she had
no children."

"As a boy I had gone down to visit Aunt Callie several times," said William.
"Being childless as she was, she doted on me as if I were her own son. She took
me out and showed me every part of the city. We would walk to the port and
look at all the ships and marvel at the sailors from many lands. We visited the
shops in the center of the city. She was an avid reader, adored Jonathan Swift,
and took me to lectures, plays, and musical performances. Newspapers and
books were everywhere in Glasgow—a sea of print, it seemed to me. But what
interested me most was Glasgow University. Aunt Callie told me that some of
the best minds in the entire world are to be found within those walls, though
few people realize it. Most assume that all the best scholars are to be found
in London and Paris. After she showed me the university, I would take every
opportunity to hang about outside the place. I watched the students walking
about, going into the taverns and coffeehouses, talking about everything under
the sun. How I wished to be one of them. Yet I knew I might as well wish for
the moon."

"But it's dreams like that that set a young man on his road," said John
Lining.

"Aye, it did seem to chart my course," said William, "though of course I
never reached the university. When I was sixteen Aunt Callie was widowed,
and it was then she asked me to come down and live with her for good. I was
sad to leave my mother but more glad than I can say for a chance at the city.

There was never any question of how I would decide, and my mother knew it. She made no attempt to keep me back. I went down and settled in with Aunt Callie and got a job in the tobacco trade. Perhaps you all know that tobacco is the commerce that now brings so much new wealth to Glasgow. Leaf from the colonies pours into that port, and we processed it into pipe tobacco and snuff. I didn't like the job so much, but I did love the smell of it. I worked in a gang, all of them mates about my age, and we chopped and ground the leaf and blended the different varieties with flavoring—cherry, rum, molasses, vanilla. Every bit of it smelled like heaven. We would end by packing it into kegs and parcels for shipment. And from all the lifting and carrying of thousands of pounds each day, we became as strong as oxen. Sparring and wrestling were our sports. Hard as nails we were."

"But then, what about your book learning?" asked John Lining. "You didn't need it to work tobacco. It would seem that it went to waste."

"No, I am pleased to say that it did not," said William. "We had another life, you see. Some of the lads—sadly not I—were on-and-off students at the university. Their hero was Francis Hutcheson, who lectures not only in Latin, but also in the English he learned at his mother's knee. What a boon for lads like myself! I attended some of his public lectures. He offers them free to anyone who will come—on Sundays, for those who must labor all week."

John Lining's interest increased. "I've read some of Hutcheson's work," he said.

"His mind is a razor," said William. "He leans over his lectern or paces about as he cuts to the heart of the most difficult questions."

"What sort of questions?" asked Robert Allen. "I've never heard of the fellow. I'm not the great reader that John is."

William deferred to John Lining in answering the question, but Lining motioned for William to take it.

"Hutcheson loves to argue that natural laws exist above and beyond the laws of the state," said William, his energy rising with his pleasure in the topic. "Because of this, he argues that men have an inalienable right to freedom of opinion, and this includes the right to resist oppressive rulers. He likes the maxim 'Action is best which produces the greatest happiness of the greatest number.' I can tell ye that he is an exciting lecturer, a fine figure of a man. In the world of ideas he is like a champion fighter in a boxing match. Only the advanced students have the nerve to match wits with him. And he cannot be swayed by the dead weight of tradition—only by the path of reason. He says that the nature of the world and its people is yet to be discovered, that we should not be content to merely accept what the ancients have written. When he talked like that, he would put me to thinking, what is the world really like? How is it that people are so different in its far-flung parts? Are they indeed so different, or do they only seem to be?"

"You can take up your studies right here on the streets of Charles Town," said Robert Allen. "Every kind is here—a veritable Babel."

Isaac Kinloch had begun to stroke his beard, appearing for the first time to be engaged. "So, in a manner of speaking, you did attend the university," he said, seemingly impressed with William's learning.

"Only in a manner of speaking," said William. "But it is true that we did, in our poor way, live a student's life. We factory lads formed a discussion group, after the manner of many of the leading citizens of Glasgow who have formed such groups. We called ourselves the Book Maggot Club, and we met weekly in the taverns and coffeehouses. We read books and talked books, and we argued about everything under the sun. At first I felt like a tongue-tied dolt—I'm from the Highlands, mind ye. But I stayed with the Book Maggots, and in time I found my tongue. I could hold my own, I can say that much. We read Jonathan Swift, Daniel Defoe, Alexander Pope, and a host of others. The truth is, I can't do without reading."

"And that is well and good," said Duncan, looking seriously at his nephew. "Learning is a precious thing—a treasure no man can take from you. But I advise you, Billy, to tread lightly in Charles Town when discussing the ideas of your Francis Hutcheson. You'll find a variety of opinions in this town. Just ask these three gentlemen here their opinion on any subject and you will get at least six different replies. I'm glad to say that all in this company have open minds, but there are those in Charles Town who will take vigorous exception to some of your ideas. You should take a care."

William nodded solemnly, more to appease his uncle than to agree with him.

Then Duncan broke out a bottle of Madeira and poured drams for all.

"To our Highland philosopher," said Isaac Kinloch, raising his glass. As the others followed suit, William bowed his head in acknowledgment, pleased, and a little surprised, to have won their respect. This was the first time he had ever measured himself in the company of established men, and he had held his own.

Soon after this the men took their leave, and Duncan and William retired for the night. When William got to his bed, he took out his little keg of whiskey and drank a small swig, savoring its flavor of sea air and moss, feeling its heat in his mouth and throat. "To the memory of Scotland," he said aloud.

2   The Indian Trade

The sun was well up in the sky when William began to come awake. He was surprised to find himself in a bed that was clean, comfortable, and stationary— no grimy, swaying hammock in the middle of the ocean. Again he had to make an effort to remember where he was—his uncle's tavern. He looked around and found he even had the luxury of no roommates, for a night at least. The three beds in this room were private, the best in the house, their price negotiable and the whole bed purchased for the night. If the tavern filled with lodgers, he would have to give way and take a space in one of the public rooms on the top-most floor, where the price was cheap and fixed by law. In those quarters complete strangers could end up in the same bed with each other, and when the beds overflowed, pallets were pitched on the floor. But for now, at least, he was quartered like a king.

A king with no prospects. The realization washed over him, and he sank further beneath the bed sheet. Though his bladder ached, he lay still, not wanting to get up and actually face the task of finding a place for himself in this new world he had entered. How even to start? All he knew was to walk the streets and look to see what might he might find. Surely one thing would lead to another.

So he rallied and rolled out of bed and pulled on his stockings, securing them with garters tied just below his knees. Then he donned a pair of blue knee-breeches and took from his pack a loose-fitting linen shirt, the one he had saved and kept clean for this occasion. He slipped into his shoes and buckled them. Then he went quickly downstairs and into the work yard behind the house, past a servants' quarters and kitchen to the privy.

Returning from the privy, he came upon a large, muscular African, very black-skinned, with a strongly chiseled face. His dress was worn and frayed, but neat.

"My man," said William, "can ye tell me where I might find a wee bow' o' water to splash on me face?"

Puzzled, the man bowed slightly and said in a strong dialect, "Sah, ah didna catch what you say."

Reminding himself that he was no longer in Glasgow, William bent his tongue to words that could be understood in Carolina. "I'm asking ye where I can find a bowl of water for washing."

"Yes, sah," said the man with another slight bow. "Theysa bucket of watah and a basin the white folks use aside the kitchen. You passed right by it."

Though his words were in English, he spoke with such an odd, musical cadence and strange pronunciation that it took William a moment to sort out his meaning. It gave him a sense of comradery to encounter another man from a far-off land whose English tongue could barely be understood in this place. He held out his hand. "I am William MacGregor, and I am glad to meet ye."

"You must be new ta this land," the man said, making a deep, polite bow to evade the handshake. "They call me Sampson. Ah ovahsee the servants and tend the hosses."

William took note—another lesson in Carolina society. Slaves occupied a position below anything he had seen in Scotland. He had known about slavery in theory, but this was the first time he had experienced it in practice. Handshakes with slaves were unacceptable even when out of the public eye.

He walked on to the kitchen, a squat structure built around a massive brick chimney, trailing a light plume of smoke. Sampson followed behind him. A stout African woman put her head out of the door. Her hair was tied up in a blue kerchief. "Sampson, where you been? Call up Tad and Cuffee to fetch some watah for laundry."

"Now Delilah, you can jus wait. Ah got 'em wuhkin' up the gyahdin for plantin'."

"They can wuhk the gyahdin after fetchin' the watah," said Delilah. "Chloe and Susan be sittin' on they hands and the washin' ain't gettin' done. Missus won't take to that."

"Ah'll see to it directly," said Sampson. As Delilah went back inside, Sampson lowered his voice and said to William, "Delilah a hahd-headed woman." William chuckled. Sampson pointed him ahead around the corner of the kitchen, and they came under a small shed roof, where there was a bucket of water on the ground and a small copper basin on a stand.

"Thas it, sah," said Sampson.

"Thank ye," said William. Sampson gave another of his slight bows, saying nothing, and William noted that he had again transgressed the rules of the social code. One did not thank slaves for what they did.

As Sampson left to go on with his work, William poured a few dippers of water from the bucket into the basin and washed his face and hands. The clean water felt so good he removed his shirt and washed his upper body more thoroughly than he had done during the entire two months of his voyage. Then he poured out the dirty water from the basin and made his way back into the tavern.

Mary was arranging chairs in the dining room. "Well," she said with a warm smile, "Lazarus is risen. We thought you would sleep all day. But we saved some breakfast for you."

"Good morning, Aunt Mary. Thank ye, I could use a wee bit of food."

Mary went to the back door and shouted, "Delilah!" She paused and listened and then called again. "Oh Delilah!" Another pause, and then William heard a curtly polite, "Yes, missus."

"Bring us that breakfast you saved us and a cup of coffee." She closed the door. "Our cook is an angel in the kitchen, but she often treads on the border of impertinence."

"Yes, I saw her earlier with Sampson," said William. "He seems to feel the same."

"Then you've met Sampson," said Mary. "Go to him for any needs you have about the tavern. He is our best help"

"He did seem a fine fellow," said William.

"He keeps the stable, and he never cuts a corner in taking his care of our lodgers' horses. We give him charge of Tad and Cuffee, the ones who do the gardening, draw the water, cut the firewood, all the heavy work. Delilah oversees Chloe and Susan, her daughter. We have six slaves in all."

Just then the back door opened and Delilah came in with a tray of food. She set the dishes before William, barely giving him a nod when their eyes met. She went quickly back outside.

"It's a little late for breakfast, you see," said Mary.

William had before him a cup of steaming coffee and a plate of eggs and bacon, just as in Scotland. But along with it was a bowl of unfamiliar gruel topped with a lump of butter and a scattering of black pepper. "I've never seen this before," he said, poking at it with his spoon.

"Hominy grits," said Mary. "We got that dish from the Indians. It is their staff of life."

"But what is it?"

Mary laughed. "If I tell you, you might not eat it. It is made it by boiling Indian corn in water spiked with wood-ash lye."

William gave her a startled look. "Lye?"

She laughed again. "Don't worry, it has all been rinsed off. The lye causes the grains to swell and slip off their skins. Then they are rinsed—several times, mind you—and pounded in a mortar to a coarse meal and spread out to dry. That gives you hominy meal. It keeps without spoiling, you see, and it cooks up quick. You have only to add it to water and simmer it for a short time. We season ours with butter, but the Indians use bear oil. They have their own names for it. We call it grits."

"It does look a bit like oatmeal grits," said William, taking a little on his spoon and tasting it.

"That's right," said Mary. "Grits are grits, no matter how they're made."

William ate with relish, still feeling pinched from two months of ship's food. For all their soaking in lye, the flavor of the grits was surprisingly bland, though they tasted good enough. He had surely eaten his share of oatmeal grits in Scotland. Many of the students who came to Glasgow for a term at the university arrived with a bag of oatmeal grits over their shoulder, and that was most of what they ate. It seemed that the staples of life were much the same everywhere. It occurred to him that were he ever to end up in Indian country, he would do all right on Indian fare.

Fortified by his breakfast, William took his leave of Aunt Mary and set out to investigate the town. First he walked north on King Street. His plan was to go to the farthest edge of the town and then explore back to the center. He could see that whereas the street along the bay was the town's wholesale center, receiving manufactured goods from England and shipping Carolina commodities out to Atlantic ports, King Street was growing up to be its retail center. Several of the small shops he was now passing catered to the Indian traders, but they also served the people of Charles Town at large, selling practical goods like saddles and bridles and all manner of gear for horses. Many were businesses downstairs and residences upstairs.

He passed by the Quaker meeting house. Quakers, it seemed, had penetrated to all the corners of the earth. The farther north he walked on King Street, the more the houses thinned out and the concentration of animals increased. He passed several stables with large pens attached, which he guessed were for putting up horses from the packtrains. As he went on beyond the town line, he came to a slaughterhouse, where cows, sheep, and pigs were butchered for the meat markets of Charles Town. Close beside it, in a great tree with gnarled, spreading limbs, a number of large, black buzzards perched, ready to swoop down on any carrion. No doubt protected by law for the scavenging service they performed, they showed little fear of the people around them.

Beyond the slaughterhouse, the town gave way to countryside. William turned around and retraced his steps, back past the horse-pens and shops. On this second pass he paid closer attention to the houses and gardens. As he neared the Packsaddle, he passed a garden in which several young women in pretty dresses were caught up in a social gathering. To his eye, they were as fashionably adorned as young women in Glasgow, and they seemed just as far from his reach. Walking on, he passed by the Packsaddle and headed on toward the center of town. He was not far from the tavern when the cheerful sound of a spinet came floating out from the window of a house he was passing. A clear soprano voice picked up the spinet's tune, and he recognized the song from John Gay's *The Beggar's Opera*. He stopped still and listened. It took him back to Scotland, to the time *The Beggar's Opera* had been the rage in Glasgow and he and his Aunt Callie had attended a recital of its songs. Of course, *The Beggar's Opera* was not a proper opera at all, but a play embroidered with engaging songs set to popular tunes. One of his mates in the Book Maggot Club would sometimes sing this very song on their tavern rounds, if they could get enough ale in him to loosen him up. But his rough tenor voice was nothing compared to this sweet sound drifting out into the warm spring air.

If the heart of a man is depressed with cares,
The mist is dispelled when a woman appears;
Like the notes of a fiddle, she sweetly, sweetly
Raises the spirits, and charms our ears.
  Roses and lilies her cheeks disclose,
  But her ripe lips are more sweet than those.
    Press her,
    Caress her
    With blisses,
    Her kisses
Dissolve us in pleasure, and soft repose.

Though the languid song made him think of Glasgow, the lush voice made him think of the young woman who was doing the singing. But as the verse ended, he tore himself away and moved on, not wanting to make a spectacle of himself by lingering too long.

He soon came to the corner of King and Broad, and there he stopped for a moment to admire the fine house on which hung the sign of John Lining, the doctor he had met last night in the Packsaddle. It would seem from the look of his home that Lining was a more substantial man in the town than his middling style of clothing and his choice of dinner company would suggest. From Lining's house William turned east on Broad Street and began walking slowly past its many stores. He entered several to examine their wares and chat with their merchants, trying to get a sense of the town's business and of any openings there might be for work. He lingered longest in John Beswicke's store, admiring his selection of cutlery—knives of several descriptions, axes, hatchets, saws, shears, and such. Much of it had been manufactured in Sheffield, but some of the simple tools appeared to have been made by local blacksmiths and artisans. William loved the look and feel of a well-wrought piece of steel. He picked up and felt the heft of several knives, mindful that he was in need of one with less blade than his father's dirk, something more suitable for butchering and kitchen duty, and even self-defense should the need arise. He found one he liked with a six-inch blade, a high tang, and a horn handle.

"Sir, you can't go wrong on that knife," said Beswicke. "It was made right here in Charles Town by our cutlerer James De Vaux. You'll not find better steel. And that handle will take rough usage and wet weather. It's deer horn, as you can see."

"I quite like it," said William, "but I don't need a knife right now." He did not want to seem too eager a customer.

"If I may say so, sir, I believe that knife is for you," said Beswicke. "I can tell by the way you handle it, as if it were made to your order. It is a bargain at 3 shillings. If you wish to buy it, I will throw in a leather sheath and a Spanish whetstone."

William inspected the knife more closely. "Sold, then" he said, closing his hand tightly around the handle, pleased with the feel of the smooth, well-shaped horn. He took his money pouch from his pocket and paid the man from his small, ever dwindling treasure. He put the small whetstone in his pocket and tucked the sheathed knife into the waistband of his pants.

Upon taking his leave of Beswicke's, he spotted a sign adorned with a painting of a tobacco plant—McKenzie's Dry Goods. He made straight for it, passing by several other establishments. As he walked inside, he inhaled deeply, savoring the warm, exotic aroma of the many kinds of flavored tobacco offered for sale. He could see at a glance that the merchandise in this place would appeal to any taste, any pocketbook: tight twists of tobacco for those who chewed it, several aromatic blends for pipes, and a variety of snuffs for those who liked their tobacco at maximum strength, a pinch at a time. Behind the counter were white long-stemmed pipes and a wide variety of snuff boxes, ranging from cheap tins to fine silver. There were other goods in the place, but it was the tobacco that drew him.

A tall man with a graying shock of red hair and a neatly trimmed beard approached him. "May I help you, young man."

"Thank ye, no," said William. "I do not myself use tobacco, but I do love the smell of it. I worked several years for the Dunlops in the tobacco trade in Glasgow."

"Did you, now?" the man said. "Most of the tobacco I sell here comes from Glasgow. You might call it well traveled. It goes from America to Glasgow and back again."

William nodded. "I saw millions of pounds of leaf shipped up the Firth of Clyde each year and millions of pounds of processed tobacco shipped out again. But I thought all of it went from us to England and the continent. I didn't know any of it came back to the country that grows it."

"Perhaps your hand mixed some of this very stock," said the man, whom William took to be the proprietor. "Look about at your leisure. Are you new then from Glasgow?"

"Sir, I am very new," said William. "This is my first full day here, and I am looking for work. Allow me to introduce myself. I am William MacGregor."

"Well, Mr. MacGregor, I am John McKenzie, and I might be able to do you some good. It would seem that providence has brought you through my door. My clerk has just quit on me, and I need to hire another. Can you read and write?"

"By all means. I have read Jonathan Swift, Alexander Pope, Daniel Defoe, a fair sample of Shakespeare."

McKenzie laughed. "Well enough. And I trust that you are also good at numbers?"

"Yes sir. I can add, subtract, multiply, and divide."

"Suppose you sold a customer a fine snuff box for seventeen shillings," said McKenzie, "and a large parcel of snuff for two shillings, two pence, and a pipe for ten pence—how much would you want in pay?"

William thought for a minute and said, "One pound would just do it."

"Very good, then. And who can vouch for you?"

"My uncle, Duncan MacGregor, at the Packsaddle Tavern. I can get a letter from him or you can pay him a visit and talk to him directly."

"Oh, yes, I know Duncan," said McKenzie, nodding approvingly. "A good fellow. So he's your uncle? Thank you, Mr. MacGregor. That is all I need to know for now. If I require your services, you will hear of it from Duncan."

William returned to the Packsaddle where he found Duncan reading the latest issue of the *South Carolina Gazette*. He seemed glad to see William as he put the paper aside.

"Well, Billy, how do you find Charles Town on this beautiful day?"

"More than beautiful," said William, taking a seat beside him. "It is a day to make everyone sing his best song. And to make it even better, I may have the prospect of work. If I do, you will hear about it before I do. I was interviewed by John McKenzie about a clerk's position in his store. If I pass muster, he said he would speak to ye about me."

"Very good," said Duncan, nodding with approval. "I know him well, and if he comes to me I will speak your praises."

"Clerking in a dry goods store is not the adventure I have come to Carolina to seek," said William, "but it will do for the time being. What I want to find, though, is work that will allow me to better myself. Have ye any advice? How is money to be made in these parts?"

"I can tell you that Charles Town is fast on the rise," said Duncan. "Many men have already made fortunes here. Some of them stay on for good and others go back to England and Scotland with gold in their pockets. Not that it is easy, mind you, but there are opportunities enough for a man who can make his way. There's many a day you'll see several dozen ships riding at anchor in the harbor, and I am not counting the scores of periaguas and trading boats that come down from the inland waterways. For the past ten years the growing of rice has been much on the rise. And in the backcountry there's long been opportunities in raising cattle."

"Now there's a possibility," said William. "I do know how to herd and tend to cattle. But on the other hand, I fled the Highlands to escape stepping in cow pies. And the same with the tobacco trade. I've just crossed an ocean to escape that, though if I get on at McKenzie's, I'll be back in it, at the retail end this time. But clerking is not my dream. In truth, I don't know what my dream is. I can hold my own talking bookish ideas in taverns and coffee shops, but no one would pay me to do that. I haven't the knowledge nor the wealth to plant rice. So I don't know what I can do that would please me. Unless it might be to take up with those packhorse trains I've been seeing. They come from a long distance, I judge. There must be money to be made in whatever it is they are carrying."

"There is," said Duncan. "Those boys are bringing in this season's beaver pelts and deerskins from the Indian country. The ones you've seen are the early birds. The town will soon be full of traders and their horses, and in just a few days this tavern will fill up to the rafters. It's true that many a young man coming to Carolina enters that trade. I did so myself when I first arrived here. Back in those days the Indian trade was the greatest enterprise in the colony, though it didn't seem so at the time I got off the ship."

"Why not?" asked William.

"Well, that was in 1716, just at the end of the Yamasee uprising—a great Indian revolt against Carolina. The Indians slaughtered traders all around the backcountry, and many a settler too. It was a sorrowful time. It was all but over by the time I got here—our militia had put it down. But the Indians were still bloody-minded and vengeful. Some of us who had been transported were assigned the miserable task of occupying the western border country that lay between our settlements on one side and the Indians and the Spaniards on the other side. As the colony's first line of defense, we were expendable. But thank God I lived through it. In the years following the uprising, the trade sprang back to life larger than ever. Leather merchants in London were willing to pay dear, and the Indians were willing to sell cheap, so there was a lot of money to be made in the middle. I worked my way into the trade and stayed at it until I had put aside enough money to get out of that and into another line of work."

"Is that when you bought the tavern?" asked William.

"In a way, but not exactly," said Duncan. "You see, in my days as an Indian trader, I often lodged here at the Packsaddle when I came into Charles Town to buy and sell. That is how I met Mary. Her father was the proprietor of this place. When he died he left everything to her—the Packsaddle is licensed in her name to this day. And he was right to trust her so. Mary was a close student of her father's business. Everything I know about the tavern trade—and there is a lot to know—I learned from her. This town bristles with taverns, boarding-houses, and grog shops, I can tell you. King Street has close to a dozen, catering in the main to travelers who come down from the backcountry. Down by the bay there are more than twice that number catering to the maritime trade. But I'll vow that there are few taverns in Charles Town that are as well run as this one is. Mary and I made a good marriage. The stake I gained from the Indian trade has allowed us to keep this place up like a proper tavern should be kept."

"I like the sound of this," said William. "Is there still money to be made in the Indian trade?"

"There is, but only if you can get in and out of it with your skin intact. It's a dangerous business, Billy. And I'll tell you why. The Indian trade, you see, is bound together by credit. London leather merchants ship goods on credit to the merchants on the harbor front—those establishments you saw when you came off ship. The merchants pass this merchandise—guns, powder, shot, hatchets, knives, cloth, and so on—they pass this to the traders on the promise of future payment. The traders then dole these goods out to the Indians in advance of payment in beaver pelts and dressed deerskins. The Indians then have to go into the woods to kill and skin the beaver and deer, and their women process the hides. If the Indians can manage to kill enough deer and beaver in a season, they can repay their debts to the trader, and then everybody else gets paid. But if the Indians come up short, if they can't find the animals, they stay in debt, and everybody along the chain of credit is pinched. And if the Indian hunters are so unlucky as to have several bad years in a row, that debt can mount up all along the line. Then the traders get pressed by the storekeepers and merchants, and they turn around and raise the pressure on the Indians. But the Indians can reach a limit on how much they can be pressed. If their debt mounts up too high, they are tempted to use their war clubs to cancel their accounts with their traders. This was one of the main causes of the Yamasee Uprising, you see."

"But that was twenty years ago," said William. "Have there been other revolts since?"

"Not another so widespread as that one, but the danger still lurks. It's there every day, and it flares up from time to time without spreading into all-out war, but from the point of view of the trader who gets brained along the way, it might as well have been a war. So when you live in the Indian country, you have to learn the Indians' ways and gain friends and allies among them. When they do pass their limit and strike back, it is especially likely to fall on young traders and packhorsemen, because they are the ones most likely to have miscalculated their actions and given offence. Many a young lad has had as his last lesson in this life that the Indians never forget an injury. They are masters at concealing dark motives."

"And yet you survived," said William. "You made money."

"I did, but in the end I felt the danger so keenly I could not sleep properly. I would jump at the slightest alarm. My health suffered. Believe me, my boy, it is a dangerous occupation for a young man. If I were you I would get on at John McKenzie's store, if you can. You will earn less, but you will meet the men of the town and learn what is what in Charles Town. In time you will find your opportunities."

Mary had come in quietly and taken a seat nearby while the two men talked.

Now she spoke up. "Not all the dangers are in the Indian country," she said darkly.

"Now, Mary," said Duncan, "don't go scaring the lad."

"It's true," said Mary. "He needs to hear it. Charles Town has its own dangers, especially in hot wet weather. That is when people come down with fevers—ague and Barbados fever especially—not to mention the bloody flux which can cut you off at any time of the year. The fevers come from the air that rises from the swamps around here, and they take their toll. That's one good thing about the higher land in the backcountry. There's not the fever that there is down here."

"You'll soon have him on his way," Duncan grumbled.

"I'm only giving him the whole story," said Mary. "I've lived in this town all my life. I know what is good about it and I know what is bad. And I'll tell you this as well, Billy. Some of the so-called lords and ladies of this town create more misery for us than the fevers do, especially if you run afoul of them. I will name no names, but they are mostly the original settlers who came here from Barbados and the West Indies. They are plantation people who have learned how to prosper from using slaves most harshly. That cruelty to some encourages them to cruelty to all. If you should happen to think that you are equal to them, they will set you straight in an instant. And if you offend them, they can hurt you in more ways than you can imagine."

"You speak as one who has tasted it," said William.

"Indeed I have," said Mary. "But that's so much history now. I've made my peace with it. I'm just saying that Duncan is right. There's trouble to be found in the Indian country. But there's trouble in this town as well. It doesn't do to be afraid of living, Billy. A young man has to follow whatever path he finds. Now," she said, slapping her hands on her knees and rising to her feet, "I'm going to the kitchen to see how Delilah is coming with that soup. We have Sam Long and his boys to feed tonight. Her turtle soup is their favorite."

As Mary left the piazza, William looked doubtfully at his uncle. "Turtle soup?"

"Of all the food God put on this earth," said Duncan, "Delilah's turtle soup is the very best. Just wait until supper tonight and you will see."

When William entered the dining room, the three men from the previous evening were there—John Lining, Robert Allen, and Isaac Kinloch—seated in their same places at the main table. They greeted William as "our philosopher in residence." Sitting at one of the small tables on the other side of the room were three deeply tanned, rough-looking young men. And back at the main table, seated across from the three Charles Town gentlemen, was a somewhat unkempt older man in a worn hunting shirt, his features rugged and his graying hair done up in a short pigtail. Beside him the seat on Duncan's left was still open. Duncan nodded toward it, and William sat down.

"That handsome dog next to you is Sam Long, " said Duncan. "Fresh from the Cherokee country. Sam's been in the Indian trade since the days I was in it." Then to Sam he said, "This is my nephew, William McGregor. He too is fresh here—from Scotland."

"I'm glad to meet ye," William said to Sam Long, shaking his hand intently. Sam nodded, silent but friendly enough.

"Those boys over there are Sam's packhorsemen," said Duncan. "There's John Coleman sitting nearest to us, and Barnaby Whitford in the middle, and Thomas Farrell."

William got up and walked across the room to the packhorsemen. Each of them rose in turn as William offered his hand. John Coleman was tall and handsome, with an aquiline nose and hazel eyes. He had something of the air of an actor, and William liked him right away. Barnaby Whitford was a shy fellow with a pockmarked face and a deep scar on his lip. His gaze wavered downward as he shook William's hand. But Thomas Farrell, in his turn, looked William boldly in the eyes, as if sizing him up. Farrel was slightly built, but with an aggressive demeanor, like a gamecock.

"I'm glad to meet all of you," said William, though the men themselves seemed not much interested in making a new acquaintance.

At that moment Delilah walked into the room carrying her kettle of soup. Seeing the fare, the men broke out in applause, pleasing Delilah so much she hazarded a brief smile.

Mary followed her in and served up the soup with a pewter ladle.

William tasted it cautiously.

"What say you?" asked Mary, watching him try it out.

"This soup could be served to royalty," said William. "Is it truly made from turtles?"

"It truly is," said Mary. "From sea turtles. But what makes it so good is the seasoning. In food, as in everything else in Carolina, you will find that the substance is British but the flavors are from all the strains that mix together here. Delilah is a master of it. I know the motions she goes through to prepare this soup, but I could not reproduce it. First she cleans and cuts up the turtle in her own particular way, and then she cooks it for hours with a meaty bone of beef. About halfway through she adds a medley of parsley and onions and some spices all her own. I know she sweetens the pot with brown sugar, and just before serving she throws in a generous glass of Madeira."

William was barely listening, and none of the others were listening at all, intent instead on eating the soup, without a care as to how it was made. They emptied their bowls and asked for more, and they would have asked for a third round had not Delilah brought in the second course—a large bowl of hoppin' John. Rice again, William noted—it indeed was a staple here. The feast ended with dessert—a heaping platter of fried pies filled with a paste made of dried peaches and brandy—hot, buttery, and very sweet. After this course, the men at the main table, now filled to the gills, settled back in their chairs and began to trade stories. The packhorsemen hitched their chairs around at their table so they could listen in.

William was anxious to hear from the newcomers, but at first it was only the gentlemen from town who spoke. Finally Duncan took the lead and said, "We've not heard much tonight from brother Long. Let's get us some rum punch in here and see if that won't encourage him to regale us with his latest adventures in the Indian country."

Delilah and one of the serving girls soon appeared with two bowls of punch: a large Delft bowl—big enough for a goose to swim in, said Duncan—for the men at the main table, and a smaller bowl for the packhorsemen's table. The men began passing the bowls around, drinking from them in turn. Some lit pipes and the room was soon filled with pungent smoke. Mary came in and took a seat at the main table at the end opposite Duncan, outside the circle of the punch bowl.

When the bowl came to William, he savored the taste of this Carolina punch, though most of the ingredients, he noted, came from the West Indies—sugar, lime juice, and a large portion of rum. Only the hot water in which it was mixed was Carolina's own.

Sam Long waited for the bowl to come past him twice before he broke his silence. Then he became every bit as loquacious as he had been reserved. "I knew I was going to have an interesting year," said Long, "when a passel of Indians came to my trading house one day and asked me to come with them and kill their grandfather." All the company sat back contentedly, waiting for the tale to unfold. "I have had some strange requests from Cherokees, but this one was more than I could fathom. I thought they were playing a joke on me. But no, they were dead serious. So I took up my musket and followed them.

"Their homestead was on the side of town nearest the woods, and when we got there, I was startled near out of my skin to see a monstrous rattlesnake coiled up in the middle of the yard amongst their houses. God almighty, this was a big one. He was coiled tight as a clock spring, ready to strike anything that came close, his rattle a-buzzing and his tongue a-going in and out." For effect, Long set an elbow on the table, his hand raised in a loose fist, and flicked his finger several times, snake-like.

"The women were all hanging near the doors of their houses, keeping their young ones in check. A pack of dogs circled around the snake, barking their heads off. And that snake just waited, his rattle a-buzz. While I was standing there, taking this in, one of the younger dogs ventured in too close, and the snake struck, almost quicker than the eye could follow. He bit him on the shoulder, and that poor little dog yelped and staggered off, slumping down as he went. In no time he was down completely, dead as a stone.

"The women commenced to yelling, 'Kill him, kill him,' and they were all looking at me. I didn't see why it should be me to do it rather than those fellows who had come to fetch me, but I picked up a stout hickory stick, long enough to give me plenty of room, and walked over to the snake and hit him several smart blows to his head. He struck and thrashed about mightily, but it was no use. He was a dead snake, dead as the dog he had just killed. We stretched him out, and he was eight foot long if he was an inch. A great snake he was. I cut the rattle off his tail and left his body for the dogs to finish."

Long got up from the table, went over to where his hat hung on the wall, took it down, and brought it over to show them. "See here," he said, "this is that very rattle." The rattle was tied to the headband, and the men examined it with great interest as he showed it around the table. They concurred that they had never seen one larger. He gave the hat a shake so they could hear the sound it made.

"This is new to me," said William. "A snake with a rattle on his tail?"

"He has no cousin in the Old Country," said Long. "You have to come to the New World to meet one of these gentlemen. But it's not the rattle you have to worry about. It's his bite that's deadly. A Spaniard I once knew described the rattlesnake this way: he has syringes in his mouth and a castanet on his tail, and when he bites you, you have just time enough to say a Hail Mary before you die."

The room had darkened with the waning light. Mary got up and lit some more candles, brightening up the room.

"Why didn't they kill the snake themselves?" asked Isaac Kinloch.

"I'm glad you asked," said Long. "There is indeed more to my story. All the people in the homestead came crowding around to see the snake, and I began to tease them. I pointed to an old man amongst them, and I said to the others, I thought you wanted me to kill your grandfather. They laughed and said, 'No, no, not that grandfather—the other one, the rattlesnake—he's the grandfather of all the creatures on earth.'

"'He's not my grandfather,' I told them. And they looked at me like they felt sorry for me.

"'He is the grandfather of all,'" they said again.

"Now I took note that while they seemed to regret my ignorance, they were willing to take advantage of it to get that snake sent on to the next world."

"That beats all I ever heard," said Robert Allen, leaning back with a twinkle in his eye. "There were some who called my wife's grandfather a son of a bitch, but they never thought to raise it a notch and call him a rattlesnake."

"It would seem the Cherokees have looked back into the Garden of Eden and taken the serpent for their ancestor instead of Adam," said John Lining.

"I don't know about that," said Long, "but I can tell you that I have never seen one of them kill a rattlesnake." He looked over at the packhorsemen. "Have any of you boys ever seen a Cherokee kill a rattlesnake?"

They all swore they never had.

"Now what I've seen," offered John Coleman, "is that they will go so far as to apologize to a rattlesnake when they suddenly stumble upon one. I've heard it with my own ears. I was with some Cherokee fellows one day when we happened upon a rattler in our path, and I swear I heard one of them say, 'Excuse us, grandfather, we are only passing through.'"

"It gets even stranger," said Long. "On occasion I've heard the Cherokees speak about a kind of snake that I have never seen and never wish to see. You'll not find one of these characters in the Garden of Eden. They call him *uktena.* They'll tell you that he lives up in the high mountains, but then they'll turn right around next thing and tell you that he lives down in the valleys in deep pools of water. And now hear this. In stormy weather, they say, this snake flies about in the heavens. Flies about! Can you think of anything to beat that? This *uktena* creature is huge, they say, as big around as the most ancient tree. He despises people, and even his glance can cause you to fall ill, or even die. And that's not all. He is horned, like a deer, and a crystal of great value and power is said to grow in the center of his forehead. Anyone who gains a crystal from the *uktena* and masters it can see into hidden things in the past and in the future. And they say that the horns that come off of these creatures are powerful charms for attracting deer. I know for a fact that many Cherokee hunters carry around a bit of horn that they swear comes from the head of an *uktena.* And its magic works on women, too. They say a charm of *uktena* horn causes a woman to come to a man in the same way it brings a deer to a hunter."

"Then could I trouble you to bring me a bit of that horn the next time you come into Charles Town," said Isaac Kinloch. "My love life has been blighted for quite a spell, and I need some relief." All the men roared with laughter.

"Well and good," said Long. "I know it sounds far-fetched. I don't know that I believe any of it myself, but then again, I can't say that I don't. I've had Cherokee hunters I've known and trusted for years tell me stories about the *uktena* in the same matter-of-fact way they speak about any ordinary creature."

"What I want to know," said Allen, "is how much rum is getting back to the Cherokee mountains? Those boys are a-seeing snakes, and I mean *snakes*." More laughter.

Long saw that the credulity of his audience had been stretched to its limit. "Everything I've told you I've seen with my own eyes or heard with my own ears. Take it or leave it."

"If I may venture to say so," said William, "the Cherokees are not the first men to believe in the existence of such monsters. The dragon in our nursery tales is much like an *uktena*, and I will warrant that our popish neighbors in Florida can fill your ears with testimony about the dragon killed by St. Michael. Even the high churchmen among us tell that tale, although it seems to me that their Protestant scepticism has now trumped their former popish conviction."

"Young MacGregor talks like a philosopher," said Sam Long. "How many times has the punch bowl been passed to him?" The men laughed.

"I can't deny it," said William. "I confess to a love of philosophy. In the coffee houses in Glasgow we often debated the nature of the red Indians. We had little to go on, I'll grant ye, but we were full of questions. Are they innocents living in nature, with a character as transparent as that of a wild animal? Or are they men the same as we? Some of my mates argued that, on the evidence of some of their customs, they are not only men such as we, but they appear to be descended from ancient Israelites."

In the packhorsemen's circle Thomas Farrell laughed loudly and slapped his hand on the table. "I can straighten you out on some of that, Mr. MacGregor. The Indians ain't red, except where they smear paint on their bodies. They are as innocent as a fox, and if you ever forget that, you will be fox-bit. And most of all, they ain't like any Bible characters I ever heard about, unless it would be the Philistines. But even there, you'd be reaching too high."

William flushed. "Thank ye kindly for that, Mr. Farrell. It's always a pleasure to meet another philosopher."

"It's a shame Thomas never had a chance to join a debating society," said John Coleman. "He goes at a conversation the way a woodsman takes an axe to a tree. Let me step into the breach, here, and turn to another topic. To give William a proper introduction to Charles Town, I'd like to recite a poem."

"By all means," said John Lining. "We would all be improved by a bit of poetry."

"You don't want to encourage him," Sam Long warned.

Coleman took a sip of rum punch and stood up to declaim the poem. "This was written by a ship captain named Martin, an occasional visitor to these shores," he said as he arranged his clothing and struck a mock oratorical pose.

Black and white all mixed together.
Inconstant, strange, unhealthful weather.
Burning heat and chilling cold,
Dangerous to both young and old.
Boisterous winds and heavy rains.
Fevers and rheumatic pains.
Agues plenty, without doubt.
Sores, boils, the prickly heat and gout.
Mosquitoes on the skin make blotches.
Centipedes and large cockroaches.
Frightful creatures in the water,
Porpoises, sharks and alligators.
Houses built on barren land,
No lamps or lights, but streets of sand.
Pleasant walks, if you can find 'em.
Scandalous tongues, if any mind 'em.
The market's dear and little money,
Large potatoes, sweet as honey.
Water bad, past all drinking.
Men and women without thinking.
Everything at a high price
But rum, hominy, and rice.
Many a widow not unwilling.
Many a beau not worth a shilling.
Many a bargain, if you can strike it.
This is Charles Town—how do you like it?

John bowed deeply, with an elaborate flourish of his hand. The men around the main table laughed and applauded.

"It is a marvel," said Isaac Kinloch, "that a poet can say in a few lines what for a scholar would require an entire book."

"That poem is surely a more balanced picture of Charles Town than what you find in the promotional literature," said John Lining. "In that genre you'll never see a word about the fevers, bad weather, scandalous tongues, mosquitoes, centipedes, and alligators."

"Not to mention high prices," said Robert Allen.

"Have another drink of punch, boys," said Duncan. "We have a fine company gathered here. There is room in this tavern for pessimists, poets, and even Scottish philosophers."

William took the ribbing in good humor as the men laughed and drank another round. They continued talking quietly among themselves, and it was past nine o'clock when the gathering broke up.

When the last guest had departed, William picked up one of the candles and made his way upstairs to his bed, still on the second floor, though now he would be sharing the room with Sam Long. Hearing Long's stories of the Indian country had pleased William immensely. He wished he could pass them on to the Book Maggots of Glasgow. What would they think of all this? What would Francis Hutcheson think?

3   Charles Town

Feeling under the weather from the night of drinking and intense conversation, William slept long past sunrise. When at last he entered the dining room for breakfast, the only other lodger still at table was Sam Long.

"Good morning, young MacGregor," said Long. "You're as slow as I am to be up and about this morning. That long ride down from Cherokee country doesn't get any easier for me."

"In my case it was the rum," said William. "I am not used to drinking it so copiously."

Long chuckled. "Carolinians are as devoted to rum as any people on earth. But to give us credit, it's not all for the love of revelry, though that does play its part. But in the main it's the water. You can't trust the water in this town. Get a bad cup of it and you're down with the flux, and you might as well move your bedroll into the privy. People hereabouts swear that if you spike your water with rum, it wards off the flux."

"That is as good a justification for imbibing as I have ever heard," said William, settling in at the table and beginning to fill his plate from the bowl of grits and the platter of eggs and bacon. "Where are your packhorsemen this morning?"

"They scattered last night. They all have places where they can stay when they come to town. John Coleman grew up in Charles Town, and his parents are still living, so he has a home here. And a lively home it is with that mother of his. She's a music teacher, and their house is always filled with song, especially when the father is home. Most times, though, he is off at sea, being a sailor as he is. Those Colemans are good-hearted people. They give Barnaby a bed while he is in town. But now, Thomas, he has a widow woman he keeps company with. When it comes to women, Thomas likes to go from flower to flower."

"I'm sorry they're gone," said William. "I was looking forward to becoming better acquainted with them. John does seem to be quite a good fellow, and I liked his poem. Thomas was a bit prickly, but he had a lot to say. I appreciate a man who will speak up. As for Barnaby, I didn't get much of a take on him. He seemed a good sort, though."

"They are a grand crew all right," said Long, "and each as different as can be. You're right about Thomas. He does have a lot to say, and he is not likely to embroider it with sweetness and light. He came up a loner, orphaned young. Both his mother and his father died aboard ship on their way from England to Pennsylvania. So Thomas came into this land alone. He was just a tad of a boy. A backwoods farmer adopted him and treated him worse than a slave. He grew up hardscrabble, but he learned all the skills of a woodsman. Put him in the woods with an axe and a knife, and he will survive. He was still a lad he when he ran off from that tyrant and stowed away on a ship and came to Charles Town. He worked on the wharves for several years before I hired him. He is the hardest worker I've ever had, and very ambitious. But he can be disagreeable. He doesn't give much quarter."

"I had a taste of that last night," said William. "He seemed to have it in for me, part in jest and part not, it seemed."

"That's just Thomas's way. Now, Barnaby, on the other hand, he's an orphan, too, but he turned out altogether different. Which shows that there's no way of accounting for such things. Barnaby wants nothing more than to please. He will always do more than his part when any work is done, and he will give you the shirt off his back. He doesn't have much to say—but he is an agreeable young fellow, loved by all."

"That leaves John Coleman," said William.

"John is a word merchant, a songster. He plays the fiddle and the recorder and is seldom seen without them. He can come up with a song for any occasion, and if not a song, a poem. He loves to have a good time, but if that was all there was to him, I wouldn't have him with me. What matters to me is that he is no shirker when it comes to work."

"I suppose you've spent long enough with those boys to know them well."

"You don't know the half of it," said Long. "Men show their true colors on that long trail to and from the Cherokees. And the same goes for living up there amongst the Indians. It's another world, and we live more in that one than in this one."

"So how long will ye be here in Charles Town?"

"It's hard to say," said Long. "We all need a break from the Indian country. We're old hands there, but it's a relief to get back here amongst our own kind, where we don't have to calculate so closely the ins and outs of everything we say or do. But in the course of time the hand of nature will come sweeping toward our backsides to send us on our way back up to the high country. The threat of a hurricane, for instance, can send us on our way, though most years the big storms come late, after we are already out of here."

"Needless to say, I have yet to experience a hurricane," said William. "We had none in Scotland."

"Well, they don't strike this place every year, but when they do, they make a mighty impression. There are no words to describe the power of that wind. Roofs are blown off, great oaks are downed, ships are cast up on land, horses and cattle are blown about, and in the worst cases many people are drowned. You should count yourself lucky if you never suffer one."

In truth, William thought it sounded exciting, though he judged it best not to say so. "When do the hurricanes come?" he asked.

"Most times late summer, early fall. Same time as the fevers. But now the fevers, they come every year, and that's what will always get us out of here for sure. It's knowing that ague and Barbados fever are about to come on that sets us to packing our horses."

"So you will be here until late summer?" asked William.

"More like the middle of summer."

"Then we'll have plenty of time for conversation. I would like to hear more stories about the Indian country."

"I'll try to oblige," said Long. He pushed back his chair to get up. "But for now I'd best get on with my business."

Long took his leave, and as he went out the front door of the tavern, he passed Duncan MacGregor coming in. Duncan came directly to the dining room. "Billy, have your ears been burning?"

"Not that I've noticed."

"Well, I have just been talking with John McKenzie, and I gave him a sterling report on your character. He wants to hire you on. You start work with him tomorrow."

"That is good news indeed," William said with a broad smile. "Thank ye, Uncle. You have been more than kind to me."

William borrowed a dressy sleeved waistcoat from his uncle so he could cut an impressive figure for the customers from the start. When he earned enough in wages he intended to obtain one of his own. He found clerking at McKenzie's to be better work than what he had known at the tobacco factory in Glasgow. Though he worked the whole store, selling whatever needed to be sold, he stuck particularly close to the tobacco counter. People from all walks of life came in looking for tobacco, and because it is such a bewitching weed, they came in repeatedly and regularly and needed no persuading to buy again.

Through the sultry weeks of May and June, William spent all his days except Sundays at his job. Duncan had been right to recommend such work as a way to learn about Carolina society. William doled out penny purchases to butchers, woodcutters, tanners, sailors, and stable hands. He particularly liked the mechanic clientele, the men who possessed the age-old skills—coopers, bricklayers, silversmiths, cabinetmakers, shipwrights, blacksmiths, brass founders, shoemakers, tailors. Some of them were readers like himself, and William enjoyed conversing with them.

Occasionally a scion of one of the leading families of Charles Town would come in for a purchase. William began to learn their names and where they came from. From the West Indies: Middleton, Lowndes, Lucas, Perry, Whaley, LaMotte. French Huguenots: Legaré, Manigault, Lauren. From Holland: Vander Horst, Vander Dussen. Spanish Jews: Cohen, Da Costa, Tobias. And among more recent arrivals in the town were many names he recognized as Scottish: Seaman, Deas, Lennox, Michie, Moultrie, Johnson, Kinloch, Pringle. He heard about the planters who were establishing the great rice plantations— Lynch, Horry, Allston, Barnwell, Elliott—but he had not yet met any of them. They were most to be seen after the summer diseases had run their course. The planters' social season, William was told, ran from December to early summer.

Though clerking had its good points, William's heart did not settle into it entirely. Many a morning it was hard to get up and take on another day. What he disliked most were the slow stretches of time when few customers came into the store. Particularly in the middle of the hot summer days the store would go dead, people staying home, out of the heat, most of them napping, he was told. But William had to stand ready and at least look alert, or else busy himself dusting merchandise, which he hated to do. On some days he became so sleepy and bored he would have liked nothing better than to lie down on the hard floor and take a nap himself.

On one such day Edward Flowers came into the store. It was the first time William had seen him since they parted ways at shipside three months back. A slightly built, older man was with him, and both were dressed to the nines. Fops, thought William, finally hitting the word that fit Flowers like a glove. He wondered why he had not thought of it sooner.

William stood up from the stool on which he had been sitting and approached the tobacco counter. "Can I be of help to you gentlemen?"

"William!" Flowers said in surprise, sounding for a moment as if they were still on ship together. But then he made an immediate adjustment in his demeanor, a noticeable distancing. "So this is where you have landed. What have you to say for yourself?"

"Not a lot," said William, feeling vaguely at fault. "I've been staying at my uncle's tavern and working here for John McKenzie."

"A chap must do what he must to live," said Flowers. "Allow me to introduce you to my good friend, Josiah Lucas. Perhaps you recognize the Lucas name. His people came from Barbados in Charles Town's earliest years. Our two families have long been friends, since back in the days of England. And Josiah," he said to his companion, "allow me to introduce you to William Campbell. We were thrown together by circumstance on the *Cecilia.*"

"William MacGregor," William corrected, reaching out to shake Lucas's hand. Lucas barely responded, the clasp of his soft hand so faint that William had the sensation of not shaking it at all.

"Ah, yes," said Flowers, "I forgot. William MacGregor." He looked at Lucas with a cool, private smile. "There's a story there," he added.

"I would be glad to help you gentlemen in any way I can," said William, raising his guard completely and adopting a formal tone of voice.

"We wish to look about," Josiah Lucas said curtly. "If we need your help, we will ask for it."

With this, the two ambled over to a different part of the store. They looked around briefly and then departed without taking their leave of William. Whatever they had come in to purchase, they seemed to have changed their minds.

As the hot weeks of July stretched out and people began wishing for the cool days of fall, the conversation at the Packsaddle turned more and more to the fevers. Rumors were already abroad, though none confirmed, of people in Charles Town down with chills and fever. Questions would swirl as to whether the feared outbreak was ague or Barbados fever. It all depended, William was told, on whether or not one's skin turned yellow. If it did, it meant you had Barbados fever. Quarantine was not necessary for either of these diseases, for they were not contagious. Common wisdom was not in accord on how they were transmitted, though most thought they were caused by miasma—bad air from the wetlands that surrounded Charles Town. This conclusion was based solely on the fact that the residents of the high country rarely came down with those diseases.

As a medical doctor, John Lining was particularly interested in the cause of the fevers, but he was not in full agreement with the majority opinion. "If they are caused by miasma," he said at supper one evening, "why do they not strike us in the cold season? Why not in the spring? We breathe the same miasma in both seasons. And yet, as we say, 'Charles Town is a paradise in spring, but a hospital in fall.' It seems to me that living in the low country is a necessary condition for contracting the fevers, but not a sufficient condition."

"Regardless of the cause, we'll take our mercies where we can get them," said Isaac Kinloch. "Were the fevers a scourge the year around, there would be no Charles Town. Even as it is, we have more deaths than births each year. It is only the steady stream of immigrants that keeps Carolina growing. Of course, there's always more than one way to look at a misfortune. It may be morbid to say so, but it must be admitted that it is disease that keeps Charles Town an open city. Because of it, there is much opportunity here for young men with talent and ambition."

"If they can live long enough to benefit," said Lining. "I dread to see another season come, with all the loss it brings."

"I just hope it is not coming early," said Sam Long. "John Coleman told me yesterday that Barnaby Whitford has fallen ill and taken to his bed. Most likely it's something he ate. He's not the strongest of lads, and he's easily laid low."

"That or bad water," said John Lining. "But I will go and take a look at him, for good measure."

"I was just about to pack up and head for the high country," said Long. "If we've waited too long, I'll be kicking myself. And now we have to lay over even longer and wait for Barnaby to get back on his feet. Surely to God it's not the fever that has him down."

"Likely not," said Lining.

The next day at breakfast Sam Long brought the news. Lining had come to him late in the evening to inform him that Barnaby did indeed have Barbados fever. The poor lad had all the symptoms: chills, high fever, he was passing blood, and his skin was turning yellow. A bad case, Lining said. He might not survive.

As William went about his duties at McKenzie's that day, his mind kept returning to Barnaby, such a quiet and shy fellow, never saying much on those evenings when he would come into the Packsaddle for a meal. And that deep scar on his lip. William wondered how he had gotten it. Who would pick a fight with such a harmless fellow? Perhaps a horse had kicked him.

This train of thought was broken by the unwelcome entrance of Edward

Flowers and Josiah Lucas into the store. They approached William directly, seeming more friendly than they had been on their previous visit.

"William Campbell," said Josiah Lucas, "you are just the person we want to see."

"MacGregor," William reminded him, looking him up and down, thinking to himself that with his curly hair and overly embroidered waistcoat this man could keep up with the silliest fops in Glasgow. "How may I help you?"

"Edward and I have a mind to go camping, and we would like to purchase a bell for our camp. Do you have a good camp bell you could sell us?"

"A camp bell? We have some hawk bells, and small bells for horse harnesses. We have dinner bells. But I'm not sure what ye mean by a camp bell."

William saw a fleeting smile on Flowers's lips, and a flash of anger coursed through him. "Yes, now I understand. Edward has told you the story of my name. Do you want to make something of it, then? And what business would it be of yours?"

"The safety of this town has long been my family's business," said Lucas. "Why would a man change his name from Campbell—a perfectly respectable name—to MacGregor, an outlawed name, a Jacobite name, a name that reeks of plotting and intrigue? We must give a thought as to whether the French have sent you here to spy on us."

William turned from Lucas to glare at Edward Flowers. "It seems you have very little to occupy your time, Mr. Flowers. Can you find nothing better to do than to spread shit over all your acquaintances?"

"Not over all of them," said Flowers with a smile. He seemed to be enjoying himself, like a man out for sport.

William turned back to Lucas. "Were I a spy, I would have kept the name Campbell, now wouldn't I? Not that I need to make a defense, but let me set ye straight on this. My father fought and died in the Jacobite cause, but that does not make the cause my own. When I sailed away from Glasgow, I left Scotland and its history behind me, and I'll not have ye bringing it in here and throwing it in my face. I don't care which side you are on, that fight has nothing more to do with me."

"My dear fellow," said Lucas, "in case you don't know, it is not a bunch of bare-assed, kilted Highlanders that loyal Britons fear. It is the subversive alliance between Jacobites and the French that worries us. That threat reaches all the way to the colonies. We all know that Britain and France are poised for a great struggle over who is to rule this part of the world. *Parlez vous français, my lad?*"

"No, I do not *parlez*. But I have had enough of your dim-witted accusations." William began removing his waistcoat, his blood on the boil. "You've come to the wrong place for your day's entertainment. I invite you, sir, to step outside with me. What is your preference? Fists or cold steel?"

At that moment John McKenzie walked over and inserted himself into the fray, having listened to it all from another part of the store. He bowed slightly to the fops. "Can I be of service to you gentlemen?" he asked calmly.

"Indeed you can," said Lucas. "You can tell me how you can expect the gentlemen of Charles Town to patronize a store that employs a Jacobite pup. Did you not know that this man has thrown off the respectable name of Campbell and taken on the proscribed name of MacGregor? What more need he do to show his true colors?"

"Surely you must know, Mr. Lucas, that even though 'MacGregor' is proscribed in Britain, it is a respectable name in Carolina," said McKenzie. "But I assure you, I will have words with Mr. MacGregor in private about his manner with our customers. I regret the fracas and can assure you that the like will not happen again. I value your patronage to the utmost."

"I'll not return so long as Jacobites are harbored here, nor will any of my acquaintances," said Lucas. He looked at William. "You should not get your hopes up for prospering in Charles Town, Mr. Campbell. You can be assured that we will keep our eyes on you. And you, too, Mr. McKenzie. You Scots are a damned clannish lot, and if we are to think otherwise, let us see it."

"Have a care, Mr. Lucas," McKenzie said soothingly. "The Scots in this town are good citizens. Have you not heard that during King William's reign the ladies complained that Scotsmen plucked Sweet Williams from their flower boxes to put in their lapels to show their solidarity with King William and the Protestants? Their loyalty is beyond question. I understand the heat of politics, but in Charles Town you need have no fear of Jacobites."

"Politics?" scoffed Lucas. "This is beyond politics. Jacobites are traitors. Hanging is too good for them, and I'll patronize no store that employs them." He turned on his heels and headed out the door, Edward Flowers following after him like a faithful dog.

"Och, William," said John McKenzie. "Prick your skin and up jumps a wild Highland boy. You cannot speak the way you did to one of the leading citizens of Charles Town, no matter how reasonable or just your cause. Josiah Lucas has many powerful allies, and he can take a bite out of my business. He will do it, too. There's no turning it around. I've seen all this before. For many of these big men, with nothing better to take up their time, the fear of Jacobites is a worm in the brain. Mere argument is powerless to cure them."

"This is a bad turn, then," said William. "I had best quit this job. I regret it, for I have enjoyed working here. But I can see there is no other way out. I have undone myself in a single moment."

"Aye, and it pains my heart," said McKenzie. "If you will, please give Duncan a full accounting of the whole story. I don't want to lose his friendship."

"That ye won't," said William. "The fault is my own."

"Not all your own," said McKenzie, "but it's you who must bear it."

William climbed the steps to the piazza, where Duncan and Sam Long were sitting side by side, staring out into the garden with sober faces. "You are home early," said Duncan. "Come have a seat. I am afraid we have had bad news."

"So have I," said William, walking over to an empty chair. "What news is yours?"

"Barnaby Whitford died this morning. John Coleman was just here to tell us."

William shook his head. His own ill fortune suddenly seemed less dire. "I am sorry to hear this. It is sad indeed."

"And what is your news?" asked Duncan.

"My news is nothing compared to the news of poor Barnaby. But I was forced to quit my job at McKenzie's. It seems Aunt Mary saw right into my future. I have already collided with the Barbados men. Josiah Lucas and a gossipy little weasel, Edward Flowers—a foppish fellow I met on the *Cecilia*—came into the store today. Lucas accused me of being a Jacobite and a French spy, no less. I invited him to step outside with me. McKenzie intervened and tried to smooth it over, but the fops were of no mind to relent. They said that neither they nor their friends would return to the store so long as I remained there. So there I was of a sudden, a liability to McKenzie's business. There was nothing to do but to quit. And it gets worse. Lucas promised me trouble even beyond this. If he has enough power to make John McKenzie march to his tune, he has enough to keep on buggering me wherever I find employ. So I'm deep in a dung hill now. I might as well be back in Scotland."

"Well now, there may be a way out," said Sam Long. "Can you rig pack-horses?"

Duncan shook his head. "I was afraid that might be in the offing, even without his getting sacked."

Sam gave a deep sigh. "A good man falls, another man appears. Is Providence against us or with us? It's hard to say. But I do know this—as soon as I see to it that Barnaby gets a decent funeral, I will go to James Crockatt and finish my purchase of goods and supplies for the coming year. Then we'll pack up the horses and strike out for the Cherokee country. So I'll ask you again, young MacGregor. Can you rig packhorses?"

"I have never in my life packed a horse as they do here in Carolina," said William, "but I am willing to learn. I would be much obliged if you would give me a chance to get on with you."

"All right then. You and I will go tomorrow to the horse-pen, and we will see whether or not you have the makings of a packhorseman."

4   How to Pack a Horse

Sam Long opened the gate, and William followed him into the dusty horse-pen. To William it looked like half a forest had been cut down to build the stout post-and-rail fence that surrounded this spacious enclosure. With wood so scarce and costly in Scotland, he was astonished at the profligate way Carolinians cut and used it.

"I know I'm going to like this work," he said to Sam. "I'll even be content to have lost my job at McKenzie's if in the end it leads to this one."

"You'd better put on this suit of clothes and wear it for a while before you thank the tailor," said Sam. "The last green packhorseman I hired lasted only half a season in Keowee before he packed up and hightailed it back to Charles Town. He caused me a great deal of trouble."

"You won't have that problem with me," said William. "But what was it that prompted him to run?"

"He got into a situation with the Cherokees. He never could get used to their foreign ways. He had a suspicious turn of mind, and through a misunderstanding he got it into his head that the Cherokees were conspiring against him. Eventually he convinced himself that they were lying in wait for him whenever he went out alone. He thought they were fixed on him, looking for a chance to do him in, and he hurled insults and accusations left and right. The Indians got into such a tangle over him, it took me a good month to straighten everything out."

"I'll steel my mind against such an attitude," said William. "I know I'll sooner master the Indian ways than I will the art of tying up packs like the ones on the horse trains I've seen in Charles Town. Though I'm confident I can learn that, too."

"You may be surprised at how complicated getting on with the Cherokees can be," said Sam. "Loading a train of horses is a damned sight easier. But tell me where we're starting from. What do you know about packing horses?"

"The truth be told, in the Highlands we didn't pack horses anything like what I've seen here. We packed goods in wicker creels slung across the backs of our *garrons*."

"*Garrons?*" asked Sam.

"The tough little ponies they use in the Highlands. Packing them is no harder than packing a picnic basket. And down in Glasgow they seldom transport goods packed on horses. Almost all light loads there are carried on two-wheeled carts."

"Well, Carolina horses ain't *garrons,* and we're not looking at carts or picnic baskets here. Your packhorse education will begin today. This herd of horses you see around you—some thirty-three head—they all belong to me and Thomas. We have them divided up into three strings of eleven, and each packhorseman has charge of a string. Only ten of the horses in each string carry packs; the eleventh is a spare in case a horse comes down lame."

William looked over the herd. The horses were all of a kind: medium in stature, with short ears, short backs, and stocky hips. They were wide between the eyes and had somewhat aquiline noses. Beyond their form, however, they were quite varied in color: bays, blacks, grays, brown chestnuts, roans, and sorrels. "I've never seen this breed except in the pack trains around here," he said.

"People hereabouts call them Chickasaw horses, and they have quite a history, if I have my facts straight. As I understand it, their founding stock was Spanish barbs that were brought into the colony from Jamaica and Florida, and some people say the Indians got hold of some horses from the Spanish territory west of the Mississippi River. The Chickasaw homeland is located at the westernmost end of the trading path from Charles Town—almost at the Mississippi River—but ten or twelve years ago about forty of them moved east to live near Fort Moore on the Savannah River. A hearty breed of packhorses was especially useful in transporting goods to and fro between those parts. That seems to be how the horses got their name, but they're used in the trade everywhere, not just to the Chickasaws."

"So this is a Spanish barb?"

"It is more than a Spanish barb. There's another line of horses that came in. After the Yamassee War there were horses of English stock that came down in packhorse trains from Virginia. The Virginia traders tried to take advantage of the temporary breakup of the Carolina trade, you see. The Spanish and English horses got together in the Indian country and gave us this fine little bastard of a breed. It didn't take long for the Carolina traders to get together and push the Virginia traders out of these parts, but we still have the offspring of their horses to remember them by."

"What is it in their breeding that makes them good for packing?" asked William.

"Everything. These Chickasaw horses are good workers, hard-hooved, and as long-winded as wolves. They're sturdy and sure-footed when it comes to carrying a load, and they can stand up to all hazards of the trail, day after day. And to top it off, they're as good for riding as they are for packing. The best of them have a smooth, single-footed gait that does wonders to ease the aches and pains of a long trail ride. People say they are coon-gaited."

"What is a coon?" asked William.

Sam laughed and shook his head. "Everything starts from scratch with you. A coon is a creature about the size of a big housecat, maybe a little bigger. He has a stripedy tail and a black mask around his eyes like a highwayman. Raccoon is their proper name. They are out from dusk to dawn everywhere around here. You'll catch sight of one before long, and when you do, you'll see what a smooth gait they have. But let's get started here." Sam walked over to a small barn where his rigging and gear were stored. "There is more to learn about packing a horse than you might think. It takes a good month for a man to learn to pack a horse smartly, and it takes a year for him to learn all that he has to know to be a good hand on a packtrain."

William followed him and stood silently watching.

"First I'm going to show you how to lair up the packs together," said Sam. "Each horse carries three packs that weigh from forty to sixty pounds each." He picked up a soiled, well-used deerskin and spread it out on the ground. Then he walked over to a stack of firewood at the edge of the pen, took up an armload, and came back and stacked it in the middle of the deerskin. Squatting beside it, he wrapped the skin around the firewood, folding in each corner precisely, forming a neat pack. Then he took a lair rope—a thirty-foot rope with a small loop in one end—and used this to bind up the pack. First he made a noose by running the rope through its loop, and with this he encircled the pack, holding it together. Then he commenced wrapping the rope around the pack, finally tying the end of the rope in a slip knot. William watched closely, trying to memorize the moves.

"Now you lair up one," said Sam. "Yours and mine will be the side packs, so you must make sure that they weigh the same, else you'll throw the horse off balance."

William spread another deerskin on the ground and placed on it what he judged to be a stack of firewood equivalent in size to what was in Sam's pack. He folded the skin over and around it as Sam had done, and then he took a lair rope and bound the pack together.

"Not bad for a first effort," said Sam. "But notice that when you pick up the packs in your two hands, yours is some lighter than the one I packed. If you was to load your horse with these two packs, he'd be listing sideways in an hour or two, staggering from the uneven weight and likely to hurt himself."

William untied his pack and added another small piece of firewood. He picked up the two packs and tested them for balance. "They feel about right to me now," he said.

Sam picked them up to check. "Yes, this will do," he said and set them down again. "Now pack a third for the top. This one can be of any weight, within reason. We often carry odd-shaped packs on top. Muskets, axes, shovels, and such go up there. The important thing here is to be careful that nothing touches the horse's withers, neck, nor any part of the body. Never forget that for all his strength and toughness, a horse has such tender skin he can feel the smallest fly on his back."

William bundled up the third pack, taking care to be neat and to make it heavier than the other two. He was already working faster than before, and this pack was more neatly got up.

"Good enough," said Sam. "Now the real packing begins." He walked over and bridled one of the horses, a handsome gray. "This fellow here is from Barnaby's string. That'll be yours, if I take you on." Sam led the horse to where the bundles were piled. He let the reins fall to the ground and fastened a leather blinder over the horse's eyes so it could not see. The gray stood stock still.

"You always put on blinders when saddling and packing a horse," he said. "And remember, the horse and the rigging both have to be free of burrs and debris, else your horse will get sores. Once that happens, you've got trouble on your hands. The sores will worsen day by day no matter what you do, unless you switch him out with the spare. But you've only got one spare." Sam took up a curry comb and carefully brushed the horse's back and sides, running his hands over them to feel the smoothness. Then he picked up a saddle pad made from a piece of an old blue duffel blanket, shook it out smartly, and placed it on the horse's back. On this he placed a wooden packsaddle made of two rectangular boards—back boards, he called them—carved out of poplar. The back boards were about two feet long and were shaped to fit smoothly against the curves on either side of the horse's upper back. They were connected at their ends by two V-shaped pieces of wood carved from forked limbs—from hickory trees, Sam noted. With the point of each V pointing upwards, the down-pointing arms were trimmed flat and dovetailed into shallow slots cut into the back boards, and all were pegged securely together. Near the front fork, the back boards on either side had slots cut through them for the strap that cinched the saddle securely to the horse.

"The packsaddle gives you something to tie to," said Sam, "and it also keeps the weight from coming down directly on the horse's spine, where it can cause injury."

Sam cinched the saddle firmly onto the horse. "You want to cinch it tight enough not to slip," he said, "but not so tight as to cause injury." He motioned for William to come over and feel the degree of tension on the cinch. "You have to be watchful. Some horses will suck in a bellyful of air just before you cinch, and then when they let the air out, the saddle will be too loose."

Next Sam affixed a crupper—a broad leather band—to the back of the pack-saddle and around the flanks of the horse, loosely around his rear end. "This keeps the load from shifting forward on the horse as it travels down hill." Then he affixed a breast strap around the horse's chest. "And this keeps the pack from slipping backward when he climbs a hill."

William walked around the horse, studying the gear, pulling on it lightly to get a feel for how tightly or loosely to fasten its different parts.

"Now we can pack," said Sam. He took the two side packs and tied them together with a sling rope and slung the two of them over the packsaddle so that they hung on either side. Then he tied the upper pack snugly on top of them.

"If the three packs are tied correctly," said Sam, "they will stay together for the duration of our journey. You have to be strong enough to heave all of them together on and off the horses."

"After heaving tobacco for the Dunlops every day," said William, "I think I can manage this."

"That's good," said Sam. "Now comes the hardest thing to learn—the half-diamond hitch that holds the three packs onto the horse. An experienced packer can throw a half-diamond hitch by himself, but it is a lot easier when two men do it."

Sam stood on the left side of the horse and William stood on the right side. He took up what he called the lash rope, about fifty feet long and thicker in di-

ameter than the ones he had used in binding the packs. The rope was tied to
one end of a wide lash cinch that had a wooden hook bound tightly to its other
end. This lash cinch ran beneath the horse's belly, with the rope strung out over
the horse and its packs in what developed into an intricate web affixed to the
wooden hook. Sam commenced passing the rope to William, giving him instructions on what he was to do before passing it back. As they went along, Sam
kept tightening and adjusting different parts of the hitch, sometimes using his
knee or his foot for extra leverage. In the end, a crude diamond-shaped rope
pattern lay on and around the top pack, and all the packs were bound to the
horse in a neat web of ropes.

"Do you have it now?" asked Sam.

"I saw it done," said William, "but I wouldn't say I have it. That is an amazing web of ropes."

"Packing a horse is a little like rigging the sails of a ship," said Sam. "It is a
spider's web of knotted ropes. Every one of those ropes has to be in place and
every knot has to be tied just right. After you do it a few times, you'll get the
hang of it. And before long it will become second nature to you. You'll be able
to load and rig a packhorse in five minutes or less."

William nodded, though in truth such speed was hard for him to imagine.

"There is one last step," said Sam. He went into the barn and came back with
a piece of linen cloth that had been treated with oil rendered from animal fat to
make it waterproof. He laid this over the rigging, tying the four corners so that
the whole pack was covered and protected from rain. Finally, he hung a small
brass bell on a strip of leather around the horse's neck. "That there is a packed
horse," he said. "Let's unpack now and see if you can pack a different horse.
You have to be able to pack and unpack quickly, and the only way to learn is to
practice."

The next time through, William repeated the parts of the routine he understood, with Sam tightening up and adjusting where needed. But when it came
to the half-diamond hitch, Sam again had to do most of the rigging. William
unpacked and packed the horse several times more, until he could do all parts
of the process acceptably, though still not perfectly.

"We have a few days before we head out," said Sam. "You should come out
here every day and practice. Each time pack two or three different horses from
Barnaby's string, so that you get to know them and they get to know you." Sam
pointed out which horses were the other ten in the string. "They sure enough
know each other, and each of them knows his or her place in the herd. They are

unhappy when they are separated from their mates, and they all look to their lead mare."

William nodded. It seemed he had the job.

"There's just one more thing you'll have to master," said Sam. He went back into the barn and came back carrying a coiled, braided whip with a wooden handle. "Have you ever handled a cow whip?" He loosed the coil and it fell to the ground. It looked to be at least twelve feet long.

"Drovers use them in the Highlands for taking cattle to market," said William. "I've tried a cow whip a few times, but I never owned one, so I never got much good at it. I've heard it said in Scotland that one mounted drover with a whip can drive a hundred head of cattle or more."

"We use them here for herding cattle," said Sam, "but we also use them to drive packhorses. Mostly the whip stays tied to your saddle. And you seldom sting an animal with it—it's the sound of the cracking that drives him. There are several ways to crack it, but the most common is what you might call the forward crack. On a clear day it makes a sound you can hear a mile away. Watch me, now."

Sam swung the handle to fling the whip forward and back, then forward again as he flicked his wrist to abruptly stop the backward motion on the end of the whip. The whip cracked and came flying forward again. He repeated this several times, cracking the whip loudly. The horses milled nervously around in the pen. "Here. You give it a try," he said, handing it over to William.

William swung the lash gingerly. He could make the backward and forward motion, but when he tried to crack it, the whip struck the ground and made no sound.

"You want to fling it horizontal to the ground," said Sam, "not hit the ground. And you don't want to hit anything solid with the whip, for that will damage it. It doesn't require much strength to crack it—it's all in the timing."

William flung the whip again, flicked his wrist, and the whip cracked weakly. He tried once more, and this time it cracked smartly.

"Now you are getting it," said Sam, reaching out to take it back again. "There are other ways of cracking it, depending on what is around you. You have to be mindful of where your mates are. A whip can cut flesh or put out an eye. A good hand with a cow whip can take the head off of a rattlesnake or kill a rabbit."

Sam swung the whip menacingly around and around over his head, then flicked his wrist, making a loud crack as the whip came flying back. "You could call that one the round-about crack," he said with a chuckle.

He returned the whip to William. "Practice these moves until you have mastered them, and you will be able to talk to your horses in a language they understand. There is a right way to tie every knot you will use, and in time you'll learn how. But the most important thing for you to understand is that you must always treat your packhorses kindly, else they will be balky, and your life will be a misery."

Barnaby Whitford had no relatives in Carolina, so Sam took it upon himself to settle his estate. This was not much of a task, for Barnaby owned very little in this world. He had lived like a sailor, spending no money during the long months in the Indian country and then emptying his pockets on rum and whores when he came into Charles Town. Sam paid the small debts Barnaby owed to John Coleman and Thomas Farrell from the little money that was still in his possession when he died. William bought his horse—Viola, a pretty little sorrel mare. He also bought his musket, hatchet, saddle, saddle bags, whip— most of his gear. As Barnaby had no will drawn up and no living relatives, Sam gave the proceeds of the sale to John Coleman's mother, who had boarded Barnaby without pay for several summers.

William now had all he needed including suitable clothing. He had gone to McKenzie's store and bought himself a black beaver hat with a broad brim and enough linsey-woolsey cloth for Chloe to sew him a hunting shirt. All of the money from his Aunt Callie's bequest was now exhausted, along with most of what he had earned clerking in McKenzie's store. But he felt pleased and confident nonetheless. Though his money be all but gone, he had acquired an occupation in this new land, and he had a fine outfit of gear with which to get started.

5   Jim-Bird

Because he was sharing lodging with Sam Long at the Packsaddle, William gained a degree of familiarity with the Charles Town end of the Indian trade. On and off throughout his stay in Charles Town, Sam had been bargaining with James Crockatt, his main supplier and creditor for the trade goods he packed into Cherokee country, gradually working his way through the list of goods that would be his stock in trade for the coming year. He wanted goods of decent enough quality to keep the Indians satisfied, but he kept a sharp eye to profitability, and he had to bargain hard with Crockatt to keep his costs down. Otherwise, at the end of the season, as he explained to William, he would find that only the Cherokees, his packhorsemen, and his creditors had benefitted from his labors, not himself. He had had a year like that in the past, he said, and he didn't want another one. In the end, he seemed satisfied with most of his negotiations, although there were a few that he had accepted only with grumbling and head shaking and the consolation of an extra round of punch at the Packsaddle.

The day before they were to set out for the backcountry, William went with John Coleman and Thomas Farrell to the horse pen, where the three packhorsemen separated out their strings of horses and bridled them. As they began cinching on the packsaddles, John and Thomas worked quickly, seemingly with no need to think about what they were doing. William did have to think about what he was doing, and by the time the other two had finished their saddling, William, though he had practiced diligently for days, had only saddled five of his horses. John pitched in and helped him finish saddling his remaining five.

"You can help the philosopher if you want to," Thomas said, "but I ain't paid to do nobody's work but my own." He leaned against the rail fence and waited for them.

"Don't pay any attention to Thomas," John said to William. "He's so contrary, if you threw him in a river he'd float upstream. After a few days of packing and unpacking these lovelies, you'll do all right."

With William's horses saddled, they parceled out the deerskins and coiled ropes they would need for bundling up the goods at the warehouse. They tied all these parcels of gear loosely onto the packsaddles, and then each man strung his horses together. William noticed that Thomas had only eight horses in his string. "It looks like you're short two," he said.

"Right you are, philosopher," Thomas replied. "Two of mine don't carry goods from the warehouse. One carries Sam's personal goods—some spirits and such—and the other is for the cook."

"The cook? Who's the cook?" asked William.

"You'll meet him tomorrow," said Thomas. "He don't like to come into town."

The three packhorsemen led the horses out of the pen and into the street. John took the lead string, William took the middle one, and Thomas followed up at the rear. They walked with their train up the sandy road, past the Packsaddle Tavern and into the heart of Charles Town to Crockatt's dry goods store and warehouse on Bay Street. Sam had been waiting for them, and as they tethered the horses out front, he went inside and began checking the merchandise and overseeing its delivery to his packhorsemen outside. The stock clerks carried out the goods, and the packhorsemen wrapped everything into bundles, and then they secured the bundles to each other and to the horses.

The powder, shot, gunflints, and gunlocks went onto John's string of horses, with the guns packed into long bundles and bound up as top packs. William's string carried several riding saddles, bridles, and a variety of small hardware: knives, hatchets, scissors, broad hoes, and brass kettles of several sizes nested together to conserve space. Thomas's string carried cloth and sewing materials bound up in bundles that were notably bulkier than the others. Again, William lagged behind in his work. And again John helped him finish.

With all the train packed, Sam walked along the line of horses, inspecting each of them, tightening and tidying up the rigging where he deemed necessary. When he was satisfied that all were properly packed, the men got the train moving and headed it back to the horse pen. Once there, each packhorseman unpacked his string and stored the bundles of goods inside the barn. John and Thomas settled down at the barn to keep watch over the packs, while Sam and

William returned to the Packsaddle to spend what would be their last night in comfortable quarters for a long while.

Before going to bed, William packed everything he intended to take with him into his saddlebags and the canvas bag that would ride behind his saddle. For something to read, he stuffed in two little duodecimo volumes of Shakespeare. These were from his most prized possession: an eight-volume Shakespeare edited by Alexander Pope and published in 1728. He also packed a bottle of ink and a small ledger in which to keep a journal. The few belongings that were not going with him went into a wooden crate for Aunt Mary to store for his return.

Then, just before putting out the candle, he sat down and wrote a letter to his mother:

July 19, 1735
Packsaddle Tavern
Charles Town
Dearest Mother,

Forgive me for not writing sooner. I have been hard at work trying to find a place for myself in Carolina, and all else, I fear, has been neglected. Uncle Duncan and Aunt Mary have allowed me to stay on at the Packsaddle, and they have continued to show me every courtesy. Had it not been for their generosity, it is difficult to imagine how I should have fared in this surprising New World. Through their good graces, I have already met several people of good stripe whom I shall treasure always.

My employment as a clerk in a dry goods store was brief, though it was long enough to introduce me to many persons in the town, both high and low. I have learned that some of the high are in fact rather low. The New World is not so different from the Old in that regard. The clerk position did not pay well, and I ran into other difficulties through not much fault of my own.

I am just now embarking on a new career as a packhorseman in the Indian trade. It is far more difficult work than clerking, but if all goes well, I shall earn more. Tomorrow we depart from Charles Town, bound for Cherokee country. Chances are you will not hear from me again until next summer, when we return here with a great load of dressed skins. I hope I will be able to send you some money then.
Your loving son,
Billy

After having barely slept, William awoke with the first light of dawn. He got dressed and went downstairs, where Uncle Duncan and Aunt Mary were already preparing for breakfast. As he placed his bags near the door, he heard someone else on the stairs and saw Sam Long coming down with his gear. Sam piled his belongings near William's and followed him into the dining room.

"We knew you boys would want an early start," said Duncan. "We are getting up a hearty breakfast to fortify you. I well remember how famished I used to get the first day out on the trail."

Delilah and Susan came into the room carrying platters of fried eggs, ham, grits, pancakes, and a pot of hot tea. Mary followed after them with a tray loaded with butter and several jars of honey and preserves for the pancakes.

"We are much obliged for such a fine table of food," said Sam. He looked over at William. "Eat hearty, my boy. You won't fare this well again for quite a while."

They ate without saying very much. And then it was time to take their leave. In the hallway Mary drew William into a warm embrace. "Dear, dear Billy," she said. William was afraid she would break into tears, but she managed to hold most of them back. "Take care that you eat well and mind your health. When men get off to themselves, they become so intent on what they are trying to achieve, they neglect themselves."

He kissed her on the cheek. "I will remember what you say, Aunt Mary. I'll take care of myself."

Mary turned away, dabbing at her eyes with a handkerchief. Duncan approached and shook William's hand. "The most important thing to remember in Indian country," Duncan said soberly, "is that it is *their* country. Avoid getting needlessly entangled in their affairs. It can cost you dearly. Believe me, Nephew, I know whereof I speak."

"I will keep my head up, Uncle."

"You'll pass by John MacDonald's cowpen on your way up," said Duncan, striking a lighter note. "Remember me to him. He is a fine fellow. He was transported here in 1716, the same as I, but on a different ship. He came on the *Wakefield*, John did."

"I will give him your greetings," said William, gathering up his gear. He nodded once more to his aunt and uncle and then went out to join Sam on the piazza.

The two had little to say as they hurried down King Street to the horse pen. William was rehearsing to himself the challenges of his new job, and Sam also seemed preoccupied. They stopped in at a store along the way and bought a large bag of rice and small quantities of jerked beef, dried sweet corn, dried beans, dried peaches, salt, tea, coffee, and several sugar loaves.

"These go on the cook's horse," said Sam.

The storekeeper sent a boy along with them to help carry the new provisions to the horse pen.

John and Thomas already had their horses packed and ready to go when Sam and William arrived. William, with Sam helping him, commenced packing his horses, while John and Thomas hurried back to the tavern to wolf down their breakfasts. Finally, Sam and William packed the food and cooking gear onto the cook's horse and two kegs of rum and sundry other items onto Sam's personal horse. They hung bells around the necks of all the horses, with the lead mare having the largest bell. From the distant sound of the lead mare's bell, all of the other horses in the train would know where she was at all times. Sam noted that they could follow her even in a thick fog. The smaller bells on the others were used to locate them when they strayed from the camp during the night. To keep them from making a great racket during the day, the men stuffed grass and leaves into all the bells each morning; only the lead mare's bell was left to ring freely. In the course of a day's exertions, however, the stuffings would gradually fall out, and more and more of the bells would begin clinking again.

The sun was well up in the sky when John and Thomas returned to the horse pen and made ready to head out of town on King Street and the Charles Town Neck Road. They opened the gate to the pen, and Sam rode out in the lead, cracking his long cowhide whip and giving a whoop. "All right, you crackers," he shouted, "let's get on the road!" John and Thomas whooped in reply and cracked their whips, and the train of horses started in motion. William took note. The next time, he would be ready to join in the whip-cracking.

Moving at a constant trot, they traveled along the same wagon road that William had explored on his first full day in Charles Town. Early morning oxcart traffic was coming in and going out of the town. The carts coming in carried naval stores, lumber, firewood, foodstuffs, and other products of the country. The carts going out carried supplies for the plantations. As their own train traveled out, they passed through long-settled country where the woods had been cut back from both sides of the road, harvested in the earliest days to build the first houses and fuel the first fireplaces of Charles Town.

After about an hour, Sam halted the train for the packhorsemen to check the rigging on all the horses. John explained to William that the packs always loosened after first setting out.

"Check them close, boys," said Sam. "There's nothing more damaging to a horse than a loose pack." William assumed this was said for his benefit, since the other two knew it well. This tightening up took only a few minutes and soon the train was in motion again.

Wagon roads led laterally off both sides of the main road they were following. These small roads led to rice plantations, and William, peering down along them, caught glimpses of substantial houses and rice fields, particularly on the right-hand side of the main road. About six miles out of Charles Town the road forked, with the left fork leading to Dorchester and the right fork, which they took, leading to Goose Creek and eventually, long after the wagon road turned into a horse trail, to the Cherokees.

William plied John and Thomas with questions about the new flora and fauna he was seeing. Thomas soon grew sullen and refused to keep answering, but John, who relished any occasion to talk with anybody, soon began volunteering information without waiting for William to inquire. This part of the country they were now in was the coastal plain, John explained, with its flat sandy soil and immense stands of longleaf pines. These pines were up to three feet in diameter at the base and very tall. Nothing much grew beneath them except a tough grass and, here and there, flowers. The trees were rough-barked and limbless for half or more of their height, with long needles and very large pine cones. It was a forest that was park-like—open, airy, and with sunlight dappling the ground below.

Deciduous trees took the low, moist ground. In some places they passed through groves of immense oak trees interspersed with other varieties of trees that John tirelessly called to William's attention, telling him all about the characteristics and uses of each kind: sycamore, shellbark hickory, swamp cottonwood. In moist, open areas, sweet gums grew thickly, with their pretty, star-shaped leaves and fragrant gum. Below the high canopy of deciduous trees were understory trees such as redbud and dogwood, and, in spots of sunlight, fragrant sassafras, from which John pulled a leaf and crushed it for William to smell. The air was pleasant in the shade of the forest canopy, but whenever they came out into the bright sun, it was mercilessly hot. William was sweating, though not so much as Viola, who was bearing her weight and his too.

They endured the blazing sun as they passed through savannahs—natural meadows—where few trees grew and where varieties of flowers bloomed that grew only in the open sunlight. Whenever they came to a stream, they stopped and watered their horses—in this hot weather, the horses drank amazing amounts. Occasionally the road skirted by swamps with stands of black gum, American beech, and magnolias—the leather-leaved trees William had admired in Charles Town, now resplendent with huge, white blossoms, luxuriously scented as if with sugared lemon water. Below the trees were cabbage palmetto and azaleas. The latter, John explained, were brilliant with color when they bloomed in the spring. Most of the space between trees and shrubs was taken by stands of tall river cane interlaced with vines, which John patiently named, pointing out each variety several times over: jasmine, smilax, and orange-flowered trumpet vine. The swampy places were thick with cypress trees, some immensely large. And yet for all the trail they covered that day, and for all the swamps and woods they passed, they were still in the thick of the settlements.

At the end of the day they had covered around fifteen miles, and the sun was sinking low when Sam turned off the road and led them to a camping place on Ralph Izard's plantation. As they approached the well-used clearing along Goose Creek, William saw a man lounging there against a large live-oak tree. Two small terriers, white with black and brown spots, circled around him, barking at the approaching packtrain, nervously wagging their cropped tails. Nearby was a substantial lean-to made of posts and small timbers, roofed with sheets of bark. A large brass kettle hung over a fire, slow-cooking. The man's horse, tethered to a tree, gave a welcoming whinny to the approaching packtrain, and all of the horses in the train perked up their ears and walked a little faster.

"You are about to meet our cook," John said to William. "Jim-Bird is his name, and you ain't never met anybody like him."

The dogs continued running around and barking until Jim-Bird said firmly, "Hush, Tazzie, hush Binkie," and the dogs got quiet. As the train pulled up, the men got off their horses and stretched their limbs.

William, out of shape for riding, was especially sore and stiff from having been in the saddle for so long. But he paid little attention to his aches and pains, fascinated as he was with the cook. He had never seen anyone like him. Jim-Bird looked to be a few years older than himself and was a half a foot taller. And to William's surprise, he appeared to be an Indian—dark skin, straight black hair, prominent cheekbones, and hooded eyes. And yet, on closer inspection, his skin was not so dark as an Indian's nor his eyes so hooded. In fact, if truth be told, on those traits alone he might be a swarthy European, perhaps a

Greek or a Gypsy. But then there was his clothing. He wore a breechcloth, leggings, moccasins, and a paisley hunting shirt. And through his open shirt front, William could see tattooing.

Sam walked over to Jim-Bird and the two of them had a short conversation. When it ended, Jim-Bird tethered his dogs to the lean-to and added some dry wood to his cook fire. Then he took up his musket and walked off into the woods. As he passed by William, he briefly met his eyes, but he made it plain that he was in no hurry to strike up an acquaintance.

"Who is this cook?" William asked Sam when the man had gone out of earshot. "What kind of name is Jim-Bird?"

"His true name is Jim Mockbird. The Indians named him Mockbird because he speaks so many languages. There is honor in that name. Indians believe the mockbird to be the most intelligent of all birds, because of the many songs it sings. And the name fits. I know for a fact that Jim-Bird speaks English, French,"—Sam counted slowly, putting out a finger for each—"Natchez, Chickasaw, and Cherokee. And maybe some others, but those are the ones I know about. We don't use his full name. We just call him Jim-Bird."

"Is he an Indian?" asked William. "He looks like one, but then again he doesn't."

John ambled over and sat down on the log with them. "That's because he is and he ain't," he said.

"He's a half-breed," said Sam. "His mother was a Natchez and his father a Frenchman. His father seems to have fancied him and taught him all sorts of things a Frenchman would know. And of course, he came up speaking the French tongue. But while he was still a boy, his father was killed in a war between the French and the Natchez, and his mother fled with Jim-Bird to the Chickasaws. She took up with an English trader there, and that fellow, too, must have taken an interest in him, for Jim-Bird not only speaks English, he has been trying to learn to read and write it."

"I take it Natchez is a kind of Indian," said William.

"That's right," said Sam. "But not just any kind. Now there's a story, I tell you. The Natchez were mound builders. They held to old, old ways, like nothing you see today amongst the other Indians hereabouts. They had a chief who fancied himself a kind of god, and he lived up on top of a great high mound, four-sided like an Egyptian pyramid, but flat on top. The Natchez didn't last long, though, once the trade came in. They got crosswise with the French and lost everything. Now they are as dispersed as the tribes of Israel. A few of them, like Jim-Bird, are living now in Four Hole Swamp, a ways up to the northwest of here. Others are with the Creeks, Chickasaws, Choctaws, and Cherokees. They're scattered all over."

"Jim-Bird has peculiar ways," John added, "but what he knows about this country and its people would fill a library. He is as curious to know the ways of the world as any man I ever met. I swear, if he had been born to wealth in England, he would be a scholar, and a good one."

William looked at the place where the woods had closed in around this unexpectedly interesting fellow. He wondered whether an Old World scholar-of-sorts could find common ground with a scholar-of-sorts born of the New World.

The packhorsemen took their time as they lifted the bundles off their horses and stacked them neatly under the lean-to. They left the packsaddles and saddle pads on the horses for a while longer.

"You got to let the horses cool down gradually," Sam explained to William. "It ain't good to cool them off too quick." The men examined the insides of their horses' hooves, using small sticks to pick out packed-in dirt and debris. They worked patiently, moving from horse to horse. Then they removed the packsaddles and pads and hung them up, along with the oiled cloths and ropes, over low-hanging limbs to keep them clear of the ground's moisture and debris. While engaged in this, they heard a gunshot in the distance. "That will be our supper," said Sam.

A short time later Jim-Bird strode into view carrying a large turkey over his shoulder. "This bird will top thirty pounds," he said. As he was gutting the turkey, William walked over and stood for a moment watching. Then he said "Mr. Mockbird, allow me to introduce myself. I am William MacGregor, and I'm pleased to make your acquaintance."

Jim-Bird stood up and shook William's hand with a gravity that seemed to come from the Indian part of his manner. Then, with nothing more forthcoming from William, he shrugged slightly and went back to dressing the turkey.

William watched him for a while longer. He had eaten turkey since coming to Carolina, but this was the first time he had seen the bird's feathers. "I would appreciate it," he said, "if I could have a half-dozen of those wing feathers. They will make fine writing pens."

Giving William little more than a glance, Jim-Bird reached over, yanked out a handful of wing feathers, and handed them to him, saying nothing. William was impressed that he knew to pull the feathers from the bird's left wing, choosing the ones with the correct curvature for a right-handed scribe. He mumbled his thanks and walked away.

Thomas sniggered, and, as William passed close beside him, he said in a low voice, "Well, philosopher, do you suppose that half-breed is impressed by your high-falutin' ways?"

William made no response and took the feathers to his canvas bag. Then he wandered back and watched Jim-Bird pull the rest of the larger feathers out of the turkey. Then he impaled the gutted carcass on the end of a spit and held the turkey close to the fire to singe off the small feathers. When this foul-smelling business was over, he cut the carcass into quarters and laid them onto a grill made of green wood suspended on small posts over the bed of hot coals. About that time John called for William to come and attend to the horses.

The packhorsemen drove the horses some distance from the camp to a pasture bordered by a canebrake along Goose Creek. All of the bells around the horses' necks were sounding freely now, and together they were a clinking symphony. The horses drank their fill of water and then began grazing on the grass and river cane. The men waited for them, lounging on the bank of the creek while John played tunes on the recorder he always carried with him in a sheath slung from his belt. Every time a tune was unfamiliar, William would ask the name of it, and before long John began announcing each one.

"This next one is 'Green Stockings'," he said. "A tune to tickle a man but soothe a beast. I learned it in a bawdy house."

"Just play," said Thomas. "Spare us the music lessons."

As the light began to fade, they drove the horses back to camp. There the men stretched a rope from tree to tree about three feet from the ground, forming a large circle to contain the horses. "I don't see how this works," William said. "The horses can jump over that rope, even run right through it."

"They can for a fact," said John, "but horses want to be together in a herd, and usually they'll not budge. Unfortunately, though, if something scares them— like a pack of wolves coming close, or a panther—they will sure enough bolt and scatter. That's why they wear the bells, so we can round them up again. And I'm sorry to say they can be spooked by most anything that takes them by surprise. What you always have to remember about horses, especially when we have them moving along in a train, is that at all times they have the hair-trigger fear that behind every rock or tree there might be a big meat-eater set to pounce on them. If they see something suddenly move out of the corner of their eye— even if it's naught but a rabbit—they are like to bolt and run. Then we have to get after them, round them up, and form the train anew. The worst thing is that when they are loaded with packs, they can hurt themselves when they bolt. It can be a real mess."

It was almost dark when the men gathered around for supper. Sam, John, and Thomas sat on the log. There was no room there for more, so William squatted on his heels. Jim-Bird tended the food on the fire, with his dogs sitting close by, watching expectantly.

"What do we have in the pot?" asked John.

"Green beans and new potatoes," replied Jim-Bird. "I bartered for them with Izard's cook, gave her some honey I got from a bee tree."

"Did you save us any of that honey?" asked Thomas.

"I wouldn't forget you, Thomas," said Jim-Bird. "I have a fawn skin near half full." From his lean-to he fetched a skin that had been removed entire from a fawn, making a bag that now bulged with honey. He also brought out, in his other hand and tucked under his arms, wooden bowls and horn cups from the cook's outfit. William, who was starving, got up and took the bowls and cups from him and handed them around. Jim-Bird ladled up beans and potatoes from the pot, and the men used their knives to cut off liberal portions of barbecued turkey, peeling off the charred skin and tossing it to the dogs. They each dipped up a cup of hot beverage from another pot hanging over the fire.

William squatted down again, balancing the bowl on his knee and setting his cup on the ground. He tried the turkey and found it good, if a little tough. The green beans and potatoes were hearty and satisfying, though the seasoning was unusual. The drink was as bitter as coffee or Asian tea, but it tasted like neither. He held out his cup and grimaced slightly as he looked at John.

"That there will get you up and going just the same as any tea or coffee," John said. "It's an Indian tea, made out of the roasted leaves of a small-leaved holly tree that grows hereabouts. The traders and packhorsemen call it black drink, but people in Charles Town call it *cassina*. If it's too bitter for your taste, sweeten it with a dollop of Jim-Bird's honey." John walked over to the kettle and refilled his cup with black drink. "Jim-Bird," he said, "tell William about this Carolina tea."

Jim-Bird looked down into the drink in his own cup and remained silent for so long that William assumed he did not care to oblige. But then he spoke, his voice quiet but strong. "The Indian people found its uses. They drank it as a sacrament, and still do. Different ones call it by different names. The Creeks call it *asi*—that's where the word *cassina* comes from. I've heard Frenchmen call it *ap-*

palachina. I like it better than tea or coffee, and it costs nothing—you just strip the leaves off the bushes and roast them until they are dark brown. I stock up on it whenever I come to the low country. It grows poorly in the high country. It's too cold up there. A hard freeze will kill it."

He fell silent again, but William was impressed—both with the tea and with Jim-Bird.

For a time they all concentrated on their food. Sam finished first, tossed his turkey bones to the dogs, and set aside his bowl. "So tell us, Jim-Bird, how have things have been for you since we last saw you?"

"I always have a good time in Four Hole Swamp," said Jim-Bird, scooping another helping of beans and potatoes into his bowl. "But I can't say the same for my time here the past couple of weeks."

"What happened here?" asked Sam.

"Not much at first. I did some hunting for the planters. They had a rogue bear killing their sheep and calves. I tracked him down easy enough, but when I found him we got into a bit of a tangle. Binkie got in too close and he sent her flying—like to have killed her." Jim-Bird reached down and scratched Binkie's ear. "The bear had some broken teeth, all rotted and black. That's why he was taking livestock. But even with that, he was skinny. Though I did manage to find a little fat on him. You tasted some of it in your beans and potatoes." Jim-Bird got up and went to the back of his lean-to and brought out his new bear skin. John pointed out to William that Jim-Bird had left the skin of the front legs entire, so that it could easily be made into a winter coat. The packhorsemen passed it around and admired it.

"But then things took a turn for the worse. I ran afoul of John Parker."

"What happened there?" asked Sam.

"Well, that driver of John Parker's lays the whip on his slaves for the slightest offense, and one of them got enough of it and took to the woods. Parker wanted me to hunt him down, but I wanted no part of it. I begged off by telling him that you would be back any day for me to go with you to the Cherokees. And I told him that if his slaves know nothing but the whip, he shouldn't be surprised if they run away. He didn't take it well, you might say. In fact, he got into a downright fury. That man's not used to being stood up to. I feared he might shoot me. I excused myself and spent most of my time in the woods after that. I think I will not be camping here again."

Sam nodded. "John Parker is a hard man. He's not the kind of fellow you can make see the light. We'll steer clear of him for a while." Sam got up and took his bowl to the bank of the creek, washed it, and brought it back and put it near where Jim-Bird kept his cooking gear. As the other men finished, they followed suit. William could see that in housekeeping as in the rest of the work, Sam ran a tight ship.

As the sun hung on the horizon in the west, they continued sitting around the dying embers of the cook fire, watching the light fade.

"I have a song for you fellows," said John. "It comes to mind every time I think of my woman waiting for me up in Cherokee country. Here's 'The Lusty Young Smith.'" The others chuckled knowingly, and even William smiled at the title, though he had never heard the song.

John played the tune through on his recorder, and then he sang the words in a fine, high tenor voice.

A lusty young smith at his vice stood a-filing,
His hammer laid by but his forge still a-glow,
When to him a buxom young damsel came smiling
And asked if to work at her forge he would go.

"I will" said the smith and they parted together;
Along to the damsel's forge they did go.
They stripped to go to't, 'twas hot work and hot weather;
She kindled a fire and soon made him blow.

Her husband, she said, could scarce raise up his hammer,
His strength and his tool were worn out long ago.
The smith said, "Well mine are in very good order,
Look here," said our Workman, "my Tool is not so."

Red-hot grew his iron as both did desire,
And he was too wise not to strike while 'twas so.
Quoth she, "What I get, I get out of the fire,
So prithee strike home and redouble the blow."

Six times did his iron by vigorous heating
Grow soft in the forge in a minute or so;
As often 'twas harden'd, still beating and beating,
The more it was softened, it hardened more slow.

When the smith then would go, said the dame full of sorrow,
"Oh what would I give could my husband do so!
Good lad with your hammer come hither tomorrow,
But say, can't you use it once more ere you go?"

All the men laughed heartily, William not the least. He wondered how the Book Maggots had missed learning this song.

"Well, John," said Sam, "that just proves what I've always said."

"What's that?"

"There's nothing like a good tool when you need one."

The men laughed again. Then Jim-Bird first and the others after him got up from their seats around the fire and went to fetch their blankets, more to be used as shields against the mosquitos that hung about them in clouds than as proof against the weather. Sam and Jim-Bird rolled up in their blankets to sleep by the lean-to, near their goods. Tazzie and Binkie lay next to each other at Jim-Bird's feet. William, John, and Thomas picked spots near the horses, where they could be on hand if something went awry during the night.

William fetched his saddlebags along with his blanket. He took out his Shakespeare and his journal, a turkey quill, and a tightly corked bottle of ink. He had resolved that each night before going to sleep, he would read a few pages of Shakespeare and write a few lines in his journal. He might be a packhorseman for now, but he would not leave civilization completely behind. He would describe what he saw during the day, or he would develop a thought that had occurred to him, or if too tired to do anything else, he would at least record how far they had traveled.

In the quickly fading light, he only had time to read a few pages. Then, with barely enough light, he trimmed the quill into a pen, set his bottle of ink carefully alongside his bedroll, and wrote a few lines in his journal. He could scarcely see what he was writing.

July 20. Today we are on our way into the backcountry. We have entered the domain of the Goose Creek men—rice planters, mostly from Barbados. I met Jim-Bird, a half-breed who fancies terrier dogs and is said to be the fount of all wisdom concerning this country and its inhabitants. He is not overly friendly, though.

I began reading Shakespeare's "Macbeth." It is high time I read what William Shakespeare has to say about Scotland. I could never find time for it while I was in Scotland, but now that I am away, I hunger for a taste of home. Though I have to say that taste is hard to come by from reading Mr. Shakespeare. As a poet he casts sentences from the fringe of what the English tongue will allow. I think I grasp it, but then I realize I do not. His language must be bitten off, chewed well, and digested. I puzzle at why he begins his play with a witch's coven. I never once saw a witch in Scotland nor knew anyone who did.

Travel: 14 miles.

6   The Road North

When they awoke the next morning, the sky was overcast and the air was heavy. After a quick bite of food, William, Thomas, and John went to pack their horses. As they approached the area where they had hung up their gear, William was chagrined to see that at least half of his had fallen from the limbs to the ground—packsaddles, pads, ropes, and all.

"You'll have to do better than that next time," said John, shaking his head. "Be sure to brush off all the litter and insects or your horses will suffer for it."

"Makes me wish for Barnaby," said Thomas. "He never once let his gear hit the ground. You might have his horse and gear, philosopher, but that's all you have of old Barnaby." He turned his back firmly on William as he went to work saddling his own horses.

"I thought I had hung it up well," said William. "I don't understand what happened."

"Well, today's another day," said John. "You can try again tonight. Now, let's pack up and get moving."

Neither of the men helped William out of his predicament, and because of this they had to stand around waiting while William desperately brushed off his gear, making slow progress as he packed his horses. He knew he could not cut corners.

Sam and Jim-Bird, who had been breaking camp and attending to their own horses, walked over to see what was going on. "What's the problem?" asked Sam.

"Some of my gear fell to the ground during the night," said William. "I don't know how it happened. I was careful when I hung it up."

"Not careful enough," said Sam. "Do a better job next time. You're holding us up. Thomas, John—don't be standing around. Let's all pitch in and get this done. We've got to get on the road."

With the help of all, they were soon on the move, heading out over Goose Creek bridge. They were passing by the rectory of St. James Church when Sam drew his horse up alongside William's. "This here is the heart of Goose Creek," he said.

"What?" asked William, still embarrassed about his gear and lost in thought about what he had done wrong in hanging it up. He was sure Sam had come to say something more about it. "I was thinking about something else. What did ye say?"

"We are right in the middle of Goose Creek," Sam said. "Much that is now Carolina began right here."

William was relieved at the change of subject. He looked around. "I can't say that I see anything special about this place."

"Carolina's history would fill but a small book," Sam said, "but a good part of it would be about Goose Creek. The Indian trade started here."

"This was an Indian town?" asked William.

"No, that's not how it was. You see, the Goose Creek men carved out some of the earliest plantations in Carolina right here in this spot. Before long, Indians showed up at their doors wanting to trade. At first it was local Indians coming in to trade deerskins to the planters for cutlery, woolens, beads and such like. But then Westos began to come over from their town on the Savannah River. That's a fair distance from here, four to five days' travel to the west. The Westos were slave-raiders who had come down from northwards of Virginia. They were armed with Dutch guns, and that was something new around here. No other Indians in Carolina had firearms at that early time. The Westos were a force to be reckoned with, and they preyed on the local bow-and-arrow Indians, who didn't stand a chance against them. After a while the Lords Proprietors back in England wanted in on what was turning into a lucrative trade for the Goose Creek men. So their men—the town men, you might say—teamed up with the Westos to monopolize the trade in Indian slaves. That notched up the slave raiding. The Indians around here mostly ended up dead, enslaved, or on the run. They were caught between the jaws of a vise—Indian invaders on one side and English invaders on the other."

"And so now, I presume, it is the Westos who rule this part of the Indian country," said William

"No, the Westos are gone now. The Lords Proprietors' monopoly cut into the profits of the Goose Creek men, you see, and the Goose Creek men didn't like it a bit. So they allied with the Savannahs—yet another group of northern Indians come south looking for advantage. The Goose Creek men armed the Savannahs with guns and sent them to clean out the Westos. Which they did. And some say that is why we call that particular stream the Savannah River instead of the Westo River. The Savannahs killed off a good many of the Westos, and the survivors fled in several directions. In this way the Goose Creek men learned the delicate art of using the Indian trade both to enrich themselves and to manage the conduct of Indian affairs."

Jim-Bird had fallen in beside them, drawn by the conversation. "Only Sam would call those people Savannahs," said Jim-Bird. "The French word for them is *Chaouanons.* It comes out 'Shawnees' in English. That's what most people around here call them. Except for old-timers like Sam."

"That's me," said Sam. "I'm an old-timer for sure, and that's why I can tell you this, too. The Goose Creek men may have started the Indian trade in Carolina, but they never took responsibility for what they had started. They never succeeded in regulating the trade, and they never had much interest in doing so. All the advantage was in the hands of the traders, or so it seemed, and the worst of them made up their own rules. They abused the Indians shamefully, ravished their wives, ruined their good judgment with rum, and when the Indians fell so deeply in debt that they couldn't pay up, some of the traders would go so far as to seize their wives and children as slaves. Said they were seizing their property in payment."

"I've heard a little about this part of it," said William. "Uncle Duncan said it caused an Indian war."

"It was one of the causes," said Sam. "A chief cause. And why wouldn't it be? The Yamasees near Port Royal rose up first. They were the ones closest to the settlements and had taken the worst abuse for the longest time. They killed their traders and then they and their allies went on to wipe out as many as four hundred settlers. This was in 1715. The uprising spread to most of the Indians we were doing business with, and a great many of the traders amongst them were cut down. Thank God I was up amongst the Cherokees. Only they and the Chickasaws stayed out of the fray. The Chickasaws were far out to the west and they were tied fast to us. God only knows why the Cherokees held back. If they had joined in, Carolina might not have survived."

"So the Goose Creek men nearly brought down the colony," said William.

"Well, they didn't feel personally responsible," said Sam. "They and the other merchants and planters in Charles Town tried every way they knew to scapegoat the traders and packhorsemen for having caused the war. And if that didn't stick, they would blame it on plots by the Spanish and the French. They even tried to blame it on black slaves escaping to the Indians and spreading slander about how bad the English were, as if the Indians didn't have a dim view of us all on their own. The cold fact is that the main cause of the war was the South Carolina colony itself. The Indians were awash in debt and were enslaving neighboring Indians to pay their way out. And they had to ask themselves in the midst of it: are we the next to be enslaved? They did what any of us would do. They rose up."

"But in the end they lost," said William. "Are they any better off today?"

"The merchants tightened up the board of commissioners that is supposed to regulate the trade, and this has made a difference, though it leaves much to be desired. The traders and the Indians are so unequal in power, we have to have some regulation for the trade to work. It ends up killing its own self if it is not well regulated."

"Could there be another uprising?" asked William.

"There not only could be," said Sam, "there has been. Just last year the Creeks murdered several traders. The Cherokees got wind of it and began throwing their weight around, trying to force us to sell more cheaply. But when we threatened to halt the trade entirely, they backed down. They hate to admit it, but they need us."

"The Indians are not as strong as they used to be," said Jim-Bird, "but they are still plenty strong enough."

"That's the way I see it, too," said Sam. "It pays to be wary. But the merchants don't like regulation. They don't like anything that cuts into their profits. So the pot's always a-boiling, and the lid barely stays on."

The pack train continued northward through terrain much the same as the day before. On both sides of the sandy road, smaller roads led off to rice plantations. In the afternoon a heavy rain fell, drenching men and horses alike. The downpour soon eased, but a light rain continued to fall, so they cut their travel short and put in for the night at James Kinloch's plantation.

As they were heading down the narrow plantation road to Kinloch's, they passed through an eerie field of dead longleaf pines with corn growing in the open land beneath them—a deadening, John called it—an area of woods being cleared for cultivation. William had not noticed any deadenings along the more settled main road, and he was fascinated by the process of clearing virgin forest from such a large stretch of land. John explained that during the previous summer Kinloch's slaves would have come in with their axes and killed the trees by cutting rings into the bark around their great trunks. Then they went to work with grubbing hoes and rooted up the saplings and small growth. During the winter some of the smaller trees were harvested to build the split-rail fence that surrounded the clearing, and in the spring the planter sent the slaves back with hoes to plant corn among the big trees that were now standing dead in the field. Some of the tree limbs had fallen off during the winter and more would fall as time went on. The newly cleared soil was soft and fertile, and the corn grew prodigiously. Deadwood falling from the trees does some damage to the crops, said John, and sometimes to people in the fields as well. But this way of clearing the woods was the cheapest way to do it. All the deadwood was gathered up and used as firewood, which was never wanting in these parts, though it sometimes came at an unwelcome price.

"They have a saying hereabouts," said John. "Love God, hate the Devil, and stay out of a deadening when the wind blows hard."

William shook his head in amazement but said no more. They were all tired and wet and rode in silence for the rest of the way. The great dead trees were like huge skeletons, holding up their bare arms to heaven with ragged Spanish moss clinging to them. Hawks and vultures perched on the limbs, hunkered down against the rain. But the woodpeckers were still active. William could hear them in the distance dining on the grubs that were in turn dining on the dead trees.

The men made camp, a task made easier by the split-rail enclosure that Kinloch had built on his place for the horses of his packtrain lodgers. After a while the rain stopped and the sky began to clear. William rechecked his gear several times to make sure it was secure on the sturdy tree limbs on which he had placed it. Jim-Bird cooked up a pot of hoppin' John—plain fare, though there was plenty of it. As daylight faded, the men laid out their bedrolls beneath a shed attached to Kinloch's barn and settled down to sleep.

William read a few pages of Shakespeare and wrote in his journal:

July 21. More than half of my horse gear ended up on the ground last night. It slowed us down. Sam, John, and Thomas were irked. I must improve.

I got further into Macbeth. He has enough ambition to assassinate a king, but he may not be wicked enough to follow through. Lady Macbeth says he is "too full of th' milk of human kindness."

For her part, she intends, as a dutiful wife, to purge herself of her feminine nature and fill herself from head to toe with "direst cruelty." What Scotland is this? Still not the one I know.

Travel: 13 miles.

William awoke while it was still dark, though a faint gray light was beginning to filter through the trees. He got up immediately and went to where he had stored his gear. Three of his packsaddles and their pads were on the ground. Gritting his teeth in frustration, he picked them up and carefully brushed them off, returning each to the limb from which it had fallen. What was it that he did not understand about how horse gear hangs on a limb? Gravity in the New World ought to be the same as in the Old World. Something was not right here.

William returned to where he had slept and found the others up and eating their breakfast—more hoppin' John. "Another three of my packsaddles were on the ground this morning," he said. "I am beginning to think we have a bad fairy doing mischief amongst us—or do ye have such in America?"

"You ain't saying that one of us is knocking down your gear?" Thomas asked testily.

"I am not. But I put it up as carefully as the rest of you, and only mine falls during the night."

"That never happened to Barnaby," said Thomas. "But then, he w'arnt no city boy. And for sure he w'arnt no philosopher. He knew how to actually do things, not just talk about them."

William turned away. He was not as upset with himself this morning, but he was getting angry. Something was awry. And yet, he had no wish to start seeing enemies everywhere. He turned his anger into energy for packing his horses and lagged only a little behind John and Thomas in getting ready for the trail.

When Sam came and checked over the train, he tightened the half-diamond hitches on several of William's horses. "You're packing them a tad slack," he said. "Pay attention to what you're doing."

William nodded grimly and said nothing.

The weather was again dreary as they continued traveling northward along the wagon road through pine forest country that was monotonously the same as the day before. The monotony was broken when, on their right they glimpsed a great expanse of swamp along the west branch of the Cooper River. Some of the cypress trees were over a hundred feet tall and must have been immensely old. The packtrain was still making its way through the flat terrain of the coastal plain, although in truth it was not perfectly flat. At every creek the land dipped gradually down to the slowly flowing stream and then rose again on the other side. These small streams were precious to the rice planters whose irrigation systems depended on them.

In the afternoon William was amazed by a great flock of raucous, bright green birds flying rapidly through a grove of cypress trees. The birds had yellow-orange heads and were about the size of doves. The whole flock was like a great, green coverlet embroidered with yellow and orange, flung sprawling through the air. Jim-Bird, who was riding nearby and was the only one close enough for William to question, said they were Carolina parakeets.

"They make a terrible racket when they fly," said Jim-Bird, "but they are dead quiet when they feed. They don't like cold weather, not a bit. Entire flocks hole up in hollow cypress trees in the winter, clinging together like bees for warmth."

"What do they eat?" asked William. "It must take a great lot to feed them."

Jim-Bird shrugged. "Cocklebur seeds, cypress seeds, sweet gum buds, mulberries, and such like as that. And also, unfortunately for them, corn and rice. The planters hate them and shoot them on sight. They make a sport of taking them down."

Jim-Bird fell silent, clearly finished with his discourse. But William was pleased. That was the most he had ever gotten out of him.

On this day, too, they cut short their travel on account of rain. They put in for the night at Alexander Kinloch's, a kinsman of Thomas Kinloch. As they approached his house and farmstead, they passed through a dense stand of longleaf pine trees. As they rode along William caught sight of two slaves attending to a mound in the shape of a cone, twenty feet or so wide at the base and twelve to fourteen feet tall. The outside of the mound was covered with a thick layer of sod and green pine straw. From the top a plume of black smoke poured out, such that the mound had the appearance of a miniature volcano. One of the men, paying closer attention to the mound than the other, poked an air-hole in the side of it with a long pole he carried in his hands. A long hollow log projected from the bottom of the mound, stretching out over a low area where two or three dozen thirty-gallon barrels were stored.

"John," William shouted, "what are those fellows doing?"

"They are tending a naval stores factory," he replied.

"What?"

"It's a tar kiln. They are turning lightwood into tar for Carolina ship captains and the Royal Navy." John saw that William would want to be filled in with details, so he reined in his horse until William caught up with him. They paused, watching the two men at work.

"I've never heard of lightwood, " said William. "Would I know it by some other name?"

"Only if you have lived near an immense, old pine forest like the one growing in this country. It is called by other names: heart wood, fat wood, fat lighter, lighterwood, lightered, and so on. When a pine tree dies, the outer wood rots and falls away, leaving the in-most wood, the heart of the tree, wood that is densely filled with combustible resin. Insects will not eat it and it will not rot. People call it lightwood not because it weighs light, but because you can use small splinters of it to light fires. Touch fire to a piece of it and it springs into flames."

"Those kiln workers spent two or three weeks tracking about in the woods," said John, "filling up wagon after wagon of lightwood. They hauled it to this kiln, which started out as a shallow clay-lined basin. They cut and split the lightwood into pieces two- to three-feet long, and then stacked them with their ends slanting down and pointing toward the center of the basin. When the kiln was piled high enough, they topped it off with an air-tight cover of sod and pine straw. Then they set fire to it through a hole in the very center of the top of the kiln."

"I never saw anything like lightwood in Highland Scotland. But if lightwood burns up in the kiln, this would seem to be self-defeating," said William.

"The object of the fire in the kiln is to make it burn just hot enough to sweat the resin, or gum, out of the wood. It drips down and collects in the clay basin floor of the kiln, and then they drain it out through the hollow log into the barrels. The kiln master can make a cool area burn hotter by punching a hole through the covering to let more air in, and he can cool it by filling up holes in the cover. It takes long experience before a man develops a sense of how hot it is inside the kiln. If it gets too hot, the thing can explode and maim or kill people. After they have got all of the tar out of the wood and drained into the barrels, they haul them down to a landing where they can be loaded onto boats and taken to Charles Town."

"Is that the end of it?"

"Not quite. After the fire goes out, a layer of charcoal—four to five feet deep—remains in the kiln. This can be used for heating or cooking, and it can be sold to blacksmiths, who use it to fire their forges."

"There seems to be no shortage of piney woods hereabouts," said William. "Tar-making must be one of the ways fortunes are made in Carolina."

"It's not as easy as it looks. You have to own a tract of forest that has not had a hot fire in a long time. Such a fire will burn up the lightwood."

"I would think it would burn up the trees and the grass as well," said William.

"Fire is no stranger to the piney woods," said John. "The pine straw catches on fire easily. Sometimes lightning will start fires. Also, when the wind is right, the Indians will deliberately set fire to the woods, and so will the cow herders hereabouts."

"I can't see why anyone would do that," said William.

"Most of the fires in the piney woods are not very hot, although they are often widespread. I have seen some that burned many thousands of acres. But it's almost as if fire and longleaf pines are the best of friends, and that goes for wiregrass as well. The thick bark protects the pines from all but the hottest fires, and the wiregrass will burn off and come back even stronger in the next growing season. The fires are the reason why the floor of a pine forest is so open. And deer and cows love to browse in the pine forest meadows.

"In addition to owning the right kind of forest, you have to have a good wagon road or access to water transport to get your tar to market. And you have to own slaves. The labor in making tar is day-in, day-out, and it is back-breaking work. And of course, it is dangerous."

"I can't seem to find an easy road to wealth in Carolina," said William.

"If it were easy," said John, "everybody would be rich."

As they unloaded and tended their horses at Kinloch's, William was discomfited to find an insect scourge that was turning out to be worse than the unrelenting swarms of mosquitoes. The further they went into the backcountry, the more ticks the packhorsemen had to pick off their horses at the end of each day. These tiny hellions were only about an eighth of an inch long. They clustered about the horses' eyes, inside and around their ears, in the folds where their legs joined their bodies, and around their anuses. When engorged with blood, the ticks swelled up enormously. The entire business of removing them was sickening. But at least the horses seemed to know that this tedious procedure was for their own good, and they stood patiently while the men picked them clean.

Worst of all was that William had to perform the same operation on his own body, taking off his clothes to search for the determined little invaders. He regularly found up to a dozen or more settled in for a meal, especially on his legs and lower trunk. The most pernicious were the newly hatched seed ticks, no larger than a grain of sand, but still capable of digging in and drinking their fill of his blood.

On this night William wrote in his journal:

July 22. Too tired to read. The bad fairy got into my gear again last night. I got up early and attended to it, so I did not hold up the others.

The insects in this country are all after my blood. My mates say the mosquitos will thin out when we reach the high country, but the ticks will be with us until the first freezing weather.

John Coleman was good enough to regale me with a wonderful account of the tar-makers of the Carolina piney woods.

Travel: 14 miles.

William again got up at first light, taking care not to wake the others. He was relieved to find all of his gear stored snugly on the top rail of a fence, where he had placed it. Relieved, he leaned against the fence and looked out over a thick stand of very large pine trees. A wind blew up, and William noticed that the sound it made as it blew through the tops of these trees was different from the sound wind makes in a leafy forest. At times it sounded like a weary sigh, and at other times it sounded like distant surf. William took in a deep breath of the clean morning air.

Later, as they were packing, John remarked on William's intact gear. "You seem to have shaken off that bad fairy, or brownie, or whatever it was."

"Aye, and I am grateful to be rid of it," said William. "But my reputation as a packhorseman has taken a hard blow almost before it's begun."

"It's nothing you can't repair," said John.

On this day they made good time, passing by several small plantations. William noted that they were now traveling more to the northwest. The horses trotted along at a good pace, and for most of the day the men stayed to themselves, wrapped in their own thoughts. They passed by the Cossada ponds, and a short distance beyond they came to Matthew Nelson's plantation, where they put in for the night.

Nelson had a prosperous enterprise. He had cut a wagon road down to a landing on the Santee River, where he operated a ferry and a shipping dock.

Because of the wagon access provided by his road, nearby planters could haul heavy and bulky products such as naval stores, and even timber, to be shipped down the Santee to its mouth, and from there to any port on the Atlantic.

After they had unpacked and unsaddled, Jim-Bird went with William to graze the horses while Thomas and John stayed back at the camp to attend to a troublesome cut on the leg of one of John's horses. While the herd grazed, Jim-Bird and William sat down to rest, each leaning back against a tree. Tazzie and Binkie, tired out from the long day's travel, lay down near Jim-Bird and fell asleep. Neither of the men spoke.

William listened to the world around him, to the horses snuffling and nipping up grass, to their bells softly clinking, and to the accompanying symphony of birdsong in the surrounding trees. All was peaceful. After a while, a new bird sent out a call in the distance: *kent, kent,* as if from a small tin trumpet. It was answered by another *kent, kent.*

"What bird is tooting that horn?" asked William.

"The warrior bird," said Jim-Bird. "One of his family answered him."

William waited to learn more, but Jim-Bird was not forthcoming. "What kind of bird is it?" asked William. "It sounds like a large one."

Jim-Bird gave a short laugh. "Larger than large. It's a great woodpecker— the lord of the forest."

"Will he come near us?"

"I can make him come." Jim-Bird took his hatchet and got up and cut a short, solid piece of wood from the limb of a low branching oak tree. Then he sat down again beside the tree against which he had been resting. "When the warrior and his family come to us, you must remain perfectly still if you want to get a good look at them. They are shyer than shy."

Jim-Bird rapped the piece of wood smartly against the tree, twice in quick succession—a two-note *ka-BLACK.* Presently they heard an answering *ka-BLACK* from a distance. Jim-Bird repeated the double rap, and they heard it answered again, followed by a chorus of *kent, kent, kent, kent.* Then the forest was silent. Jim-Bird motioned for William to stay still. Presently they heard the swoosh-swoosh of powerful wings overhead. Jim-Bird moved one finger to point, and William carefully looked up at a nearby sweetgum tree, an old, large one, dead and devoid of leaves. Four huge woodpeckers clung to its trunk, two parent birds and two large, gawky youngsters. They presented such a stunning sight that William could barely contain a gasp. The father bird looked to be almost two feet long from head to tail. Their bodies were glossy black, with a curved streak of white feathers running from their cheeks down their necks to their backs and lower wings. They had ivory-colored beaks, and the two males—the father and a young one—had scarlet crests on their heads. All four of them scrambled around the tree, hopping on their powerful clawed feet from place to place, animated and quick in their movements, all the while calling *kent, kent.* Their piercing yellow eyes looked this way and that as they all scampered up the tree with the agility of squirrels. The mother found a likely spot to mine for grubs and began chipping away at the bark with the ivory-colored chisel that was her beak, first from one side and then the other, until she put her beak under the bark she had raised and with a quick twist sent it flying. She had knocked off a piece the size of a man's hand. She kept on this way, proceeding to peck away until she got a fat grub, which she quickly ate. The youngsters evidently were on their own. She did give way, however, when one came crowding in to try her spot.

William was fixed on the birds and did not see Tazzie awake from his nap. Tazzie must have looked up to see what the men were staring at so intently, for he suddenly spied the birds and ran out barking. Binkie awoke in a flash and followed him. The woodpeckers flew silently away, swooping up and down on their great wings until they blended back into the forest.

"God almighty!" said William. "I have never seen a woodpecker so large. The wingspan of that big male must have been at least three feet."

"The warrior bird is the mightiest flyer in the forest," said Jim-Bird.

"Why is he called a warrior bird?"

"Because he wears black on his body and red on his head. Those are the colors of warfare and death. And the sound of his beak pounding on a tree is like the sound of a war club when it strikes the head of an enemy. He lives in the deepest parts of old forests. Usually Indian warriors only see him when they are traveling far from home to raid their enemies. It is a good omen to see him, or even to hear him. The Indians say that the warrior birds were on hand at the beginning of the world, clinging to clouds, with the tips of their long tails hanging down in the water."

"It is not hard for me to imagine that," said William.

That night he wrote:

July 23. I am again too tired to read Shakespeare. Jim-Bird is all they say he is. He knows this country in a different way from the others. He knows it from the inside out. I have got him talking some, but he does not yet regard me as a friend.

Travel: 22 miles

7   MacDonald's Cowpen

The day dawned clear, the light so bright that everything in sight seemed to have sharp edges. The men were still at their breakfast when Sam told them to start packing—he wanted to cover good distance on this day to make up for lost time. They wolfed down the last of their food and got in motion.

As they were about to depart from Nelson's plantation, William saw that the rising sun was more to their right than it had been on previous days.

"You can set your compass to the northwest," said John, "and you can leave it there until we reach Keowee. First we will have the Santee River on our right hand, then it will be the Congaree River, and when we hit the high country it will be the Saluda River. We'll have this wagon road for a while yet, and then it will turn to a horse trail for the rest of the way. With that you'll know for sure you're on the Cherokee Path. Of course, we've been on it since we left Charles Town, but a lot more of it now goes through settled land than it once did. It's a good path all the way, rain or shine, if you don't mind getting wet."

As they moved briskly along the sandy road, the day began heating up. For some distance they trotted along with no stream or standing water appearing across the path or near it, and the horses began to get noticeably thirsty. No one else seemed concerned about this, so William said nothing, but he was relieved when they came at last to a fine watering hole. The waters of Eutaw Springs welled up prodigiously out of twin spring heads and rushed out cold and clear to form a small, steep-sided creek that ran northward into the Santee. It was the finest water William had yet tasted in Carolina, as pure as a Highland stream. Both men and horses drank their fill, the refreshing water so cold it made their eyes blink.

But Sam allowed no lingering. When the last horse had lifted its head from its last drink, he cracked his whip and set the train in motion. And on they went, pushing the horses hard, using whoops and whip cracking to keep them at a steady trot, only occasionally letting them rest by slowing to a walk. All along the way the high ground was taken by immense stands of longleaf pines, with little underneath except wiregrass, pine needles, and large pine cones. These pines, it seemed to William, were the bullies of the forest. Only on the low ground along the little creeks running off to the right were there leafy trees. For the midday meal Jim-Bird rode from man to man handing out dried peaches and strips of jerked beef as hard as whit-leather—and the train kept moving. As the horses grew tired, the men had to work harder to keep them at a trot.

In the middle of the afternoon, the lash rope snapped on the third horse in William's string. The half-diamond hitch went slack, and as the bundles began to slip, the horse staggered and struggled to keep his footing.

"Whoa up," shouted William, halting his string of horses. Thomas stopped behind him. When John saw what had happened, he spurred his horse forward and halted his own string, bringing the entire train to a stop. William got down from his horse and was inspecting the two ends of the broken rope when Sam came riding back.

"What the hell is going on?" asked Sam. "I'm trying to make good time here."

"This lash rope snapped," said William.

"Didn't you inspect it before you tied it this morning?"

"I surely did, but I saw nothing amiss."

"Well, you didn't look close enough, did you? You got to do better, boy. This holding up the train is getting to be a habit with you, and it is a habit I can ill afford. Tie the two ends together and throw another hitch—and I'd appreciate it if you'd be quick about it."

John dismounted and came over to lend a hand. The two of them stood on either side of the horse and tidied up the bundles and tied a fresh hitch. Jim-Bird and Thomas rode up to watch the proceedings. Jim-Bird leaned over to inspect the two ends of the broken rope, where William had tied them together in a square knot.

"What do you make of it?" asked John.

"Can't say. I've seen plenty of lash ropes loosen up, but I don't recall ever seeing one break like that."

"Maybe it ain't the rope, but the man who tied the rope," said Thomas. "None of Barnaby's ropes ever broke. In fact, I can't remember him ever holding up the pack train."

"Why is it," John said to Thomas, "that you never had anything good to say about Barnaby while he was alive—all you could do was pick at him—but you sing his praises now that he is dead and gone?"

"I did not pick at Barnaby," Thomas snapped, and he turned away and rode back to his string of horses.

The train was soon moving again and the horses clipped along without further incident. The road ran along the high ground paralleling the Santee, the way measured out by the crossing of small creeks that ran down to their right toward the river. John named them—Webb's Creek, Mill Creek—helping William get the country set in his mind.

"Way yonder to the left," John said, "is Four-Hole Swamp. Now that is as great a tangle of wood and water as you'll ever see. There are cypress trees growing there that must have been seeded when God was still a boy. They're as big around as a house and reach almost to the clouds. It's hard to get back in there. It's mostly covered over with blackwater. But there's some high ground. Some settlement Indians live on patches of it in there."

"Settlement Indians?" asked William.

"That's right. They're not like the ones who live all in one nation and speak the same language and have the same ways. Settlement Indians are from the broken nations. They come from all over and bunch up together, needing each other as neighbors to make up a settlement, even if they don't understand one another's tongues. There's a few Natchez living there who've come all the way from the French colony in the west."

"You mean Jim-Bird's people?" asked William.

"Every people is Jim-Bird's people," said John. "Natchez, Chickasaw, French, English, Cherokee. You name it. I don't know that he claims any one over the others. But yes, Jim-Bird often visits in there. Mostly to see his woman friend."

William looked in the direction in which John had indicated the swamp lay. He could see nothing of it, but he could imagine it. And he could imagine Jim-Bird spending time among the people there.

As they rode through the last half of the afternoon, the land rose gently and the air began to feel drier. William was conscious of their leaving the settled plantations behind. They had entered a border country that was only sparsely populated by settlers.

Sam still pushed them along. He allowed the horses to drink whenever they came to a creek, but he did not dawdle. Both men and horses were wearing out. Very late in the day the land dipped and they entered a grove of poplar trees, so tall and towering it took William's breath away. The immense trunks, limbless up to forty feet or so, were like columns holding up heaven itself. It felt as if they were in a cathedral, though it was a bit gloomy in the fading light of the setting sun. After a while, as William looked ahead down the line of horses, he could see more light in that direction—they were coming to a clearing.

"MacDonald's cowpen dead ahead," Sam announced loudly, with evident pleasure. He had pushed them hard enough to reach his goal. Within sight of the homestead, the woods began to thin out, with stumps remaining where trees had been cut for building materials and firewood.

Sam halted the train of horses in front of a modest but neat house close by the road. Like rural houses in parts of Scotland and England, it was framed up out of heavy, squared timbers set as posts in the ground, with its horizontal framework made of like timbers, all pegged together. William had seen many houses like this. The large interstices in the framework were filled in with wattles made of wooden withes woven together in basket-weave fashion, all of it plastered over with thick clay daub, making a tight, well-insulated construction. Like the rest of this cowpen, the house was carefully built and well tended. On its south side there was a tidy garden of herbs and multicolored flowers.

A tall, gray-haired man came out of the house and walked up to meet Sam, who remained on horseback. The man looked strong and fit, tempered by his hard life on the frontier. He and Sam exchanged pleasantries for a few minutes. Then Sam cracked his whip and shouted: "Let's put them up for the night, boys!"

The men guided the train of horses into a horse-pen hard by a barn a short distance from the house. As they entered the pen, several lean, medium-sized herd dogs ran out to challenge Tazzie and Binkie, who bristled and barked as if ready to fight. The dogs, though, were acquainted with each other, and once the ritual of territorial claim had been honored, they fell into sniffing and tail wagging.

The packhorsemen stored their bundles inside the barn and cooled down the weary horses, cleaning their hooves and picking off ticks before taking off the saddles, pads, and bridles. Then they stored all their gear under a shed roof built off the side of the barn. The horses drank from a small stream that ran through the horse-pen, and Sam purchased corn from MacDonald to feed them. They badly needed this grain to help recover the energy they had expended in traveling this far.

As the others walked from the barn to the house, William stayed behind for a few moments to look out over a cowpen of about three acres, containing, it would seem, about twenty cows and their calves. A stout wattle fence closed in the area, and the stream that ran through the horse-pen ran through the cowpen as well. Inside the large pen was a smaller pen in which there were several strong posts set into the ground for tethering the cows for milking. A crew was busy with the evening milking, one of them a young woman with reddish blonde hair, the others young African slaves. They were laughing and talking among themselves as they worked.

Memories of William's boyhood in Scotland washed over him. He knew that after they had taken the milk they wanted from the cows, they would drive them through the gate into the large pen, where their calves would find their mothers and strip out the remaining milk. The calves would suckle off and on all night, until the next morning when the cows would be driven out to pasture, leaving the calves behind. And just like in Scotland, there would be no problem calling in the cows at the end of the day. Their udders would be distended, and they would want to get back to their calves and to the salt that William could see scattered atop tree stumps inside the pen. Were it not for his hunger, he would have stayed near the cows longer, savoring the familiarity of this pleasant scene. But he tore himself away and headed on toward the house.

As William was on his way, a young black boy came up to a pigsty that adjoined the cowpen and raised a large conch-shell trumpet to his lips. The sound he produced was so loud it must have been audible a mile away. In a few minutes the hogs came running from the nearby woods, squealing and grunting, the large ones flouncing along in front at an amazingly rapid pace, with the little ones bringing up the rear, their legs a perfect blur. These creatures were long-snouted and long-legged, with sharp, thin backs. They looked more like greyhounds than hogs. William was fascinated and moved closer to watch them. Some of the hogs took notice of him, and they did not meet his eye timidly, but with a mixture of fright and defiance like half-wild creatures. He found himself thinking about what he might grab up as a weapon if he needed one. They ran on into the pen, which the boy, whom William now engaged in light conversation, referred to as a "hog crawl."

Just then William heard his name being called. He turned away from the hog crawl and ran to the house, where the others, yet again, were waiting for him. John MacDonald was standing with them outside, and when William came to a breathless halt beside John Coleman, MacDonald looked him up and down. "You must be new to this crew," he said. "I ain't seen you before."

"Yes sir, I am new. Barnaby Whitford came down with jaundice fever in Charles Town and died from it. I am filling in for him."

MacDonald shook his head sadly at the news of Barnaby and looked away at the ground beyond them. "I am sorry to hear that," he said quietly. "Barnaby was a good, steady fellow. He had a bright countenance." He looked back at William. "I am John MacDonald," he said, holding out his hand.

"And I am William MacGregor," William said, impressed as he felt Mac-Donald's strong and sure grip.

"You ain't the first MacGregor to eat at my table," said MacDonald. "You wouldn't be ary kin to Duncan, would ye?"

"I would, indeed. Duncan is my uncle, my father's brother. He sends you greetings."

"Great God," said MacDonald. "I knew your father! Duncan and I go way back. We were mates in the old country. We spent a bad day together at a place called Sheriffmuir." He shook his head. "It was a lot worse for your father than for Duncan and me."

"Yes, it was," said William. "His last day on earth."

"David MacGregor," MacDonald said slowly, staring off again. "He was a good man, your father was. The three of us talked each other into joining up with Bobbing John to fight for the noble Jacobite cause to bring the Stuarts back to the throne. A lost cause if ever there was one. We should have saved our breath, and our blood. You must have been just a tyke back then."

"I was less than a tyke. I was still in my mother's womb."

"That's right," said MacDonald. "I remember David worrying about Margaret. He pined for her."

"I wish he had pined enough to have stayed home with her," said William. "I still marvel at her being able to put food on the table for the two of us. Life is hard for a widow."

MacDonald looked at him squarely and grimly. He reached out to shake William's hand again, then he pulled him into a quick embrace and patted him on the back.

"And here we are once again, waiting for the philosopher," said Thomas. "I guess we'll get to the food directly."

"Go on in," said MacDonald, stepping back and motioning them before him toward the door. "The womenfolk are putting it on the table."

MacDonald's house had one room with a large fireplace off to one side. The rear of the house was partitioned off for John's bedroom, a small service area, and a stairway to a loft where the young people slept. A shed roof off that end of the house covered a second small bedroom. The main room was furnished with a long trestle table, with peg-leg benches on either side and ladder-back chairs at the ends. The table was set with wooden trenchers for the men. Several small children were playing around the table, hungrily eying the food being brought in by their mothers in bowls of mottled gray and black pottery. MacDonald shooed the children outside to await their turn to eat later with the women. The men took their seats, and MacDonald, who sat at the head of the table, started passing around the bowls of food, while the women continued to bring in more.

The women were well known to Sam and the others, but MacDonald introduced them for William's sake. There were two of them, Betsy and Liza, MacDonald's married daughters. Their husbands were off tending to the business of the cowpen, one looking after the outlying herd, the other overseeing the cutting and squaring of timber to be floated down the Santee River.

Just then a third daughter appeared in the door, Rosemary was her name, a maiden of about sixteen, her reddish-blonde hair no longer tied back, as when she was milking, but hanging loose about her pert oval face. She had lively green eyes that surveyed the room with evident amusement. William liked the look of her and was pleased that she would be helping with the serving.

In fact, he liked everything about this place and was feeling very much at home. MacDonald's connection to his father had taken him by surprise. After days of riding deeper and deeper into unfamiliar land, he had come to a small piece of Scotland with ties to family and home. He wanted to return to the conversation they had begun outside, but he held himself back until they had filled their trenchers and eaten enough to take the edge off their hunger. Then he said, "So you were at Sheriffmuir, Mr. MacDonald."

"Aye, I was there at that great catastrophe, following Bobbing John like a fool. Duncan and I were solid lucky to get out of it alive. Alive, but in deep trouble. They caught us both and transported us out."

"What about Rob Roy?" said William. "Some say he was at Sheriffmuir and some say he wasn't. Did ye see him there?"

"No, I never saw him that day," said MacDonald. "I've heard it several different ways. Some say that Rob Roy understood Bobbing John's folly from the outset and held back his men from the battle. It could be that he did. But I also heard that he was posted with his men ten miles away, and that when he heard that the battle had already started, he came forward to join in, but he got there too late to do any good."

John MacDonald looked down the table and saw that the trenchers of the packhorsemen were almost empty. "Rosemary," he said to his youngest daughter, who was now standing near the table listening intently, "bring in that kettle of potatoes. The stomachs of these men are bottomless pits."

Rosemary disappeared and soon came back from the kitchen with a small kettle and made her way down the table, asking each man in turn whether he wanted more, which all of them did. When she got to William, she blushed prettily as she spoke to him, perhaps because he was new to her. As she leaned in to serve his plate, the sleeve of her dress brushed against his shoulder. He had hardly thought of women since he had left Glasgow, what with so much new experience washing over him, demanding all his attention. But now his thoughts were turned that way, and he was glad he was sitting, not standing. He could have sworn she smelled of rosemary. Or was it just the suggestion of her name? Her direct gaze and quick smile made his heart jump.

She left the room, but soon she was back with a pan of hot berry pie. Her sister Betsy came after her with a big pitcher of buttermilk, cold from the spring house, and the two of them worked their way around the table. Again the sleeve of her dress brushed over William's arm as she spooned a generous serving of berries and crust onto his trencher.

While the men ate their pie and drank their buttermilk in contented silence, Rosemary still lingered by the table. After a few moments, she spoke up. "Can I ask ye a question, MacGregor?"

William, who was savoring a bite of pie, choked and had to clear his throat with a drink of buttermilk. "Aye," he said, still coughing a bit, "ask me anything."

The other men laughed.

"Why were ye inquiring about Rob Roy MacGregor? Are ye ary kin to him?"

"So ye've heard about Rob Roy?" said William, pleased that she knew of the old country, though she had never lived there.

"My father has told me stories of him," she said.

"I am indeed kin to him," said William. "I am related to him both by marriage and by blood. Not that I knew him well, mind ye. I've barely met him. But he married my cousin Mary, of Comer. And there's a blood connection from five generations back. My line and his sprang from Gregor Dubh MacGregor III of Glen Gyle."

"Who the bloody hell is that?" asked Thomas.

"A well-remembered chieftain of the MacGregors of Glen Gyle," said William. "He had two sons. Rob Roy comes from the line of the elder son. I come from the younger son's line."

"The lesser one," muttered Thomas.

"That's so," William said. "The other line is the first family of the Mac-Gregors of Glen Gyle. Our line is the second."

"Did ye ever go out raiding for cattle with Rob Roy?" asked Rosemary.

"No. He was an old man when I was a boy. But I've seen him at clan gatherings. His famous red hair had turned white. There was always a great crowd gathered around him—he was well loved. I shook hands with him once. I never will forget it. He told me I have the makings of that great grip for which he was famous. I'm sure he said the same to all the boys, but I felt like I was the only one, like I had been blessed by a king."

"What great grip is he famous for?" asked John Coleman.

"Anyone could hold out a knife or a sword to him," said William, "and he would grasp the blade so very tightly between his fingers, the other person could not pull it away."

"Now I'm getting interested in this Rob Roy," said Jim-Bird. "Tell us who he is."

William looked over at John MacDonald, deferring to his elder to tell the tale.

"You tell it," said MacDonald.

"To Clan Gregor," said William, "Rob Roy is the greatest chief who ever lived. But to many Scots he's naught but an outlaw. His father was Donald MacGregor, the fifteenth chief of the Children of the Mist—that's the Gregors. His mother was a Campbell. Rob Roy was a smart and stealthy raider and a fearless master of all weapons. Not a tall fellow, but very brawny. Some call him pony-built: small but strong, as a pony is to a horse."

"The law has always been after him," said John MacDonald. "Especially the Duke of Montrose. There was bad blood between those two. I heard that even after Sheriffmuir, Rob Roy continued raiding Montrose and his friends. Bold as a terrier dog." He cast a merry look to Jim-Bird, who chuckled.

"He was captured twice," said William. "But he escaped execution both times. In his later years he lived quietly at Balquhidder, and he died peacefully just last year."

"Och, he's dead then," MacDonald said quietly. He fell silent for a moment, giving death its due. Then, just as quickly, he turned back to life, the spark returning to his eye.

"Rosemary," he said, "some of these men want their cups refilled."

Rosemary sighed, tearing herself away from the stories and going out to fetch a pot of tea. In a short time she returned and began making her way with it around the table. When she came to William, she said: "*An gabh tu cupa tea Uilleam?*"

"Do I? Och, you speak Gaelic. *Tapadh leat, bhitheadh sin math.*"

Smiling, she poured him a cup.

"What did he say?" asked John Coleman.

"He said, 'Thank you, that would be nice,'" said Rosemary.

"Of all my children," MacDonald said, "Rosemary is the only one who has cared to learn the old ways."

With their bellies full, the travel-weary men began to grow sleepy. They got up from the table and went outside to smoke their pipes and enjoy the night air. The women and children quickly closed in behind them to claim the vacant table and the remaining food for their own dinner.

William was expecting another night on the ground, but John MacDonald was more hospitable than the planters with whom they had taken lodgings in nights past. Perhaps it was the scarce company of his fellow man out here on the frontier that prompted MacDonald to open his house to travelers. The floor of the main room was theirs for the night.

Sam, William, and John fetched their bedrolls and laid them out. The floor was hard but there would be far fewer of the mosquitos they had contended with in nights past. Thomas and Jim-Bird stayed at the barn to sleep close to the horses. John MacDonald retired to the small bedroom off the main room. Rosemary, Betsy, Liza, and the children climbed up to the sleeping loft.

In the guttering light of a candle, William wrote:

> July 24. On this day I enjoyed fine country food in the country palace of one John MacDonald, who fought with my father at Sheriffmuir. I was served at table by a golden angel of a Scottish lass (now Carolinian) as perfectly at home in this landscape as any native deer.
>
> Travel: 35 miles, no less.

8   Border Country

When William began to come awake the next morning, it was with the memory of how tired he had been the night before. From the way he lay, he seemed not to have moved a muscle the whole night long. He heard the MacDonald women moving about, and as he opened his eyes he could see from the diffuse light in the room that outside the sky was overcast.

Rosemary came striding past him carrying an armload of kindling and firewood. Her bare foot brushed him ever so slightly—whether purposefully he did not know. This time he was sure he smelled a whiff of rosemary.

"Wake up, sleepyheads," she said. "A new day is dawning—a drizzly one." Then she knelt in front of the fireplace and went about building a fire.

Her presence affected William the same way it had last night. He got up and out of his blanket rather awkwardly, concealing the bulge in the front of his pants, and went outside, where a light rain was falling. As he made his way to the privy, he noticed parts of the farmstead he had not taken in the evening before. An outside kitchen, a smokehouse redolent with the smell of smoky fires and cured pork, a spring house next to Rosemary's dairy, a crude chicken house, a corncrib, and two small slave houses.

Coming out of the privy, he met John Coleman waiting to come in, so after he exited he waited for John under the eave of the chicken house and walked with him back to the house. John led the way past the kitchen around to the back porch, where there was a pan of water and a piece of soap on a shelf for washing up. As first John and then William cleaned theirs hands and faces, Sam arrived to take his turn. William followed John back into the house and found breakfast under way. Thomas and Jim-Bird had already come in and were sitting at the table with John MacDonald. The three sisters were serving up platters of fried eggs, fried slices of ham, hominy grits, pancakes, butter, honey, and cups of cold sweet milk. A small, cheery fire burned in the fireplace, and the children played about the room noisily, unable to go outside because of the rain. The women continually tried to shush them, and Betsy finally sent them out to play in the barn.

With all this good food and good company inside, and with the wet drear outside, the men were in a mood to linger over their meal.

"So, William," said John MacDonald, "are ye a-taking up packhorseman work for good or just for the season?"

"I'm taking it up for good, for the time being," William said. Thomas gave a snort, which William ignored. "I had a short career as a clerk at a dry goods store in Charles Town, but I got so crosswise with two of the town's grandees, it became convenient for me to seek another career."

Thomas snorted again.

"It's not hard to get crosswise with that crowd," said MacDonald. "The planters don't have any trouble eating my beef and cheese and butter, but when I drive my cattle to market past their plantations, they get as edgy as can be. They hate the very idea of my cows getting anywhere close to the crops in their fields."

"If I may ask," said William, "were you a cowherd in the old country?"

"Aye, indeed I was," said MacDonald, leaning back in his chair. "Before the Jacobite rising came along and undid me, I had got myself up a good little herd of kyloes. But it was good-bye to all that and to everything else when they shipped me out. Once I got here to the colony, they forced us to go out to guard the western border. I thought I had come to the end of the earth. But all things work for the good, and it was out there that I found Martha, God rest her soul. After we married, I went to work for her father, and when he died, she inherited a small part of his herd. With careful husbandry we built up to what you've seen here, as well as quite a bit you haven't seen."

"I'm impressed by the size of your dairy herd," said William. "I understand where the beef goes—I saw the slaughterhouses in Charles Town. But what becomes of all that milk? There could not be much market for it around here."

"We sell some of the butter and cheese to plantations downriver, but my family and my slaves consume the rest of it, along with milk and clabber. We work hard and eat big. If there's any left over, it goes as slop for the hogs. But the greater part of my stock is for beef, not for dairying. I have six hundred head of free-range cattle, more or less. We drive about a sixty of them to Charles Town each fall, as well as any hogs I can spare. Rufus—that's Betsy's husband—he and his cow-hunters are out with the cattle now, driving them along to fresh forage as they need it. You ask me where the milk goes? Those cow-hunters alone eat a ton of cheese. And the timber crew eats twice as much. That's the hardest work there is."

"I was wondering about that," said William. "Logging and cowkeeping are such different trades. Does a cow-hunter have to be a woodsman too? Along the way I have seen plenty of natural savannahs for grazing."

John Coleman intervened. "William asks a lot of questions," he said, offering MacDonald a reprieve from answering.

"It's enough to drive a person to distraction," said Thomas, pushing back his chair to leave. But then he settled back again, perhaps remembering the rain outside.

John MacDonald, however, was enjoying himself, glad to talk about his work and his life. He waved away the suggestion that he might feel otherwise. "The canebrakes are good for grazing in winter, and the wiregrass savannahs in the piney woods are good the rest of the year. But clearing timber from the land and cowkeeping can go together. If you have a good location for getting your timber into a big enough river, the more land we clear, the more forage there is for cattle. And of course, there's money coming in from the timber itself. Aaron's crew cuts down and squares up pine, poplar, and cypress timbers, and then they drag them on timber wheels to the bank of the Santee and tumble them in. Once they get them in the water, they form them up into rafts and float them downriver. We sell and trade some of it along the way, but from the mouth of the Santee most of my timber is shipped to the sugar islands. But that's sure enough hard work, that timber work."

MacDonald was holding forth on his own now, with no more prompting needed from William. "Carolina is a fair place for a cow-keeper. There is enough green forage in the canebrakes to keep the cows alive through the winter, though they get a bit thin before the break of spring. Not nearly as skinny, though, as the Highland cows back home. Back there, those kyloes are some pitifully thin creatures by the time spring comes. Right, William? You know what I'm a-talking about."

William nodded. "I do. I know it well."

"I don't see how they could get much skinnier than these Carolina cattle at the end of a hard year," said Thomas. "I've seen some mighty lean cows."

"I will guarantee ye," said MacDonald, "that at the end of the coldest, hardest winter in Carolina, the cows here would be positively fat compared to Highland cows at the end of any winter in Scotland. Tell him, William."

"It's true," said William. "In the Highlands, we grazed our cows free-range, but we had precious little hay to give them in the depths of winter. Mind ye, these are but wee cows to start with. They have to be to survive. Full grown and fat, they weigh barely 400 pounds, and sometimes as little as 200. But even at that we still lost some to starvation each year. It didn't help that we had to take blood from their veins to keep from starving ourselves."

"You drank their blood?" said Thomas.

"Aye," said John MacDonald, "that we did. You would be surprised, Thomas, how good it tastes cooked with oatmeal and onions. Black pudding we called it. We did all we could to get the cows and us both through hard times, but they didn't always make it. It was pitiful. We were all pitiful. At the end of winter many of the cows were so weak they had to be lifted up bodily and helped out to pasture."

"But once they began grazing," said William, "they could put their weight on quickly. They were nothing if not hardy. And they could hold up to being driven through rough country and over long distances. They had their good points, those little shaggy cows."

"But when ye say 'skinny cows,'" said MacDonald, "Carolina cows are out of the contest."

Coming out on the short end of this argument, Thomas puffed up. "Well, I guess I'm just too ignorant to sit at this table," he said. And this time he did get up and go outside.

"What's amiss with Thomas?" asked MacDonald after he had left the room.

"He's is a bit thin-skinned these days," replied Sam. "More than usual, that is. I think it's on account of Barnaby dying on us. Thomas can't just grieve and get it over with like the rest of us."

Rosemary came in with a pot of hot tea. "Is anybody ready for more?" she asked. All the men held up their cups and watched with pleasure as she went around the table filling each one.

"What's worse here than in Scotland are the varmints," said MacDonald, barely pausing in his discourse. "In Scotland it was the two-legged varmints that gave us the most trouble. Here it's the four-legged ones. Wolves are the worst problem. Then panthers. And now and again a bear will try to pick off a newborn. Oft times, though, these horned cattle can hold their own. They'll form a protecting circle around their heifers and calves, and it takes a brave varmint to go against those lowered horns. Now the hogs, they can nearly always take care of themselves. Not even a panther is anxious to take on a full grown boar hog. A hog will even kill and eat rattlesnakes, which is the damndest thing

I've ever seen. The snakes sometimes bite them, but if the hogs are fat enough it seems to do them no harm. Those hogs can make it on their own. During the day they range a far piece into the woods, but if ye put out a little food for them to eat and a dry sty in the hogcrawl for them to sleep in, they'll come home for the night. If ye get careless, though, and neglect them, they'll go wild and you'll not see them again. They're not like cattle. They can get along without us."

"What about the two-legged varmints," asked William. "Do you lose many cattle to theft?"

"We do lose some each year, but it's not nearly the problem here that it was back home. In Scotland you'd get so many cattle lifted, you had to lift in self-defense. Here it's mainly the Indians. From time to time they kill a cow or a hog, especially when their hunting is bad. Most times they use a bow and arrow and you never hear a thing."

MacDonald sipped his tea, and everyone was quiet. William knew it was time to stop asking questions.

"I love the herding life," said MacDonald, as if to put a cap on all that he had said. "And there is no country more beautiful than this. I love to be out in it every day. But if things get tight here, our wealth is in our livestock, and we can drive them somewhere else. The one thing I wish for is a bigger breed of cattle. That's what I am working on. I am breeding bigger stock into my cows as fast as I can do it."

Sam stood up from the table and stretched, then walked over to the door, opened it, and looked out. "Well," he said, "I do believe this rain is going to let up. Let's get out there and pack those horses so we can get on the road."

As William inspected his gear, he quickly went over each of his lash ropes foot by foot. Noticing what seemed to be a limp spot in one of them, he examined it more closely and felt a pang in the pit of his stomach. Someone had taken the thin point of a sharp knife and gone inside the rope to cut through more than half of its fibers. The surface of the weakened place had been rubbed with animal fat and dirt to conceal any stray severed ends. It was set to snap in the course of a day's travel just like the other one had. William coiled up the damaged rope and stowed it in his saddle bag. Then he substituted one of the extra lash ropes they carried with them.

As he lashed his packs onto his horses, his mind was reeling. Who could be doing this—the downed gear, the cut ropes? And why? Sam could have no conceivable reason, unless perhaps it was a way in which he tested his new men, to see if they could handle such problems. Whether John Coleman had a reason or not, it was hard to see how he could have done it. He had hardly been out of William's sight since they arrived at the cowpen. The two of them had spent the night in the house. Which left Jim-Bird and Thomas, both of whom had slept in the barn and had plenty of opportunity. Thomas certainly had an edge on him. And Jim-Bird, well, who knew what was going on with Jim-Bird? But why would either of them want to undercut him? One thing was certain: he had trouble on his hands. From now on, he would stay on the alert.

With his horses packed, William mounted Viola and looked over at the rest of the crew, who were also mounted and ready to depart. Which one was the snake in the grass? He hated the fact that he now had to regard his mates with suspicion, when all he had wanted was to gain their trust. Yet he had no choice but to face this problem.

John MacDonald and his daughters came out to see them off, standing by and watching as they formed up the horses into a train. Tazzie and Binkie waited eagerly at the fore, ready for another day's adventure. "Let's go, you crackers," said Sam, and the packhorsemen cracked their whips and whooped as they moved the horses out. William gave more than a simple crack. He swung his whip round about in an elegant circle over his head and brought it back sharply, making a crack loud enough to be heard, he hoped, in Charles Town. Partly he was serving notice to his unknown enemy, but also partly, if truth be told, he did it to impress Rosemary. As they rode past the house, she was standing near the flower garden, waving good-bye with her father and sisters while the children played in the yard around them. This was a picture William wanted to etch into his memory. When he waved back, he thought her quick smile and tilted head might be for him alone.

John was now the only one in whom William had any much trust. He pulled up beside him as they headed out onto the trail, wondering if he should say something to him about the rope. But he thought better of it and turned instead to the other pressing topic on his mind. "Godamighty, that Rosemary is a pretty girl," he said. "If only she weren't such a young one."

"She ain't young for the border country," said John. "Many of these border girls marry at thirteen or fourteen. But when their father is protective, they can get a man in a mess of trouble. I'd not want the likes of John MacDonald coming down on me." He looked back to see where Thomas was, then lowered his voice. "You know, Thomas is sweet on Rosemary. But he's not yet said anything to her for fear of her father. The thing with Thomas, of course, is that he would never be in it just for the woman. His ambition is to get into the horse and cattle business."

"I didn't see him paying the least attention to her," said William.

"You wouldn't," said John. "Thomas is so secretive he'll never disclose any-thing unless it suits him."

William reined in Viola until he had fallen back with the horses in his own string. He had to think. He did not like the idea of Thomas having his sights set on Rosemary. He himself had no claim on her, but the memory of her smile and the tilt of her head made him feel warm and interested. He did not fear John MacDonald; he understood him. Rosemary could be his, he thought, but he would have to be ready to settle down with her. John MacDonald would ac-cept no less. And the truth was, he was not ready to settle down, especially not as a cow-hunter back here in the border country. He had come to Carolina to find a new life, not to lock himself into the very one he had turned away from as a lad in Scotland. The best thing would be to forget Rosemary, to stop think-ing about her. Though he knew that it would not be easy.

A mile or so up the trail they heard the faint bark of a dog as they ap-proached a great, wide, stump-filled wiregrass savannah—an old deadening in which only a few scattered trees were still alive and standing. Tazzie and Binkie answered with barking of their own, running a short way toward the clear-ing and then stopping to hold their territory, still barking. William looked be-yond them and saw a large herd of cattle in the distance, on the far side of the open land. A cow-hunter on horseback, whom William took to be MacDon-ald's son-in-law, waved his broad-brimmed hat at them. Beyond him, two other cow-hunters, African slaves, rode slowly among the cattle. That was a sight rarely seen in Scotland—cow-herders on horseback. William waved back at MacDonald's son-in-law, and the Africans waved in return.

Upon leaving behind the grazing range of MacDonald's cowpen, the pine forest closed in around them again. "Does this pine forest go on forever?" William asked Jim-Bird, who was riding alongside him.

"No," he said, "not forever, but it is much bigger than you might imagine. We will start seeing a few oak trees mixed in with the pines tomorrow. And two days after that the trees will be mostly oak and hickory with only a few pines mixed in. But if we were to swing down to the Southwest from here, it would be piney woods all the way to the Mississippi River. And I've heard people say the pines go west of that river a ways."

"That is a lot of pine trees."

"You are right about that."

As they followed the road paralleling Halfway Swamp, the land was still flat, the soil still sandy. Everyone except William was in good spirits. But

William kept to himself, feeling grim and wary over the treachery he had discovered earlier in the day. In the afternoon, the spirits of the others were dampened as well when the sky clouded up again and a hard rain came and got them soaking wet. But they pressed on until they reached Captain Russell's plantation near the junction of Ox Creek and Halfway Swamp Creek, where they put in for the night.

"Captain Russell was one of the first to settle in these parts," John explained to William, though William had not asked him about it. "He was the commander of Old Fort Congaree, which we'll come to in a couple of days. When the fort closed down, Russell married well and became master of this plantation. It has long been a stopover for travelers going to and fro on the Cherokee Path, and on the path to the Catawbas as well."

The plantation had obviously been long established, despite the rough countryside around it. The main house was made of logs. In fact, it was two houses side by side, with a covered breezeway in between them. A white-haired man wearing a broad-brimmed straw hat came out to meet them.

"Good evening, Captain," said Sam, tipping his hat. "Have you room for us here tonight?"

"Welcome, Sam," the old gentleman replied jovially. "We have plenty of room, and we're lonesome for company. While you attend to your horses, I'll tell Mrs. Russell to throw some extra beans into the pot."

It turned out that Mrs. Russell was famous in this neck of the woods for putting on a good table. After dinner, the men savored a round of rum punch and continued to exchange their news.

"Did you hear tell of any Germans landing in Charles Town?" asked Russell. "We're expecting some new settlers for these townships up here."

"As a matter of fact," said Sam, "about a week before we set out, I did hear of a shipload of Switzers putting in. I thought they might be headed this way."

"A few of them may be coming here to Amelia Township," said Russell, "but most are going to Orangeburg Township over on the Edisto River."

"What townships are these?" asked William. "We've come through nothing but wilderness for two days."

"The townships," said Captain Russell, "are a scheme devised by governor Johnson to salve the worries of the citizens of Charles Town about their neighbors, both near and far." He turned back to his punch as if that were explanation enough.

"What neighbors are they worried about?" asked William. "The Indians?"

"The Indians are just one part of it," said Russell. "They also worry about the slaves all around them, outnumbering them two to one, though they import more every day. Every so often people in Charles Town get caught up in terror of a slave insurrection. And they worry about the Catholics—the Spaniards to the south and the Frenchmen to the west. Every way they look, they feel in danger. Governor Johnson's solution is to set up a string of townships back here in the border country and populate them with poor Protestant farmers from Europe. They are enticed here with an offer of fifty acres of free land for each person, plus a waver of quitrents for ten years, plus other help from the public coffer. And with that we get white settlers to offset the black slaves and the Indians, as well as Protestants to offset the Catholics."

"It seems to be working," said Sam, "from what I've seen around here lately."

"It's starting to," said Russell. "I've already helped several families of Switzers settle on the north fork of the Edisto. They are hard workers. They plan to cultivate wheat, corn, hemp, and flax. And for quite some time we've had some adventuresome cow-keepers in the cane swamps along the Edisto."

"It's fast becoming a polyglot country," said Sam, not altogether approvingly.

"It is for a fact," said Russell. "But the young people of all tongues are learning to speak English. We get along well enough."

When they had finished their punch, Captain Russell offered them pallets on the floor of the downstairs of his house, but William declined and went out to sleep in the barn. He meant to keep an eye on his gear and horses.

In the barn, he piled up a mound of cornshucks and laid his bedroll on it. Mrs. Russell had generously offered him a lantern with a short stub of a candle burning in it—enough of a stub for him to read a few pages of Shakespeare before taking pen and ink to his journal.

July 25. Macbeth. Emboldened by the soothsaying of a witch, Macbeth assassinates the King of Scotland and takes the crown for his own. But frightened by the soothsaying of a second witch, who predicts that his friend and fellow nobleman, Banquo, will father a line of future kings, thus threatening his reign, Macbeth has Banquo murdered. Do the English assume that all Scottish affairs of state hinge on the doings of witches? And that Scots are so bloody-minded that they see assassination as a ready road to political ambition?

So much for Shakespeare. My own life has become almost as dramatic. I have had quite a day. From a cut lash rope I found out for sure that I have an enemy among my mates. And also, it would seem, I've taken an arrow in my heart from Cupid's bow. As we rode along today I kept thinking of Rosemary. I didn't want to, but I couldn't stop myself. And I kept wondering whether she thinks of me.

It's either Sam or Thomas or Jim-Bird who is trying to undercut me. I don't think it could be John, though he might know about it.

Travel: 10 miles.

Beyond Captain Russell's, the terrain at last began to change. The land was clearly rising now, and they began seeing oaks mixed in amongst the pines, just as Jim-Bird had said. They were finally leaving the coastal plain behind. For much of the day the packtrain followed along a ridge that lay between two watersheds, the streams on their right running down into the Congaree River and on their left into the north fork of the Edisto River. In the late afternoon they made their way down a long hill, crossed Beaver Creek, and encamped for the night.

No longer knowing whom to trust among the men, William found himself turning for companionship to Tazzie, Jim-Bird's male terrier. Binkie stayed close to Jim-Bird, but Tazzie had been warming to William as the days had gone by. The dog liked having his ears scratched and examined for ticks. Often, when William sat down, Tazzie would come up to him and gently bump his nose against his leg to get his attention.

"In Britain," William said to Jim-Bird, who was sitting nearby on a log, "they call these little dogs feisting curs."

"I've heard them called feists," said Jim-Bird, "but that never made any sense to me. A feist is a fart. These dogs are not bad for farting."

"Yes, but they're so small, you see, they can lie in the laps of their master. Then when the master lets loose a silent but rank wind, the dog can be blamed for it."

Jim-Bird chuckled. "That is not the reason I keep them. I keep them because they don't eat much. And because they are eye-dogs—they keep their eyes on the world about them more than they do their noses. That makes them good for hunting squirrels. If you have a dog that can keep track of a squirrel in a tree and run it around so you can draw a bead on it, you'll never go hungry."

"What I like about them," said William, "is how bold their spirits are."

Jim-Bird nodded. "They are brave to a fault." He reached out to scratch Binkie's back above her tail, while Binkie closed her eyes with pleasure. "They're bred small, but they think they're as big as any dog they see. They are always ready to take on anything. Especially Tazzie. I have to be careful to keep him out of fights he should have more sense than to get into. In every other way he's a smart little fellow."

"He is for a fact," said William. "I've noticed how he and Binkie watch your every move. They almost always know what you intend to do next." William scratched Tazzie's ear. "Yes, you're a smart little fellow," he said to the dog.

"Tazzie," said Jim-Bird, and the dog looked up at his master, fully alert. "Tazzie, fetch my hatchet."

Tazzie jumped up, looked around, saw where Jim-Bird had been chopping firewood, trotted over, and picked up the hatchet's handle in his teeth. Then he came trotting back to Jim-Bird and dropped it at his feet.

"Tazzie, chop that wood," said Jim-Bird, pointing to a stick on the ground nearby.

Tazzie stood wagging his tail, looking at Jim-Bird, who looked around to see William's face.

"He may be smart for a dog," said Jim-Bird, "but he's not *that* smart."

July 26. First Tazzie warmed up to me, and now, evidently, so has his master. If Jim-Bird is the bad fairy, he is a master of deceit. I am sleeping near my gear every night now. Let the bad fairy try it again, and we will find out who he is.

Travel: 18 miles.

For much of the next day the packhorsemen drove their horses along the rough wagon road through dune-like, sandy hills, as if near the sea, though the closest surf was some sixty miles behind them. Coming at last to the other side of the sand hills, the road sloped down toward Old Fort Congaree near the Congaree River. As the packtrain descended, it gradually entered the dense, darkly shaded floodplain forest that lined the margins of the river. It was a hard passage. They had to ford Sandy Run Creek and Savanna Hunt Creek, both of which ran deeper here in the floodplain than did the streams on higher ground, to which the packhorsemen had become accustomed. Recent rains had swollen the creeks, and they had to take extra care in driving their horses across the fords. At the end of the day they came to Brown's store on Congaree Creek, where they camped.

As they sat around the fire that night, William asked about Old Fort Congaree.

"It ain't far from where we're a-sittin'," said John. "What's left of it. Carolina built it just after the Yamassee War, in 1718 I guess it was, on a neck of land that has Congaree Creek on one side and the Congaree River on the other."

"After the war," said Sam, "Fort Congaree was supposed to be the place where the Cherokees and Catawbas could come to trade—the expectation being that the trade could be supervised there by a Carolina Indian agent. The problem was, the Indians didn't want to go to the trade, they wanted the trade to come to them. So Fort Congaree was abandoned as a bad idea only four years after it was built."

"But there's a store here now," said William. "There must be at least some trade to be had."

"I'll say one thing for the Brown brothers," said Thomas, "they picked a sure enough good place to put a store. That fort idea just came at the wrong time. This here is right below where the Saluda and Broad rivers join to form up the Congaree, and it's close by the crossing of two strong trails, the north-south one we're on and the east-west path that runs between Fort Moore on the Savannah River and the Catawbas. A store sittin' here can be supplied by horse and also by batteaus and periaguas coming up the Congaree from the Santee."

"It's true," said Sam, "the Browns have a good head for business. Thomas Brown had a store at the Catawbas until their numbers got so low it wasn't worth his while to stay amongst them anymore. That's when he set up this one. His brother Patrick is in with him for now, but I've heard it said that Patrick is talking about moving to greener fields on the Savannah River at Fort Moore. They say he's wanting to get in on the Creek and Chickasaw trade. That's where things are opening up."

"Well, if it's the Indian trade he wants, he'd be smart to go to Fort Moore," said Thomas. "This store here is going to be more and more selling to the new settlers coming in. We're right in the middle of Saxe-Gotha Township. It might not look like much now, but as more Germans and Switzers come in, the Indian trade will be drying up and the settler trade will be swelling. But those Bible-thumpers had better look sharp if they want to avoid being skinned by the Browns. This ain't no paradise they're coming to."

"There's more than one way to get skinned," said Sam. "They had better be smart about the Indians, too. They're putting down roots right on the border between the Indians and Carolina, and the Indians still have the run of this place for now."

July 27. We are crossing the divide between the Carolina settlements and the Indian country. I have lived all my life under written law. Am I now to live under unwritten law? Two kinds of law at once? No laws at all? This will be a different world, like nothing I have ever known before. Uncle Duncan tried to tell me I was going to a different world, but only now do I begin to have an inkling of what he was saying. Compared with this, Charles Town was not a new world. It was but a change of scenery in the old one.

No time for Shakespeare these days. Rosemary will not stay out of my thoughts. I am trying to forget her. One good thing is the bad fairy has not returned.

Travel: 19 miles.

9   Macbeth

The next morning began with no surprises. William's gear was firmly in place on limbs above the ground. A few horses had strayed into a canebrake during the night, but the packhorsemen easily rounded them up in the early dawn light by following the tinkling of their bells. Jim-Bird had gotten up early and cooked a pot of hominy grits and boiled up a kettle of black drink. The men ate quickly and got on their way. After a little more than an hour on the trail, they made their usual stop to inspect the rigging of their horses and tighten it up where tightening was needed.

Jim-Bird's terriers took this opportunity to do some foraging at the edge of the woods. Binkie was the first to investigate a great hollow log moldering in the underbrush. Tazzie quickly joined her, both of their forequarters squeezed together inside, while outside their stubby tails were up and wagging rapidly. Soon they were yapping in high excitement, straining to get at some creature inside the log, each making it harder for the other to push forward. Then suddenly they tucked their tails and backed out quickly. Binkie had a baby raccoon in her mouth. But just as she was giving it a shake, the mother raccoon came flying out of the log as if shot from a cannon, her fur on end and her fangs bared—a perfect fury of a raccoon. Binkie turned to flee with her prey, but the mother raccoon caught her stub of a tail in her teeth and bit down hard. With a sharp yelp, Binkie dropped the baby raccoon and took out running straight for William's string of horses, the mother raccoon in close pursuit, with Tazzie charging after the raccoon, his hackles raised, barking furiously.

Had it been only the dogs, they might not have spooked the horses—the dogs were always underfoot. But the ruffled raccoon barreling straight down on one of the horses was all it took to set it kicking and running for safety. With this, the other horses in the string bolted, magnifying the general sense of imminent danger, which in turn led several horses in the other strings to bolt and scatter as well, running helter-skelter up the trail or into the woods. William had dismounted to tighten his rigging, and Viola bolted with the rest, leaving him helpless to do anything but start out after the runaways on foot.

Jim-Bird, who was still in his saddle, headed quickly for the fleeing lead mare. Pulling up next to her, he grabbed her halter and rode alongside her until she calmed down. Some of the other horses calmed with her, bringing most of the runaways under control.

Three of the horses, however, had run into the woods, where, encumbered by their packs, they had stumbled and fallen and were now thrashing madly, weighed down by their packs and unable to get to their feet. William reached them before the others, taking off his hunting shirt as he approached and wrapping it around the eyes of the first horse he came to. Thomas and John were right behind, blindfolding the other two horses to calm them. Then Sam came and helped them unpack the downed horses and get them on their feet again. Fortunately no bones were broken, but the horses were scratched and bleeding and two of them were lame. The packhorsemen cleaned them of debris and treated their wounds with a salve of bear fat and herbs. Then they repacked the loads of the two lame horses onto two of the spares, leaving only one more spare for the rest of the journey.

Sam was of no mind to linger. Everyone helped with the repacking, and as soon as the train was back together, they set off again. William rode along grimly, angry at the world. Not a bit of that melee had been his fault, but it was his horses that spooked first. It made him look bad, though there was not a bloody thing he could have done about it.

Sam rode over and fell in beside him. "We came out of that one all right," he said. "Those little dogs can be a pain in the ass, but we have to put up with them if we want Jim-Bird with us."

William nodded, understanding that he was not being blamed.

"The horses seem to know we are coming into Indian country today," said Sam. "They know as well as we do that from here on we'll have no more of the safety that comes from having planters and cow-keepers about us. That means more danger from wolves and panthers. And we have to look sharp for Indians and outlaws. It's not unknown in the backcountry for a gang of outlaws to stampede a pack train and steal some of the runaway horses with all the goods on their backs."

"Outlaws?" said William.

"That's right," said Sam. "Where else would you find outlaws but out where there ain't no law? They are to land as pirates are to the sea. These rogues live in the backcountry as if they were in a kingdom of their own. They hunt deer for meat and skins, and of course the Indians don't like that. They raise a little corn and beans on land that don't belong to them. They have amongst them a few Indians who are outcasts from their own people, and a few escaped black slaves. They've come into the settlements from time to time to trade horses, most of which are stolen. They come down into these parts from the north, from the backcountry of Virginia and North Carolina. As those lands get settled, they move down here. Every year there's more of them than before."

Sam rode on ahead and William relaxed. Maybe the tide had turned. He was no longer drawing blame for everything that happened. He studied the country around him, admiring the beauty of the oak and hickory trees. In the battle of the trees the oaks and hickories were now becoming dominant over the pines. The double ruts of the wagon road, having grown increasingly faint in the past few days, had become a single-rut horse trail. It paralleled the south side of the Saluda River through land that was hilly and pleasant to the eye.

Late in the day they came to Eighteen Mile Creek—so named because it was eighteen miles from Congaree Creek. They rode along its bank for a mile before fording it and encamped on the other side. From here on they would be sleeping in the open every night and eating nothing but trail food. Jim-Bird tried to put the best face on it by cooking up a thick soup made mainly with dried sweet corn and dried peaches. Perhaps he was also trying to make amends for the havoc set in motion by his dogs.

July 28. Since I have taken to sleeping near my gear, I have had no more trouble from my bad fairy. Ill luck befell us today, but this time it did not land on me. I would forget the past occurrences were it not for the cut rope I have in my saddlebag. That cut is no product of my imagination.
Travel: 19 miles.

The next day the trail followed closely along the south side of the Saluda River, crossing a great many creeks—Little Rocky Creek, Beaverdam, Great Rocky Creek, Hollow Creek, and several others whose names William could not keep in mind, though John called out each one for his benefit. The hills grew steeper. The subsoil of this land, visible in the banks that were cut along the streams, was a richly colored red-orange clay. At the end of the day they crossed the headwaters of the western branch of the Saluda River and camped in a forest of the largest trees William had ever seen. These were black oaks and chestnut oaks, he was told. Some of the black oaks were ten feet in diameter, with enormous, bulging roots extending out from the bases of their perfectly straight trunks, which tapered up forty or fifty feet to the first limbs.

"I've seen black oaks so tall you could not shoot a turkey out of the top of them with birdshot," Jim-Bird said. The chestnut oaks, which were also very tall, were renowned for their acorns, which were large and not too bitter. According to Jim-Bird, the Indians liked to roast them and pound them into a meal for soups and stews. Widely interspersed among the oaks and hickories were large poplar and beech trees. The floor of this cathedral forest was as clear as a park in Scotland.

That night the packhorsemen dined on three large bass that Jim-Bird had taken with a green-cane fish spear with a fire-hardened point. Grilled over hot hickory coals, they were deliciously tender and well flavored.

"Up yonderways," said Sam, pointing toward the north, "is the site of Saluda Old Town, the namesake of this river. The Saludas were a mysterious bunch of Indians who moved in there about twenty years after Charles Town was first settled. They may have been kin to the Savannahs, the ones who drove out the Westos."

"Were they slave catchers like the Westos were?" asked William.

"They were. That was the business back then. For a time they joined with the Congarees and Catawbas, and together they preyed on the Cherokees and sold them to us as slaves. Well, not to me. I wasn't here then, but to the Carolina traders. Just as I was coming into the trade, the Saludas picked up and moved north, up to Pennsylvania. That was about the time the Indians hereabouts were warming up for the Yamassee War, and the Saludas had worn out their welcome by then. After the uprising, the trade in Indian slaves died out. Some of the Indian slaves on the plantations had plotted with the rebels, you see, and those plantations got hit first. People were wary of keeping Indian slaves after that."

"I'm thankful the trade is only in deerskins these days," said William. "I would not care to be a slave trader."

"Let's just hope the deerskin trade will last," said Sam. "Deer are getting mighty thin in some places already."

July 29. My mother thought her world would last forever. But it has not. The very ground is crumbling beneath her feet, if she would only admit it. Likewise, the Westos and Saludas must have thought they had found a fine business opportunity in Carolina. But it did not last. Now I hear that my new profession is already on the wane. It would seem that the New World is just like the Old in that change is the only constant condition. I wish it were not so, but there is naught I can do about it.

Travel: 18 miles.

The next day they traveled without incident through dense woods from sunup to sundown, until at the end of it they came to Buffalo Swamp and encamped. A great flock of turkeys feeding in a glade near the swamp ran into the woods as the packtrain approached.

"Tonight," Jim-Bird said to William as they were cleaning up after dinner, "you will hear a serenade by the wolves and panthers who live in this swamp. They sleep under cover by day and come out at night to hunt deer."

"I will steel my nerves for it," said William.

In the evening twilight he found time to read a few pages of *Macbeth*.

July 30. Lady Macbeth was right. Macbeth does not have the constitution for murder and assassination. He cannot sleep. He complains that his mind is full of scorpions. He begins to see ghosts. He behaves oddly, and Lady Macbeth must make apologies for him. A grim tale.

Travel: 22 miles.

The farther north they traveled, the higher the hills became. The horses began to sweat and breathe hard as they ascended the steeper grades. Still traveling beneath a canopy of enormous trees, they crossed Ninety-Six Creek—that is, ninety-six miles from Keowee—then Wilson's Creek, and Black Ram Creek, and then they came to Coronaca—a well-known campground, it would seem, from all the remains of old campfires scattered about. Here they spent the night. They were stretching out their travel each day as they drew closer to their destination. Everyone was weary of the trail.

William retired early from the others to get back to *Macbeth* in the fading light.

July 31. Macbeth searches out the witch's coven again. Now the witches' goddess, Hecate, scolds the three witches for trafficking in riddles with Macbeth without inviting her infernal majesty, "the close contriver of all harms," to play her part. The witches all meet again and cook up a proper witch's cauldron of revolting stuffs capped off with a cup of baboon's blood.

Now Macbeth is in their evil clutches. They calm his fears, but they warn him to beware of Macduff, one of his noble comrades. With this advice Macbeth determines he must kill poor Macduff. Mr. Shakespeare seems to assume that this is how the Scots solve their problems. And worse yet, Macbeth's assassins can only get their hands on Macduff's wife, children, and servants, whom they—yes—murder. Macbeth thinks his troubles are over.

Though I too am a Scotsman, I believe I can find better ways to solve my problems.

Travel: 24 miles.

They started out the next day still heading toward the northwest and still crossing small tributaries of the Saluda River. It was yet early morning when they drew up their horses at the sight of a large panther walking leisurely up the trail a short distance ahead. John, who was at the head of the train, drew down on the creature, fired, and missed. Unperturbed, the great tawny cat sat down on its haunches and calmly turned its head to look back at the packtrain.

"Bloody hell," muttered Thomas. "It's the devil himself."

"That is one strange panther," said Jim-Bird. He looked around for his dogs, but it was too late. They had just caught sight of the cat and were tearing off up the trail, barking madly, legs flying. Jim-Bird tried to call them back, but to no avail. The cat lowered its ears, crouched, and flicked its tail. Jim-Bird stood up in his stirrups, gave the loudest whistle William had ever heard, and the two dogs skidded to a halt, turned around, and came trotting back to the horses with their tails tucked between their legs. The panther rose to its feet and ambled into the woods without bothering to look again at the train.

"That beats all I've ever seen," said Sam. "Panthers don't show themselves in the open like that. You should have let the dogs have a go at him, see if he was real or a ghost."

"Either way, they would not have come out of it well," said Jim-Bird. "I'd just as soon not have my dogs eaten by a cat."

They got under way again, pushing on through the growing heat of the day, crossing Marrow Bone Creek, Mulberry Creek, and the several branches of Turkey Creek. When they came to Apple Tree Creek, John announced it triumphantly. The Saluda watershed was behind them. Apple Tree Creek drained toward the west, into the headwaters of the Savannah River.

Just past Apple Tree Creek the trail forked. Both forks, John explained to William, went to the towns of the Lower Cherokees. The left fork ran southwest to the more southerly towns. The right fork, which they took, continued northwest toward Keowee and the more northerly towns.

Late in the afternoon a ripple of unease began to run through the horses. It started in John's string at the front of the train, with first one and then another of the horses snorting and tossing its head. As the ripple passed through William's horses, he rode in close beside them, talking soothingly. They settled down and William heard the unease pass to Thomas's horses behind him. He turned around to look, and as he did his eye was caught by the foliage of a large oak limb overhanging the trail—a broad tawny face with wide-spaced gray eyes looked out.

"Thomas!" he shouted, pointing to the limb. "The panther!"

Just as Thomas looked up, the cat sprang down onto one of his horses. The horse reared and kicked, making a blur of cat, packs, and horse. The other horses scattered. The cat hung on but could not get his teeth and claws into the bucking horse. It bit futilely at the top pack and then gave it up, leaping to the ground and bounding off into the woods before anyone could get a shot at him.

It took a while to gather up the horses. The cat had pounced on the one carrying Sam's special goods. The horse was frightened, but not much hurt. He had a scratch on his hindquarters from the cat's hind claws, but it was not as bad as it might have been. As Thomas rubbed salve on the wound, John noticed a wet place on the pack. "What happened here?" he asked. He investigated and found the shattered pieces of a roundlet of brandy. "That's good liquor wasted," he said, shaking his head.

"But it explains the mystery of the panther," said William. "He is a cat drunkard, addicted to brandy."

"I believe you are right," John said with a chuckle. "He lies about the trail like a wastrel, waiting for the next train to come along and bring him another drink."

"Never does an honest day's work," added Jim-Bird.

The packhorsemen laughed, even Thomas joining in.

They did not try to travel much further. They were close to Barker's Creek, and when they reached it, they encamped for the night.

After supper, daylight lingered. William moved a little apart from the others and sat leaning against a tree to finish reading *Macbeth*. The play ended, and he closed the book just as the light was beginning to fade. He got up to return the book to his bag.

"What's that you've been reading, philosopher?" asked Thomas, who was sitting with the others at the fire.

"*Macbeth*. It's a play by William Shakespeare."

"A play?" Thomas said with interest. "I like a good play. Tell us the story. Don't keep it to yourself."

"It has five acts," said William. "It's too much to tell. There are witches, ghosts, and spectres running around, murder and mayhem. It's complicated."

"You mean we're too dimwitted to understand it?" said Thomas.

"No, I mean it's too complicated for me to be able to tell it."

"You're just putting us off," said Thomas. "You've heard plenty of stories from us. It's your turn to tell us one. Tell us about these witches and ghosts."

"All right, I will try," said William, squaring up for the task. He returned to his earlier place by the fire. For a moment he was silent, thinking back through the story. Then he began.

"Macbeth and Banquo were thanes, Scottish nobles, and great heroes, much beloved by Duncan, the King of Scotland. One day the two of them came upon a coven of three witches, and not by accident. The witches had lain in wait for them because they had some predictions to impart. One witch predicts that Macbeth, who was thane of Glamis, would also be made thane of Cawdor, and would even be made King of Scotland. Another witch predicts that Banquo would not himself be king, yet he would be the founder of a lineage of kings." William paused and glanced around at the others. They were listening.

"Macbeth and Banquo doubt the predictions of these three weird sisters, but word soon arrives that the Thane of Cawdor has committed treason. King Duncan has sentenced him to death and conferred his title on Macbeth, who is now Thane of both Glamis and Cawdor."

"So a thane would be what we call a lord?" asked John, interrupting.

"Yes," said William. "A Scottish lord. But here's where the trouble starts."

"The trouble started with those witches," said Jim-Bird.

"Yes, but it gets worse," said William. "Macbeth tells his wife about the witches, and Lady Macbeth starts thinking on how to hurry along their predictions. She knows Macbeth has ambition enough to contemplate assassinating the king, but she is not sure he is wicked enough to carry through with it. She vows to egg him on until he does the deed and whatever else must be done in its wake. And she succeeds. Macbeth plies Duncan's two guards with wine, and when all are asleep he goes in and stabs King Duncan to death. Then he stabs the two guards. When the household gathers, he blames the dead guards for killing the king, saying they were put up to it by the king's two sons. The sons then have to flee to save their lives. One of them, Malcolm, goes to England, and the other one goes to Ireland."

"He cleaned out the whole pack of them," said Sam.

"That he did," said William. "But Lady Macbeth was right to fear that her husband did not have the mettle to carry through with the plot. He got it this far, but for Macbeth that was one step too many. He begins to show signs of madness. He is unable to sleep. He begins thinking about the witch's prediction that Banquo will be founder of a line of kings. How can that be, he wonders, if he himself is to be the king?"

"It would have to mean that Banquo would replace him on the throne," said Sam.

"That's right," said William. "So Macbeth sends out assassins to murder Banquo, which they do. But this only worsens Macbeth's madness. His mind is now full of terror—he doubts, he fears, he sees the ghost of Banquo, he behaves oddly in company, and Lady Macbeth has to make excuses for his queer behavior."

"She saw it coming, didn't she," said Thomas. "Macbeth don't have what it takes to be no king."

"Not that kind of king," said William. "Macbeth has become fascinated by the witches. How do they know what they know? He seeks them out again, and this time he finds them in the company of Hecate, their goddess. The witches call up apparitions, who make more pronouncements to Macbeth. One tells him to beware of Macduff, the thane of Fife. Another tells him that no man born of woman can harm him. And a third one tells him that he will be safe in his fort at Dunsinane until the forest of Birnam Wood betakes itself there."

"Until what?" asked Thomas.

"Until the trees of Birnam Wood move themselves to his castle."

"That should keep him safe for a while," said Sam.

"That's what Macbeth thought, too," said William. "Who ever heard of a traveling forest? Who ever heard of a man not born of a woman? So he took those two pronouncements as good news. The only problem was this fellow Macduff."

"He's going to have to kill him," said Thomas.

"Yes, he sends his assassins after him. Macduff is not home when they get there, but they go at it anyway and kill his wife, children, and servants."

Sam shook his head. "What had *they* done?" he muttered.

"Meanwhile," William pressed on, "word comes that Malcolm, the king's son who went to England, has got up an army of 10,000 Englishmen. Macduff is with him, and the two of them are leading the army back against Macbeth.

Macbeth orders his men to scour the countryside and hang any of his subjects who show fear of the advancing English."

"That would be all of them," said Jim-Bird.

"Yes, had he men enough to carry through. But things are beginning to unravel for him now. News comes that the English army has been sighted near Dunsinane and that all these thousands of soldiers are carrying leafy branches from Birnam Wood as camouflage. Macbeth is confounded. Birnam Wood has, in a sense, come to Dunsinane. But still he takes comfort from the fact that no man born of woman can harm him."

"There ain't no way around that," said John.

"Well," said Jim-Bird, "if a man can't kill him, maybe a woman can. Where's Lady Macbeth?"

"No, that's not it," said William. "And anyway, she's already killed herself."

"Good riddance to her," said John.

"Let's get on with it," said Sam.

"Macduff, the fellow whose family was slaughtered, now finds his way to Macbeth, and the two take up swords. Still keeping his faith in the witches, Macbeth tells Macduff that he is not afraid of him because he cannot be killed by any man born of a woman. Macduff then informs him that he was cut from his mother's womb, not born from it. This bit of news spells the end for Macbeth, and he knows it. They go at each other until Macduff kills Macbeth and cuts off his head. Then all hail Malcolm, the new king. Malcolm's first royal act is to decree that all thanes are henceforth to be known as earls, the first ever in Scotland." William sat back and slowly rubbed his hands together, gazing into the campfire, his tale at an end.

"That's the dumbest story I ever heard," said Thomas. "Any man who allows his wife to lead him around by the nose like that Lady Macbeth did with this fool can't be much of a man. And even the greatest fool who ever lived would know to stay away from witches. So none of it makes sense from the start. That Shakespeare feller ought to give up trying to write plays. He is too ignorant to live."

"He's been dead for over a hundred years," said William. "People with learning say he's the greatest writer ever."

Thomas stood up. "Are you calling me ignorant?"

William stood up as well, squaring away at him. "I'm talking about what people say about Shakespeare," he said. "I'm not talking about you."

Sam broke in. "Enough of this. I'll have no fighting. Now, cool down, the two of you, and let's all of us get some sleep."

Thomas and William walked away from each other, but it was clear that, more than ever, there was no love lost between them.

"I thought it was a good story," Jim-Bird said to William as they all headed for their bedrolls. "It was about how power ruins people. We need stories like that."

William lay awake for a long time. The moon rose fully round and began its climb up the eastern sky. After a while he held out his hand and looked at it in the moonlight, testing how much light was available to see by. Finding there to be quite a lot, he sat up and scrawled a few words in his journal.

August 1. All Scotland needs, Shakespeare seems to say, is to have a few thousand English soldiers on her soil to oversee the Scots' salvation. Which to Shakespeare, I suppose, means turning Scotland into another England.

When I told this story to my mates, I had two surprises. One was the degree to which Thomas despises me, an antipathy so deep I don't know its source. He seems to think I have a low regard for his intellect. In truth, I cannot claim to have a high regard for it, but I recall no instance in which I have said as much.

The other surprise is that Jim-Bird is even more intelligent than I had yet realized.

I am now all but certain that Thomas is the bad fairy who has been be-deviling me. But I need to be sure, so I will bide my time.

Travel: 27 miles.

The next day's travel was still to the northwest and across many creeks: Hen Coop, Briar, Little Beaverdam, and Beaverdam. Then they came to Six-and-Twenty Creek, another of the milepost creeks that told them how far they were from Keowee. They crossed it and continued on to Three-and-Twenty Creek, where they encamped for the night.

August 2. I keep coming back to the question of why *Macbeth* is such a witch-ridden play? I know there are witches in other Shakespeare stories. But in this one it is the witches who pull the strings of the puppets at play on the human stage. Is it because Englishmen assume that Scotland is so benighted, so backward, so savage that its only hope is to knuckle under to the English? Does Scotland seem as wild and barbaric to England as the Indian country seems to Carolina? What if William Shakespeare had met Francis Hutcheson? What kind of Scotland would he have staged for us then?

Travel: 25 miles. Tomorrow Keowee.

On this last day they traveled rapidly, ticking off the milepost creeks: Eighteen, Twelve, Six. By the middle of the afternoon they found themselves atop a hill above the Keowee River. In the distance, on the opposite side of the river, they could see the town of Keowee, neat and compact, on the nearest high ground above the floodplain.

10   Keowee

The train of weary horses plodded down the sloping path, worn deep by heavy use and years of eroding rains, until they came to a broad expanse of bottomland. Now the path was bordered on both sides by stands of mature cornstalks wound with vines of ripening beans. It crossed a small creek and continued on across the cornfield to the eastern bank of the Keowee River. A broad rippling ford stretched across the river to the other side where the path into town resumed, lying hard against a steep hill. William sat back in his saddle and watched as Sam, always mindful of the horses, checked to see how deep the water was running in the river's channel. When fully loaded, packhorses can lose their footing and drown, weighed down by their packs. Unless someone gets to them quickly and cuts their lash ropes, their doom is certain in a depth of water that would not otherwise drown them. Sam rode his horse across and back, reporting that the deepest water in the ford was safe enough for them to take the horses across fully loaded. Even so, the men set a slow and easy pace in getting to the other side. Having come so far with so little loss, they did not want their luck to end just before reaching their destination.

Once across, they swung south a short distance through the floodplain and then rode up a rise to Keowee. William was all eyes as they entered the town, which was unlike any he had ever seen before. Each of the Cherokee households consisted of several small buildings spaced neatly around square yards, and these households in turn surrounded an open space in the center of the town, a kind of commons, heavily used, its smoothly packed ground sparse of vegetation. "Is that where they hold their fairs?" he asked John, pointing to the commons area.

"You could say that," said John, "if you can have a fair without a market. It's the town yard. Most of what happens in Keowee happens there—politics, ceremonies, games, dances. That great, round building at the end of it yonder, with that tall, cone-shaped roof, that's their town house. It's like a cross between a coffee house and a town hall. And sometimes it's a bit like a church, if heathens can be said to have a church. In all, it's where the men like to spend their days in the company of each other. The house on the other end of the yard is where the chief lives."

William paid careful attention. He knew that ignorance was a handicap in a place like this and that he had to learn as much as he could as quickly as possible.

Sam halted the lead horse near a pair of small but strongly built log trading houses, closely spaced beside each other and facing onto the town yard. Both were padlocked. The one on the right had a cribbed wooden chimney plastered with clay. The other one had no chimney, and William surmised it was used only for storage. Peg-leg benches sat by the front sides of both buildings.

A crowd of people—men and women of all ages and a great throng of children—soon assembled to watch the unloading of the new train of goods. Many of the women were naked above the waist, which William found a pleasing spectacle. A handsome Indian woman fully clad in a blue dress approached Sam and talked with him intently for a few minutes. The two were not demonstrative in their affection for each other, but from the familiarity between them William could see that she was Sam's woman. It was also evident from her demeanor that they were discussing a serious matter.

From around her neck the woman removed a cord with a key dangling from it and handed it to Sam, who used the key to unlock the padlock on the door of the store that had the chimney. John Coleman began unpacking his lead string of horses, and they all helped carry the goods inside where they piled them more or less in a heap, neatness not being the first order of business. The men of the town were particularly attentive as they unpacked this first part of the train: the guns, powder, shot, cutlery, and tools. The other two strings were unloaded in turn, and before long the job was done.

Sam walked over to speak to William. "After you've helped with the horses, come back and find me. I'll be in yonder homestead." He pointed to an area behind the store where a house and several other buildings surrounded a small, square yard.

William went with John and Thomas to take the horses to the edge of town, to a horse pen encircled by a high, strong, post-and-rail fence. They unsaddled the horses and stored the packsaddles, riding saddles, and all the other gear inside a crude barn. Thomas carried his own saddlebags and bedroll into a small, neat log cabin close by. It had a split-shingle roof and a cribbed wooden chimney. William saw that someone, maybe Thomas himself, had planted a few peach and apple trees around and about it.

Several young Cherokee men and women wandered up and gathered in Thomas's yard to wait for him. When he came out, they greeted him fondly. "They like to help him with the horses," John explained.

Thomas looked over and saw William watching him. "Well, philosopher," he said, "you've seen where I live. Now what about you? Where do you plan to spend the night?"

"In a tavern, I suppose," said William, who had given no thought to where he would be staying.

"A tavern? John, can you tell the philosopher how he can get to the nearest tavern, and after that to the opera house?"

William flushed with anger, but he held his temper and said nothing.

"Why not try keeping a civil tongue," John said to Thomas. "We will all pay a price if we can't get along." He turned to William. "There are no taverns in Keowee, William. The best way to get a roof over your head is to take up with a woman. But you're not ready for that yet, I don't care how many pretty tits you've seen today. You can get yourself into a big tangle if you don't know what you're doing. Sam will take you in until you learn your way around."

"Where do you call home?" William asked.

"I stay at Tugalo," John replied. "That's a town southwest of here, about two days travel. I look after an old trading post there. But tonight I'll be sleeping at Sam's. My woman, Tskwayi, is coming from Tugalo with her brother to meet me and should be here directly. I hope she'll think to bring along my fiddle."

John and William left Thomas with his Cherokee companions and walked back to the trading house. Circling around behind it, they entered the square yard that formed the center of Sam's homestead. Jim-Bird was standing off to one side of it talking to a middle-aged man who wore a kind of turban of red cloth wrapped about his head. Sam was surrounded by women and children in the middle of the yard. Besides his own woman, there were several others who were about her age, some of them wearing cloth dresses, others wearing short deerskin skirts and nothing else except glass trade beads around their necks. A number of naked children played about the yard while a few younger ones clung to their mothers's skirts. Two older women stood apart from the rest, both wearing short deerskin skirts and necklaces of bone and shell beads. The oldest of the two had her hair done up elaborately in a kind of bun and wore shell ear ornaments like long, thick pins stuck through slits along the outer rims of her ears. She smiled pleasantly, surveying the gathering around her.

When Sam saw that William and John had arrived, he waved at William to come over and join him. "Welcome to my home," he said as William approached. "Let me introduce you to some of these people. This here is Rose, my woman. And these are her sisters and their mothers. Every one of them belongs to the Bird clan. Pay attention to that, now, because in Keowee you need to always take note around you of who's in what clan."

"I am pleased to meet ye, Rose," said William, taking off his hat and giving her a bow. "My clan is MacGregor."

Rose smiled and nodded her head in greeting. "MacGregor," she replied politely.

Sam chuckled. "Keowee clans are not going to be quite like those in Scotland."

William nodded to the other women, but there was nothing he could say to them, lacking, as he did, any knowledge of their tongue.

Sam spoke to them in Cherokee, and they all smiled at William and nodded again. "I told them you would be staying with us for a time," said Sam.

"Thank ye," William said to them in English, smiling and nodding back. If only he could speak to them in Cherokee. He began to wish for an out.

Sam, who must have seen his discomfort, said, "Go over there to where Jim-Bird is. He'll introduce you to the king."

"The king?" said William.

"That fellow in the red head cloth. You need to go pay your respects."

William exchanged a parting round of nods with the women and then turned and walked across the yard to Jim-Bird. "This here is William, our new packhorseman," Jim-Bird said to the red-turbaned man. And to William he said, "Meet King Crow, the chief of Keowee."

"It is indeed a pleasure to meet ye," said William, shaking the king's hand.

"You got Barnaby's horse," said King Crow in clipped but completely intelligible English.

"Yes, I am sorry to say that I have had to come in Barnaby's place. He died of Barbados fever, a very bad disease in the low country."

"Fever. Very bad, sure, sure," said King Crow. "Very bad in Charles Town. Cherokees fear going to Charles Town in warm season. Keowee has little fever. English say air is good here."

"Indeed it is," said William, breathing in deeply. "I am pleased to be here, sir."

"You want woman?" asked King Crow.

"Beg pardon?" said William.

"You need woman. She give you house, bring you firewood, cook, fuck, teach you to talk Cherokee. I have good woman for you, Tuti, my sister's daughter. She was Barnaby's woman. Good woman for Englishman."

"Thank ye," said William, wondering what words were proper for declining such an offer. "Thank you very much for your concern. But I think it would be best for me to get along on my own for a while, learn my way around before I take up housekeeping."

"Sure, sure. Plenty time. Plenty time," said King Crow. "You listen to Sanee and you will do good." Then he turned and left them, walking over to where Sam was talking with the women. For all William knew, one of those women with whom he had been smiling and nodding was Tuti, the match King Crow was trying to make for him.

William looked at Jim-Bird. "Who is Sanee?"

"That's 'Sam' in Cherokee," said Jim-Bird. "When Cherokees talk, they can't put their lips together to make an 'm' sound. You'd not think it could be that hard, but for them it is. They can't do it until they learn to speak English."

William tried it out, saying "Sam" without closing his lips. It came out "San."

"So why didn't you take him up on the woman?" asked Jim-Bird. "Tuti would be a good one for you."

"As it stands now," said William, "I am riding Barnaby's horse, shooting his musket, and wielding his hatchet. I'm almost living in his skin. I can do without taking up with his woman." He shook his head, still amazed at the offer. "Now tell me about this so-called king. Keowee doesn't seem to me to quite measure up to a kingdom. Why isn't he Governor Crow, or Mayor Crow?"

"Well, he's no governor because there is no Cherokee state, and he's no mayor either. He's the big man in the towns close around here as well as in this one. They all look to him as the man who matters most. To the English that makes him a kind of king."

William nodded. He could get used to an Indian king. "By the way where do I take a piss in an Indian town?" he asked.

"Away from the yard," said Jim-Bird. "Any place you can find a little privacy."

William wandered off to the other side of one of the small buildings and relieved himself. When he came back, Jim-Bird was gone, and so he walked back over to where Sam was visiting with his family. A girl of three or four years, naked and full of fun, ran over and stood with both of her little feet on one of Sam's feet, wrapping her arms around his leg. "Walk, Papa," she said. Sam took a couple of steps, the little girl riding on his foot, and then he reached down, scooped her up, and kissed her cheek. He turned to William. "This fussy little bird is my daughter, Little Wren." He set her down on the ground, then said to William, "Come with me and I'll show you around my household."

The buildings of Sam's homestead seemed to differ little from those of the Indians, except that they were slightly larger. Following him into the main house, William felt a rush of recognition. The packed dirt floor was like the floor in the Highland house in which he had grown up, and here, too, was a hearth in the center of the floor and a smokehole in the peak of the roof above. He remembered the blackened roof timbers and thatched roof of his mother's house and how a hard rain would drip through the roof in brown drops. Sam's house was different from his mother's house, however, in that the central part of the roof was held up with four large posts. Nor did his mother's house have sitting and sleeping benches built in against each of the four walls. Here there were no bedsteads, no tables, no chairs, only the built-in benches.

They ducked out through the low door and continued on around the court-yard to a second, smaller house. This one was circular with a conical roof. Its floor had been dug down into the earth a foot or so, and it had thick walls and thick thatch on the roof. "This is our *asi*—our winter house," said Sam. "When the bitter cold weather sets in, we sleep in here. It's also our guest house. Jim-Bird stays here. You can stay too until you find a place of your own. You two will have it to yourselves most of the time, but now and then you'll have com-pany, mostly the traders and packhorsemen traveling to and from the Middle and Overhill Cherokee towns."

"Like the Packsaddle," said William.

"But closer quarters," Sam chuckled.

Moving on around the compound, he showed William the small chicken house where his laying hens nested. Next to it was a low-limbed peach tree where the chickens roosted at night. There was a fowl yard enclosed by a stout wicker fence to keep out dogs and varmints, but it seemed not to be in regular use. The chickens were out ranging free.

On the third side of the courtyard Sam had a small smokehouse for cur-ing and storing meat. William breathed in the pungent smell of wood smoke and aged, salted meat. Beneath a shed roof built off of this smokehouse was a shaded area where Rose did much of her cooking over an outside hearth. Not far around the courtyard from the smokehouse was a small, neat, tall building. Sam identified it as the corncrib, though it looked like none that William had seen among the English. Built up on six sturdy posts and tightly plastered with clay, its floor stood just above the height of a stooped-over man. In the shaded area beneath the floor were crude benches on which some of the women were now sitting to escape the heat of the day. This seemed to be a place for people to take their leisure. From here they could see what was going on both in the town yard and at the store. "Up there in the crib is where we put everything that has to be kept safe from moisture and mice," said Sam.

He led William back to the cookshed beside the smokehouse, where some of the other women were putting out food. "Let's eat a little," said Sam. "The Indians don't have regular sit-down meals like we do. It's every man for himself. Try some of this bean bread." He picked up a neat parcel a little larger than a deck of cards and handed it to William. It was warm and moist.

"What is it?" asked William as he unwrapped it.

"A kind of dumpling," said Sam. "It's made of hominy meal and cooked beans. They wrap it up in cornshucks and simmer it in water."

Peeling back the shuck, William took a bite and found it agreeable. The taste was familiar, now that he had grown accustomed to hominy grits.

With his sheath knife Sam cut off a few pieces of barbequed venison and put them into an Indian pottery bowl. From an English teapot he poured a cup of tea, and then he handed the cup and bowl to William. Sam poured himself a cup of tea and motioned to William to take a seat on a bench. Sam sat down beside him and heaved a sigh. "A long trip," he said. "I'm glad to be back in Keowee. Glad to be back amongst my Birds." He chuckled softly.

"I don't think I understand this clan business," said William. "I take it that being a MacGregor does not apply in Keowee."

"That's right," said Sam. "Cherokee clans are different from what you are used to. It takes a while to get onto it, but I might as well get you started. It goes like this. These Cherokees are divided up into seven clans: Bird, Wolf, Deer, Paint, Blue, Wild Potato, and Twister. My wife is a . . ."

"Wait," said William, and he tried to repeat the clan names. He left out Paint and Wild Potato, but on the second try he named them all.

"Now," said Sam, "my wife is a member of the Bird clan, and all of these women around here are her sisters and her mothers. They are the ones who cooked up this feast."

"How can your wife have more than one mother?"

"The Cherokees divide up their kinfolk differently than we do," said Sam.

"This is where it starts to get complicated. The first thing you've got to understand is that blood kinship is very important to them—even more important than for you Scottish Highlanders. Now, here's the main thing: they trace blood only through women. So all the members of a clan—both male and female— are born of mothers of the same blood. As they see it, a man doesn't pass his blood to his own children. He is their father, and yet they are not of his blood. A man's children belong to his wife's clan, not to his own."

"How strange," said William.

"You get used to it," said Sam. "It all makes sense if you just let go of what you think you know from back in our world and take this one on its own terms. A man is not king in his wife's house, but he is in his sister's house, because that's his clan, you see. Those children are of his blood. When he says 'jump,' his sister's young'uns have to jump. When a woman needs help keeping her children in line, she calls on her brother, not her husband. Even better, she calls on her mother's brother, if he is still living. He would be the man who is king over all in that house."

"Would this uncle live there?" asked William.

"No, he would live with his own wife, just as her brothers live with their wives. But an uncle or a brother comes running when a niece or a sister calls. The best way to think of a Cherokee clan is as a little republic of women who are in league with their mothers' brothers, their own brothers, and their sons, all of whom, as married men, live in other republics. You either belong to a particular republic or you do not, and the only way you can be a member is to be born of one of the women of that clan. To a woman, all of the clanswomen of her mother's generation are like a mother to her, and so she calls all of them mother. And to these mothers, all of the children of the clan are just the same as sons and daughters to them, and that is what they call them. And so a child looks not only to his own mother for comfort, but to many mothers."

"So that's how they have more than one mother," said William.

"That's right. And you can see how this makes for a system in which the old women of the clan are so highly respected. You need to remember that. The old women are the mothers from whom everyone in each of these little republics has gained his right to belong. They hold a great deal of power. For example, you don't want to get on the bad side of the old white-haired woman with the shell ear pins. Her name is Hawk's Mother. She's held in great esteem not only amongst the Birds but in all of Keowee. She's one of the king's sisters, you see. The eldest of them."

William looked around to find her, but she was no longer in sight. "I'll keep that in mind," he said. "What about your own household? Does it run the same way? Is it Rose's blood that rules here and not yours?"

"That's right," said Sam. "I think of it as my house, but if I ever got so crossed up with her that we were to go our separate ways, the house and the children and everything in it would stay with her and the Birds. Anything I consider all my own I keep in the store."

As the sun sank on the western horizon, King Crow and the Bird women and their children departed from Rose's homestead and returned to their own. John and Jim-Bird, who had disappeared for a time, came back, and Thomas came in from his cabin to get some food. After all had eaten their fill, they gravitated to the benches beneath the corn crib. Sam walked across the court-yard to the house and came back with a bottle of rum.

"I want to thank you boys for your good work in getting our skins safely to Charles Town and our trade goods back here to Keowee. May this coming sea-son be better than the last."

"Hear, hear," the men said.

"We'll drink to that," said John.

Sam took a swig from the bottle and then raised it to the men and handed it off.

"William here could have slept under his own roof tonight," said Jim-Bird, as William swallowed down some of the fiery rum and passed the bottle to him.

"How's that?" asked Sam.

"King Crow offered him the vacant spot in Tuti's bed," said Jim-Bird.

"What's the matter, William, ain't she good enough fer ye?" asked Thomas.

"I haven't the least idea how good she is," said William. "Everyone from Charles Town to Keowee has told me to proceed with care in dealing with the Cherokees. I'm not about to move in with a woman I've never laid eyes on."

"I'll say one thing in favor of the king's offer," said Sam. "There are advan-tages in taking up with a Bird woman."

"How's that?" asked William.

"The clans often fall out with each other," said Sam, "and when they do, it can put a wicked spin on the doings of the traders who are aligned with differ-ent ones of them. Every little thing gets a different meaning when it's one clan pitched against another. And that ain't good for business. Of course, there's also some trouble that comes with all of us being paired off with Birds—me with Rose, John with Tskwayi, and Barnaby, as he was, with Tuti. It tends to make the Cherokees in the other clans jealous. They get to thinking that the Birds have all the advantage with the trade. And jealousy in an Indian town can lead to serious complications. So we're caught both ways, in truth."

"Is everyone here in bed with the Birds?" asked William.

"I ain't in bed with any clan," said Thomas. "I save up my lovin' and take it back to Charles Town. I don't want to get tangled up in no clan quarrels. I've had a taste of that in my day, and I didn't like it one bit."

"Excuse me for saying so," said John, "but when you get involved with a clan, you don't cause a quarrel, you cause a war."

"It's the truth," said Thomas. "I ain't delicate enough for their way of doing things."

"And what about you, Jim-Bird?" said William. "Do you have a woman in Keowee?"

Jim-Bird shook his head. "I'm way too young to be married."

They all laughed.

"Didn't you see Jim-Bird looking in the direction of Four Hole Swamp as we skirted it?" John asked William. "There is a certain girl in that band of settlement Indians that lives back up in there. Let's just say that Jim-Bird steers clear of the clan wars around here. Which is wise, I must say."

"Do the clans ever come to blows with each other?" asked William.

"They hardly ever fight openly," said Jim-Bird. "They have ways of working things out between clans, to keep things smoothed out."

"Like what?" asked William.

Thomas gave a loud sigh. "Spare us," he muttered.

"No, go ahead and answer him," said Sam. "He'll get us all in trouble if he don't learn about all this as fast as we can teach him."

"Well, for one thing," said Jim-Bird, "they have to marry outside their own clans, so however they might regard their husband or wife's clan, they have to get along somehow. And then there's the feast of the green corn that comes along every year to get things balanced up and straightened out. The king and the priests put on ceremonies to soothe the ruffled feathers in the clans and try to get everyone to forgive the year's injuries that have been done to them. But if blood has been spilled between clans, they'll not be of a mind to forgive. They'll want revenge. That's the usual way to settle a blood score."

"Even short of spilt blood, the green corn feast don't always get its business done," interrupted Sam. "The first thing Rose told me when we pulled into town was that this summer's ceremony was barely over before the Birds and

Wolves were picking at each other again. It's getting worse between those two every year. Seems like they'll never work their way out of it."

"Some say there actually is spilt blood there," said John. "And others say there's not."

"Is there no constable or judge to settle their dispute?" asked William.

Thomas snorted.

"No, there's not," said Sam. "When a man kills a member of another clan—man, woman, child, it doesn't matter which, but let's say a man has been killed—then the dead man's clan believes it is their right and their duty to take vengeance on the killer's clan. It makes no difference if it was an accident. To them no death is accidental. A killing is a killing, and that's that. They will not rest until they satisfy 'crying blood.' That's what they call it—spilt blood crying for vengeance. They will try to kill the killer, but if they can't lay hands on him, they'll kill a fellow clansman of the killer. One's as good as another. And once that's done, the matter is over. The clan of the first killer has to accept it. There are no more killings. That keeps a never-ending feud from breaking out."

"But it is harsh justice," said William, "if the one killed in revenge was innocent of causing harm. Especially if the first killing was but an accident."

"It is indeed a hard business," Sam agreed. "And it hangs over this Bird and Wolf affair, which don't quite shake out the way it ought to. I surely do wish they would clear it up. It's gone on for years, green corn feast or no."

"It's the witchcraft accusation that's the fly in this ointment," said John.

"Witchcraft?" asked William.

"Yes, witchcraft," said Sam. "You didn't leave that behind in the Christian world. It's here, too, though not exactly in the same way we know it. What happens here is that every so often someone will die unexpectedly. We would call it death by natural causes, or an accident, or God's will, or what have you. But the Cherokees are as likely to say the death was caused by a witch. Their kind of witches can be either a male or a female, and for them it is the spirit of the witch that goes out and attacks the victim. So, witchcraft ain't something you can ever see happen. If you could, then there could be clan vengeance. That's the rub, you see. Nobody ever sees anything."

"But of course, there's always suspicion," said John.

"That's right," said Sam. "So the clansmen of the victim will get to conjuring against the clansmen of the suspected witch, and then someone in the suspected clan might happen to die. So, by their law, you now ought to be even. But it don't end the way it ought to, because nothing is out in the open, you see. You can't be sure that the avenging clan actually did the conjuring, much less that the suspected clan was guilty. So the clan that was suspected of the first killing is likely to now consider itself a victim and get busy and conjure right back. Or so it seems when somebody else in the other clan happens to die. There's no end to it. There's all this frustrated lust for vengeance bubbling beneath the surface and suspicions and accusations being constantly muttered. After a while, you don't know how to sort out what is real from wild imaginings. I'll tell you, I hate being caught in the middle of it with the Wolves and the Birds. It's the biggest stewpot of nasty intrigue I ever had to sit next to."

"It sounds like Shakespeare's Scotland," said William.

"Yes and no," said Sam. "After you've lived with it for a while, you'll see how much this Cherokee witchcraft is a horse of a different color from the good old witchcraft we know back home. Here it's not about who's in league with the Devil. But just what it is about ain't easy to explain. If you want to know more, get Jim-Bird to tell you the finer ins and outs of it. He understands Indian things better than the rest of us. But do it in private. I'm with Thomas now. I don't want to hear anything more about it tonight. I'm in favor of a song from John."

Thomas reached for the bottle and took another pull of rum. "I don't see no point in trying to ferret out what the Indians think," he said. "They've got the deerskins we want, and we've got the goods they need, and all that remains is how to bargain for the exchange of one for the other. That right there is all we need to know. That's enough."

Thomas passed the bottle to John, who swallowed down a swig and then said, "Thomas, one of these days you will want to know more than that about what the Indians are thinking. I'll lay money on it."

John's fiddle, which his woman had indeed brought from Tugalo, lay on the bench beside him. He took it from its case, tuned it, and struck up a tune—"The Irish Washerwoman." For William it was a great relief to hear the familiar sound of a merry fiddle in the midst of such a strange new land. John followed the first tune with a few bars of "Man Is for the Woman Made," and then he droned on the fiddle as he took up singing the song.

Man is for the woman made,
And the woman made for man;
As the spur is for the jade,
As the scabbard for the blade,
As the digging for the spade,

As the liquor's for the can,
So man is for the woman made,
And the woman made for man.

As the scepter's to be sway'd,
As for night's the serenade,
As for pudding is the pan,
And to cool us is the fan,
So man is for the woman made,
And the woman made for man.

Be she widow, wife, or maid,
Be she wanton, be she stay'd,
Be she well, or ill array'd,
Whore, bawd, or harridan,
Yet man is for the woman made,
And woman made for man.

John followed with more fiddling, this time a jig. The men, still tired from
their long journey, listened, but none wanted to frolic. Finally John put his
fiddle back into its case. "I've done my best to get you sweethearts a-dancing,"
he said, "but you fellows are all done in. I say it's time for some sleep. Tskwayi
and I are heading out at first light for Tugalo. In case you're not up then, we'll
say our good-byes now."

"Keep your head up when you get there," said Sam, "and your eyes open."

"I always do," said John. "And now more than ever."

With this, they adjourned and scattered out to their beds for a night's rest.

August 3. My first day in Keowee, and already I have found there is
more in this Cherokee world than our philosophy dreams of. We don't
even agree with them about what a mother is. They believe in witches far
more assuredly and concretely than we do. My mind reels. Common sense
will not be enough for me to understand these people. Our common sense
is not common to them, nor I presume, is theirs common to us. Add to
this the difficulty of their tongue and I feel far at sea. So far I have learned
but a single word, and that of little use. Asi. Hot house. My new home.

According to my records, we traveled 302 miles in fifteen days. We
have come from the very center of Carolina's commerce and culture out

through its farming and cattle land and across the border into another world that lies beyond. Does this not make me a Carolinian? I think so, for I am feeling less a Scotsman every day. I have now seen all the various ways devised to make a living in our new land: rice plantations, pitch and tar, timber, and cow-keeping. And now I have arrived at the most far flung of all, the Indian trade. I shall try my hand at it and see how I like it.

Travel: 23 miles, the last of 302.

The Trading House

William awoke to darkness in Sam's winter house. Looking around for the door, he saw the faint glow of early dawn. No sound came from Jim-Bird's bed, but it was too dark to see if he was still there. William dozed a little and then awoke again. Now there was enough light to see that Jim-Bird had indeed already arisen, but still William lay abed, glad to be off the trail. Finally, when he heard people stirring in the courtyard, he got up and went to a patch of weeds to relieve himself. Returning, he found Rose at the cookfire, stirring a kettle of gruel.

"Good morning, Rose," he said, trusting that in her life with the traders she had learned at least a little of their language. "Is Sam about?"

"Sanee got up early," Rose replied. "He is in trading house. Jim-Bird too. John and Tskwayi are gone to Tugalo." She dished up a bowl of the gruel and handed it to him. "This is *ganahena*."

William nodded and smiled as he took the bowl. "Hominy grits," he said, "*ganahena*." He drew his knife to cut off some of the venison left over from yesterday and added the pieces to the bowl. After finishing off his breakfast with a cup of strong black drink, he headed for the trading house. Upon entering it, the morning sunlight fell away and it took some moments before he could see Sam and Jim-Bird moving about, stocking goods onto shelves along the walls. Besides what came in through the doorway, the only other light in the store filtered in through small openings in the chinking and down the wood-and-clay chimney.

"Give us a hand, William," said Sam. "We'll soon have customers coming to take first pick of the new stock. I want to be able to put my hand on what I need. You can start there." He pointed to a pile of bags of powder and bullets.

"Where does it go?" asked William, heaving a heavy bag of powder onto his hip.

"Over yonder." Sam nodded toward a corner at the opposite end of the store from the fireplace. "It ain't healthy to mix fire and gunpowder. Keep that in mind when it comes to parceling it out. You'll be using the horn measuring cup—it holds a pint—and you'll want to clean up any little bit of it that you spill. Better yet, don't spill any. A stray spark could cause a lot of mischief in here."

William carried the bag over and deposited it in the corner and then returned for the next one.

"When you get done with the powder," said Sam, "carry the bullets over there too. Do all that and you'll be earning your keep. Those bullet bags look small, but they weigh the same as the powder, fifty pounds each."

William carried bag after bag until he had finished the job. Then he stood for a moment and looked around. Now that his eyes had grown accustomed to the dimness, he could see things clearly. Towards the middle of the store on high shelves were stocks of cloth goods, reminding him of John McKenzie's store: lightweight Osnaburg linen, scarlet and blue woolen strouds, plain duffel blankets, shag end blankets, caddice for garters, calico, striped flannel, large and small silk handkerchiefs, and white shirts.

"They seem to favor scarlet and blue strouds," said William.

"That's right," said Sam. "The women use it for their skirts and the men for their arsecloths and leggings. It wouldn't be my favorite thing to wrap between my legs, but they don't seem to mind."

William walked around the store, looking further. Near the fireplace were the guns, gunlocks, and flints. Here also was cutlery and other hardware: hatchets, large and small knives, broad hoes, scissors, and brass kettles. Also snaffle-bit bridles and a few saddles. As William was inspecting the saddles, a large yellow tom cat strolled over and wound around his legs. He reached down to pet him, and the cat gave an appreciative purr and humped his back up against William's hand.

"What's his name?" asked William.

"We just call him Pussy," said Sam. "That's name enough—he's the only cat in Keowee. He keeps the mice out of the cloth."

"The Cherokees call him Wesa," Jim-Bird added. "They can't make the 'p.'"

"It's the oddest thing," said Sam. "It's not that they can't put their lips together at all. They just can't do it and talk at the same time. Of course, there's some of their sounds that I can't make come out right either."

Out in the floor near the doorway Sam had built a counter for laying out merchandise in the brighter light that was there. On a shelf nearby he had pretties on display. William looked them over and again saw many of the same items that were sold in McKenzie's store: brass hawk's bells, needles, thimbles, buttons, binding, horn combs, earbobs, vermillion, brass wire, red and yellow ribbons for women's hair, and a great many strands of glass beads. "What do ye keep in the other house?" he asked.

"Deerskins," said Sam. "They'll start piling up come winter. Though there's more to it than just putting them in there and shutting the door. Every so often we have to take them all outside and shake out the worms and maggots before they can do their damage."

"We didn't have to shake out worms at McKenzie's store," laughed William.

"I reckon not," said Sam. "And it would be nice to be paid with money instead of deerskins. I'll have to teach you how we do our ciphering around here."

"I'm ready to learn," William said.

"All right, then, here we go," said Sam. "Our unit of currency is an average dressed deer skin that will weigh about a pound. If it's of a mature buck, it'll weigh about two pounds, and every so often one will weigh as much as three pounds. Beaver skins are something else. With them, it's not the quality of the skin that matters, but the fur that's on it. When a hatter buys a beaver skin, he takes off the hair to make felt and throws the skin away. So you've got to make sure the fur is good. The Indians don't bring in near as many beaver skins as they used to, but when they do, a prime beaver pelt is worth as much as a large buckskin."

Sam stopped to untie a bundle of knives and lay them up on a shelf. Then he resumed the lesson. "A one-pound skin is called a chalk. It shows as a tally mark made by a piece of chalk on a board or by a quill and ink on a piece of paper. So, if a customer purchases five chalks of merchandise, he can pay that debt off with five average skins, or with three average skins and one large buckskin."

"Or with two buckskins and one average skin," said William.

"That's right, you've got it. They're just like pieces of money—you add them up. When that customer brings in those five dressed deerskins, or whatever combination he's brought you that adds up to five, you draw a slash mark through the five chalks, and the customer can see that his debt is paid."

"What about fractions?" asked William.

"It ain't that exact a science. We have stilliards to weigh the skins, but the Indians don't trust scales to be fair. Most of them are pretty good at judging the weight of their skins by feel. Some skins are a little under a pound, but others are a little over. So it averages out in the end. You can't cut it so fine with this currency as you can with shillings and pence. But don't go trying to cheat them. They always know what's their due."

"I wouldn't think of cheating them," said William.

"Well, you'd be surprised what temptations come over you when you're out of reach of the law."

"The Indians have their own kind of law," said Jim-Bird. "You're never out of reach of that."

The morning was still young when some of the men of Keowee started coming by to hang around the front of the trading house. Cherokee men, it seemed, took little pleasure in staying at their homesteads where the women and children held sway. They liked to be out and about, and the trading house seemed to be a favored destination. The older men sought the shade beneath Sam's corn-crib, while younger ones sat or lounged near the benches on either side of the doors of the two trading house buildings. They seldom stepped inside the store unless they intended to purchase something. Out in the plaza other young men played games and practiced martial skills. From time to time a lounger would go out to join the play or a player would come over to sit down to rest. Whenever Jim-Bird took a break from his work in the store, he would join the loungers on the benches, catching up on the gossip from the town.

During the course of the morning several men came into the store to make small purchases, mostly gun flints, powder, and bullets. Sam told William to watch and learn as he conducted the business. It was almost noon when a young man came to the door, pausing just outside to talk to his friends on the bench. A young woman accompanied him and stood waiting behind him, a packbasket on her back.

"Here come two Birds," Sam said quietly, narrating the scene for William, as he had done throughout the morning. "Scar and his sister, Tsiskwaya—Sparrow in English. Scar will be wanting to outfit for the winter hunt. He's always one of the first to come in."

As the two entered the store, William noticed at once the source of the man's name—a jagged scar just at the hairline on his forehead. Scar came over and solemnly shook Sam's hand.

"I need 200 bullets and three measures of gunpowder," said Scar in barely intelligible English. "And 15 flints." He held up his hand and showed five fingers three times.

"I'll let you have that much," said Sam, "but you still owe me 25 chalks from last year."

"I will hunt better this year—kill many deer," said Scar.

"I hope so. We can't let you dig this hole of debt much deeper." Sam fetched him the merchandise. "That'll be four chalks for the bullets, one for the flints, and three for the gunpowder—eight more chalks in all. Now you owe me 33 chalks." Sam showed Scar the tally marks in his ledger and counted them off: 33 chalks.

"I also need duffel blanket," said Scar, "and Tsiskwaya needs brass kettle and small knife."

"That would come to 12 more chalks," said Sam. "You know I can't let you have that much. I'll throw in a little knife. It's worth less than a chalk. I'll toss it in with the flints. Get your bill paid down, and then we'll talk about blankets and kettles."

Scar did not plead his case further. As they moved away toward the door, Sam muttered to William, "I hate turning down a Bird. I'll hear back about it from Rose."

Scar and his sister had just reached the doorway when another young man and woman arrived outside, each pair abruptly blocking the way of the other. No one stepped aside as they stood in silence.

"This should be interesting," Sam whispered in William's ear. "Those other two are a brother and sister of the Wolf clan—the Gunsmith and Otter Queen."

The two couples stood stubbornly blocking each other at the doorway. Civility obliged them to speak to each other, but none would be the first.

Finally, Tsiskwaya turned to her brother and asked him a question in Cherokee. Scar smiled and shook his head no. She then answered her own question, and Scar laughed. The two shared their joke as if the other pair were not present.

The Wolf woman, Otter Queen, then turned to her own brother and asked him a question. The Gunsmith shook his head no, and, like Tsiskwaya, Otter Queen answered her own question. The Gunsmith laughed heartily, looking squarely at Scar and Tsiskwaya, who did not laugh with him. For a moment longer the four stood in their tense impasse, until finally the Gunsmith and Otter Queen moved slightly to one side and let Scar and Tsiskwaya pass by and walk outside. Then the other two came in.

"What was that all about?" murmured William.

"Wait till they're gone and I'll tell you," said Sam.

The Gunsmith walked over and shook Sam's hand. "I want winter stock" he said. "300 bullets, four measures of gunpowder, and 15 flints."

Sam fetched these from the back of the store. "You still have three chalks to your credit from last year—all this comes to 11, so that makes it 8 chalks you now owe me."

"I want more," said the Gunsmith. "One duffel blanket, one hatchet. And Otter Queen wants good knife and earbobs."

Sam fetched a heavy blue wool blanket, a hatchet, and a knife. He handed these to the Gunsmith, who admired the thick nap on the blanket and the keen edge on the hatchet. He looked the knife over and handed it to his sister.

"William," said Sam, "bring over the earbobs for Otter Queen."

William found the box of earbobs and brought them to the counter for Otter Queen to make her choice. She pulled out a pair—white glass beads suspended from brass wire hoops—and handed them to William. He started to hand them over to Sam.

"No," she said in English, turning her head to one side and pointing to her ear. She wanted him to put one of them through the small slit in her earlobe. William was flustered. He had been admiring her bare-breasted beauty with glances, but now he looked squarely at the whole of her for the first time. She was perhaps eighteen years of age and aptly named, for she was as curvaceous as any otter and as quick and graceful in her movements. He looked dumbly at the earbob and then at her ear, and then he awkwardly slipped the brass wire through the small opening in the lovely flesh of her earlobe. She flashed a smile at him and turned her head to the other side so he could attach the other bob. When she moved her head the white beads dangled prettily against her dark skin.

"Now, fetch her that hand-mirror under the counter so she can see herself," said Sam.

William picked up the mirror and held it in front of Otter Queen. She smiled broadly and said, "Oh my." William was surprised at so English an utterance. There was nothing else English about her.

Sam had his ledger open and was making the new marks. "That will be 8 chalks for the blanket, two for the hatchet, one for the knife, and two for the earbobs. That comes to 13 in all. Added to the 8, that makes 21 you owe me." Sam showed the ledger to the Gunsmith.

The Gunsmith nodded that he understood the numbers, and then he turned away and began stuffing his purchases into Otter Queen's packbasket. The weight of the packbasket made her beautiful breasts all the more taut and enticing.

After the two left the store, Sam said, "Her name in Cherokee is *Tsi:tu:*"—he drew the vowels out long as he pronounced it. "That's their word for otter. To them the otter is the most beautiful of animals. To the traders that young woman is the most beautiful of otters—it's the traders who named her Otter Queen. You should see her swim, showing off that tidy little fanny of hers. It wouldn't matter if she couldn't speak a word of English, but the fact is that there are few in this town who can speak it so naturally. Her father was one of the earliest traders in the Cherokee country."

"Then she is part English?" William said with surprise.

"She doesn't think of it that way," said Sam. "Her mothers are Cherokee, so by their measure she's a full-blooded Wolf."

"She doesn't look English," said William.

"Her features came out more Indian than white."

"Is she attached to anyone in particular?" William tried not to sound as interested as he felt.

Sam gave him a long look. "No. She does as she pleases. They all do, if they are unmarried. No one thinks the worse of them for it. All the young men lust after her, as you might suppose, but to a man they are wary of her. Mind you, she is a Wolf."

"Why does that matter?" asked William.

"It's that Bird versus Wolf business," said Sam. "It's the worst tangle they've got going amongst the clans around here, and she's square in the middle of it."

William fell silent. Jim-Bird had come in from outside in time to hear most of this conversation. He chuckled, and William glanced at him. "What is so funny?"

"Otter Queen caught your eye," said Jim-Bird, "but now you are having second thoughts."

"As well you should," said Sam.

William smiled lamely. "I'm willing to talk about the Gunsmith instead. He seems a fine fellow. How did he get his name?"

"He's the handiest with guns as any around here," said Jim-Bird.

"More so than Jim-Bird, if that be possible," said Sam.

"He can even repair a gunlock," said Jim-Bird, "if he can find the parts. He can carve as neat a gunstock as you would want. And he's a clever hunter and a deadeye shot. Often he can get in close enough to take down a deer with a head shot, so as not to damage the skin."

"What I like about him is that he never ends a season in debt," said Sam.

"Unlike Scar," noted William. "Which reminds me to ask, what was it that passed amongst the four of them when they met up at the doorway?"

"You were out there, Jim-Bird," said Sam. "Explain it to him. And watch the store for me while you're at it. I'll be at the house."

Sam left, and Jim-Bird and William leaned against the counter, looking out through the doorway as they talked together.

"It's Wolves and Birds," said Jim-Bird. "The problem Scar and the Gunsmith had was that their sisters were with them. When there is trouble between two clans, it's most often going to be the women who needle each other. The men on their own will usually try to get along. That's just the natural way with Cherokee men and women. The men have to get past their differences if they are going to take on their real enemies—neighboring Indians—or embark on anything that requires them to pull together on behalf of the town. But with the women, what they care most about is their clan. What you saw happen there was those two women besmirching each other's clans. It was Tsiskwaya who started it. She asked Scar why is it that wolves meeting in the woods are always smelling each other's asses. Scar claimed not to know, and she replied that it's the only way wolves know how to say hello to each other. Now, that was a shot over the bow. So Otter Queen fired back. She asked The Gunsmith what that little black spot is that's always there on top of bird shit. He said he didn't know, and she informed him, 'Oh, that's bird shit too. Everything is shit when birds get together.' Of course, the Birds didn't find that to be humorous."

William shook his head. "Slurs like that would set off duels amongst the clans where I come from."

"Not here," said Jim-Bird. "They will take the greatest of pains not to spill the blood of another clan because that would set the wheels of vengeance in motion. You cannot exchange blood for harsh words. So they keep on attacking each other with a hundred veiled barbs of sarcasm. It goes on and on. Someday somebody will push too far, and blood will finally be spilled."

"Can't the king settle it?"

Jim-Bird shook his head. "We call him king, but he's not like an English king. He's not much more than first among equals. The most he can do is try to persuade everyone to be on good behavior. In ancient days, they say, the chiefs had more power. But today they do not. So it falls to the clans to handle things their way."

William and Jim-Bird tended the store for the remainder of the day. William waited on the customers while Jim-Bird stayed close at hand to make sure he got the price of everything right. By the end of the day, William knew the value in deerskins of a good part of what they had in stock. In late afternoon, when the trade fell off, they spent some time straightening the store. Jim-Bird tidied up the stock and William swept the floor and knocked down spider webs, which, it would seem, were at their worst in late summer, just as in Scotland. Finally they closed up, locked the door on the trading house, and went to Sam's for supper.

Thomas joined them there. He had been out all day tending the horses with his Indian helpers, whose company he said he much preferred over the loungers at the trading house. After they ate their supper, they sat beneath the corn-crib for a while, but with John gone to Tugalo, there was no prospect of music. Thomas took the first opportunity to return to his horse-pen, and Sam went into his house to be with his family. William and Jim-Bird lingered on the benches and watched the darkness gather. It was not long before William's thoughts strayed to Otter Queen and the arousing memory of having touched her beautiful brown body.

"Tell me more about the Birds and the Wolves," he said to Jim-Bird. "How did that trouble get started?"

"It was right after I first came here—three years ago, maybe four. The Birds accused a Wolf woman—a grandmother of Otter Queen—of being a witch."

"Tell me exactly what that means," said William. "If Indian witchcraft is not about God and the Devil, what is it about?"

"It is about good and evil, but they just don't call it God and the Devil. For the Cherokees a witch is a man or woman who is thoroughly evil, from the inside out, in a way that none can readily explain. A witch can cause all manner of mischief, the worst being death itself. A witch can remove his own guts, and by doing that he can change into the semblance of another person, or even into another animal—usually an owl or a raven. Or he can change into a spirit that no one can see. He can fly to the home of a sick person and go to the sick bed, and no one knows he's there. He goes to work and steals the days, weeks, months, or even years of life remaining to the person who is ill. The witch adds this stolen time to his own life. If not caught, a witch can live to be quite old."

"Do ye believe that?" asked William.

"The part of me that is Indian believes it," Jim-Bird said. "The part that is white does not."

"Do ye think Otter Queen's grandmother flew about stealing life from sick people?"

"It's not what I think that matters, it is what the Birds think. In a single winter they lost three of their clansmen to illnesses that struck suddenly and took those people away in no time at all. They suspected a witch was at work, and so they looked around and decided on the old woman. She was very old and not as friendly as she might have been. It is rumored that the Birds hired a conjuror to work magic against her, but nothing came of that. Finally, they accused her publically. But the Wolves rallied around her. They said that it was only that her liver was sour. She was ill-tempered and had too sharp a tongue, but she was not a witch."

"Was that enough to defend her?" asked William.

"It was if the other clans stood with the Wolves, and they did. But the Birds were not satisfied. Last winter the old Wolf woman did finally die. We thought that would be the end of it, but it did not even slow it down. The Birds still feel they have been wronged by the Wolves, cheated of satisfaction. It's getting worse, not better."

"Then what can ever bring an end to it?" asked William.

"If I knew that, I could be king of Keowee. In witchcraft, everything that happens is fogged in mystery. Nothing is seen, nothing is certain. They say that if you can strip away this mystery—expose the witch for who he or she is—it is enough to cause the witch to die. If you can't do that, if you only have your suspicions, you can still sometimes sway the sentiment in the town against the witch and have him or her executed. But neither of those things happened. They never had more than a suspicion of the old Wolf woman, and the town wouldn't go along with it and give them an execution. So she seems to have lived out all her days. At least so it seems to most people around here. But some of the Wolves speculate that the Birds may have finally caused her death by conjury. The old Wolf woman died suddenly, just fell over beside her fire one night. In the natural course of things old people do sometimes fall over and die. But that doesn't stop the suspicions."

"I'm beginning to think I will myself have to believe in the existence of witches if I am to understand this place," said William.

"That is truer than you might think," said Jim-Bird. "Sam's homestead is often caught up in it, especially when old Hawk's Mother is here. She seems a pleasant sort when there are only Birds around, but when it comes to the Wolves this threat to her clan has made her more vengeful than a man on the war trail. She is always on the lookout for the enemy. That's why you want to steer clear of Otter Queen. The one they had accused of being a witch was Otter Queen's actual grandmother, in the English way of naming kin. Otter Queen's mother, Pretty Baskets, was born of that old woman. And Otter Queen was born of Pretty Baskets. Now, no one has ever accused Pretty Baskets of being a witch. She just isn't the kind to be one. She's open and friendly and anyone can read her like a book. But old Hawk's Mother has been muttering for some time about Otter Queen. There's something about her that stirs suspicions. Otter Queen is more like her grandmother than she is like her mother. Not that she's particularly ill-tempered. But she's not overly friendly either. She keeps to herself, which would cause no comment if she did it in a shy way. But shyness is not in her nature. She has a direct way of looking at you that can sure enough give you a chill."

"That's not what she gave me," said William. "She gave me a warm feeling that hasn't gone away yet. How could anyone accuse that beautiful young woman of being a witch? It's the craziest thing I ever heard. And ye sound like ye half believe it."

"It may sound crazy to you," said Jim-Bird, "but the Birds take it seriously, and so do some of the other clans. And I have to say that I am as wary of Otter Queen as are the other men of this town. It's not that I believe that she's a witch, but neither do I see her behaving in a way that would lift the suspicion from her. It is her nature to be as she is, and that means that this trouble that has settled on her is not going anywhere until the whole problem between the Wolves and the Birds gets solved."

"And no one knows how to solve it," said William.

"That's right."

They fell silent. For William this was a lot to think about. Jim-Bird soon got up and went to bed, but William went into the *asi* and got his journal and pen and ink and came back out to the cookshed. He raked up the coals in the fireplace and added a few small pieces of dry wood. When they flared up into a small, bright fire, he wrote in his journal:

August 4. Today I learned the essentials of how the business of the deerskin trade is conducted. My time in McKenzie's store has prepared me well for this work, which is not hard to learn. I find my attention wandering elsewhere. There is a young woman in Keowee who is so beautiful she makes my knees go weak. The Birds accuse her of being a witch. She is no witch, not in the enlightened world that I know. But in Keowee the enlightenment has not yet thrown much light.

12   Otter Queen

William settled in at Keowee. In September the summer heat abated, though not so much as it would have done in Scotland. The mornings were cool enough, but midday breezes felt warm on his face, and by afternoon it was hot. Since that first day when she had come into the trading house with her brother, Otter Queen had returned alone several times to make small purchases: some strings of glass beads, a needle, a thimble. William usually managed to position himself to wait on her, and they would exchange a few words. She had learned to call him Willy, as did other Cherokees—their B-less version of "Billy." William would have liked to engage her in conversation beyond the business at hand, but he could never keep quite enough of his wits about him to do so.

It was Otter Queen who made the first move, not in the store but in the middle of the town yard. It was early afternoon, the sun was hot, and no customers were coming into the store. Everyone was in the town yard watching two men run along beside each other and throw wooden shafts to slide along the ground. William was not sure what kind of game this was, but from the way the onlookers shouted and gestured, they were obviously keenly interested in whatever was going on with those shafts. As he stood in the door and watched, Sam spoke up from behind the counter where he was working on his ledger. "Go on out there and join the crowd. I don't need you here. The store will be still as a tomb until that chunkey game is over."

"I don't mind if I do," said William, and he sauntered out and made his way through the crowd until he had a good view of what was going on. The two players were familiar to him: Scar of the Bird clan and the Gunsmith of the Wolf clan. They were dressed only in their breechcloths, but both were dripping with sweat from their exertions.

Standing close to where the two players were about to start their run for another round, William saw that one of them, the Gunsmith, was holding a stone disc, perfectly round and highly polished. It was about three fingers wide, with a circumference that looked as though it could just be held within the encircled fingers of one's two hands. The playing ground was a swept lane of smooth, hard-packed clay, about three yards wide and perhaps forty yards long.

From the near end of the lane, the two men started out running at half speed. Then the Gunsmith cast out the disc to roll ahead at a fast speed down the lane. The two ran along behind it, and when the disc slowed down, they both cast their shafts, underhanded, so that the shafts slid along the clay lane in pursuit of the rolling disc. The shafts and the disc all came to a stop together in the same vicinity. The two men walked over to examine them, and then Scar picked up his shaft triumphantly. Evidently he had won the round. The Gunsmith showed no emotion as he retrieved his shaft. Scar picked up the disc and they returned to the starting line.

Intent as he was on the game, William did not notice that Otter Queen had appeared at his side. "Good day, Willy," she said brightly. "Who is winning?"

He looked around, pleased to see her there. Her facility with English still surprised him. "I don't rightly know. I don't know how the game is scored."

"You win a point if the *gatayusti* is closest to your shaft when she stops rolling and falls over."

"The *gatayusti* is a she?"

"That's how the men think of it," Otter Queen said. "And you can guess how they think of their shafts." She smiled at him, her white teeth beautiful against her dark skin.

"Yes, I think I can," he laughed. "And I agree that she is a beauty. So smooth and polished and perfectly round. She looks to be made of granite. That is a hard stone to be so finely fashioned."

"Yes, she is treasured in Keowee," said Otter Queen.

"Who owns her?"

Otter Queen appeared surprised at the question. "She belongs to Keowee. King Crow looks after her. He is the one who brings her to the game. And he stays and watches while they play."

"To protect her?"

Otter Queen laughed. "A hard stone like that can take care of herself. It is the players who have to be protected from her. This game can get out of hand."

William watched the players starting out on their next run and tried to see what Otter Queen might be talking about. He could not.

"How could the game get out of hand?"

"It's not the game itself, it's what they bet on the game," she said. She turned to a woman standing on the other side of her and exchanged some words with her in Cherokee. Then she turned back to William. "Those two have bet the bullets they bought at the store the other day. Scar has nine points and the Gunsmith has six. It takes eleven points to win the game. My brother is not as reckless as some. He will stop if he loses his bullets. But some would keep on until they had lost their guns and axes and even their clothing if King Crow were not here to put a stop to it."

"I've known gamblers like that in Scotland," said William.

They fell silent and turned their attention to the game. For William it had become even more interesting, now that he knew what was at stake. Scar, already deeply in debt at the store, could not afford to lose those bullets. He watched as the two men finished their run, the *gatayusti* rolling out before them. They threw their shafts, which slid along close together, but when the *gatayusti* rolled to a stop, the Gunsmith's shaft was the closest—so close the stone fell over on top of it. That put the score at nine to seven.

Otter Queen began cheering loudly for her brother, and now the Gunsmith had a run of scores, taking each of the next three points. The Gunsmith was ten, Scar nine. The next point could give the Gunsmith the game—and Scar's bullets.

Scar was visibly perturbed. He looked over in Otter Queen's direction and began talking loudly. Then he went over to an old man on the other side of the yard. They spoke briefly, and the man reached into a pouch hanging at his waist. He pulled out a small wad of something and put it into the pipe he was smoking. Then he blew smoke on Scar's chest and arms and down onto his legs. Scar returned to the playing field and made ready for the next roll of the disc.

"What happened there?" William asked.

"Scar is accusing me of bringing him bad luck," she said quietly. "He said that he was winning until I appeared. He hopes the old man's smoke will protect him and change his luck."

"Is this because of the bad business between the Birds and the Wolves?" asked William.

"Yes. They think of me as a walking curse." She laughed a little, but without amusement.

The two men again rolled the *gatayusti* and ran after it, casting their shafts. The crowd called out for their favorites. This time Scar's shaft was closest when the *gatayusti* stopped rolling and fell over. Ten to ten. But Scar was still grim-faced, and he did not look in Otter Queen's direction.

"That should make him happy," she said. "But he has ruined the game for me. I want my brother to win, but if he does, Scar will want to string me up for the birds to eat."

The two men lined up and started running. Scar rolled the stone down the lane. The two of them trotted along after the *gatayusti*. Otter Queen shouted out her encouragement, but to William's surprise it was Scar's name she called out, not her brother's. If Scar heard her above the shouts of everyone else, he did not show it, but it seemed to William that he must have heard.

When the *gatayusti* slowed down, the two men slid their shafts toward it along the lane. The shouts of the bystanders rose to a high pitch. The two shafts slid to a halt, one on either side of the *gatayusti* as she stopped rolling. But, remarkably, she did not fall over. The shafts were so close on either side of her, they seemed to be holding her up. The two men ran up and looked, and each claimed that his shaft was touching the *gatayusti*. Because of the dispute, they left the shafts where they were.

King Crow walked over and looked closely at the *gatayusti* and shafts. He plucked a blade of grass and ran it between Scar's shaft and the *gatayusti*. Then he did the same to the Gunsmith's shaft, and the blade of grass dragged and stuck.

"She is touching the Gunsmith's shaft," King Crow announced, Otter Queen murmuring the translation to William. "The game goes to the Gunsmith."

With the decision coming from King Crow, a member of Scar's own clan and chief of the town, Scar could not contest the decision. But he was not able to conceal his anger, and the look he cast in Otter Queen's direction was full of spite.

William found his own anger rising toward Scar.

"What can I say?" said Otter Queen. "Even when I lose, I win. Or is it that when I win, I lose? Either way, it is time for me to go home and get out of Scar's sight for a while. He'll get drunk and forget about me. Maybe I will see you another time, Willy."

"I do hope so," said William. He watched her go, admiring the poetry of her lithe young body as she walked away into the crowd.

In the late afternoons, after Sam locked up the store, William would often walk up to the men's swimming pool in the Keowee River, some distance upstream from the town. Sometimes Jim-Bird would come along, and sometimes not. The women also had a pool in the river, but it was downstream from the town. According to Jim-Bird, these respective locations could never be reversed, the reason being, strange to say, that the Cherokee men feared being weakened by the power of menstruating women who might be bathing upstream from them. It seemed that Cherokee men and women regarded themselves almost as separate peoples. There were many situations in which they were expected to keep their distance from each other, each sex defending itself from unwanted influences from the other. William found this of interest, but for him the argument for separate pools was not convincing—he would have welcomed the possibility of chance encounters with the other sex. Even without that potential for drama, however, it lifted his spirits to strip off his clothes and dive into the pool at the end of a hot day to cool off and wash away the sweat and grime. If Jim-Bird came along, there was the special treat of Tazzie and Binkie, who would dive off the bank after Jim-Bird and splash comically into the pool. The little dogs would swim about for while, seeming both happy and uncomfortable at the same time, and then they would go paddling back to shore.

As September wore on and the days cooled more, Jim-Bird came along less often. Other men and boys of the town were also less likely to be about when William arrived at the pool. Cherokee men would come to the pool early in the morning, at the first light of dawn, for some kind of washing ceremony to which they were devoted, but they did not like to swim purely for pleasure when the days were cool. Perhaps it was because of his Scottish blood that William paid little mind to being cold and wet. The truth was, he greatly enjoyed being alone at the pool.

On one particularly fine day when he had the pool all to himself, he lingered long, falling into a kind of reverie. Idly treading water, he watched a pair of shy wood ducks fly close to the water in a fast beeline down the river until they were out of sight He slowly turned, looking all around. A belted kingfisher lit on a dead branch that reached out over the water. The bird sat there for a few moments and then set his sights on something in the water below, cocking his head to one side. Suddenly he dove off the branch into the water and disappeared. A moment later he popped up, flapped the water off his wings, and flew back to his perch, where he swallowed the small fish he had caught. As if in triumph, he let out a harsh, rattling cry, like the sound a boy makes when running along clattering a stick of wood against a paling fence.

"Willy! Willy!" A voice from the bank entered his reverie. A woman's voice.

William looked round and saw Otter Queen standing on the bank, holding his breeches in her hands.

"Willy, I got your breeches," she said as she danced a little dance and waved them in the air.

William laughed and began swimming toward the shore.

"Willy, come get your pants," she shouted.

As he neared the bank, she whirled around and ran like a doe into the woods.

William scrambled up the bank and put on his shirt, which covered his nakedness a bit. Then he pulled on his stockings and his shoes and took out running up a steep hill in the direction Otter Queen had taken, following a little creek that coursed swiftly down into the river. But he could catch no sight of her. After a short distance, he stopped and listened.

Behind him he heard, "Willy."

He spun around and ran in the direction of her voice. Again he could not find her. And again she called to him from an unexpected direction. Not only was she fast, she could move in utter silence through the litter on the forest floor. How did she do that? He came to a cloistered place thick with laurel bushes, on the high ground above the river.

"Willy," she said from behind his back. He spun around to chase her, but she was right there, standing her ground. He almost fell into her.

She laughed to see him dressed only in his shirt, stockings, and shoes. He reached out for his breeches, but she held them behind her back. This time, however, she did not run.

Reaching around her, he felt her warm body against his wet, cool skin. She did not resist but moved closer to him, and in the next instant she reached beneath his shirt and grasped his member, quite gently, with a loving hand.

William stopped in his tracks. The thought of his pants left his mind. The possibility that she might be a witch never entered it. He cupped the delicious curves of her backside in his two hands, and she put her other arm around his neck and clung to him.

"Oh, Willy, what is this I feel beneath your shirt?"

William could not think of a witty response. In fact, he could not think of anything. The faculty of speech completely failed him.

He ran his hands up and down the curves of her body. She reached down and untied the belt around her waist and her skirt fell away.

"Oh, Willy," she said, "what is this thing that is trying to push between my legs?"

William was almost dizzy, feeling awash in desire. She drew him down to the mossy ground. Novice at love that he was, he immediately began trying to have her. As he fumbled, Otter Queen helped him get to where he wanted to be.

William began thrusting with abandon, quite oblivious to the fact that he was rutting half naked with a fully naked Cherokee woman in the light of day in a not-so-private woods. He ejaculated almost immediately. Then, after a pause, he began thrusting anew, and before long he came again, his pleasure keener than before.

"You do it like a rabbit," she said. "In such a hurry. All humpy-hump and no play. You should learn to do it like an otter."

"How would that be?"

"Otters wind around each other. They take their time. They sing otter songs. And then, when they have played enough, they do it."

"Well, from now on I will pay more attention to the otters I see on the river-bank," William laughed. "I will study their every move. As a philosopher, I take instruction wherever I can find it."

"Let's go back to the water and wash," Otter Queen said.

"Can ye go into the men's pool? I thought it was a violation."

"Do you care if a woman is in your pool?"

"Not at all."

"Then neither do I."

They went back to the river, but they did not stay long in the water. Had it been up to William, they would have remained there through the night, but Otter Queen said she had to go home.

On the shore they stood together putting on their clothing, he taking longer than she, not only because he had more pieces to don but because he kept stopping to admire her. So long as women come in such glorious packages, he thought, there is little chance that the human race will die out. But then that thought led to considerations of possible consequences. "What will the Gunsmith say about this?" he asked as he tucked in his shirt.

Otter Queen shrugged. "Maybe he will hear about it, maybe he won't. There are always eyes and ears in the Keowee woods, but they don't see everything. Not that it matters to me. My body is my own, and I do with it as I please."

William listened to her voice as if she were singing one of John's ballads. He loved the lilt of her Cherokee accent. Her facility with the English language continued to fascinate him. "You speak our tongue better than anyone else I have heard in this town," he said. "Is that because of your father?"

"Yes," she said. "He liked to see me laugh."

He looked at her quizzically. "I don't understand."

"My father loved to play with his language. He was always making puns and asking me riddles. I had to pay close attention and learn his language well in order to be able to understand what was funny about the things he would say to me. If I understood and laughed, it made him happy. Do you want to hear a riddle?"

"Yes, ask me one," said William.

"I have teeth and yet can't eat, can't crunch corn or bread of wheat, still I'll fix you fairly neat."

"What is it?"

"A comb. You knew that."

"No, I didn't."

"Then you are not trying. I'll tell you another one, and you must try harder. This did not come from my father. He wouldn't tell me one like this. I learned it from Barnaby."

"The packhorseman?"

"Yes, the one who died. Here is the riddle. What does a cow have four of that a woman has only two of?"

He smiled. "Teats."

"No, legs," Otter Queen laughed. "But now I know what you have on your mind."

"Yes, indeed," William laughed. "It is all I can think of. Will we do this again?"

"Tell riddles?"

He laughed again. "You know what I mean."

"Yes, we will do it again—if you will stop eating rabbit for dinner."

"I will not so much as look at a rabbit. And I will not eat one for the rest of my days."

She laughed. "Willy, you are so, so serious." Then she put out her hand to motion for him to stay where he was while she turned to leave. "Let me go first and get a headstart. Then you take the main path. I will take a different one. If the eyes and ears of Keowee have not yet found us out, it would be good to keep it that way."

"Go on, then," he said. "I will wait."

As he watched her walk out of sight, he was already hungering for their next meeting. That night he wrote in his journal.

September 5. Today Otter Queen gave me a lesson in Cherokee love-making that I will not soon forget. If she is a witch, then I am bewitched. In celebration I took out my roundlet of whiskey and drank a swig.

Philosophical reflection for this day: avoid rabbits—observe otters.

William and Otter Queen continued their secret lovemaking into October. They would meet at prearranged places in the woods, and when their ardor had cooled, they would say their good-byes and return separately to town. Neither of them felt secure enough in their relationship to let the fact of it be known to others.

But keeping their distance in public was not easy, so strong was their desire for each other's presence. Otter Queen began coming to the trading house on the flimsiest of pretexts, and William had to pretend that he had no special interest in her. She befriended Sam's daughter, Little Wren, and sometimes after making a small purchase in the store, she would sit on a bench outside and play with the little girl for a long time. One day Otter Queen came into the store carrying a gourd bowl and a pipe made entirely of river cane—a section of small-diameter cane was fitted as a stem into a bowl made of a short length of large-diameter cane. But the bowl of a pipe should be stone or clay. Sam teased her, saying that she would burn off her nose if she smoked from that pipe. She smiled and asked to borrow a piece of soap. Then she asked for some water for her gourd bowl.

Little Wren, who had seen Otter Queen crossing the plaza to the store, was now hanging about the doorway, waiting for her new friend to come out and play. Though her Bird mothers did not like for her to spend time with Otter Queen, her father did not object. When Otter Queen came out of the store with the bowl of water in one hand and the soap and pipe in the other, Little Wren fastened quickly to her side, and they sat down together on a bench out front. William wandered over and stood in the doorway, watching them.

Otter Queen dissolved some of the soap into the water, as Little Wren watched patiently. Then she showed Little Wren how to dip the bowl of the pipe into the soapy water and blow bubbles. Little Wren was thrilled. She practiced until she could send out a steady stream of bubbles. Then she ran around the yard in front of the store, blowing bubbles before her. When she tired of that, she began trying to blow very large bubbles that would jiggle and shimmer in the sunlight until they left the pipe and floated away. The men lounging nearby watched and laughed. William, too, was captivated by the scene— more than he should have been. Only a prod from Jim-Bird broke the spell, and he turned away and went back into the store. He noted to himself that he had to be more careful. Jim-Bird, from the strength of his prod, seemed to suspect something. Others were probably speculating, too.

The speculation ended abruptly one day when Thomas showed up at the store. His visits were infrequent, preferring as he did his own little kingdom of horses and young wranglers away from the center of town. For a while he chatted with Sam and Jim-Bird, ignoring the presence of William. Then finally he turned and spoke to him.

"Where have you been going off to every day, philosopher? I hear tell from my boys that you've taken to walking in the woods. Now, what would a philosopher be up to in the wild woods?"

"I go where I please," said William.

"Right you are. No need to explain."

William turned away to go back to his work.

"But let me ask you this," said Thomas. "What was that I was saw there on your pants? Some hairs it looked like to me."

"What are ye talking about?" William said sharply, though he was trying not to get riled.

"Looked like dog hairs, right there on the fly of your pants. Long dog hairs. But then, I ain't never seen no long-haired dogs in Keowee. Now, they might be wolf hairs. Could that be? Wolf hairs brought back from your walks in the woods?"

"Shut your bloody mouth!" said William, whirling around to face him. He pointed to the door. "Let's take this outside, Mr. Farrell. It's time for a philosophical discussion between you and me. I've been wanting to share my philosophy with ye ever since we left Charles Town."

"My pleasure," said Thomas, and he followed William outside. But no sooner were they out the door than he rushed William from behind and caught him by the neck in a choke hold.

William brought his elbow back in a sharp blow to Thomas' belly. Thomas gasped for breath and loosened his hold. William spun around, got a leg behind him, and toppled him to the ground.

The Indians in front of the trading house quickly formed a circle around the combatants as the fight edged out into the town yard. Others came running, eager for the show. Sam came out of the store, but he made no move to break up the fight. William and Thomas were trading punches now, with William getting the best of Thomas, moving lightly on his feet, feinting in and then backpedaling, landing the stiff left-right combinations he had learned from his hardscrabble mates in Glasgow. Thomas landed some blows, but William landed more, and Thomas's face began to show injury. He had a swelling below his left eye and was bleeding from his nose. Cursing and breathing hard, he pulled a knife from a sheath on his belt.

"Is that the knife ye used to cut my lash ropes?" William taunted, feinting at him. "I've got a *sgian mhor*, too, but I'll leave mine in its sheath. I don't need a *sgian mhor* to whip your arse." William grabbed up a stout hickory stick that had been dropped to the ground by a child when the fight began. "In the Highlands we boys fought with single-sticks about the length of this one." William used both hands to try to flex it, feeling its strength. "Just about like this," he said.

Thomas lunged at him with the knife, but William punched him hard with his stick and kept punching whenever he came in. Thomas could not get close enough to cut him. As the punches with the end of the single-stick began to take their toll, Thomas pulled back.

They circled each other. Finally Thomas made a desperate charge, braving the punches and blows from the stick, bulling his way forward to get in cutting distance. He made an underhand thrust with his knife, but William came down with the stick on his lower arm, striking with all his might.

Thomas cried out, dropping his knife and grasping his arm. William then gave him a whack on the side of his head, hard, but not full strength, and Thomas fell to the ground, stunned. After a moment he moved, but only weakly. He could not rise. William made sure of it by pinning him down with his stick.

"Don't ye ever touch my gear again," said William in a low, clear voice. "Next time I'll crack your head and spill your bloody brains."

Thomas said nothing.

"Do ye hear me?" said William.

Thomas nodded.

"Say it then. Say you will never touch my gear again."

"I never will," murmured Thomas.

"Never will what?"

"I never will touch your gear."

"Again. Say 'again.'" William pressed hard with the stick. "You never will touch my gear again."

"I never will touch your gear again. Now let me up. You broke my bloody arm."

William pulled back the stick and stood looking down at him, breathing deeply to catch his breath.

Sam walked over to the two men. "Get to your feet," he said to Thomas.

"My arm is broken," said Thomas.

Sam reached down and felt along it. "No, it's not," he said. "Get up."

William helped him rise, pulling him up by his good arm. Thomas tried out the other one. It had a dark, spreading bruise, but it seemed to be in one piece.

"Now you two shake hands," said Sam. "We are few among many in this place, and we have to get along with each other. If you two go at it again, I'll dismiss the both of you and you'll be on your own getting out of Indian country."

They shook hands perfunctorily. Thomas retrieved his knife and sheathed it. Then he walked off to his cabin without looking back.

The onlookers began an excited discussion of the fight, imitating some of the moves William and Thomas had made on each other. William could see that he had gained in their estimation for having bested Thomas with a lesser weapon—a stick of wood versus a knife. Cherokee men valued courage, and this fight had proved that William's courage was the greater.

October 5. Today I had a philosophical discussion with Thomas Farrell. I drove my argument home with a single-stick. He made my relations with Otter Queen known to all and insulted me one time too many. There is no question that it is he who has been my bad fairy. The beating I gave him will weigh on him, but enough is enough. We have settled our score, and he knows now the philosophy I learned from my Gregor clansmen before I learned any book philosophy.

Sam was not happy with our brawl, but he let us play it out. Then he warned us to never do the like again. He is right. We are a paltry handful in someone else's country, and we must be united if we are to hold our own.

Philosophical thought for the day: if philosophical disputation took this form at the University of Glasgow, it would be less frequently indulged.

By the next day everyone in Keowee knew how the fight had started, and thus it became known to all that Otter Queen and William were lovers. But the sky did not fall. Otter Queen told William that the Gunsmith approved of their relationship, as did her mothers and their brothers.

It was Sam's reaction that William dreaded most, but several days passed without a word from Sam, though he was noticeably distant. William finally realized that he himself would have to initiate the conversation. He waited until a time when no one else was in the store, and then he confessed what Sam already knew—that he had a romance going with Otter Queen.

"You can't say you've not been warned about what you're getting into," said Sam. "But what's done is done." That was all he had to say. He turned away and went back to work.

For several more days Sam continued to be chilly and formal with William.

But then one morning Sam leaned on the counter like his old self again and said, "Maybe there will be benefits to your pairing off with Otter Queen. I've never thought her to be the witch the Birds claim she is. Maybe your being with her will strengthen her standing in the town and clear up this trouble between the Birds and the Wolves. It's gone on long enough, and this might be the key for getting past it. But it's not over yet, so you need to move on out of my winter house. My Birds aren't happy anymore to have you amongst them. You'll have to take up with the Wolves."

Later that same day, the Gunsmith stopped in at the store and struck up a conversation with William. It seems the Wolves had shot a fat bear and had plans to barbecue it as the centerpiece of a great feast. William was welcome to attend. Later, William had a feeling that the feast had to do with him and Otter Queen, but no one said as much. Not even she would tell him what was going on.

The Wolves lived on the opposite side of the town yard from the Birds. William had dealt with many of the Wolves who had come into the store to make purchases, but on the day of the feast he found himself amongst so many of them at once that he felt unexpectedly ill at ease. I have been living with the Birds too long, he said to himself.

Otter Queen did not come over to greet him, even after he had been there for a while. She stayed with her clanswomen and pretended to pay no special attention to him, though he did catch her looking at him a time or two, and once she flashed him a little smile.

It was awkward keeping company with the Wolf men, most of whom spoke little or no English. Finally two young ones came up to William carrying sticks about the length of the one he had used against Thomas in the fight. Though no words were exchanged, they made it plain that they wanted instruction on how to fight with such a weapon in the Highland way. He showed them some moves that imitated sword play. Though adept at so many other physical feats, Cherokee men were strangers to the use of swords. The youths were awkward in their first attempts, but soon they were picking up the moves.

The Gunsmith walked over to William in the company of an older, ruggedly built man who had an antique war club stuck in his belt. The man might not know how to use that club in the Highland way, but William had no doubt he could easily crack a skull with it. By the scars on this fellow's body it was evident that he was no stranger to combat. William handed off his single-stick to one of the young men and turned to the Gunsmith and his companion.

"Willy," said the Gunsmith, "this man is Five-Killer. He is brother to Otter Queen's mother. Uncle, you say in English. He is Otter Queen's uncle. Also my uncle." The Gunsmith glanced proudly at the older man, then looked back at William. "He wants to talk to you, but he speaks no English."

"And I speak no Cherokee," said William.

The Gunsmith nodded. "I will help you." Then he indicated to his uncle that he should begin.

"You go into woods with Otter Queen," said Five-Killer, the Gunsmith translating.

William braced himself. This did not seem to be a good start.

"What will you do for her?" asked Five-Killer. "She is young girl. She has not known many men."

"We fancy each other," said William. "We wish to live in a house together."

"She is blood of my blood and dear to me. Will you give her English goods and take care of her?"

"Yes, I will take care of her in every way."

"Her mother must agree," said Five-Killer. He motioned to a round-faced woman of about his same age who was standing near Otter Queen but looking toward Five-Killer and William. The woman came walking over to them.

"This is Pretty Baskets," the Gunsmith explained. "She is Five-Killer's sister, mother of Otter Queen and of me."

Pretty Baskets nodded to William as she approached. She had once been a trader's woman and could speak better English than her brother. She motioned for the Gunsmith to stay quiet, and then she spoke for herself.

"You and my daughter want a house of your own?" she asked.

"Yes, we do."

"You take good care of her? Provide for her? Never hit her?"

"Yes," said William. "I will take care of her. I promise to always protect her."

William glanced over at Otter Queen and saw that she was watching them. The young women with her were flushed with excitement and were also looking in William's direction.

"I will be good to her," said William.

"The Wolves will build a house for my daughter," said Pretty Baskets. "You must bring goods from your store and wood for the first fire. After that, you may live together. But remember what I tell you now. Otter Queen is dear to the Gunsmith, and to Five-Killer, and to me. We will watch everything you do."

The feast lasted late into the night, with dancing that went on and on. It was almost dawn when William returned to the homestead. The next day at the store, bleary and hung over, William told Sam the news. "I think perhaps I am married," he said. "At least, I have held court with the uncle of the bride, and I seem to have passed muster with him. And the mother gave her blessing. Then we danced all night. Was that a Cherokee wedding?"

"As close as you will come to one," said Sam. " But it's not as binding as a Scottish wedding. She can kick you out any time she wants."

"I hope she will never want to," said William. "Have ye any advice for me?"

"I wouldn't know where to start. You will have to learn as you go. The bad blood between the Birds and the Wolves will be your first problem. You don't have a mother clan of your own to align with. You'll be seen as being squarely in the Wolf camp. That puts you in good with the Wolves, but now you're on the outs with the Birds. It won't be easy. Your strategy should be to stand above the trouble and not take sides."

"I shall endeavor to do that," said William. He took a deep breath. He could hardly fathom the change his life was taking, especially with his head swirling as it was. "Before I forget it, I want to thank you and Rose for taking me in as a free lodger in your winter house. I regret that by following my heart, I had to betray the Birds. Not that I actually did betray them, but I know they think I did. I'll soon be out of their way. The fox out of the henhouse, I suppose they would say."

"I believe that would be the wolf out of the henhouse," said Sam. "One last word. The more the Wolf clan folds you into their bosom, the more likely you are to forget that you are here to trade skins and further your fortune. So keep in mind what you've come for—to make yourself some money to take back to Charles Town. You didn't come to Keowee to be an agent for the Wolf clan."

On the morning of the day that work was to begin on Otter Queen's house, William walked over to the Wolf quarter to see how things were going. A throng of Wolves were there, both men and women. The women had gotten up a large supply of cooked food, and now they were busy bringing in bundles of river cane to weave together for the wattle-and-daub walls. Five-Killer was laying out the house, and some of the men were digging holes for the posts that would provide vertical structure. Evidently they had an exact idea of the house they were going to build—the timbers they brought to the site were already cut to length. Everyone seemed to know his job, and William could see he would only be in the way if he offered to help. He watched for a while and then returned to the store and worked there until late in the afternoon.

At the end of the day he left the store and went out to the woods to collect some deadwood for Otter Queen's fire. He was surprised at how cleanly scavenged the ground was in the nearest part of the woods. Only after walking a long distance did he find enough wood to make a large bundle, which he tied up and slung over his back.

When he returned to the Wolf quarter with the firewood, he found to his astonishment that Otter Queen's house was already up—complete but for a few finishing touches. They had even put up an outdoor cookshed for her—four posts and a bark roof.

He had not realized that he and Otter Queen would be in their new house that very night. Returning to Sam's, he got the key to the store and gathered up a blue duffel blanket, a hoe, a hatchet, and a brass kettle for Otter Queen. He also picked out a knife for Five-Killer and a string of glass beads for Pretty Baskets. He entered all of this into the account book, to come out of his pay at the end of the season.

Otter Queen started the first fire in her new house with coals from her mother's hearth. She cooked bean bread in her new brass kettle. The other Wolves stayed around until dark and then went home, tired out from the day's work.

William and Otter Queen immediately banked the coals of their fire and retired to their bed. With all its newly cut wood and freshly split river cane, the inside of the house was wonderfully fragrant. So too was Otter Queen, her hair dressed with bear oil mixed with spicebush and sassafras. It seemed to William that his marriage bed smelled of the garden of Eden.

Later he got up and went out to the cookshed and built up a small fire to give him light for writing in his journal.

October 10. Otter Queen and I have built our nest. Rather it was built for us by the Wolves. And rather, the nest is hers, not mine, and I do not rule this roost. But what a thing is love. Quite as powerful as Newton's gravity, it has knocked me out of my orbit. I confess to being pleased to be spinning in this new one.

It is not by accident that I have begun to read "Romeo and Juliet"— the story of a young man and woman knocked out of their orbits in Old Verona.

Marriage Bed

In his new life with Otter Queen, William went to bed earlier at night and stayed in it later in the morning than had ever been his habit. Privacy was scarce in Keowee, and this was one place where he and Otter Queen could find it. Their delight in each other's bodies was still keen, and they would wind their limbs about each other as they talked late into the night. William had much to learn to be a good Cherokee husband. He pressed Otter Queen to tell him tales of Cherokee life, and he tried to learn more of the language. Lying in bed one night, he put his finger on her ear. "What is this in Cherokee?"

"*Tsile:na,*" she said. "*Tsi*—'my.' *Le:na*—'ear.'"

He practiced saying it, working hard on the long "e" sound before the "n." "Sihlayyna."

"Ts," she said, trying to show him with her tongue how to put a "t" sound before the "s."

"Tsihlayyna," he said.

She nodded. It was good enough.

Then he touched his finger gently to her eye.

"*Tsik'to'li,*" she said.

The stressed "k" and "o" were difficult. He kept trying until she was satisfied. Then he touched his finger to her arm.

"*Tsinoge:na,*" she said. Another long "ay."

He touched her leg.

"*Tsinvsge:na,*" she said.

"Tsihnuhsgayyna." The "nuh" was nasalized and took some practice.

Then he touched his finger between her legs.

"*Tsile:stahlv:ʔi,*" she said.

He shook his head. "That is too hard to say. I'll keep to the English. Coney."

"Coney?" she said with a smile. "I have never heard it called that."

"It's also the English word for rabbit."

Otter Queen laughed so hard that tears came to her eyes. "Now I understand," she said, barely able to speak, "why Englishmen do it so fast. They do it like rabbits."

"I'm not English, I'm Scottish," laughed William, and they began tussling with each other, playing like otters until he finally managed to get on top and make love to her like a Scotsman. Then they settled back again, still not ready to sleep.

"I have a riddle for ye," William said.

"What is it?"

"What is round, split in the middle, surrounded by hair, and water comes out?"

"*Tsile:stahlv:ʔi?*" she asked.

"No, your eye. But now I know what ye have on your mind."

Otter Queen laughed so hard she gasped for air. "Oh, Willy," she said when she could speak again. "You make me happy."

William came up short on sleep that night. The next morning they had to rise with first light because Pretty Baskets was coming for a day of basket-making. William staggered about feeling wooly-headed as Otter Queen built a fire against the October chill.

"Why does your mother have to come so early?"

"We have a lot to do," said Otter Queen. "I can't have a house without baskets."

They were still eating their breakfast when they heard the slap of a hand against the outside wall of the house. Then, without further ado, Pretty Baskets came in through the door carrying several hoops of cured, brownish-yellow cane splits. She and Otter Queen talked with each other briefly in Cherokee, and then the two of them went outside and kindled another fire for their work. William went out and stood leaning against a post of the cookshed. Otter Queen offered commentary as they worked, though William's interest in their project was not great. He simply liked to watch Otter Queen do things, no matter what it was.

As he looked on, she and Pretty Baskets put most of the cane splits into a big pot of cold water and left them there to steep and become pliable. Of the remaining splits, they put half of them into a pot of water containing butternut bark and roots, which would dye them black, and the other half into a pot of water steeped with blood root to dye them red. They weighed down the splits with rocks and set the two pots beside the fire to simmer, tossing some wood ashes into each pot to speed up the dyeing.

"Now," said Otter Queen, "we must go out and collect some cane of our own to pay back Pretty Baskets for these splits she brought us. You have to come along."

"You didn't tell me about this," said William. "How long will it take? I can't be late to the trading house."

"You have to come with us, Willy. Collecting cane is dangerous."

William's foggy mind began to clear. "What is dangerous about it?"

"We have to go very far from the town to get it. All the cane nearby was used up long ago. The nearest canebrake is now so far away that Creek raiders sometimes lurk there. We need a man with a gun to protect us." She looked at him and shrugged. As she saw it, there was nothing to debate. They were going whether he came with them or not. And so she was right, there was nothing to debate. He had no choice but to come.

Pretty Baskets spoke up, exchanging a few words in Cherokee with her daughter. ·

"There is some cane growing along Cornhouse Creek," said Otter Queen. "It is not the best canebrake, but it is the closest one. If we go now, you will not be very late getting back to Sanee's."

Resigning himself, William took up his musket, dirk, and hatchet and followed them on a very long walk away from the town to the canebrake, where the three of them worked together cutting down canes and dragging them out of the brake. William helped them strip off the leaves, and he gathered up rocks to weigh down most of the canes in the water of the creek, where they would be left until another day. The remaining canes had to be made into splits for Pretty Baskets.

William could not help them make the splits. It was beyond his ability. He watched as the women worked quickly, using small, sharp knives to smooth the joints and split the cane lengthwise into halves and then quarters. Large stalks were divided further until the splits were the width they desired. When they had finished, they bundled them together to take back to Keowee. William offered to carry part of the load, but Otter Queen refused, saying that the other men in Keowee would ridicule him if they saw him carrying basket splits.

"There is woman's work and there is man's work," she said. "Carrying is woman's work."

He started to argue, but Pretty Baskets waved at him to be quiet. William closed his mouth in bemusement. The petticoat government of the Cherokees was surprisingly stubborn.

It was late in the morning when he finally got to the store. Sam just shook his head and said nothing. Fortunately, it had been a slow morning, with few customers coming in to trade. William found extra work to do to make up for being tardy, and since Jim-Bird seemed to be spending most of the day on a bench out front, William felt he was holding up his end of the work well enough.

When the workday was over, he was glad to get home again. He found that the two women had thinned down all of the splits by shaving away the inner core with their knives. They had each started weaving a basket, though only the bases were woven so far, with splits splaying out on all sides. Pretty Baskets had gone home for the day, and Otter Queen was busy with the evening meal. It pleased William to have a home to come to, a woman's world in which to rest.

For the next three days Otter Queen and her mother wove baskets. The first one that Pretty Baskets made was a pack basket woven of undyed splits. With its flaring rim, it had roughly the shape of a large inverted bell, with a capacity, William estimated, of about three bushels. A woman carried her packbasket by wrapping a broad tumpline around and under the flaring upper part of the basket and then tying the strap around her upper chest. Even though the packbasket itself was very light, it could carry great weight and bulk.

Otter Queen's first production was a large storage basket, also woven out of undyed splits. This one had a four-sided base that rose to a roundish rim, but unlike the flaring packbasket, the sides of the storage basket came straight up. Otter Queen's weaving was as tight and neat as her mother's.

In the days that followed, the two women produced a fine mat with a red and black border for Otter Queen and William to use on their bed, several additional storage baskets, some food-serving baskets, a basket for gathering berries, a sifter for making cornmeal, and several sieves with different sizes of mesh.

Otter Queen's last basket was what she called a doubleweave, an intricate work she produced by herself the day after Pretty Baskets had stopped coming. This basket was not large, but it was quite beautiful, and William was amazed at her handiwork. The smooth side of the cane splits faced both the inside and the outside, which was accomplished by weaving it seamlessly and folding it back on itself to make two layers, with a different pattern of black and red against the natural splits on each side. Having finished one of these, she started another, and in the end she showed him how the two pieces together made a small covered hamper. The piece that was the cover was slightly wider in girth than the other and only about half as deep. The two baskets could be used separately or together. When Otter Queen finished the last touch, she put the two pieces together and held them up for William to admire.

"I am proud of this," she said.

October 19. Otter Queen and her mother have woven us a houseful of baskets, light, strong, and pretty to behold. The patterns they weave have names. One is Pebbles and Stones. Another is Snake Tracks. Their baskets marry art and utility.

I have been making my way through Romeo and Juliet. Master Shakespeare shows us the impetuous side of young love. There is no stone wall young lovers will not breach, no parent they will not defy, no prince whose laws they will not flaunt. They are not tempered by wise counsel, though the stage become littered with the dead.

The enmity between Romeo's house of Montague and Juliet's house of Capulet is quite as strong as that between the Birds and Wolves of Keowee. And yet this enmity does not keep the lovers apart. The friar is wiser than he knows when he says:

Young men's love then lies
Not truly in their hearts but in their eyes.

Romeo had only to see Juliet, and she to see him, whereupon both of them cast aside their families' choice of intended marriage partners. This tale strikes close to home.

William woke up shivering. Otter Queen was already up and about, and the blanket had come off him.

"Get up, Willy," she said. "There was frost last night. We must get to the chestnut grove before the others."

"No, come back to bed for a little while," he said, reaching out to grab her.

She stepped back, out of reach. "Frost," she repeated. "This is a chestnut morning. We have to hurry."

Grumbling, William dragged himself up and got dressed. Otter Queen had a kettle of water simmering on the fireplace, and he made a cup of black drink, though she was so impatient to leave that he had to add some cool water to it so he could gulp it down quickly enough to suit her. She objected when he took out his knife to cut himself a piece of hard, barbecued venison.

"We have to go now," she said, tying her packbasket onto her back with a cloth tumpline. "I will show you how to eat while we are on the way. The woods are full of food."

"Yes, but has it been cooked?" He cut off a piece of meat and followed her out the door.

They headed out of town toward the northwest, walking faster than usual. It was a beautiful frosty morning, the trees well along in their turn from green to autumn colors. Before long Otter Queen stopped at a grove of smallish trees with beautifully colored oval leaves. "Here is food," she said. "And it doesn't have to be cooked."

"These are not chestnuts," said William.

"They are persimmons, silly." She stooped over and picked up a plum-sized fruit from the ground and put it into her mouth. While eating the flesh, she spat out flat black seeds, one after the other. "Very good and sweet," she said, "but only if they are all the way ripe. Rotten ripe, as my father used to say."

She handed one to William and he tasted it. It was sweet and good, a fine treat. He ate it eagerly, spitting out the seeds. Then he picked up another and popped it into his mouth, biting into the flesh, soft as custard, sifting out the seeds with his teeth. But almost at once the inside of his mouth began to pucker, and he spit out the fruit, and then spit again, but he could not get rid of the astringency.

"That one was not quite ripe," laughed Otter Queen. "I told you, they have to be rotten ripe. Don't try the ones that are pretty and plump. They have to be wrinkled and squishy or else they will turn your mouth inside out."

"So it seems," said William, still spitting as he looked more carefully for his next one. "The good ones are good, but the bad ones are very bad."

"Everyone loves persimmons," said Otter Queen. "They ripen in cold weather, when we are hungry for fruit. And they hang on the trees for a long time. They don't all fall at once. Sometimes you can still find a few of them hanging on bare trees when there is snow on the ground. We will come another day and gather persimmons."

After they had eaten their fill, they continued on to the chestnut grove. The spreading tops of the great, towering trees—some a hundred feet tall or more—with spreading tops that formed a dense canopy of lance-shaped leaves beginning to turn yellow and light brown. The rough-barked trunks rose straight up like columns, and the forest below was as open as a parkland. Only spots of sunlight penetrated the canopy, and it was utterly quiet except for the falling chestnuts. Here and there a brown leaf floated silently to earth. William could see that the chestnut burrs were opening up both on the ground and in the trees. The chestnuts inside them were a rich brown color, much like the ones he had seen, but rarely tasted, in Scotland. There they were a delicacy. Here they could be gathered free in the woods by the bushel.

"Deer always know when the chestnuts are ripe," said Otter Queen, pointing with her toe to a scatter of deer dung on the ground. "A chestnut grove is a good place to hunt."

When Otter Queen's packbasket began to fill up, she removed it and set it on the ground. As William bent over and picked up chestnuts, he collected them in his hat until it was full, and then he emptied them into the packbasket. Otter Queen did likewise, bending over and picking up chestnut after chestnut, collecting them in the front of her skirt until she emptied them into the packbasket. Watching her, William became aroused, and he walked over to her from behind and hugged her. He reached around and cupped her breasts in his hands and pulled her to him, and she felt his arousal. She made to move away, but William held on and kissed her on the back of her neck.

"I have some unfinished business from this morning," he said.

"It's too cold for love in the woods," she said.

"Never fear. I will warm you up."

She made as if to move away, but he held on.

"Willy—you are acting like a rabbit—or a dog!" She laughed and reached around to feel his arousal.

"Maybe a little of both," he said as he caressed her. From the way she was breathing, he knew that she was relenting.

They walked over to a clump of weeds and lay down on a pile of leaves. William hiked up Otter Queen's skirt and then and there they made love with a minimum of Otter play. Though the air was cold, it did not seem so in their ardor for each other.

They had gathered a load that was as large as Otter Queen could manage. Her basket was not full, but it was heavy. William offered to carry it, but she reminded him again that carrying was a woman's job. He shook his head, finding this difficult to accept.

"When a baby is born," she said, "people will ask, 'Is it a pack basket or an arrow?' A girl or a boy? Maybe one day we Cherokees will own enough horses to do our carrying for us, but until that day, this is woman's work. You cannot be a man in Keowee if you do woman's work."

The chestnut grove was not so far from the town, and they got back in time for William to put in a full day at the store. When he returned home in the late afternoon, Otter Queen had roasted some of the chestnuts and used them to make chestnut bread, a hominy dumpling wrapped in corn shucks and boiled like bean bread, only mixed with roasted chestnuts instead of beans.

Taking a bite, William closed his eyes and savored the sweet, nutty flavor. "This is fit for the gods," he said. "Here I am in the wilds of America eating better than the grandees in Glasgow."

"You are easy to please," she replied.

From time to time William would ask Otter Queen to tell him about the trouble between the Birds and the Wolves. He wanted to hear the story as the Wolves would tell it. But she would never comply. "We are happy, Willy," she would answer. "I do not want to talk about the Birds."

Late one night, after having witnessed, earlier that day, a bitter scene in the town yard between old Hawk's Mother of the Bird clan and a woman from the Wolf clan, William asked her again. When Otter Queen tried to turn him aside, he pressed on. "They say you are a witch," he said.

Otter Queen was silent for a moment. He could not see her face in the dark. "All right," she said. "We will not be happy tonight. Instead I will tell you the story of the Wolves and the Birds. But it is hard to explain this to an Englishman."

"I am a Scotsman," said William, playfully poking a finger against her side.

She laughed a little. "Scotsman, Englishman, there is not much difference."

He chuckled. "See, you are still happy."

"Just wait. If I go on with this I will end up crying."

"I will comfort you," he said.

She sighed. "You can't, Willy. Not about this. But here is the story. It started between my grandmother and a woman of the Bird clan—an old woman who was Hawk's Mother's sister. My grandmother and Hawk Mother's sister had always been friends, and no one knows what it was that went wrong between them. But something did. They stopped speaking. It must have been something that one of them said to the other. Then the Bird woman suddenly became ill and died. And that is when the Birds began saying that my grandmother was a *tshki:li*."

"What is a *tshki:li?*"

"A *tshki:li* is a large owl, the kind that has tufts of feathers on its head like horns. The English call it a horned owl."

"They said your grandmother was an owl?"

"A horned owl. A *tshki:li*. They meant that she was a witch."

"I do not understand this," said William.

"That is because you don't know anything about horned owls," said Otter Queen. "A horned owl is a secretive bird that only flies about at night, or in half-light. It is large and frightening, with furious yellow eyes that look directly at you when you come upon it. Its call can make your heart stop when it comes from you know not where in the darkness. When you hear it, you do not know if it is just an owl or if it is a witch disguised as an owl. Witches can change their shape, and the horned owl is their favorite shape. Everyone knows this, Willy."

"I have heard this bird," said William. "We were sitting by the fire one night on the trail from Charles Town and there was one in a tree close by. John called it a great horned owl, but no one said anything about a witch. It is true, though, that it had an eerie call. Hoo, hoo, hoo."

"That is not how it sounds," said Otter Queen. "It makes such a deep and throaty sound, it could come from a human chest. It goes, hoo, hoo-hoo, hoo, hoo."

"Yes!" said William. "That was it exactly. But it was not so frightening as the howl of a wolf, or the screech of a panther in the night."

"Wolves and panthers don't fly. The horned owl is terrifying because of how silently it flies in the darkness and swoops down and kills other birds while they sleep. It plunders baby birds from their nests, even from the nests of crows and hawks, who themselves are fierce in the daylight but are helpless in the dark. This is how it is with witches. They plunder peoples' lives in the same way, under the cover of darkness. You must know about this. You must have witches in Scotland."

William laughed.

"This is not funny," she said.

He tried to explain his amusement. "While we packhorsemen were on the trail from Charles Town, I read a story about witches in Scotland. It did not seem to me to be a true story. And now here I am again talking about witches in Scotland. That story is following me."

"Do you or don't you have witches in Scotland?

"Some people there believe that witches exist. Only ignorant and backward people believe this, not enlightened people. But enlightened or not, everyone in Scotland has heard stories about witches, and so in that way they do exist, as stories."

"Tell me a story about a Scottish witch."

"I am a poor storyteller," he said, "but I will try. I will tell you one my mother used to tell me. I have heard others tell it, too. In this story there was a great hunter of Glen Gyle who had been hunting all day in the high Trossach Hills. At twilight he returned to his hunting hut, and he and his two dogs lay down to sleep by the fire, with his rifle and his *skian dhu*—his black dagger—nearby. A storm came up. As the wind and the rain beat against the hut, a weather-beaten cat, soaking wet, pushed its way in through the door. The dogs saw her and bristled and growled. The man sat up.

"'Sir,' the cat said, 'I beg you to protect me. My sisters have treated me badly.'"

"The hunter knew at once what this talking cat was, but she looked so bedraggled and forlorn, he pitied her."

"Was she a witch?" asked Otter Queen.

"Wait and see," said William. "The hunter said to her, 'I have no use for your kind, but come to my fire and warm yourself for just a few minutes.'"

"'Thank you, sir,' said the cat, 'but I am afraid of your dogs. Will you first bind them with this long hair?' It was a curiously long hair she handed him. He took it and looped one end of the hair around the necks of his two dogs, and he seemed to tie the other end of it around a roof beam.

"The cat, seeing the dogs bound by the long hair, walked confidently over to the fire, sat down on her haunches, and began licking herself dry. As she did, she grew larger.

"'It is just that when my hairs are heated, they expand,' she said. But she continued to grow larger and larger, and then suddenly she changed into the likeness of the Goodwife of Glen Gyle, an old and respected woman known by all in those parts.

"You see," said Otter Queen. "She had only taken the shape of a cat. She was a witch."

"So it seems," said William. "The old woman said to the hunter, 'I am the queen of my sisterhood, and it is I who have been ravaging the lives of the people in the countryside. Your time has come.' With this, she lunged at the hunter, but at the same instant the two dogs sprang at her, teeth bared."

"'Seize, hair!' she cried, and the hair clasped itself tightly around the dogs' necks. But it failed to clasp itself around the roof beam, where the hunter had only pretended to fasten it, and so the dogs kept coming. They each grabbed onto one of her breasts with their teeth and the pair of them dragged her from the house into the raging storm. As soon as the rain wetted her, she shook off the dogs, changed into a raven, and flew off towards her home.

"The two dogs limped back into the hut. They licked the hunter's hands and then fell dead at his feet, done in by the bedraggled cat, who was also the Goodwife of Glen Gyle, who was also a raven."

"It is much the same in Scotland as it is here," said Otter Queen.

"There is more," said William. "The hunter returned to his home the next day, but his wife was not there when he arrived. Toward evening she came home, and he asked her where she had been.

"'Nursing the Goodwife of Glen Gyle,' she said. 'It seems that she got her feet wet yesterday and has fallen ill. She is very sick. All of the neighbors have come to her aid.'

"'I will go to look in on her as well,' he said.

"When he reached the house of the Goodwife of Glen Gyle, he found a great crowd of worried people gathered around her. The hunter walked over to her bedside. 'Good to see you again, old cat,' he said, and to the horror of everyone present, he stripped the bedclothes off of the old woman. She snarled at him, and the people in the room were aghast to see the wretched body, the bleeding breasts, of a witch.

"The hunter told the people around her bed the story of what had befallen him in his hunter's hut, and the bite marks on the witch bore out his tale. And with her true identity revealed, the witch began to die before their eyes. But even as she died, she would admit no wrong. She said she had made love to the Devil and would do it again when she got to hell. Then she laughed a horrid laugh until she was dead. The people brought torches and burned her house to the ground with her body in it."

"Do you mean that she became a witch after sleeping with the Devil?" asked Otter Queen.

"Yes, that is how Scottish women become witches. At least, that is what some people say."

"Well, that is not how it is here. We had witches among us long before we ever heard about the Devil."

"If your witches don't come from the Devil, where do they come from?"

"No one knows where witches come from," said Otter Queen. "Some say that their lineage goes back to a terrible *tshki:li* who used to range about in the mountains near here. But where did that *tshki:li* come from? I think witches have been here since the beginning of things. Wherever there are people, there are witches."

"Now you have to tell me a story," said William. "Tell me about the witch in the mountains."

"I would rather tell you that than tell you about the Birds. But with all this talk of witches, I am wishing for the light of day."

"I'll protect ye," said William, reaching his arm around her.

She drew his arm in tight. "Listen, then. Here is the story. A long time ago, a horrible monster ranged through these mountains. She could remove her guts and then take on any shape, human or animal. In her real form she was an old woman whose body was stone, and for this reason she was named *Nunyuhuwi*, 'Stone Dress.'"

Otter Queen paused and made William practice saying the name in Cherokee. Then she went on, "Her favorite food was human livers. The forefinger of her right hand was a long, bony awl. She could make herself invisible and stick her bony finger into you and you would never feel it. This is how she stole livers. You would not know anything about it for a day or two, but then you would start to feel ill and turn yellow, and soon you would be dead.

"She liked to prey on hunters who were out in the woods. When they would set the woods on fire to drive game, she would smell the smoke and come looking for prey. The hunters feared her, and for this reason they usually hunted in groups.

"The trouble was, you never knew what she would look like. The hunters stuck together, because if one were to go alone to a spring for a drink of water, you never knew whether it was Stone Dress coming back or the hunter himself.

"In time Stone Dress came down from the mountains and began witching people closer and closer to the town. People would go missing while out collecting firewood or for cane or chestnuts. Something had to be done. So the people dug a deep hole on a trail—like a wolf pit—and they carefully covered it over with sticks and dead weeds. They built a big fire nearby as if they were driving game, and sure enough, they soon saw an old woman coming along the trail toward them. She had the appearance of a respected old woman whom the hunters knew well, and some of them wanted to warn her about the trap. But cooler heads stopped them from doing so.

"The old woman never suspected the trap. She fell into the pit, and then her true nature came out. She began screeching and thrashing about with her bony finger, trying to stab the hunters who gathered around the rim of the pit. They fired arrow after arrow at her, but the arrows only bounced off of her stony flesh. She kept jumping at the hunters, higher and higher, and they were afraid she would escape.

"Then a tufted titmouse came along and perched on a limb above the pit and began to sing." Otter Queen paused and asked William, "Do you know this bird? It is small and grey and has a crest on its head."

"Yes," said William. "I have seen it."

"Well, the tufted titmouse perched on the limb and sang *un, un, un*. They thought the bird was trying to say *unahwi*, 'heart,' and so they fired arrow after arrow at Stone Dress's chest, where her heart should be, but the arrows still bounced off.

"Then a chickadee came along." She looked at William. "Do you know this one? The tiny gray bird with a black cap?"

"Yes, I know it," said William.

"The chickadee came and perched for a moment on Stone Dress's awl finger. The hunters shot their arrows at that hand, and with this Stone Dress began to whirl madly around in the pit, trying to evade the arrows. Finally, an arrow pierced her hand—her right hand, the one with the awl finger—and she fell dead. Then they knew that her heart was not in her breast where it should have been. She carried her own beating heart clutched in that dreadful awl hand.

"So that's how people learned that the tufted titmouse is a liar. The hunters were so angry at him, they cut off his tongue, and to this day his tongue is still short and everybody knows he is a bird you cannot trust. But you must always listen to a chickadee. The chickadee is a truth-teller, and we are always happy when this little bird comes around. You often see them both together, the tufted titmouse and the chickadee. Each seems to enjoy the company of people, and their songs are so similar you have to be very careful to distinguish one from the other. It is the same way with people. You have to be careful to distinguish truth-tellers from liars." Otter Queen squeezed William's arm. "Do you hear me, Willy? Do not believe them when they say I am a witch."

William laughed. "How could I ever believe that?"

"You keep laughing," she said, "but it is not funny." There was a catch in her voice, as if she might cry. "When you are accused of being a witch, it is impossible to disprove. It is an accusation about how you are deep inside, Willy, not about something you have done. They can keep on saying it forever, like they did with my grandmother. But she was not a witch. And neither am I." William became aware that Otter Queen was quietly weeping. He tightened his arms around her and felt helpless. There was nothing he could do about what the Birds were saying about her.

In a little while she stopped crying, and they lay in silence for a long time. William was almost asleep when she spoke again.

"Willy, are you awake?"

"Yes," he murmured

"Do you remember the question that people ask about the packbasket or the arrow?"

"About a girl or a boy?"

"Yes, that question."

He nodded. "I remember it."

"I think you might ask me that."

William raised up from the bed to look at her, but it was too dark to see her face. "Are ye with child?"

"I think so. I talked with my mother about it and she thinks that I am."

"A child," said William, falling back down beside her and gathering her back into his arms. "I can hardly believe it. A child." He was quiet for a moment, taking it in. Then he said, "This bairn will be a Highlander twice over. Once for the Scottish Highlands and again for the Cherokee Highlands. A Wolf and a MacGregor."

"A Wolf," Otter Queen said quietly.

William did not try to argue. He held her until he fell asleep.

Before leaving for the trading house the next day, he wrote in his journal.

October 30. It seems that I am to be a father. If it is a boy, we will name him Francis, after Francis Hutcheson, the Scottish philosopher who searches for truth; but if it is a girl, we will name her Chickadee, after a Cherokee bird that can tell nothing but the truth.

After such news as this, it seems of little consequence to report on the progress of Romeo and Juliet, but the play has drawn me in. Master Shakespeare's story bears out the adage that love is blind. It does not, however, sustain the adage that love conquers all. Juliet's father, not having been informed that she has secretly married Romeo, has forced her to agree to marry Paris. Romeo, meanwhile, has been banished to Mantua. As the two lovers careen about, trying to rejoin each other, everything begins to come apart. Otter Queen keeps asking me to tell her the story. I tell her that I will do so after I have finished reading it for myself. But now that it is going so badly, I do not want to tell her about it at all.

Last night, before she told me about the baby, we exchanged stories about witches. It seems there is not much difference between the witches of Scotland and those of Keowee. Both there and here witches are said to be humans who become inexplicably evil and who are somehow able to take on the appearance of other people, or even animals. Both in Scotland

and in Keowee it is said that witches wish to harm all who are around them. And both there and here it is said that a witch who is unmasked will die. How is one to explain these similarities, unless witches really do exist? And yet I do not believe that they do.

Philosophical thought for this day: people everywhere are basically the same.

14   Verona

As William read the final pages of *Romeo and Juliet,* tears came to his eyes. Otter Queen saw it happen.

"How could words on paper bring a man to tears?" she asked. "It is time for you to tell me this story. It must be a terrible one if it makes you cry."

"It is sad," he said, "but it is not terrible. It has a strange effect. It has made me feel that I am larger and wiser than I was before I read it."

"Then you must tell it to me," she said. "I told you about the trouble between the Wolves and the Birds, now you must tell me this story."

"You might be disappointed," he warned her. "Much of this will be strange to you. The world of Old Verona is not like the world of Keowee."

"Verona," said Otter Queen, trying out the new word. "Is this a town in Scotland?"

"No, it is in Italy."

"Is that near England?"

William drew in a long breath and slowly let it out again. "It is difficult to tell you about the world I came from. Italy is not near England. England and Scotland are right next to each other, but Italy is farther away. But Italy is closer to England than it is to Keowee. So perhaps it is not wrong to say that it is near England. Now here is the story. Once upon a time in Verona."

"In Italy," Otter Queen added.

"Yes, once upon a time in Verona, in Italy, there were two clans, the Montagues and the Capulets. There was trouble between them, not unlike the trouble between the Birds and the Wolves in Keowee. Whenever the young men of one clan happened upon the young men of the other clan in the streets, they would taunt each other into anger, and fighting would break out. They were disturbing the peace of Verona, and the townspeople had grown weary of it."

"I thought you said it would be strange to me," said Otter Queen. "It is just like here, except that the Birds and the Wolves do not break out into fighting. Not in the open. They fight each other with conjury."

"Just wait," said William. "Some of this will be strange. One day the Prince of Verona found the young men of the two clans at each other's throats in the streets, and he gave a warning to both clans. If they ever disturbed the peace again, he thundered, he would execute the combatants on the spot."

"Kill them?"

"Yes, hang them by their necks."

"How does the Prince of Verona have such power?" asked Otter Queen. "King Crow would never say such a thing to the young men of Keowee, not even if he had the power of the English behind him. It is up to the clans to restore order on their own."

"I told you it would be strange. Where I come from, many people think the Prince's power comes from God. He can do almost anything he wants. But let me get back to my story. It so happened that Romeo of the Montague clan went to a masquerade—a place of music and dance—put on by the Capulets."

"A feast," said Otter Queen. "We would call that a feast. Everyone likes to come out and eat someone else's cooking."

"Yes, a feast," said William. "Romeo and his friends went to this Capulet feast wearing masks so that none would recognize them as Montagues. Juliet was a daughter of the Capulets. She was young and very beautiful—like you. The moment Romeo set eyes on her, he forgot about every other woman in the world. He was just as I was when I first saw you. And as Juliet danced, she saw that his eyes were fixed on her. She thought he was very handsome."

"But he had on a mask," said Otter Queen.

"Not one that covered all of his face like a Cherokee mask. It only covered the part around his eyes. She could see that he was handsome."

"It must have been a raccoon mask," said Otter Queen.

William laughed. "Yes, he was like a raccoon, with black around his eyes. So she saw him and she liked him—she liked his looks, just as he liked hers. So they moved closer to each other until they were able to find a private place where they could stand together. They talked, they touched hands, and they kissed. But later Romeo learned that this beautiful young woman, whom he so greatly desired, was a Capulet; and Juliet learned that this handsome young man was a Montague. This made them very sad."

"Now, I do not understand this," said Otter Queen. "Even Birds and Wolves can marry each other. We all must marry into a clan other than our own, and it often happens that relations between the two clans are not on the best footing. There are only six other clans besides your own. So every clan has to be able to marry into every other."

"That may be true in Cherokee, but not in Verona," said William. "No one wanted these two to get married. Neither clan would permit it. But in spite of the difficulty it was sure to cause them, Romeo and Juliet secretly married, and they became lovers."

"Which came first?"

"They married first."

"Before they were lovers?"

"Yes, that is the way it is done in Verona."

"And in Scotland, too?"

"Yes, if a girl is to keep her honor, that is how it must be done."

"How does she keep her honor."

"By marrying before she lies with a man."

"With any man?"

"Yes, with any man."

"Then how does she know who she wants to marry?"

"I told you this would be strange," said William.

"Yes, it is strange. But I am listening. What happened next?"

"It so happened," said William, "that Romeo had a sharp-tongued, hot-tempered cousin named Mercutio. Mercutio liked to show off by being clever with words. He would take the words of others and turn them into puns and mockeries and veiled insults. He was not a fool, but he liked to play the fool."

"Puns are funny," said Otter Queen, "but insults are not good. He sounds like a Bird. I don't think I would like Mercutio."

"Well, Romeo did. They were fellow clansmen. One day Mercutio came upon Tybalt, a famous warrior of the Capulets. Mercutio played the fool with words, making Tybalt so angry he drew his sword, and they began to fight.

"But the prince, you remember, had forbidden the two clans to fight. So Romeo ran over and put himself between Mercutio and Tybalt, begging them to stop before the prince found them out. But Romeo should not have done this, because in the thick of battle, a warrior like Tybalt could not so easily be calmed. While Romeo was in the way of the fight, Tybalt thrust his sword under Romeo's arm and stabbed Mercutio."

"Oh, no," murmured Otter Queen.

"At first it seemed that Mercutio was not badly injured. He kept on talking. But he began to fail, and then he slumped down and died. Tybalt and his kinsmen tried to flee, but Romeo was full of anger and ran after him."

"This was crying blood," said Otter Queen.

"Yes. So Romeo overtook him, and the two of them began to fight. Romeo ran Tybalt through with his sword and Tybalt fell dead. Romeo was horrified when he realized what a foolish thing he had done. Not only was he now in trouble with the prince, but he had killed a Capulet, one of his wife's own kinsmen."

"There was nothing wrong with that," said Otter Queen. "Any Cherokee would say it was his duty to take blood revenge, a Capulet for a Montague. Juliet should have been relieved that the one he killed was Tybalt himself and not some other Capulet. Tybalt was the very one who killed Mercutio, so that came out well. Are you sure you have this story right?"

"Yes, I am telling it to you just as William Shakespeare wrote it," said William. "Romeo's killing of Tybalt might have been a good thing in Keowee, but it was a bad thing in Verona. The prince meant every word of his threat to execute any of them who ever fought again. And as for Juliet, it broke her heart that Romeo had killed her kinsman."

"But if he explained it to her," said Otter Queen, "if he told her that it was Tybalt who killed a Montague first, then she would not blame him."

"That is not the way it is in Italy," said William. "So Romeo felt terrible for what he had done. He feared that Juliet would never forgive him. And he also knew that the prince would be sending out soldiers to arrest him. So he fled to another town—to Mantua—where he would be safe."

"Is Mantua also in Italy?" asked Otter Queen.

"Yes."

"Then he did not go far."

"No, but he went far enough. He and Juliet were now separated. Neither knew what the other was doing. They could not talk with each other. Juliet was filled with pain. She despaired of her life. Her beloved husband had killed her beloved kinsman, which was almost unbearable to her. And to make things worse, her father was trying to marry her off to a man named Paris. She did not have the courage to tell her father and mother that she had secretly married Romeo."

"This is a mess," said Otter Queen.

"It gets worse. Juliet went to a medicine man and told him of her desperate plight. He came up with a plan. He gave her a medicine that would put her to sleep so deeply that she would seem to be dead. Her kinsmen would put her body in a Capulet tomb and everyone would go away and leave her there, thinking they would never see her again. But in two days she would wake up and be just fine."

"Wait," said Otter Queen. "That can't be right. His people would bury her for two days, and then she would wake up and be just fine? If they buried her, she really would die."

"A tomb is not like a grave," said William. "A tomb is a small stone house they put you in when you are dead."

"We put the dead in houses, too. In their own houses, underneath their beds. That's where a person is buried."

"I've never heard of doing that," said William.

"Where else would you want to be buried? Your bed is the one place in this world that is most your own. So of course people are buried beneath their beds. But you can't dig them up in two days and expect them to be alive."

"In a tomb you are not buried. They just lay you out on a stone slab. But you have not heard all of the plan. Listen now. The medicine man promised Juliet that he would tell Romeo what was happening to her so that Romeo could go to the tomb and be there when she woke up. Then the two of them could flee to safety in Mantua, away from their kinsmen and from the prince.

"And so that is what she decided to do. She went home and took the medicine, and she seemed to die. Her kinsmen put her body in the tomb, thinking she was dead. The medicine man sent a message to Romeo explaining everything, but then the real trouble began, because the message never reached him. All he heard was what everyone else heard, that Juliet had died. He went to the Capulet tomb and found her there all laid out, so deeply asleep that he thought that she was truly dead. This was more than he could bear. In despair he quickly drank some poison he had brought, and he fell to the floor beside her and died."

Otter Queen made a little sound of exasperation.

William went on. "When Juliet woke up, she found her Romeo dead. She was beside herself with grief, utterly distraught. How could she live without Romeo? She grabbed up Romeo's dagger and plunged it into her breast, and she died."

Otter Queen shook her head. "I know you have the story wrong. Juliet would not have killed herself because of this, no matter how much she loved Romeo. She would have understood that it was because Romeo had killed Tybalt that he took his own life, and in this way he must have thought that he had satisfied the blood revenge that the prince was trying to take on both the clans. Then the Capulets would be so grateful that it would end the feud and bring the clans back together again. It doesn't make sense that she would kill herself after he had done that. It would dishonor the good he had done."

"But this is the way Shakespeare wrote it," said William. "I told the story exactly as he did. And you haven't heard the ending yet. Listen. This is my favorite part.

"A cry went up in Verona when the people heard the news of Romeo's death and of Juliet's second death. The prince came to the tomb, as did the Capulets and the Montagues. When they saw the two dead lovers and heard the whole story of how their deaths had come about, clansmen of both houses gave voice to their sadness and mourned for Romeo and Juliet. Their deaths seemed to be sacrifices that overcame the hatred between the two clans, and as they realized this, the Capulets and Montagues clasped their arms around each other in tearful forgiveness."

William picked up the book and opened it to the last page of the play. "Here is what the prince said on that sad day in Verona.

A glooming peace this morning with it brings,
The Sun for sorrow will not show his head.
Go hence to have more talk of these sad things.
Some shall be pardon'd and some punished.
For never was a story of more woe
Than this of Juliet and her Romeo.

William closed the book. "It still brings a tear to my eye," he said.

"I do not think it is such a sad story," said Otter Queen. "I think there are parts of it that you have wrong, but if the Capulets and the Montagues did reconcile with each other, then that makes it a better story. Forgiveness between clans is a good thing. It makes sense for her to kill herself if she did it for the good of their clans, but not if she did it because she and Romeo could no longer make love to each other. He was only her lover. She was not bound to him as if she were his slave. You don't have to die if your lover dies. You can find another lover after you have grieved."

William felt oddly off balance. He had told one story and Otter Queen had heard another. He was beginning to realize that he might never be able to think like a Cherokee.

November 15. I told Shakespeare's story of Romeo and Juliet to my own Juliet tonight, but she had her own ideas about what the master intended. She insisted it was not a tragedy at all. It was a story about how clans should get along with each other. All the while I had thought it was a tragedy about love.

Philosophical thought for this day: People everywhere are not basically the same.

I would like to hear the Book Maggots take up this question: Can two contraries be true at once? Can it be said that people everywhere are basically alike and at the same time are in many ways different? My head is swimming.

15   Cause of Death

When William came home at midday to eat a bite of food, Otter Queen did not greet him with her usual good cheer. He saw that her eyes were red.

"What is wrong?" he asked. "You have been crying."

"I don't know why I cry," she said. "I should be used to this by now."

"To what? What happened?"

Otter Queen sighed. "Little Wren found her way here today. She wanted to play with the bubble pipe. But I was busy with persimmons. I told her I had no time for bubbles, but that she could help me rub some persimmon pulp through a sieve. She was starting to do that—I gave her a sieve of her own to use—but then Rose came and snatched her up. She scolded her right in front of me, telling her to stay away from my house. Now why would she say that to that little girl, as if I were the greatest danger in the town? I am sick to death of this trouble. I cannot even sit in my own yard without it coming to me. I love Little Wren, Willy. She is just like I was when I was her age. I can barely remember my father anymore, but when I look at Little Wren, I say, there I am, there in that little girl who is growing up with an Englishman for a father. Why would anyone think I would want to hurt her? Why would they tell her such things and keep her away from me?" Otter Queen began weeping anew.

William sat down beside her and put his arms around her. He hated this helpless feeling. "We will have our own little Otter Queen," he said. "Or Otter King."

She gave a little laugh and pulled away from him and wiped away her tears. "I am better now," she said. "This little one inside makes me cry too easily. Usually I am strong."

"There must be something we can do about the Birds," said William. "I will talk to Sam."

"You will waste your words," she said. "It won't do a bit of good."

Back in the store that afternoon, William waited until there were no customers inside and then broached the subject with Sam and Jim-Bird. "Otter Queen was in tears today because of that business with the Birds," he said.

"What's happened now?" asked Sam.

"Little Wren found her way to our house, and Rose came after her and snatched her away. Rose scolded her as if she had wandered into a dragon's den."

Sam shook his head. "I hope you're not asking me to rein in my woman. This is Keowee, don't forget."

"I know that," said William. "But maybe the two of us could do something. I'm with the Wolves and you're with the Birds. Maybe we could bring the two clans together and help them make peace with one another."

"It don't work like that," said Sam. "I wish I could help you, but experience tells me that when clans are at odds with each other, the best advice for outsiders is to step aside."

Jim-Bird weighed in. "Sam is right. The way of the clans has been around longer than your new ideas about reason. Science and suchlike may be the pride of Scotland, but all of that falls on deaf ears amongst the clan matrons of Keowee. Don't bother to waste your breath on it."

"And remember that you have your own interests to protect," said Sam. "I've warned you before and I'm warning you again—if you get caught up in clan affairs, you will pay a price. I promise you."

At that moment a group of young men came into the store, and the traders went back to shopkeeping.

It was almost closing time when Rose came bursting into the store looking for Sam. "Little Wren is very, very sick. She vomited and then she had a fit. Now she is just lying there. I have never seen her so."

Sam ran out of the store without a word, Rose on his heels.

William and Jim-Bird locked up the store and followed them around back to Rose's house, where they went in and stood just inside the doorway, looking on. Little Wren's small body lay on a bed. She was salivating and was drenched in sweat. Her breathing was shallow. Sam had his hands cupped around her face.

"She has no fever," he said. There was fear in his voice. "What could it be?"

The little girl tried to hold up her arms to him, but she was too weak to do so. He leaned down and kissed her. Rose stood behind him and gripped his shoulders, and they watched helplessly as Little Wren's breathing became shallower and shallower, fading away to no breath at all. The light in her eyes went out. Sam gathered her up and tried to force more breath into her, but it was no use. Her little arms and legs hung loose, and her head fell back, her eyes fixed on nothing.

Rose began wailing loudly and tearing at her hair. The sound brought her clan sisters and mothers running, and the house filled with tumult. William and Jim-Bird stepped outside, and in a moment Sam joined them. He was rubbing his head as if he had been struck a blow. Tears flowed down his face.

"How can it be?" he said. "She was happy and healthy this morning. How can it have happened so quickly?"

William did not know what to say. Jim-Bird, too, was just shaking his head.

Rose came out, looking wildly about for Sam. Running to him, she grabbed his arm and shook it. "It was that *tshki:li*—that Wolf *tshki:li*! Little Wren was with her today!"

William could see what was coming next. Without a word to Sam and Jim-Bird, he turned and left Sam's yard and ran across the town yard and into Otter Queen's house. She was kneeling by the fire, spreading persimmon pulp on a slab to dry. She looked up, startled to see him come bursting in.

"Little Wren has died," he gasped.

Otter Queen's mouth fell open, her eyes wide. She could not take it in. "What are you saying, Willy? She was here only this morning. She is not dead."

"Yes, she is. It just happened. She vomited and had a seizure and died. The Birds are all aflutter. They say it is because she came here today."

Otter Queen closed her eyes and took a deep breath. Then she opened her eyes and looked at him."Now what do I do?" she asked.

William fetched his musket from where it leaned against the wall near their bed. He loaded and primed it and then took up his dirk and hatchet and stuck them in his belt. "Stay inside," he said.

The news flew around the town, and in no time a crowd began to gather outside Otter Queen's house. People from the other clans were choosing sides. The sound of Bird and Wolf voices, shouting and arguing, came in through the door. "Liver-eater!" someone called loudly. "Come outside. Let us see your hands. Have you grown an awl for a finger?"

"Are your guts still in your body?" someone else shouted.

"Leave her alone," another voice said loudly. "Otter Queen is no *tshki:li.*"

William stepped outside and faced the crowd. Otter Queen followed, but he pushed her back. She stayed, standing just outside the doorway.

The Birds were out in force. Old Hawk's Mother was foremost among them, thrashing about, talking furiously with all who would listen. Her jerky movements were those of someone on the verge of doing something mad, impetuous. Sam and Jim-Bird came pushing through the crowd and strode over to stand with William. Thomas, too, came and joined them.

William reached out for Jim-Bird and pulled him over next to him. "Translate for me," said William. Jim-Bird nodded.

William looked over the crowd, which had now grown silent. The Birds appeared implacable, barely containing themselves. But he knew they were as human as he was. Surely they could hear reason if it were spoken clearly. "The Birds are mistaken about Otter Queen," he said. "My wife does not have an evil bone in her body. I know her better than any of you do, and I swear to this with my very life. Otter Queen loved Little Wren as if she herself were one of the child's mothers, as if she herself were a Bird. She would not have harmed a hair on her head. Little Wren did not die by Otter Queen's hand. The true cause of her death lies elsewhere. If you look for it with calmness and with reason, you will find it. In the meantime, I will tell ye this." He cocked his musket. "I will flat kill anyone who tries to lay a hand on Otter Queen."

King Crow stepped into the space that had opened up between William and the crowd. "We do not know what has happened today," he said to the people before him, "but it is time for everyone to calm down. Cool your tempers. We will go to the town house and drink black drink together; make our hearts white. We will talk about this, and we will find out what it means that our Little Wren has died so quickly. The peace of Keowee has been upset. Let the seven clans come together in the town house, and we will sort this out." He turned to William. "Put your musket down, Willy. It will misfire and set your yellow hair on fire." All but the Birds laughed, and the crowd began dispersing.

Sam headed for the council at the town house. Thomas went back to his horses. William was going to sit at his door and keep guard over Otter Queen, but Jim-Bird had other ideas. "We will take Otter Queen to her mother's house," he said. "Her brothers will protect her. You and I will go find out for ourselves what happened to Little Wren."

"How can we do that?" asked William.

"It looked to me like death by poison," said Jim-Bird. "Perhaps we can discover what she was doing when she fell ill. We will start at Sam's chicken house. She often played there."

William nodded. It seemed a reasonable course. They walked with Otter Queen to her mother's house and then crossed the plaza and circled around in the yard of Sam's household. They did not know what they were looking for, but they examined the ground for anything they could find. As they approached the chicken house, the hens began puk-pukking, and a rooster ruffled his feathers and made sounds of alarm, more at Jim-Bird's two dogs than at the men. Tazzie and Binkie steered clear of the rooster. William and Jim-Bird continued their search, their eyes combing every inch of the yard. They found nothing. They moved on to the corn crib. Nothing. To the cookshed. Nothing.

Then suddenly Jim-Bird stopped in his tracks and pointed to a small gourd bowl that had been set on the ground against the back side of the smoke house. They went over to investigate and found that it contained water—soapy water— and beside it was a stalk of a weed. The stalk was hollow—Wren's version of a bubble pipe.

"Soap never killed anyone," said William.

"It was not the soap," said Jim-Bird, picking up the stalk and looking at it. He showed it to William, who examined it more closely and held it up to sniff it.

"I see what you mean," William said. The two of them looked at each other in silent agreement and set out for the council. Neither spoke as they crossed the town yard.

At the town house they ducked inside through the low door. The interior of the large conical room was dimly lit by the small fire that burned in the hearth in the center of the room and by the last bit of fading daylight that fell weakly from the smokehole in the peak of the roof above. The fire, which crept along a spiral of dried river cane that had been laid down inside the hearth, was almost smokeless and burned brightly.

William carried the bowl of soapy water and the section of weed. As his eyes adjusted to the darkness, he began to recognize some faces in the audience that filled the room. King Crow was in clear view, standing by the fire with a white deerskin wrapped around his shoulders. Evidently the beloved old men had just finished the opening ceremony of drinking black drink together. The talking part of the council was only now beginning.

"You have all heard of the death of Little Wren," said King Crow. Jim-Bird translated quietly for William. "It was sudden and strange, very strange. No one knows what has happened. No hand was seen raised against the child. Some of the Birds say that they do see a hand, the hand of a *tchki:li*, but Sanee, the father of Little Wren, says he does not. The Birds point to Otter Queen. Sanee and his English brothers stand in her defense. So where is the truth? It is like a rabbit that runs this way and that and then leaps into brush and cannot be found.

"This trouble between the Birds and the Wolves did not begin on this day. Green corn feasts have come and gone, come and gone, but still no forgiveness has settled between these two clans. And now the old wounds have been opened again. The peace of Keowee is upset, and we are so busy looking at each other in fear that we fail to keep watch for our enemies from a distance, our Creek enemies, who are always ready to fall upon us. They will not fail to see that we wear long faces and fight among ourselves. How long before they come to mount an attack against us, to drive us out and take our gardens and our hunting ground? We must bring an end to this trouble between the Birds and the Wolves. We must restore the harmony of Keowee. Let us speak to this now. Let us speak to harmony."

Rose stood up immediately and began talking. "Harmony will return when we unmask the *tshki:li* in our town and deal with her. This morning my little daughter was happy and healthy. But then I looked around and she was gone, and I found her in the house of Otter Queen. I brought her home, and it was not long afterward that she began to vomit. Saliva ran from her mouth. She collapsed and died. What else could this be but spoiled saliva? How could it be more clear? Otter Queen's grandmother was a *tshki:li*, and Otter Queen is a *tshki:li* too."

Five-Killer, Otter Queen's uncle, stood up. "None but the Birds ever thought Otter Queen's grandmother was a *tshki:li*. The people of Keowee did not agree, and the Birds were not allowed to execute her."

Rose stood up again. "We had no proof against the old woman. But we have proof against the young one."

Old Hawk's Mother stood up. "I needed no proof about Otter Queen. I already knew it. She is just like her grandmother, always aloof, standing apart from everyone else. She never wants anyone to see what she is doing."

Five-Killer rose again. "Otter Queen is her own company. There is no crime in that. She does not need a crowd of people around her to keep her happy. Remember that her father was an Englishman. That can make a person different, but it doesn't make her a *tchki:li*."

"You have not explained why she is always disappearing into the woods," said Hawk's Mother. "What is she doing out there all alone? Does she seek the company of animals? Of horned owls? Of ravens?"

William had heard enough. He stood up to speak, pulling Jim-Bird up with him to translate. "I am not a son of a Cherokee mother," William said and paused for Jim-Bird to relay his words. "I have not been long in your town. But I have answers to some of the questions that my good friends, the Birds, have been asking here today. No one knows better than I why Otter Queen was going into the woods. She was going there to meet me. I can tell ye that we were not communing with owls or ravens—we were doing what men and women do when they are alone. And I will wager that many of you have gone into the woods to do the same." Some of the people laughed.

"Going into the woods to meet her lover does not make Otter Queen a witch, and neither does the death of this child after visiting her house." William reached down and picked up the bowl of soapy water and the hollow weed. Then he walked to the light of the fire and held them out in his hand so that they could be seen clearly by everyone.

"Little Wren came to Otter Queen's house today because she wanted to play at blowing soap bubbles. But Otter Queen was busy at work. She was up to her elbows in persimmon pulp and had no time for playing with bubbles. She invited Little Wren to help her make persimmon strips, but Rose came and took the child away. And now we know what happened after that. Jim-Bird found this gourd bowl and weed in the yard of Little Wren's homestead. After Rose brought her home, Little Wren tried to play with bubbles by herself. She got this little bowl that ye see in my hand, and she put water and soap in it. She didn't have a bubble pipe, and so she decided to make one. She looked around until she found a weed with a stout, hollow stem." William held up the purple-streaked piece of weed, and the people sitting close enough to recognize it gasped.

"It is *kanesása*—water hemlock," Jim-Bird said to the others.

"That's right," said William. "In the land where I come from we have a plant like this. We call it cow bane because cows sometimes eat it, and when they do, they fall ill and often die. We also call it child's bane, because children sometimes try to make whistles out of it, and when they put it to their lips, they fall very ill, and often they die in just the way poor Little Wren died today. This is a very sad day for the Bird people. It is a sad day for all of us. We all loved Little Wren. But now you can see that Little Wren did not die because of a *tshki:li*. She died because she was too young to know enough about the mortal danger of water hemlock. That, as we can all see, was the cause of her death."

William sat down, satisfied that he had put the matter to rest.

Old Hawk's Mother got to her feet. "You have told us nothing, white man. Had it not been for Otter Queen, Little Wren never would have learned to blow bubbles from a pipe. It is a strange and unnatural thing, those bubbles. Other Cherokee children do not play with such things. It was the *tshki:li* who prompted her to do this and caused her to be dead."

Some of the Birds spoke in favor of this argument. Others, however, sat in silence. Rose herself seemed to be wavering.

A man of the Paint clan stood up. "I think we have heard enough. It is plain to me that the child died of her own hand, although she did not intend to. It is sad for the Birds, and for all of us. But the *tshki:li* accusation does not hold. I say we should hear no more of this."

Many people in the townhouse agreed. "Yes, yes, he is right," they began to say. "Let us hear no more of this."

It became clear that this was the consensus and the dissenters had fallen silent. King Crow declared it so, and the people got up and slowly filed out of the townhouse. But Hawk's Mother still had her jaw set, and so did some of her senior clanswomen.

November 20. Oh that this day were struck from history. Little Wren died suddenly and horribly this afternoon. The Birds made it worse by seizing it as proof that Otter Queen is a witch. But Jim-Bird had his wits about him and found that Little Wren had made a bubble pipe out of a section of child's bane. We took the evidence to the townhouse and I argued the case. Today reason entered the ring with Superstition in Keowee, but she won no more than a draw.

"Old Hawk's Mother will never give me any peace," said Otter Queen. "My life in Keowee is misery."

William sighed and stared up at the bark roof above their bed. Time had passed and Otter Queen's feelings were still the same. "There is nothing we can do about the Birds," he said, "this is the town where we live. This is our Verona."

Otter Queen sat up suddenly. "There *is* something we can do, Willy! If this is Verona, we can go to that other town."

"What are you talking about?"

"We can do what Romeo and Juliet were trying to do in the story. We can go away. We can go into the woods and find the Gunsmith and his crew and finish the hunting season with them. It would not be forever, but for a little while I would not have to be stared down by the Birds every time I go to the river to fetch water."

"And maybe when we come back, things will be better here," said William.

"Oh, Willy, are you thinking about going hunting? Would you do this for me? I know the Gunsmith would be happy if we want to join him. Hunting for deerskins is hard work, and it's cold out there in the woods." She leaned over him and laughed. "But we have always liked the woods."

"I don't know what Sam would say," said William. He was thinking hard about it now. "I can't go if it would leave him short-handed. But on the other hand, he might be glad to see us out of town. We've put him in a bind, making him straddle between Birds and Wolves."

Otter Queen kissed William and pulled him into her arms and for a moment he just held her tightly, feeling her belly against his, knowing that deep inside her a child was forming. Then he got up and dressed.

He went directly to the store, arriving before Sam and Jim-Bird did. When Sam came in, William got right to the point.

"Otter Queen wants to go join up with the Gunsmith's deer hunt. She wants to get away from the Birds for a while, let things calm down around here. If it's all right with you, I will go with her to protect her and keep her company. And I may try my hand at deer hunting."

Sam thought about it for a moment then nodded his head. "I can see the sense of it. I can't even say I'm surprised to hear about it. Something needs to happen, and this sounds good enough. We can get by without you for a while. Just remember what I've said all along. While you are serving the Wolf clan, you can't be serving me. So you'll lose out on quite a bit of your pay for the season. You might be able to make it up in deerskins, but that would take some hard work. Do you know what you're getting into?"

William laughed and shook his head. "I never do, it seems."

"A hunter is on a lower rung of the Indian trade ladder than a packhorseman is, if you can imagine that. You will be out there in the winter weather with your nose freezing and your clothes caked with deer blood and guts. The farther to the southwest you hunt—and you have to go in that direction, because that's where the deer are—the more likely you are to run into a Creek who will want to add your scalp to his collection. In that light you're a tad better off than the Cherokees are, for the Creeks might spare you as an Englishman, though you can't count on it. And don't forget to add in the fact that the Cherokee hunters are not going to be overjoyed to have a white hunter at work in their territory. That is what you're in for, and more than that most likely. But if this is what you want to do, go ahead and do it."

William was feeling happy. "It is what I want to do, so long as I'm not leaving ye short of help."

"We're well into the slack season now," said Sam. "Most of the hunters are stocked up and in the woods and won't be back with their skins until February. That's when the work picks up again, and I'll need you back here. So don't be the last to come in. Try to be the first. That's all I ask of you."

Jim-Bird had come into the store and had listened attentively to this conversation. Now he cleared his throat. "Sam's description of the profession of deer hunting is not likely to attract many hopefuls, but I'm already bored with the slack time around here. It's not as though I have a woman's bed to crawl into at night, and there's hardly any work for me to put my hand to. If I go on the hunt with William, I might be able to get him back to you alive. I know I'll be more entertained on a deer hunt than sitting here by the fire waiting for February to come. If you could get along without the both of us, I would like to go as well."

"Go on then," said Sam. "I don't need you. I'd just as soon keep your wages in my pocket. Thomas can give me a hand if I need any help."

William grinned broadly at Jim-Bird. "This is better yet! We'll be taking some experience to the Gunsmith and not just a raw recruit."

"I have precious little real experience to offer," said Jim-Bird. "I've killed quite a few deer in my day, but I've not hunted them for skins since I was a boy with the Chickasaws."

"Just take a normal hunt and multiply it by a hundred," said Sam. "That's all you're in for. No more than that."

Otter Queen's mood brightened the instant William returned home with the news. He had not seen her so happy since their first days as lovers in the woods. She decided that they would leave in two days, and she started rushing about, getting up the supplies they would need for the season. She borrowed some venison jerky from Pretty Baskets, and she packed a watertight bag of parched corn and another of rice, along with strips of fruit leather she had made from the persimmon pulp. From her uncle Five-Killer she borrowed two deer-head decoys and two large bottle gourds for carrying water. She told William that when he was purchasing his powder, bullets, and flints, he should buy an extra blanket and enough duffle for her to make a waistcoat and cape for him and a matchcoat for herself. The coldest part of the winter was before them, and their hunting camp in the bush would give them less shelter than William was used to having.

William and Jim-Bird likewise worked at getting up what they would need in the coming months. On the night before their departure, they fetched their horses, Viola and Caesar, from the horse-pen, along with packsaddles, and they tethered them at Otter Queen's house. Before retiring, they assembled and packed all their goods and supplies onto the saddles.

Because they wanted to make good distance on their first day of travel, and because the late November days were short, they got an especially early start the next morning. They tied their packs on to the horses while it was still dark, and at the first crack of dawn they were ready to go. Five-Killer and Pretty Baskets came out to see them off.

It was cold and overcast as they took the trail out of Keowee, the three of them walking, leading the two horses. Tazzie and Binkie, excited at this break from routine, trotted happily out in front. They were headed toward Tugalo, where John Coleman ran the trading house. The hunting camp was farther on.

To take advantage of the shallowest crossings of the creeks and rivers they encountered, they first took a small trail that ran due north until they came to a larger trail that skirted the edge of the mountains. They turned onto it and followed it to the west. The worst thing about winter travel was the water crossings, but on this trail many of the streams they came to were so small they could jump across them. Others they crossed on raccoon bridges—the trunks of large trees that had fallen across streams—while the horses waded across. On raccoon bridges it only took one slip to tumble into the cold water, but on this day they managed to cross them all without mishap. Wider streams, like Little River and Flat Shoal River, they had to wade across, taking off their leggings and footgear and fastening up the rest of their clothing to keep it above the water.

After they crossed Flat Shoal River the trail turned southward. The hills they were crossing were rather high, with long ascents and descents and frequent outcroppings of rock. They crossed Oconee Creek and Cane Creek and continued on to Coneross Creek. When they reached it, they saw that the woods on the other side of it had been burned over.

"Did hunters do this?" William asked as they were wading the creek. He was remembering Otter Queen's story of the old witch and the smoke of the hunters that drew her.

"If the creek were deeper," said Jim-Bird, "I would say so. But that would not be the case with a little creek like this one."

"Why not?" William asked.

"The reason to set a fire is to drive game into the bend of a river or a big creek. The deer have to jump in and swim, and then the hunters can shoot them easily. It works with bears, too."

"That's not very sporting," said William.

"The Indians don't hunt for sport. They hunt to fill their bellies and pay their debts."

"This one must have been started by a camp fire," said Otter Queen. "If it were summer, it could have been lightning, but not at this time of year."

On the other side of the creek they unpacked the horses and bedded there for the night, enjoying the luxury of a large fire on the already blackened ground. They ate a light dinner of venison jerky and persimmon strips and then curled up in their bedrolls as the fire burned down to coals. In the fading light of the embers, William wrote in his journal.

November 29. We have left Verona behind and are on the road to Mantua. We have made it as far as Coneross Creek—about 17 miles.

The next day they continued traveling toward the southwest, and the hills gradually declined in elevation. The sky became cloudy as the morning progressed, and by noon it began spitting snow. Their discomfort was magnified when they had to wade across a ford at Chauga River. Their only consolation was that the water was not so deep that they had to unpack their horses and carry all the bundles across on their backs. The sky grew darker, and the snow fell harder and began accumulating on the ground. They were still six miles from Tugalo. They trudged on, and in late afternoon the town came in sight, situated on high ground on the opposite bank of the Tugalo River. On both sides of the river the heavily used trail was furrowed deeply into the ground from many years of traffic and erosion.

They forded the river and made their way toward John Coleman's trading house. Compared to Keowee, Tugalo had obviously fallen on hard times. Many of the houses were in poor repair, and some were even worse—abandoned and falling in on themselves. Few people were to be seen moving about.

When they reached the town yard, William stopped to look with amazement at the town house, which was built up on top of an earthen mound that stood about twelve feet high.

"That's one of the few mounds in this part of the country that's still in use," said Jim-Bird. "There's lots bigger ones than that around here, but they're covered over with trees and surrounded by woods."

The trading house was closed, but Jim-Bird knew the way to the homestead behind it where John Coleman lived with his woman, Tskwayi. As they approached the house, two dogs came out barking and showing their teeth, and Tazzie and Binkie were more than ready to show theirs. It was only with some difficulty that Jim-Bird kept the dogs separated and prevented a general melee. The door to the house opened and John stepped out holding a musket. He had a hatchet and a long knife stuck in his belt.

"Are you expecting company, John?" asked Jim-Bird.

"Jim-Bird! William! Can it be? And Otter Queen too! I heard that you two were building a nest. Welcome all of you. Come in and have some food. What in hell's name are you doing out here?"

"We are looking to join up with the Gunsmith," said William. "We thought we would get a few skins of our own, get a jump on the trade."

John laughed. "You'll be lucky to recoup your powder and shot." He turned and led them into the house. "Tskwayi," he said gaily, "add a little food to the pot for this company that's come draggin' in."

Inside, they gathered by the fire, warming themselves. All enjoyed a round of rum while they caught John up on the news from Keowee. He was saddened to hear of the death of Little Wren. Otter Queen could not bear to hear them talk about it and went outside to start unpacking the horses. William and Jim-Bird soon went out to help her. Afterwards they returned and settled in for the night.

"Well, I've got to say that you've not picked the best year to be joining the Gunsmith on his hunt," said John, as they sat around the fire eating their supper. "We've taken a hard hit in these parts from marauding Creeks. It's the worst I've ever seen. Back when the chestnuts were coming ripe, we held a dance in Tugalo, as we always do in the chestnut season. Everything went well until we noticed that two people who had left to go out to the bushes had not returned. The men took up arms and fat lighter torches and went looking for them. And they soon found their bodies. Both had been killed with hatchet blows to the head, and both had been scalped.

"The mourning cry went up, and everyone went on their guard. We were pretty sure the killers were Creek revenge-raiders, but no one could catch sight of them. During the next two weeks, they killed five more people—*five*—and every time by a carefully planned ambush. It scared these people around here half to death. And what no one could figure was how those marauders were getting past our dogs." John paused to take seconds from the stewpot, but no one followed his lead. They were listening.

"The last of those five they killed—it was the seventh one in all—that one was the most terrifying. The killer stalked a house that was a little removed from the others, a little too far from its neighbors. When the young man who lived there came outside in the early morning and went around to the back of his house to pee, the marauder jumped him—killed and scalped him. Now I hate to say it, but as bad as it was that this fellow was killed, that wasn't the worst part of it. The killer crept into the man's house, looking for what he might find. He found the house empty, but then he heard someone approaching from outside. He jumped into the dead man's bed and pulled the blanket over his head. The dead man's mother came in. She spoke to him, thinking he was her son. The marauder grunted and kept himself covered. She fished out some winter squashes that had been roasting in the coals, and then she left the house. As she was walking away, she happened to look back and saw a man running for the woods. She yelled, and when people came running, they found the body of her son beside the house. He had been struck in the head by a hatchet and then, like I said, he was scalped. What terrified everyone the most was the idea that you could be inside your own son's home, taking roasted squashes out of a fire, and under a bedcover there could be a killer hiding."

"So was it over?" asked Jim-Bird. "Seven dead and no more?"

"Yes and no," said John. "There's an old man here whose habit it is to climb a certain tree every day and look out to see what he can see. He was the one to catch sight of two men at a distance from town. From their dress and their way of moving, he knew that they were Creeks—they were the killers. Taking his time, he came down from the tree and went to the town house to tell the head warriors of Tugalo what he had seen. The warriors hatched a plan and quietly spread word of it to the rest of the town. You've never seen anything like it. The people of Tugalo went about their business as if nothing was amiss, and they organized a dance for late afternoon. And they sent out all of their best young warriors to lay a trap for those killers. As soon as the music for the dance began, the killers came creeping in closer to town. But those warriors were waiting and closed in on them. They got one of them pinned to the ground, but the other one broke free and took to his heels. Even though he was an older fellow, he was a swift runner, and devilishly clever. He eluded our best warriors and got away.

"The fate of the captive was never in doubt—death by torture, you could be sure. But I've got to say, as horrible a murderer as he was, I could not help but feel pity for him. They tied his hands behind his back. They stripped off his clothes and put a rope around his neck and tethered him to a slave post in the town yard. All he could do was run in a circle and kick at his tormentors, who were mostly the relatives of the people he had murdered. They consigned the poor bastard to the little fire." John looked at William. "That means that they stuck flaming splinters of fat-lighter into his body. When he fainted, they would douse his head with water to revive him. His head, mind you, not the parts that were burning.

"Before he died, he let it be known that he was a kinsman of one of those Creek emissaries who were murdered by the Cherokees here at Tugalo back during the Yamasee War. He said the fellow who was with him, the one who got away, was his uncle. And he named him. He was proud to do it. The uncle's name is Bloody Mouth, and Bloody Mouth, too, he said, was avenging that same Creek fellow who was murdered here in Tugalo twenty years ago. There was more than one murdered, but it was only this one they were avenging. I think the murdered emissary must have been a brother to Bloody Mouth and an uncle to this younger one that was getting tortured. Crying blood can cry for a long time, it seems."

"If you'll pardon my saying so," said William, "Tugalo is not so impressive a town. It's hard for me to imagine that anything that happened here could have been so momentous as to still inflame men to vengeance twenty years later."

"Tugalo is down on its heels right now," said John, "but on a certain night in 1715, the history of Carolina spun around like a compass needle on its pivot, and the pivot was right here in this town. Do you know about the Yamasee War?"

"I know that the Indians rose up against the traders and raided the plantations and that most of the colonists had to take shelter inside the walls of Charles Town."

John nodded with approval. "You've been learning your history. We all grew up on this tale. My parents remember that time well, but I was just a tyke. They say that at first it seemed that all the Indians throughout the entire region might be at war with them. But on the other hand, maybe not. So how could they go about finding out who their enemies actually were? They knew the Catawbas were against them, but they managed to beat them in a single battle and brought them around. But they still did not know what the mood of the Cherokees might be.

"According to the story I was told, they learned from an old Cherokee trader that there was no love lost between the Lower Cherokees and the Creeks, meaning that the Lower Cherokees might be willing to side with the English against the Creeks. So the Carolinians sent a colonel by the name of Maurice Moore back up in here with an army of Carolinians to find out what he could and to try to talk the Cherokees into staying with the English. But unbeknownst to Moore as he traveled upcountry, he was shadowed all the way by Creek scouts. He came here to Tugalo and met with the Conjurer, who was the chief of this place. The Conjurer told Moore that he was willing to go to war against the Yuchis and the Shawnees and the Apalachees, but he would not go to war against the Creeks. It seems that not all the Lower Cherokees were at odds with the Creeks, just some of them. That made matters more complicated.

"The next thing Moore did was to send George Chicken and John Herbert, officers in his army, northwest of here to Little Chota, up yonder at the head of the Chattahoochee River, to meet with Caesar, another big man amongst the Cherokees. They found that Caesar was stirring up the young warriors of his town to go to war against the Creeks. The old men there were counseling them to not go to war, but the young warriors were dancing all night, singing for blood.

"All of which left our people in a quandary. They could now see that the Cherokees were not a unified nation, as they had hoped. No one leader had power over all the Cherokee people."

"Reminds me of the Highlanders in Scotland," said William.

John laughed. "Right you are. But here's what happened that led to all this murder that we've just seen around here. While George Chicken and John Herbert were off at Little Chota, and while Maurice Moore and his army were still here in Tugalo, twelve headmen of the Creeks and Yamasees arrived at Tugalo—this very town—as ambassadors under the white flag of peace. Now what was Moore to do? Should he side with the Conjurer and try to negotiate a peace with the Creeks that might spread out to the English, or should he side with Caesar and go to war against the Creeks, whom he knew had killed some of our traders and had struck some of our settlements?

"As he was trying to decide about this, Caesar and his warriors came down to Tugalo and decided it for him. In the dead of night, Caesar and his men crept into the town house—the same shabby town house you saw when you rode into town—and murdered all twelve of the Creek ambassadors. Other Creeks were visiting in other Lower Towns, and King Crow and the warriors of Keowee played a part in killing them off as well. With this, the history of Carolina took a turn. All of the Cherokees were now solid with the Carolinians, whether they wanted to be or not, because they were all now at war with the Creeks and they needed the Carolinians to back them up. The upshot of it was that with the Cherokees as allies, the Carolinians were able to survive the Yamasee War. But unfortunately, the breach that was opened between the Cherokees and the Creeks has not healed to this day. That's because the Cherokees violated a revered rule of all Indians everywhere, including the Cherokees themselves—namely that ambassadors under white colors are entitled to immunity from harm."

"The bane of the Indians," said Jim-Bird, "has always been their inability to form lasting alliances with other Indians. The Christian nations have their faults, but at least they understand the importance of forgiveness."

"Thank you for the sermon," said John, "but don't talk to the Indians about forgiveness. Twenty years have gone by, and we still live in the shadow of the massacre of those Creek ambassadors. The vengeance goes on."

"Do you think the other raider is still out there?" asked Jim-Bird.

"Bloody Mouth? I'm sure he is, and you need to keep that in mind. He's got to take revenge for his nephew now, as well as for his brother."

"He took seven scalps," said William. "That more than settles the score in a case of crying blood. He lost his brother and his nephew—that's two—and he's taken the lives of seven. Wouldn't he be satisfied with that?"

John shook his head. "This ain't a case of blood revenge amongst the clans, where one life satisfies one other. In this vengeance Bloody Mouth is not subject to any rules. He will kill until he is satisfied or until he is dead, whichever comes first. He came to avenge his brother, but you can be sure he is staying to avenge his nephew. As a trader, though, you have less to fear than the Cherokees do. The Indians these days are hesitant to kill a trader. They know they can upset the trade for themselves if they start in on that. That's what they learned in the Yamasee War. They might hate our guts, but they need the goods we provide for them." John looked at Jim-Bird. "I don't know where that leaves you. You are in with the traders, but you are half Indian."

"That's why I have these dogs to protect me," said Jim-Bird, reaching down to scratch Binkie's ear. Everyone laughed, glad for the mood to be lightened.

"They're small but they're brave," said William, patting his leg for Tazzie to come over to him.

"Where do you expect to find the Gunsmith's hunting camp?" asked John.

"He usually camps a day south of here," said Otter Queen.

John nodded. "I know that place. Near the junction of the North and Middle Broad Rivers. There used to be good hunting in that country."

"Sometimes the Gunsmith edges over toward the Oconee River," said Otter Queen.

"Now, that territory is claimed by the Creeks, and don't forget it," said John. "Not with Bloody Mouth and his like marauding about. Tell the Gunsmith to stay in close this year. He shouldn't press his luck." He got up and went over to get out his fiddle. "We've had enough bad news for one night. What we need is some music." He looked at Otter Queen and smiled. "I would like to sing a song for Mistress Otter Queen and her husband." John chuckled at himself and shook his head. "There hasn't been a lot to do around here, you see. The story of flaming love between William and Otter Queen has inspired the bard in me. I built this new song upon an old riddle song. I was planning on singing it for you when I got back to Keowee. But since you've come here first, I'll introduce it now." He glanced at William. "You might be surprised at how much gossip runs around these parts. A man's life is not his own. And now it's captured in song forever."

"Then so be it," said William. "Let's hear it."

John first played the tune on his fiddle. William knew the tune, if not the song, and he sat back and watched Otter Queen's face as John sang the words in his clear, high voice, droning along on his fiddle.

On a fair and bright autumn day,
A Scots-born lad thought he would play,
He went to the river and he jumped in,
Thought he would have him a little swim.

A beautiful maid came tripping by,
She saw him there and she did sigh,
Come, my boy, where the sweet fern grows,
I'll teach you things that you don't know.

To the bank the lad did make his way,
And amongst the ferns the two did lay,
She taught him well, she taught him free,
Now, she said, will you marry me?

He cleared his throat and scratched his head,
I had not thought to marry, he said.
Any wife of mine must a great wit be,
I'll marry you if you answer these riddles three.

Oh what is longer than the way,
Or what is deeper than the sea?
Or what is whiter than the milk,
Or what is softer than the silk?
Or what is louder than the horn,
Or what is worse than woman scorned?

Said she, twice three is six, my dear,
The hardest riddles I ever did hear.
She cocked her head, she closed her eyes,
Just wait, she said, you'll be surprised.

Oh love is longer than the way,
And hell is deeper than the sea.
The snow is whiter than the milk,
And the down is softer than the silk.
Thunder is louder than the horn,
And the Devil is worse than woman scorned.

Your wit, said he, is sharper than a knife,
And I must have you for my wife.
No beauteous maid of such high worth,
Could e'er be found on all this earth.

Otter Queen had listened intently. When the ballad ended, everyone's attention turned to her. Embarrassed, she blushed and hugged William, hiding her face against his chest.

"Now, now," said John, playing a brief refrain on his fiddle. "I didn't mean to embarrass you." He played a little more and then put the fiddle down. "You all will be the first to know that I'm thinking this may be the last year I will trade at Tugalo. There just ain't enough business anymore to make it worthwhile. And all the people here wear long, haggard faces. I've hardly had my fiddle out of its case this season. Life is too short to live thisaway."

"What will ye do?" asked William.

"I haven't worked it out that far," said John. "Maybe go across the mountains to one of the Overhill towns."

This brought the conversation to an end. Everyone was tired and needed sleep. William and Otter Queen took one of the beds in John's winter house and Jim-Bird took another. Jim-Bird kindled a small fire in the hearth, all that would be needed to keep them warm within the thick, tight walls.

November 30. If Tugalo is not enmeshed in Thomas Hobbes's war of all against all, it is the closest thing to it. And it is as dirty a war as one can imagine. What can it mean that Otter Queen would rather be here than in Keowee?

We made 13 miles today.

The next morning the three of them rose early once again for another long day on the trail. They said their farewells to John and Tskwayi and set out, crossing Toccoa Creek and heading off toward the south. They threaded their way through the gentle piedmont hills and were glad to have no large streams to cross. In the afternoon they picked up the North Fork of the Broad River and traveled along its course to where it joined the Middle Fork. Otter Queen had been to this place several times before, and she knew the way to the little creek where the hunting camp was likely to be.

They made good time, and in the middle of the afternoon they came to the Gunsmith's camp, located just where Otter Queen said it would be. The camp consisted of a cluster of lean-to sheds near a small stream that ran into the North Fork of the nearby Broad River. The hunters had set up several poles on which deerskins could be cleaned and several racks where skins were being stretched and softened. In past years a large poplar tree had fallen at the camp, and they had chopped out several basins in its trunk for soaking and treating deer skins.

The Gunsmith's hunting party was made up of three of his clan brothers and two clan sisters. All of the men had their arms at the ready when William, Otter Queen, and Jim-Bird came into view. The Gunsmith and his brothers looked bewildered. They were not expecting company. When Otter Queen explained the circumstances of their coming, the Gunsmith told her that his outfit had their hunt well underway. It was the first of December, and they had already killed many deer. Otter Queen would have to establish a small outfit of her own with William and Jim-Bird. They would be together at the camp, but they would be separate in the hunt.

All were amenable to this, and the three newcomers picked out a spot where they would build their shelter, and here they unpacked their horses. For the night they threw up a rough lean-to and built a large fire. They were exhausted from having traveled so far on foot. Laying down a carpet of pine boughs inside the lean-to, they rolled up in their blankets and settled down to sleep. But first William wrote in his journal.

> December 1. Our journey from Tugalo to the Gunsmith's hunting camp was uneventful. The Gunsmith is not overjoyed to see us, but he seems to be willing to tolerate our being here. Tomorrow we set up our camp, and after that I begin my career as a deer hunter.
>
> Travel: 21 miles.

17   How to Skin a Deer

They awoke early the next morning, glad for a clear dawn and the prospect of a sunny day. Their first order of business was to build a shelter that would keep them dry and tolerably warm during their stay in the woods. Jim-Bird and Otter Queen knew just what to do. They selected a spot by a small oak tree. And about eight feet out from the tree Jim-Bird and William planted a stout post with a fork on its upper end, positioning it so that the fork of the post was at the same height as the fork of a stout limb on the young oak, about nine feet above the ground. They then lifted up a strong roof beam, placing one end in the fork of the post and the other securely on the limb of the oak tree.

Next they cut four long poles, set their wide ends into the ground, and laid their tapering ends across the ends of the roof beam. With a pair of these peaking at each end of the beam, they now had an open frame in the form of a wide A. They filled in this frame with additional poles laid parallel to the first ones and then attached numerous small cross beams down each side, making the framework of a roof. Small open spaces at either end of the roof beam would allow smoke to escape from the hearth that would be positioned directly below.

Next they cut numerous lengths of large-diameter river cane to form the walls at the two open sides of the frame, leaving an opening in the middle of one side for a doorway. Then the three of them went into the woods to collect sheets of bark to cover their shelter. They found a downed poplar tree—a big one—and Otter Queen tested it to see if its bark had rotted enough to be easily removed. She used her hatchet to cut a ring around the large trunk and then cut a slit lengthwise along the bark. Using the edge of her hatchet, she pried it up.

"This is good," she said. "It will come off."

Jim-Bird cut and trimmed a tree limb to use as a spud to pry the sheets of bark from the trunk, and they fell away easily. Otter Queen collected the ribbon-like fibers of the inner bark and bundled them for later use as cordage. After several trips to carry the bark back to the camp, the men put the sheets in place against the roof, while Otter Queen used the fiber to tie them down. This bark-covered shelter would be their home for the next couple of months.

Otter Queen dug out a shallow hearth pit in the center of the structure. She sent the men to gather a large quantity of small green pine boughs, and as they brought them in, she laid them on the ground for their beds, the springy sides up to create enough loft to keep the cold ground from draining away their body heat as they slept. From poles in the roof they hung gear, goods, and food, including some dried and smoked meat they had brought with them. The meat was greasy, especially the bear meat, and they tried to position it where its dripping would cause the least unpleasantness. When at last they were finished, they stood outside and admired their handiwork.

"It is a good camp," Otter Queen said.

William could see that it was quite neat compared to the Gunsmith's camp. Judging from that one, he knew to expect the ground in and around their own camp would eventually become darkly covered with blood, grease, and the by-products of worked deerskins.

Close by their camp they set another horizontal pole, this one high up between two trees. On both trees they cut the lower limbs back to short stubs to serve as rungs on which they could climb up to hang meat that was to be cooked and barbequed. It would be safe there from dogs and scavengers. Otter Queen explained that they would also drape dressed deerskins over this same pole, covering them with oiled cloths to protect them from the weather.

It took an entire day to build the camp.

December 2. Today the three of us constructed our little shelter in the woods. I will not call it snug, but at least it will keep us dry in a tempest. If I want a bite of dried meat, I have only to draw my knife, reach up, and cut off a piece hanging from the roof. Tazzie and Binkie have free run of the camp, as we call our little house, and they don't mind in the least the fat that comes dripping down from the meat. In fact, they keep their eyes peeled for it and do us the service of cleaning it up.

The next morning, Jim-Bird and William were ready to begin their hunt. William felt ambivalent at the prospect, glad to be going out for a new adventure, but regretful to be leaving Otter Queen behind in the camp.

She assured him she would be safe. She would not be alone—her clan sisters were there in the Gunsmith's camp. And she had plenty of work to do. There was warm clothing to be made from the blue duffle they had brought along. There were the horses to look after and preparations to be made for processing the meat and skins they would be bringing in.

"And I need for you to watch after my dogs," said Jim-Bird. "Tie them up until we are well away."

"I will like having them here," said Otter Queen. "They are good company." She gave William a hug. "Do not worry about me, Willy."

"That's right," said Jim-Bird. "You'll have worry enough trying to get close enough to a deer to kill one. Have you ever done it?"

"Only once," said William, "back in Scotland during a hard, hard winter. We were all so starved you could count our ribs. I used an old musket that had been my father's and I shot a red deer—poached it from a gentleman's estate. I was still a young lad, didn't have the muscles I have now. But I managed to drag it home through the snow. Thankfully another snow came right along and covered my tracks."

"Well, I don't know if your red deer are like our Carolina deer," said Jim-Bird, "but let me tell you some things you'll need to know if you hope to have any luck at all. The first thing you must always keep in mind is that a deer's senses are amazingly sharp. If you rattle sections of deer antlers together, a buck can hear it half a mile away. Their eyes are much better than ours, especially when it comes to spotting any kind of movement. When a deer is looking in your direction, even from a hundred yards in the distance, the slightest move from you can send him running. They see quite well in dim light and even in almost total darkness they can still see a little. And, of course, they can smell anything. You have to be careful about the smells you bring with you, though there are several ways to mask the human scent. And when you are on the move, always try to keep the wind to your face. Then your scent won't be going out before you. Deer do the same—when they travel they try to keep the wind to their faces to catch the scent of anything they are approaching. So if you are waiting in a stand, look downwind to watch for their coming. But if it's too windy, you'd do just as well to remain in camp, because deer don't like to be out when the wind is too strong or too changeable."

William nodded, wondering how he managed to bag that deer in Scotland. His mother may have been right when she said it was a blessing from God.

"Deer live in a territory of some two or three square miles," Jim-Bird went on. "As they move about to forage, they come to know the details of their territory—how it looks, how it sounds, how it smells. If they sense that any-thing has changed, they are immediately on guard. If in doubt, stick up your tail and run! That is a deer's philosophy. And your philosophy as a hunter should be: walk a little, watch a lot. Pretend you are a panther."

William nodded, remembering the panther on the trail from Charles Town.

"When it snows heavily," said Jim-Bird, "it changes the look of the deer's territory, and they don't like that. So if we get a heavy snow, we'll do just as well to stay in camp, because the deer will lie low for two or three days until it melts off, or until they get so hungry they have to go out to get food."

"It seems to me that we are wasting a good day," said William. "It's not too windy and it's not too snowy. If the lessons are over, I'm ready to go."

"That's all the lessons for now," said Jim-Bird. He reached into the hearth and picked up a piece of charcoal and rubbed it on his hands and face. William followed his example. Jim-Bird pointed out that he was putting some on each of his eyelids. "You don't want to be flashing skin-colored signals each time you blink your eyes."

With blackened faces they stood and wolfed down a hearty meal of grits be-fore finally starting out. Otter Queen gave them parched cornmeal and per-simmon strips for their shoulder bags. Because the parched meal was already cooked, they would only have to add a little water to make it edible.

From camp they struck out to the south. The Gunsmith and his outfit had been hunting to the west and northwest. But even so, the deer to the south would be wary from having so many people moving about in the wider region, especially because of the gunshots, the sound of which carried a very long way. Jim-Bird noted that they were fortunate that rut was about to begin. The does would soon be moving about quite a bit, and the bucks would be following them with keen interest.

Before long they came across a scatter of black pellets on the ground. William saw them first and pointed them out to Jim-Bird, who leaned over and in-spected them. "Doe turds," he said.

"How do you know that?" asked William. "Why not a buck?"

"Because they are less than an inch long, and there's only about fifty of them. If it had been a buck, they would be over an inch long and we could count up to seventy or more."

Jim-Bird stepped on the dung, once with each foot, smearing the soles of his moccasins in it. "This will give us a covering scent," he said. "That's what we need in rut season."

William likewise stepped onto the dung, scuffing his shoes thoroughly to scent them.

"Right now the deer are out building up their strength for the rut," said Jim-Bird, "so we want to find us a grove of chestnuts or white oaks. The deer will be after the mast."

As they moved along, William tried to imitate Jim-Bird's way of walking, putting his foot down flat to keep his heels from crunching into the forest litter. If Jim-Bird snapped a twig, he would stop and stand still for about three minutes before moving again. "They have sharp ears," he whispered, "but a short span of attention."

As they approached a stand of large white oaks, Jim-Bird pointed toward an area on the ground about two feet in diameter where the leaf cover had been scraped off. "That's a buck's scrape," he whispered, his words barely audible. "And look here." He pointed up to a low, overhanging branch that had been chewed and broken. "This is how a buck marks his territory. He's showing the other deer how big he is by how much damage he can do. Don't touch anything near this scrape or we'll never see the buck that made it."

Further along, Jim-Bird bent over and looked at a scuffed place in the bark of a dogwood tree. "Here's where one rubbed his antlers," he whispered. "They do it on trees that have strong scents. It can be any of them—dogwood, chestnut, sassafras, cherry, pine, cedar. They have scent glands on their foreheads and they add these other scents to their forehead scents."

"Why do they do that?" asked William.

"I don't know," said Jim-Bird. "To impress the girls, I guess."

There were plenty of signs of deer, but no deer in the flesh. In mid-morning they came to a place where an animal trail crossed a small stream. "They drink early in the morning, then just before noon, and again in the late afternoon," Jim-Bird said quietly. "Let's set up a blind downwind from this spot and see if we can bag one coming in for the noon drink."

They found a small depression and piled a little brush in front of it, forming a low screen. Then they lay down behind the screen, each with his musket half cocked. Jim-Bird leaned his musket through the screen on the ready, aimed roughly at the juncture of the trail and the stream. William started to do likewise, but Jim-Bird shook his head. "Two together won't work. We'll get crossed up. You just back me up."

They heard some jaybirds shouting alarm. "Pay attention now," Jim-Bird breathed, barely forming his words. "The heralds of the forest." Or at least that's what William thought he said. Crows began cawing high overhead and then a squirrel barked close by. Presently a herd of three does came warily up the trail. They paused and sniffed the air, their ears switching about, fully alert. Then, ever so cautiously, they moved on up to the stream and one of them drank.

Jim-Bird waited until she had drunk her fill and began to amble away. He cocked his hammer at full, and when it clicked she stopped to look back. At that moment he fired, the ball striking her clean through the lungs. She bolted into the air and kicked and then ran into the woods, the other two streaking away in other directions.

"Let's wait a few minutes," said Jim-Bird. "She won't get far."

William uncocked his musket, and after a wait they followed in the direction the doe had taken. From the drops of blood on the ground, she was easy to track. They found her about fifty yards away, dead in a heap.

Jim-Bird immediately knelt beside her, pulling his knife from its sheath. He said something in Cherokee and then set to work, cutting a shallow slit from the doe's crotch up to her breastbone, taking care to not cut into her guts. As they began to bulge out, he pulled them further out and then took his knife and cut around the inside of her chest, severing her diaphragm. Reaching in, he cut the guts free from the windpipe and esophagus and pulled them out. Then he went back in to cut out her heart and lungs. It was like gutting a calf, William noted. He watched Jim-Bird sever her heart and lay it aside on some clean leaves. Then he cut out the liver and laid it on the leaves beside the heart.

"What are you going to do with those," William asked.

"That's our supper tonight. I'll warrant you've never tasted better."

Jim-Bird finished cleaning the carcass, taking care to empty the bladder into a small medicine bottle he had in his shoulder bag. "This will come in handy as covering scent," he said. With his hatchet he cut a gambrel from a stout oak branch and inserted the two pointed ends between the bones and Achilles tendons of the doe's hind legs. He cut strips of bark from some small pawpaw trees, tied them together to make a rope, and tied the bark rope to the gambrel. Throwing the rope over the limb of a tree, he hoisted the carcass up into the air to skin it. "People think you have to use a skinning knife," he said, "but you don't. It's much better to pull the skin off. If you use a knife you're likely to cut into the skin and damage it."

With a few deft cuts, beginning at the hind legs, he pulled the skin downward and free. He held it up for William to see. "This here is what we are after. It's going back across the sea to where you came from, and when it gets there, they're going to turn it into gloves and pantaloons and bookbindings and everything under the sun. But for now we'll roll it up and take it with us. This carcass we'll leave hanging and come back to butcher it later."

Before leaving, Jim-Bird cut off the doe's head with his hatchet and chopped into her skull and removed her brains, which he put into a container made from a large section of cane, tightly corked, which he had brought along in his shoulder bag. "Otter Queen will use these for tanning," he said.

Finally, from his shoulder bag Jim-Bird pulled a handkerchief and tied it onto a tree branch near the deer's carcass, leaving it there to flutter in the breeze. "The smell and look of this should be enough to keep the wolves away."

"Let's go back to the blind and wait for the next herd," said William. "I'd like to get in at least one shot today."

"We can try," said Jim-Bird. "But it's not likely that we can make two kills at the same place. Not on the same day."

They returned to the blind and Jim-Bird sprinkled some of his newly collected deer urine onto the ground. They lay there for several hours. William's muscles ached and the cold soaked through his clothing, all the way into his bones. His rifle was pointed through the brush at the ready, but he wondered if his finger would be working well enough to pull the trigger by the time he got a chance to take a shot.

In late afternoon they heard some turkeys calling in the near distance. "More heralds of the woods," Jim-Bird whispered softly. And sure enough, a young buck soon approached and stopped and sniffed the urine scent. Then he raised his head and curled his upper lip. William fired his musket. The shot was at an awkward angle. The bullet penetrated the heart but also the guts. The buck died instantly, but when they cut him open, they saw that the gut shot had ruined the meat.

So they took only the skin, the liver, and the brains and abandoned the rest of the carcass. They went back to the doe and finished butchering it, dividing the meat between them to carry, and then they set out for camp. It was growing dark, but a bright moon was rising, and by its light they found their way back.

"That doe must have been in rut," said Jim-Bird, "else that buck would not have curled his lip. Rut will change the way we hunt."

"I just learned how to hunt this way," said William.

"It will be this way plus some new tricks," said Jim-Bird. "It's all in learning to think like a deer. If they can do it, you can too."

Otter Queen was pleased to see them return with two skins, though she was less than happy to have only one carcass. Speaking a few words of Cherokee, she took a tiny piece of liver and handed it to Jim-Bird, who said a few words in Cherokee and threw it into the fire, burning it to a cinder. Then she fried the rest of it in some bear oil and served it to them with some Jerusalem artichoke roots she had dug up and roasted. William and Jim-Bird ate heartily, leaving only a few scraps for the dogs. The liver was as good as Jim-Bird said it would be.

December 3. I shot my first Carolina deer today. The killing of such a large animal leaves a hole in the world. It makes me want to fill it in somehow, to do something to atone for killing it. The Indians say words before making a kill and later they throw a small piece of the liver into the fire as an offering. I am tempted to try that, though I don't know what god I am appeasing.

Uktena

The next day the wind was blustery and none of the hunters went out. William and Jim-Bird spent most of the day on the Gunsmith's side of the camp. As a gift, William took along a small portion of the cane sugar he had brought from Charles Town. The treat was well received.

The day after that the wind had calmed and the air was cold and crisp. They returned to the hunt, but they did not kill any deer. The does were indeed coming into rut. William and Jim-Bird caught sight of several that were not browsing as usual but were moving about with agitation, their tails stuck straight out. Twice they saw bucks following the scent of does, blundering carelessly, taking risks. But they could not get a clean shot.

"We'll get some tomorrow," said Jim-Bird as they headed back to camp empty-handed. "Be glad you're not a buck right now. You would be having a perpetual stiff one and would be out to impregnate every doe in the woods. Somehow you would know that the rut's not going to last long, and you'd be wanting to make the most out of the time you have. It would make you careless and exposed to hunters, not to mention the tangles you'd be getting into with the other randy bucks. Something like Thomas Farrell when he goes to Charles Town."

"How far I have fallen from my days in the Book Maggot club," said William. "Last year at this time I was sitting in a coffeehouse in Glasgow discussing the philosophy of Francis Hutcheson. This year I'm stumbling through the woods in the wilds of America discussing the philosophy of a buck with a stiff prick."

The next day they returned and set up a blind in a clump of small cedar trees near a scrape. Jim-Bird had brought along some sections of deer antlers. "Let's see if we can call in a buck for a fight," he said. He rattled the antlers together moderately hard, made a sound that was a kind of grunt-snort, and stamped his feet on the ground. Then they took shelter in the blind and waited silently for a long time. But no buck took the bait.

"There ain't no fighters out there today," whispered Jim-Bird. "So let's try this." He made a shrill bleating sound like the cry of a distressed fawn.

Presently a doe appeared, fully alert, looking for the fawn. And trailing closely after her was a very large buck, who cared nothing for the fawn but only for the doe. William drew down on him and felled him with a good lung shot, while Jim-Bird got off a shot at the doe and brought her down.

"This buck will easily bring us the price of two skins," said Jim-Bird as they went to clean and skin them.

Later in the day, Jim-Bird shot another doe. They were pleased with their day's hunt. They had the equivalent of four skins, maybe five, and they butchered all of the meat that they could carry away, leaving the rest to hang on the chance that they might return and butcher more of it. It would keep for days in the cold weather.

December 5. Our hunt is still going well. Jim-Bird knows enough about our quarry to keep us in business. And it is a business. Whatever Indian hunters were in ancient times, they are now engaged in the business of killing as many deer as they possibly can. They are so good at it, the herds in their usual hunting grounds are getting thin.

Late in December a heavy snow fell and lay on the ground for several days. The deer were bedded down, not moving about. William and Jim-Bird took advantage of this time to repair their clothing and equipment and to rest up from the hunting they had done. They had already accumulated a large store of skins, and Otter Queen was hard at work processing them. William offered to help, but she would not let him. "You would ruin them," she said. He was amazed at the efficiency with which she worked, and he liked watching her as she moved about. The baby that was quickening in her belly did not seem to slow her down at all. Though she would not let William touch the skins with a tool, he did find little ways to help her.

Her first task for each hide was to deflesh it soon after it was brought in, and for this she laid it on a beam made from a section of a small maple tree. The beam was set solidly in the ground and came up at a slant to about waist high. She bent over the hide, working with a scraper, removing all bits of muscle or fat that still adhered to the skin. This did not take much time—she could do three or four hides in an hour. She allowed William to move the skins on and off the beam for her.

The next step was a lye bath in one of the dug-out basins in the large poplar log in their camp. She knew how to mix the wood-ash lye and water to just the right strength. If the lye water were too weak, she explained to him, it would take forever to treat the skins; but if it were too strong, it would ruin them. She could not explain how she knew when it was just right. Using rocks to hold down the skins in the lye solution, she left them there to soak, periodically returning to shift the skins about to ensure that the lye water got to all parts of them. She would not let him help with that, though her hands and lower arms reddened from the corrosiveness of the lye, even after going to the creek each time to wash them off. "A man is not careful enough to do it right," she told him.

After three days or so of soaking the skins in the lye water, Otter Queen judged them to have been in long enough and pulled them out one by one, wringing the lye solution back into the basin to be used again. Then, she took the hides to the creek and immersed them there, weighing them down with rocks and leaving them overnight to let the moving water rinse out more of the lye. She let William do this part, though she went along to keep an eye on the operation.

The next step was tedious and required a great deal of effort, but William was not allowed to put his hand to it, except to once again help her lay each skin over her beam. With a scraper that had an edge, but not too sharp an edge, she started at the neck of the hide and scraped away the hair and the membrane in which it was embedded. Though the membrane had been loosened by the lye, she still had to bear down hard, while at the same time being careful not to cut into the skin itself. It required three or four hours of concentrated labor to scrape each skin clean, and once she started, she had to keep on until the job was done, or else the skin would be damaged.

Otter Queen let William help her take the newly scraped skins back to the stream for another overnight stay beneath the rocks, where the water rinsed out the remaining lye and mucous. When they took them out of the water, she showed him how to squeeze out the moisture until they were almost dry. Now they had a scraped skin, but not yet a tanned one.

The next treatment was a kettle of warm water in which a handful or two of pulverized deer brains had been stirred into a soupy solution. Again the skin was weighed down and left to soak overnight. The next morning she would pull the hide up, wring it out over the kettle, put it back in, and then pull it up and wring it out again, repeating the process several times to work the brain solution well into the skin. After wringing it out for the last time, it could be dried and safely stored. This was a half-dressed skin and was acceptable to some traders. But a full-dressed skin was worth more and required yet another tedious procedure—softening.

Otter Queen softened all her skins. For this she used one of the frames that William and Jim-Bird had made for her, each constructed of four strong wooden poles, crossed and secured at their extremities to make a rectangular space about seven feet high and five feet wide. To prepare a half-dressed deerskin for a frame, Otter Queen used an awl to make small perforations all the way around its edges. Then she took cordage and threaded it through the holes, sewing the skin to the frame and stretching it out flat. To stretch the hide more thoroughly, she pushed against it with her hands and fists, as well as with a softening stick, which was made of a piece of hickory about the length of an axe handle, chisel-shaped on one end. As she worked, stretching the skin in all directions, the skin would gradually slacken and she would retighten the cordage. This stretching both softened the skin and finished drying it out. When she had it soft enough, she buffed it velvety smooth on both sides, using the coarse surface on the end of a dried-out leg bone of a deer.

The skin was now all but finished. For the last step she laid it over a dome-shaped frame made of bent saplings, which was positioned over a bed of coals in a small fire pit. She threw small pieces of punk—rotten wood—onto the coals, creating a dense cloud of smoke. She would smoke the skin for an hour or so, carefully tending it and moving it around several times to get it evenly treated. Then she turned it over and smoked it on the opposite side. She liked this step, so close to the end and requiring so little labor after all that had gone before. She even let William adjust the skin and turn it for her, provided he followed her instructions.

When the skin came off the frame, it was fully dressed. Compared to a half-dressed skin, it was flexible and soft, more like cloth than leather. Even if soaked through with water, it would keep its flexibility as it dried.

January 3. Otter Queen is working her fingers to the bone. Each skin requires hours and hours of labor. Besides the skins, there are all the other duties she has to attend to keep the camp going. And still she is happier here than in Keowee. As for me, I am cold and would rather be at home—if Keowee can be considered home. The baby is growing in her belly. It is starting to show.

In early February the hunt began to come to an end. The deer herds had been thinned out and the surviving deer were especially wary. To make the best use of the short time remaining, William and Jim-Bird began using drives to round up and kill some of those that were left.

Jim-Bird would set up a stand at a location where deer were likely to pass, and William would be the driver. He would start out at quite a distance from Jim-Bird and would walk through the woods, noisily making large zig-zagging loops as he gradually approached the stand. If any deer were around, they would walk or trot ahead, keeping just out of sight of William, and when one came within range of the stand, Jim-Bird could take a shot. If a deer were rushing too fast, Jim-Bird would bleat like a fawn or make an unusual whistle to momentarily freeze it in its tracks.

They killed a few more deer in this way, but then several days went by without a kill. Trying a new approach, they began going out individually, using the two deer decoys Otter Queen had borrowed from Five-Killer. These were entire deerskins, including the head, with all the hair left on. The head was stuffed, and small cane hoops had been placed inside the neck to fill it out. Jim-Bird spent an entire evening teaching William how to use one. First he demonstrated. Bending low, he draped the skin over his back, holding his left arm and hand up through the neck. With his musket in his right hand—it would be cocked, he explained, if he were in the woods—he manipulated the head and neck with his left arm. He put the head down as if to graze, then he would lift his arm suddenly so the head seemed to look around. He would even pretend to lick his side, as deer do when they are nervous. He made grunting calls to entice other deer to approach. Pretending that one had come within range, he tossed the skin aside, drew down and took a mock shot. "Dead on!" he exclaimed. "Clean through the lungs!"

William had little hope of succeeding at this, but he spent much of the evening practicing, to the great amusement of Otter Queen.

"One of the hazards," Jim-Bird told him, "is that you can draw fire from other hunters who take you for a deer."

"There's not much danger in my case," said William. "I am unlikely to fool either man or deer."

And indeed he did not. They killed only six deer using this technique, all of them taken by Jim-Bird. But all in all they were pleased with their hunt as the season came to a close. They had killed just over 120 deer, forty skins for each of the three of them, with Otter Queen holding out several of the best skins for William and Jim-Bird to use for clothing.

Joining with the Gunsmith's crew, they decided to stage a feast to celebrate the end of the hunt. Weeks earlier, Jim-Bird had spotted claw marks on the hollow trunk of a dead sycamore tree. What would make a better feast than bear meat? So Jim-Bird and William went out with their muskets. Jim-Bird let Tazzie and Binkie come along, since a sleeping bear would have no nose for dogs nor for anything else. But Binkie was well into a pregnancy, and she soon gave up on the adventure and trotted back to camp. The two men and Tazzie went on.

When they finally neared the hollow tree, Jim-Bird put out his hand for silence. Standing still and listening, they made out the sound of soft snoring coming from inside the tree. Jim-Bird looked at William and smiled. Then he went to work and cut himself a long, slender pole. He took out a cord and tied one end of it to the small end of the pole. Then he tied a handful of shredded cedar bark onto the other end of the cord. He shimmied up a slender poplar tree that was growing in the open space beside the dead tree, and then he took out a steel-and-flint and struck a fire in the cedar bark. Using the pole, he swung the ignited tinder over and down into the hollow tree. Soon they heard a snort, and then a rustling inside the tree. And then a large, sleepy bear came up and out of the top of the open trunk and began climbing down the tree.

"Shoot him, William!"

William shot, but he only wounded the bear, bringing him fully awake, enraged.

"Take up my musket," shouted Jim-Bird. "Shoot again!"

The bear hit the ground and Tazzie charged in and began circling around him, barking furiously. Paying little attention to the dog, the bear headed toward William. Feeling surprisingly calm, William took careful aim with Jim-Bird's musket, pulled the trigger, and dropped the bear in his tracks.

"Get the dog," shouted Jim-Bird as he clambered down his tree. "Don't let him spoil that skin."

They skinned out the bear and butchered the meat and carried back as much of it as they could. The Wolves rejoiced at their arrival. The men went to work preparing the meat for the barbeque hurdles, and the women cooked sweet dishes with the sugar and honey they had been hoarding for just this occasion.

All ate heartily, and they talked merrily long into the night around the fire at the Gunsmith's camp.

Later, after they had gone to bed, William awoke in the middle of the night to find Otter Queen struggling in her sleep, making unintelligible sounds of fright. He put his arm around her and shook her gently, and she woke up.

"Willy" she said, clinging to him. "What a terrible dream!"

"Was someone after you?" he asked.

"I was in the woods, and I thought I saw a clump of red leaves in the water. I leaned over to look closer. And then the head of a huge red *uktena* reared up out of the water."

"What is an uktena? I have heard that word, but I can't remember where."

"It is a serpent. A great serpent."

"That's right. Sam told us about uktenas on the first night I met him, back at the Packsaddle. They are monstrous snakes."

"Oh, Willy," she said, rubbing her face against his chest as if to make the image go away. Then she pulled back and looked at him. Her face was grim. "He towered over me, Willy. His head was huge, as big as a rum keg, and he was hissing and dripping water on me. He had horns, and such teeth! And he knew I was there. His eyes—they were looking at me."

"It was just a dream," said William. "There is no uktena here."

"No dream is ever just a dream. It means something."

"What does it mean?" he asked.

"I don't know," said Otter Queen. "Uktenas can be either good or bad. You never know which they are bringing. They are scary, though, no matter what. You have to be very brave to get what is good, if he is bringing good."

"And if he is bringing bad?"

"Then you have to get ready and be alert for whatever is coming."

"If you were a Christian," said William, "you could pray for St. Michael to come slay the uktena for you. St. Michael does not bother to ask if a dragon is good or bad."

"Well, he should," said Otter Queen. "With an uktena, you never know."

19   Bloody Mouth

Otter Queen put on her matchcoat, once blue but now after so many weeks in the woods, darkly soiled with grime and deer blood. As she tied her pack-basket about her shoulders and picked up her hatchet in her hand, Tazzie started jumping up and down, wagging his stump of a tail. He knew they were going for firewood. Tazzie had grown to love Otter Queen and preferred to spend his time with her instead of Jim-Bird. Often at night he would creep into her bed and curl up at her feet to sleep. During the day she would give him tidbits to eat, and he had taken to watching her as closely as he did Jim-Bird, studying her every move to anticipate what she was about to do next. Binkie, on the other hand, was not interested in what Otter Queen was doing. Greatly swollen with the puppies that were soon to be born, she awoke from a nap and watched Otter Queen for a moment without raising her head from her paws. Then she closed her eyes and went back to sleep.

As Otter Queen headed outside, Tazzie went in front, leading the way out the door. They passed by William, who sat in the yard cleaning his musket.

"Where is Jim-Bird?" asked Otter Queen.

"Over at the Gunsmith's," said William. "They are laying plans for get-ting our skins back to Keowee." He glanced at the hatchet in her hand. "Don't go far."

"I won't," she assured him. "Tazzie will look out for me."

William went back to his work, cleaning the musket carefully and arming it with a fresh gun flint. When he had finally finished with it, he set it aside and noted that Otter Queen had not yet returned. Standing up, he looked in the direction in which she had gone. There was no sign of her for as far as he could see. He picked up the musket and loaded and primed it and headed out to meet her.

He had hardly left the camp when he saw her packbasket and hatchet lying on the ground. The forest floor was disturbed—signs of a struggle. His heart began to pound. Whirling around, taking it all in, he spotted something white lying on the ground a stone's throw from the scuff marks. Tazzie! He ran over, expecting the worst. One of the little dog's front legs was bloody and an ear was torn—he had taken a heavy blow to his head. He appeared to be dead, but when William put a hand on his chest, he could feel a heartbeat. But where was Otter Queen? He stood up and again turned all around, but he could see nothing more. He fought to keep his head clear. He walked quickly around the perimeter of the scuffed area, studying the ground, looking for signs of which way to go, but he could find none. For a moment he stood paralyzed, but then his mind cleared again. Jim-Bird would know which way to go. And the Gunsmith. They would see more than he could see. Grabbing up Tazzie's limp body, he ran toward the camp. "Jim-Bird! Gunsmith!" he shouted. "Otter Queen has been taken. Hurry!"

He handed Tazzie over to one of the Wolf women and then ran to pull on warm clothing. He grabbed up a bag of cold meal in case they had to stay for some days in the woods—he was not coming back without Otter Queen. With his hatchet and dirk in his belt and his gun in his hand, he ducked outside and ran back to where the struggle had taken place, the Gunsmith and Jim-Bird following closely on his heels. It made him sick to see Otter Queen's packbasket lying there on the ground. But at least it was not her scalped body.

After looking around for a few moments, the Gunsmith said, "Someone hid in those bushes. She fought hard."

"Here is blood," said Jim-Bird, pointing to the ground.

"Tazzie's ear was torn," said William.

"Where was the dog?" asked the Gunsmith.

William pointed to the spot, and the Gunsmith walked out beyond it and began walking in a wide circle around the area of the struggle, scanning the ground. Then he stopped. "Here," he said. "More blood. This is not the dog. One of them is hurt." He looked and found more blood, and then, following on in that direction, he found the disturbed forest litter that revealed the trail.

William and Jim-Bird ran to catch up, and the three of them plunged into the forest.

"Creek marauders," said Jim-Bird.

The Gunsmith grunted in agreement. "We are going west," he said, "toward Creek hunting ground."

It soon became apparent that Otter Queen was laying down a trail. The Gunsmith and Jim-Bird found small vines that had been uprooted, leaves torn half through, faint scuff marks in the litter, twigs snapped and left dangling. And most tellingly, they began finding tiny tufts of blue wool ravelings from her matchcoat.

Otter Queen's captors had a head start on their pursuers, who had to travel less rapidly, slowed as they were by the task of picking out the faint signs that guided them on their way. To make things worse, it was growing dark and they would soon be unable to see any clues at all.

In their last bit of light they came to a creek crossing, with soft, moist soil on both sides. Jim-Bird and the Gunsmith bent over to examine the footprints.

"Only two of them," said the Gunsmith. "Otter Queen and one other."

"He's a big man," said Jim-Bird. "You could bury a cat in one of his footprints."

The Gunsmith got down on his knee to examine the footprints more closely. "There is still some blood," he said. "It is the man who is wounded. Not Otter Queen."

At least they knew that much as they stopped for the night. Only one wounded man for them to fight if they could catch him. They built no fire and ate only a little parched corn to take the edge off their hunger. They sat together with their backs to each other so that they could doze off intermittently while one kept watch in case the marauder backtracked and came after them.

As soon as the dawn light began to rise, they were on the trail again. The Gunsmith continued as their main tracker. It seemed to William that it was because the Gunsmith could look without focusing on anything in particular that he was able to spot small disturbances in the normal pattern of things. By mid-morning they found the place where the two had spent the night. The Gunsmith pointed out where one of them had slept. It was Otter Queen, he thought, because of the small signs she had left, very faint signs—she obviously had great fear that her captor would see her doing it. A twig was snapped. A leaf was torn half through. But where had the man spent the night? The Gunsmith and Jim-Bird began circling about, scanning the ground. Jim-Bird found the spot some thirty yards away, behind some foliage.

"He is using her as a decoy," Jim-Bird said, "trying to draw us in. We must be careful."

They moved on and had only gone a short distance when the Gunsmith stopped suddenly. "Sycamore bark," he said, "and no sycamore tree nearby." He picked up the piece of bark and inspected it front and back. "There is something here." He showed it to the other two. On the smooth side of the bark someone had dabbed seven drops of blood with a fingertip. "Is she bleeding, too?" the Gunsmith wondered.

"It must be a message," said Jim-Bird

They stared at the piece of bark, unable to comprehend it.

Then suddenly an image flashed through William's mind. "Tugalo!" he said. "Seven is the number of people Bloody Mouth and his nephew murdered there. God help her. She's telling us that Bloody Mouth has taken her."

They threw down the bark and pushed on, trying to go faster, still heading westward into Creek territory. As the afternoon went on, the Gunsmith got the impression that Bloody Mouth was slowing down. Was his wound wearing him down, or was he up to something? Late in the afternoon, with a slight breeze in their faces, the Gunsmith stopped and sniffed the air. "Smoke," he said.

Neither William nor Jim-Bird could smell anything.

"Bloody Mouth has built a fire," said the Gunsmith. "To lure us in. He's setting up an ambush."

Now that their prey had stopped, they moved more slowly and carefully. They did not want to give themselves away or fall into his trap. Instead they would set one of their own.

Jim-Bird soon smelled the smoke, still upwind, and before long William could smell it, too. After going a short distance further, they stopped to lay a plan of their own.

"Willy, go straight ahead," whispered the Gunsmith. "I loop left. Jim-Bird, you loop right. Make no sound. No sound. Go slow. When you see Otter Queen, stop. Make no sound. Look for Bloody Mouth. If you cannot see him, go slow, slow. Crawl on your belly. Stop when Otter Queen is in musket range. Go no further. No further. If you go to her, he will kill you. We kill him first. Then we go to her."

William nodded. He checked his hatchet and dirk in his belt, and then, gripping his musket, he moved ahead alone. He crept through the woods until he saw the glint of a fire in the dimming light. It was a welcome sight, even though he knew it was a trap. Dropping down to the ground, he moved in closer until he saw her hunched over beside the fire. His heart raced. He could hardly contain himself. Everything in him wanted to run to her and grab her up and hold her safely in his arms. But she would not be safe in his arms. His head knew it, but his heart did not. He listened to his head.

Edging forward, he looked for Bloody Mouth but saw no sign of him. So this was as far as he could go—he had to stop. Like stalking a deer. No sound. Moving very, very slowly, he folded down a clump of weeds and inched himself over them to gain some insulation against the cold ground for the night ahead. He slowly moved his musket into place, pointing it in the direction of Otter Queen.

The last lingering daylight faded. A cold night it was, and a long one. He was glad she had a fire.

William did not sleep at all. With the first, faintest light of dawn he moved ever so slowly to position himself behind his screen of weeds so that his face, just his face, would be visible to her as the light rose. He guessed the distance to be about forty yards. Otter Queen was awake. Now and then she would look around a little, although not as if she expected to see anything. Yet he was sure that she knew they had followed her and that Bloody Mouth had set her there as a trap. The dawn light grew stronger. William stayed perfectly still, not moving a muscle. Finally he saw her freeze for a moment when her eyes swept past him, and he knew that she had seen his face. She turned her head slightly to the left and upward. She seemed to be gesturing with her gaze toward a large cedar tree. William scanned the tree. Was Bloody Mouth in it? Had he too seen William's face? Was he already drawing a bead on him? William inched back, letting the weeds close until he could just see out. All was still. Then he saw one of the branches tremble in the cedar tree, very slightly, about a quarter of the way up from the ground. Bloody Mouth was there. What to do? How to get the bloody bastard out of the tree?

The trembling branch had revealed Bloody Mouth's general vicinity in the tree. William wondered if he could determine the exact location. If so, he could shoot the son of a bitch. It was a large, robust cedar, with dense foliage. He could see the angle that most of the limbs took from the trunk, and he could estimate the approximate line of the trunk. He slowly cocked his musket and calculated where the trembling limb must intersect with the trunk. That is where Bloody Mouth would be perched.

William pulled the trigger and fired. He heard a yelp. In the next instant a second shot rang out and a musket ball ripped through the foliage near his head. He saw the cedar boughs shake as Bloody Mouth fell, or else climbed down quickly, through the limbs of the tree. One way or another, he was coming to ground. William dropped his musket, grabbed up his hatchet in his right hand and his dirk in his left, and struck out for the tree madcap, as fast as he could run, yelling at the top of his lungs, a Highland charge of one on one as he closed the distance.

A large figure of a man came out of the foliage wielding a hatchet, running directly at him. If William's bullet had hit him, it had not done much damage. Bloody Mouth wore a dirty hunting shirt, a breechcloth, and leggings. His face was painted black, with vermillion streaks coming down like rivulets of streaming blood from his vermillion-encircled mouth.

His eyes were fixed on William's head, but William, following an elemental rule of combat he had learned in the Highlands, kept his own eyes on Bloody Mouth's hatchet. As they came together, Bloody Mouth struck with his hatchet, aiming at William's head. William parried solidly, catching Bloody Mouth's hatchet in the crook of his own, and with his left hand he thrust forward with his dirk. Bloody Mouth wrenched his body to avoid the dirk, and as he did, he went tumbling to the ground, brushing past William, who spun around and went for him with his hatchet raised.

Bloody Mouth rolled quickly and sprang to his feet. Having gained a better opinion of William, he circled with his hatchet set for a more careful blow. Now it was William who was at risk, too much in the grip of hatred, and both of them knew it.

A bullet flew by, just missing Bloody Mouth. It had come from the Gunsmith's side of the clearing. Bloody Mouth flinched but stayed with the fight. He wanted very much to kill William. Then a second musket fired from the other direction, and William saw a scatter of threads fly out from Bloody Mouth's hunting shirt. Jim-Bird's bullet had at least grazed him, and for a moment Bloody Mouth stopped in his tracks. William broke away and moved to reposition himself between Bloody Mouth and Otter Queen. Facing Bloody Mouth anew, he raised his hatchet in his right hand and his dirk in his left. Let him come. He was ready. Bloody Mouth hesitated. William could see him calculating. He did not know how many companions William had with him. There were at least two, reloading or charging at him now from the woods. And he knew that this white man before him was no easy prey. Deciding to cut his losses, Bloody Mouth turned and ran. Jim-Bird and the Gunsmith ran after him, but Bloody Mouth sped swiftly and disappeared into a large canebrake. There could be no following him into that. He had only to be still, and the rattling ground litter would broadcast the location of anyone foolish enough to chase in after him and suffer the business end of his hatchet. So Jim-Bird and the Gunsmith gave it up. Jim-Bird stayed at the canebrake's edge as a lookout, while the Gunsmith went back to his sister.

William had already reached Otter Queen and was cutting free the rawhide thongs that tightly bound her wrists and ankles. Her eyes were red and her hair disheveled. She had deep scratches in her legs from having been forced to run through smilax and blackberry briars. Cutting the last cord, he took her into his arms. At first he could not speak and could only hold her tightly. Then at last he murmured, "I am so sorry this has happened to you."

"I knew you would come," she said. "But I was afraid Bloody Mouth would kill you. And then he had such terrible plans for me. He talked to me with signs. He said he was taking me to the Creek hunting camp and I would be his slave and my baby would be raised a Creek. Every time we stopped, he would tell me this again."

William's anger was pulsing. "I'll hunt down the bloody bastard and kill him," he said. "Jim-Bird will stay here and keep you safe. The Gunsmith and I will track him down."

"No!" she said emphatically. "You must not do that! You have to stay with me, Willy. Get me away from this place. I want to go now. Let's get out of here." The Gunsmith had come up beside them, and she turned to him and threw her arms around him. "I thought he would kill you," she said and began to cry. "I didn't want you to die because of me. Tell me you won't go after him."

The Gunsmith glanced at William.

William took a deep breath and let it out slowly. "She's been through enough. Let's take her home."

William retrieved Bloody Mouth's musket from the cedar tree and set out for the camp, backtracking more or less the way they had come. When night fell, they built a big fire and roasted a turkey that Jim-Bird had killed along the way. After they had eaten, they sat silently by the fire. No one asked Otter Queen what had happened on that day she went out to gather firewood. They waited until she offered to talk about it.

Finally she spoke. "I went to the place where I usually go to find firewood," she said. "There is always new deadwood on the ground there after a storm. Tazzie was edgy. He was sniffing the ground and sniffing the air. His hackles went up, and he growled and edged toward a clump of bushes, his legs all stiff. I thought it must be a raccoon, or maybe a fox. But then I saw a little patch of red through the leaves. I saw it, and then I didn't see it. A cardinal, I thought. I went over closer to take a look. I was just curious. I was so near the camp—I had hardly left it. It did not occur to me to think of danger. Then Bloody Mouth came bursting out. He paid no attention to Tazzie, such a small dog. He was coming for me. It all happened in an instant.

"Tazzie jumped up in the air—you know the way he jumps straight up—and he bit into the front of Bloody Mouth's breechcloth and held on for dear life. He had Bloody Mouth's prick in his teeth. It happened so quickly. Bloody Mouth was dancing around, trying to beat Tazzie off with his fist, but Tazzie held on. Then Bloody Mouth hit him with the blunt side of his hatchet. I think he was afraid to use the blade, afraid he would cut himself. Tazzie fell to the ground and I turned to run. I think Tazzie was dead. The next thing I knew, Bloody Mouth had me. I still had my hatchet and I spun around and tried to fight, but he was too quick and too strong. He knocked my hatchet to the ground and grabbed me by my hair. I thought I was as good as dead. I thought he would scalp me. But instead he started dragging me away. I think he was so angry and embarrassed at what that little dog had done to him that he decided then and there to save me for something special, something more cruel than a chop in the head. He wanted to get even. Tazzie really bit into him. I think he severed a blood vessel, because Bloody Mouth couldn't stop the bleeding, not for a long time."

"That helped us track you at first," said Jim-Bird. "After that it was the signs you left."

"I had to be careful," Otter Queen said. "Once he caught me uprooting a vine. He hit me hard, twice, and said he would kill me if I did it again. Did you find the sycamore bark?"

"Seven spots of blood," said the Gunsmith.

"I had to do it behind my back. I stuck my finger on a smilax thorn to get the blood."

"You might like to know," said William, "that Tazzie was still alive when we last saw him. He was not conscious, but he was breathing."

Otter Queen smiled a little. "I hope he is all right."

After a while the fire died down. As they had done the night before, they arranged themselves with their backs against each other, all four of them facing in different directions, and they took turns sleeping.

As they approached the hunting camp the next day, they fired their muskets into the air as a sign of celebration. All of Otter Queen's kinsmen came running out to greet her, Tazzie trotting along with them. When the little dog saw Otter Queen, he picked up speed and came running, tail wagging, leaping up against her and pawing at her skirt. One of her sisters had sewn up his torn ear, and he was almost as good as new.

"What a brave dog you are," said Otter Queen, and she picked him up and tried to hold him in her arms. But he squirmed too much and she put him down again.

After spending a little time with her kinsmen, Otter Queen headed for the shelter, William following after her. Inside, she went over and lay down on their bed. "I did not think I would ever get back here again," she said.

William sat down beside her and put his hand on her belly. "The bairn is none the worse for wear," he said. "I felt a kick."

"The bairn kicks like a fawn," she said.

They were silent for a moment and from the silence came some small squeaking sounds. "Binkie must have had her puppies," said William. He followed the sound to a far corner on Jim-Bird's side of the camp and returned with a tiny, sightless puppy in one hand. He put it into Otter Queen's cupped hands, and she cuddled it up against her face. Then her lips began to tremble.

"Poor little thing," she said softly. "Whatever will become of you?" She began to weep.

William stood looking at her helplessly. She handed back the puppy, and he returned it to the litter. As he came back to rejoin her, she waved him toward the door.

"I'll be all right," she said. "I need some time. Let me be alone now."

Pain stabbed his heart as he kissed her on the cheek and then went outside to join the others.

February 7. Otter Queen is lucky to be alive. Bloody Mouth captured her just outside our camp. He only spared her because he wanted to save her for a slave. She kept a cool head, and we got her back alive. But she is changed. She is sad and distracted, and not just a little. Something has happened inside her. Though she is back, I still fear for her. And I fear for our child. I can't say why, but that is how I feel.

The Devil's Piss

As they bundled their deerskins and packed their gear to return to Keowee, Otter Queen's melancholy deepened. For the first time in months she began to talk about the Birds. She dreaded going home.

William tried to strike an optimistic note. Time had gone by. The Birds would have their minds on other things—on the coming of spring, on the clearing of fields and the planting of corn. Otter Queen ceased speaking of her unease, but William suspected this was only for his sake. She had lost her joy for the small moments of life, and she had lost the sense of humor that he so loved.

The Wolves bided their time and waited for a clear day that promised to have several other clear days coming along behind it. Then they set out to the north, toward Tugalo. All five of their horses were loaded with as much as they could bear, and every one of the Wolves carried a heavy pack on his or her back. Even Otter Queen insisted on carrying a load, though William made sure it was not too heavy, and even then he worried about the baby.

Burdened so, their pace of travel was slower than it had been when they came down to the camp with nothing but their gear and supplies. Arriving at Tugalo in late afternoon, the town seemed even more dismal than before, with few people out and about. When they reached John Coleman's store, they found it locked tight. Someone had chopped at the door with a hatchet, whether trying to get inside or merely showing their anger, it was not clear. William and Jim-Bird walked around behind the store to John's house, and it too was shut tight, though a thin plume of smoke wafted out of the smoke hole in the roof.

Jim-Bird slapped on the side of the house. "John!" he called. The door opened and John stuck his head out. When he saw who had come, he leaned his musket against the inside doorway and came out to greet his visitors.

"Well, if it ain't the Keowee Wolves," he said, looking out at the horses and crew. "It appears you've had a good season after all. Come settle in for the night. But first you'll need to put all your packs into my store for safekeeping. And you'll want to leave a guard with the horses all night, else you might not have horses come morning. We have a pot of venison stew on the fire. We'll add some water to it and cook up some rice."

"We have barbequed bear," said William.

"Bring it on," said John.

Jim-Bird went back to help the Gunsmith and his crew of Wolves put the skins in the store and build a fire in John's winter house. William went inside with John.

"How many of those skins are yours and how many are the Gunsmith's?" John asked him.

"I'm coming out better than I thought I would," said William. "Jim-Bird and I took a hundred and twenty or so. The Gunsmith and his crew did better, of course. There are more of them and they started earlier."

"Not to mention they've had a mite more practice."

William chuckled. "That too," he allowed. Then he sobered. "We had a bad time of it a few days ago," he said. "Bloody Mouth surprised Otter Queen while she was out gathering firewood. He would have killed her on the spot, but Jim-Bird's Tazzie went after him and bit into his crotch, which was as high as the little fellow could jump, and tore him up some. It rattled Bloody Mouth so bad, he took Otter Queen with him, intending to take her back to the Creeks for a worse fate than a mere knock on the head. But we tracked him down and got her back."

"Did you kill him?"

"We got a couple of shots at him, but he got away into a canebrake. I wish we could say we brought his scalp with us. We could have given it to the relatives of those seven he murdered here."

"That's mighty thoughtful," said John. "But we've had such a bad year in Tugalo, I'm not sure Bloody Mouth's scalp would do much to soothe our nerves. We're all taken up now with the Paints swilling rum."

"What do you mean by that?" asked William.

"Well, first you have to understand that Paint clan has had an extra hard time of it here lately. They lost three of their people to that rampage by Bloody Mouth and his nephew. Then at the end of the deer season a gang of Creek marauders came into their hunting camp and stole most of their skins. And this comes on the heels of a long run of bad luck that's been going on for years. I remember the day when the Paints were big beaver trappers around here. They were on top of the world. But things started going downhill for them when the beavers started to disappear."

"Come to think of it," said William, "I've hardly seen a beaver pond in these parts. There were more on the trail from Charles Town than I've seen up here."

"They've come back some down there," said John, "but up here they're all but trapped out. In the old days there was one beaver pond after another in this country. But beaver trapping was a favored trade. It takes some skill to trap them, but once you manage to do it, you only have to take off the skin and dry it. With a deer, your work just begins when you get the skin off. But the hatters don't care about the beaver's skin, they only want the hair for felt."

"It's hard to believe people could clear out all the beavers in the entire country," William said.

"Once they got the knack of trapping them, it went right fast. And it changed the land around here, too. Once you kill all the beavers out of their ponds, their dams start to give way in spring floods and the ponds go dry. Most of the little meadows and canebrakes you see in this part of the country used to be beaver ponds. So, that's what happened to the Tugalo Paints. They went from being on top of the trade to being on the bottom. And one disaster followed another. Now that the Creeks have taken their deerskins, they'll not be able to pay down their debts this year, and it's hard to see how they can pay them down next year, being so deep in the hole as they are. Which means they can't get new guns, can't get powder, can't get shot. And to make things worse, they recently managed to get their hands on the better part of a keg of rum."

"That should make things better, not worse," said William. "It would for me."

"Then you've never seen Indians drink rum when things are going bad. It's when they've lost all hope and can't see how they're going to make it in the world that they drink themselves into oblivion and don't want to stop. They blame it on the rum. They say it entices and seduces them like a beautiful woman who captures their minds. They'll sell the last thing they own for one more drink. They would swim in rum if they could. And the drunker they become, the more they lose the restraints that normally govern them. A quiet man becomes a mad bear, foaming at the mouth, intent on punishing people from other clans who have slighted him. He'll even punish members of his own clan for the constant demands they place upon him. After he sobers up he will say, in all innocence, "'Twas not me that did it, 'twas the rum.'"

"I've heard that said in Scotland," said William.

John shook his head. "I hate to see it around here. They injure themselves. They fall asleep in the snow and freeze to death. They fall into cooking fires and burn themselves. I once saw a drunken young man boast that he could eat fire, and right there in front of our eyes, before anyone could stop him, he picked up hot embers and put them in his mouth and scarred himself for life. When the men get like this, hellbent on oblivion, their women hide the children, and if they can, they move their men's weapons out of the way, too."

"It is not just the Indians who get crazy drunk," said Tskwayi, speaking up from her work at the cook fire. "I've seen traders just as bad. Rum is the Devil's piss."

"I can't argue with that," said John. "And what I hate even worse than a staggering drunk trader is the rogue trader who encourages the swilling of rum amongst the hunters. They will intercept Indians coming in from their winter hunt, ply them with rum, get them shit-faced drunk, and then cheat them out of their skins—leaving the traders back in the houses empty-handed and the Indians hopelessly in debt." John waved his hand. "Don't get me started. I'll go on all night."

"You were telling me about the Paints," said William.

"The Paints." John shook his head. "Their clan is falling apart here. Some have abandoned Tugalo. The ones who are still here spend their time hatching desperate schemes to right their fortune by any means they can think of. And the worst of it is, it's not only the Paints. There are others around here almost as desperate. Tugalo has become too grim a place for me. As soon as the last hunting crew comes in, I'm packing up and getting out of here for good. But I've not let on about this to anyone around here. If the people of Tugalo knew I was leaving, wouldn't any of them bring in the skins they owe me. They'd wait me out. I've even been advancing a little credit against next year's trade just to make them think I'll still be here."

Otter Queen arrived with some dried bear meat and joined Tskwayi at the fire, where the two of them began talking together. In a little while Jim-Bird came in. The Gunsmith and his crew were tired, he said, and would stay in the winter house and eat their own provisions.

"I will take some rice and stew to them," said Tskwayi.

"I think we can call that soup now, instead of stew," said John.

They all laughed at that, even Otter Queen.

William and Otter Queen slept in the extra bed in John and Tskwayi's house and Jim-Bird slept in his blanket on the floor near the fire. It was well past midnight when everyone was awakened by a commotion outside. The men took up arms and went out to find the Gunsmith fending off two drunken Indians who were trying to take two of the horses. The Gunsmith was brandishing his hatchet.

"Don't hurt them," said John. "They don't know what they're doing. They won't remember anything about this tomorrow."

The traders rounded up the drunken horse thieves and tied their hands behind their backs. Trussed up in this way, they could not keep their balance and fell to the ground, where they were easily kept down. Tskwayi and Otter Queen had come out to watch. "Run over to the Paints," John said to Tskwayi, "and tell them to come fetch their rum-hounds. We want to get some sleep before this night is over."

After a little while some Paint men came and took the two miscreants in tow. They did not scold them. Far from it, they treated them gently.

"They hate it when their young men act like that," said John as he and his guests went back inside. "But they forgive them because they know how terrible those drunkards are going to feel when they sober up and learn what they've done. I sometimes think the Indians have found themselves in a world that leaves them no possible place to be. So they drink 'the water that takes away their wits.' And in that state, for a brief time, they have the illusion of power. But all they do is hurt themselves and everyone else around them."

The remaining trip home was uneventful but exhausting. They camped for a night on Cane Creek and arrived at Keowee late in the afternoon of the next day. They shot off their muskets as they approached the town. The Wolf clan turned out in force to welcome them home, and everyone was happy. Everyone except Otter Queen.

February 12. We are back from our season in the woods. I am glad to have had the adventure, but I can't say I would ever do the like again. I now know what the Indian hunters have to endure to survive in this changing world of theirs. If I am going to be in the deerskin trade from now on, I'll do it from this side and not that one. But at least I know what the other side is like. It gives me compassion for the men whose debts we hold, though that sentiment might not serve me well as a trader.

Nor did our venture do for Otter Queen what we had hoped. We thought it would make things better, but in the end it has made them worse. I don't know what to do to help her. She's a Cherokee and a woman, and I'm a Scot and a man. The gulf has never seemed so wide.

21   "The Sun for Sorrow Will Not Show His Head"

On the next morning after their return, William went to the trading house carrying one of the two bundles of skins belonging to himself and Otter Queen. Sam and Jim-Bird were already at work, preparing for a busy day of trading.

"I was just telling Jim-Bird how I thought you fellows weren't never getting back," said Sam as William came in and dropped his bundle to the floor. "The hunters have been coming in every day, unloading their skins, paying off old debts and taking on new ones. I was counting on Thomas to give me some help, but he claims not to have any helpers he can trust enough to leave with the horses for very long. I don't believe it, but I'm not going to argue with him. Like as not he'd just make trouble for me if he got in here. He's better with horses than with people. And it's the horse work I'm paying him for, not this."

"If I could have gotten here a day sooner, I would have," said William. "I was happy to have my season in the woods, but that's some hard living out there. I am glad to be halfway back to civilization."

"Keowee is civilized enough for me," said Sam. "I wouldn't trade it for no other."

"I meant no criticism of Keowee," said William. "I was more than happy to get out of Charles Town last summer, you may recall. Though I'll admit that I did find myself thinking fondly of that place when I was lying out there in the woods with my teeth chattering."

"We all do toward the end of the season," said Sam. "But it don't last long once we get there."

"I am never fond of Charles Town," said Jim-Bird.

"That's right," said Sam. "You are fond of Four Hole Swamp and that little Natchez girl."

"That's paradise to me," said Jim-Bird.

William smiled, glad to be back with Sam and the trading house. He left and returned to Otter Queen's house for their second bundle of skins, brought it back to the store, and dropped it on the floor beside the other one. "There's forty skins in each bundle," he said. "One is mine and one is Otter Queen's. She said to put hers into my account."

"You will need to unpack them," said Jim-Bird, "so Sam can inspect them."

"If they are as well cleaned and dressed as Jim-Bird's are," said Sam, "there ain't no need to inspect them. Every one of his is neat as a pin. Did Otter Queen do all of these?"

"Every one," said William. "She wouldn't let me touch them."

"Then carry them over to the storehouse and stack them with the others. I'll trust your count and put them in the book. But when the other hunters come in, you will want to unpack and inspect every last bundle. There's some hunters that are slapdash in their skinning and dressing. I give half-credit for some of the damaged skins, but those that are too rough, I refuse them."

Just then a hunter came into the store with two women companions. All three were carrying bundles of deerskins on their backs. Soon the Gunsmith and his crew came in as well, and so it went for the rest of the day. William was totally absorbed in unpacking skins, inspecting them, and packing them up again. He had to negotiate with hunters who insisted that the heaviest of their buckskins were worth two or even three chalks. He had to consult with Sam to negotiate how much credit he could allow some of the hunters whose season had gone badly or who were already too heavily in debt to come out on top.

Finally the day of trading ended, and Sam, William, and Jim-Bird retired to the benches beneath Sam's corncrib. The Gunsmith, who had lingered at the store, joined them. Sam brought out a bottle of rum and passed it around. They spent some time on the story of Bloody Mouth, but then moved on to other talk. William stayed for another round of rum and then another, preferring the light banter of the men to the melancholy of Otter Queen's house.

February 13. I can't say that I regret being back in Keowee. I only wish that Otter Queen could share in this sentiment. It seems she dreads the dawning of each day.

For several weeks William immersed himself in the daily routine at the trading house. At home things continued to be gloomy. Otter Queen seldom left her house, and she had little to say to William when he was there. Her hair, which she had always kept up neatly, now was often disheveled.

"You need to get out and about," William said to her one evening. "It will make ye feel better."

"If I go out of the house, I will see the Birds with their pinched, pissy faces," she said. "That makes me feel worse."

"You could go sit by the river. You know that would lift your spirits. Just sit there and let the river talk to you. You could watch the birds in the trees, the real birds, the ones that fly and sing and make ye happy. If ye keep on sitting in the house like this, it will make ye crazy."

She looked at him with chagrin. "Do you think I am going crazy?"

"I don't know what's happening to ye. I just know ye need to get out and be in the world." He wanted to say something about the baby, about how she needed to come back into life for his sake, but he did not think that would help.

"All right," she said with a sigh. "I will go to the river tomorrow. You are right. It will probably make me feel better."

When William returned home at the end of the next day, the house was dark inside. The fire had gone out. Otter Queen was lying in their bed with her face to the wall. William brushed at the ashes in the hearth and found a few live coals. He added some twigs and soon had a bright little fire going. He nursed it, gradually adding larger pieces of wood. Otter Queen did not stir, and he did not know whether she was asleep or awake.

"Did ye go to the river today?" he asked.

There was no reply. The silence stretched on. Then finally she rolled over and faced him. "Yes, I went to the river, and I listened to the water and watched the birds and washed my face and hair, and it did make me feel better. But on my way back, who should I meet but old Hawk's Mother, of all people. I rounded a turn in the path, and there she was, bending over and digging up a root. I surprised her and she tried to conceal what she was doing. And what do you suppose? Did she show herself to be the grand clan matron everyone thinks she is? Did she act like a human being talking to another human being? No. She showed her true nature to me. She asked, 'Did the *tchki:li* get tired of hunting deer? Did she come back to Keowee to hunt human livers? And what is that ugly lump in her belly? Is that a baby *tchki:li*? After this one is born, we will know what to think if our Keowee babies start dying.'

"That is what she said to me, Willy. No one was there to hear it except me. No one would believe me if I told them that she talked to me that way. They would call me a liar and say it is proof that I really am a *tchki:li*. I stood there thinking all that. I knew I should walk past her and say nothing. But Willy, I didn't have the strength I needed. It scares me that I am not myself any more. I know I am not because I did something I should never have done. Willy, I slapped her face." She shook her head, pained as she recalled the scene. "I slapped her face and it made her furious. It would make anyone furious, but not like that. She spewed forth a stream of nastiness such as I have never heard. I could not even understand her, only a word here and there. I turned and walked away, but it was too late. I know what will come of it. Things will get worse for me. Can you imagine that, Willy? That things will get even worse than they already are?"

"What can she do?" asked William. "If she were to tell others what you did, she would have to give a reason for it, and how can she do that? She would lose the respect of the clans if she told them how she insulted you."

Before Otter Queen could answer there was a tap against the side of the house. Then the Gunsmith ducked in through the door. Otter Queen sat up.

"What happened today?" the Gunsmith asked her, coming right to the matter that had brought him there. "People are talking. They say you insulted Hawk's Mother on the path to the river. Everyone is astir. They are saying that you stay in your house all day and only go out to heap insults on the Birds. And it's not just the Birds who are talking."

William just shook his head. The truth was even worse—a slapped face, not a mere insult.

The Gunsmith sat down beside his sister. "What is wrong?" he asked. "What is happening to you?"

"What is wrong?" she repeated. "What is happening? For me Keowee has become a black cloth down in a dark pit. That is what is happening. By day I cannot shake the feeling that I am being pursued. It is worse than being stalked by Bloody Mouth. With him we all knew who the enemy was. And he was out to get all of us, even if I happened to be the one he caught. But here, everyone else lives normally, everyone but me. Why do I have to endure this? Why do I even have to go on living? I don't feel like working. I don't feel like eating. And I have such terrible dreams when I sleep."

"Something is wrong here," The Gunsmith said, a new urgency rising in his voice. Then he began talking to her in Cherokee. He seemed to be taking charge of things, and she was obviously heartened by his words.

After the Gunsmith left, William asked her to explain. "He says it sounds to him like conjury," she said. "He thinks someone is conjuring against us and making me ill. I think he is right, Willy. He told me to begin fasting. He will come for me tomorrow at dawn and we will go to the divining pool. He will bring someone with him who can clear away the smoke. If the Birds are conjuring against us, we will find out about it and answer it."

William nodded and said nothing.

March 1. It seems to me that the hole we have now fallen into is getting deeper. Now we are delving into conjury. Tomorrow morning Otter Queen will go with the Gunsmith to the divining pool. He will bring along a conjurer to get at the cause of her distress. It is a fool's errand, surely. And yet this is the world we are in. Conjury against conjury. What else can help us? I find myself unwilling to relinquish hope. I will go with them.

William and Otter Queen were up and dressed before dawn. They built up the fire and as it burned down to coals they waited in silence. Presently the Gunsmith tapped against the side of the house and came inside, followed by an old man whom William had often seen in the town yard. The old man wore a turban of white cloth wrapped around his head, and about his body he wore an old-fashioned deerskin matchcoat painted with odd designs. For a walking stick he carried a long staff made of white wood. The Gunsmith introduced him as Old Fox of the Wild Potato clan and explained that people trusted him to discover hidden causes. He was so old, the Gunsmith noted, that he was above all the strife amongst the clans. He could look at things impartially.

William looked on as the old man walked over and touched his fingers to Otter Queen's temples. Then he touched her wrists. Next he began to question her. The Gunsmith explained that he was asking her whether she had eaten any unclean foods or broken any of the many rules and avoidances that life required of her. She said that she had not. William thought of the slap she had given the old woman, but then he noted to himself that she was already falling ill before that happened.

Next Old Fox drew Otter Queen close to the fire, and they both stood gazing into it. The Gunsmith motioned to William to step outside. They were not allowed to watch what would happen next. From inside the house they could hear Old Fox intoning an incantation, his voice rising and falling with evident feeling. The Gunsmith explained quietly that the old man was imploring first the fire in the hearth, then the river, and then the sun to raise Otter Queen up, step by step, to the seventh level of heaven and restore her to health.

"Does he not have any gods to pray to?" asked William. "We need help, but he is only asking it of dead things."

"Dead things?" The Gunsmith looked at him quizzically. "Fire is living. So is River, and Sun know better than we how to live. When we join our lives to theirs, they help us live in health." He shook his head, finding the ignorance of white men hard to believe.

The incantation ended and Old Fox and Otter Queen came outside. Old Fox led the way out of the yard, with Otter Queen following close behind. William and the Gunsmith brought up the rear, keeping a careful distance. "Now we will go to Long Man and find out what is happening to my sister."

"Where does he live?" asked William.

"Long Man is river," the Gunsmith said.

"And the river is a living being?" asked William.

"Yes, he is Long Man."

"So the river is not a river," said William. "It is not a channel in the earth with water running through it."

"It is channel with water," said the Gunsmith, "and it is also alive. How can you not know this? Have you never heard Long Man talk to you? Has he never healed you? Has he never made you feel better?"

William remembered the advice he had given to Otter Queen only the day before. "Yes," he said, "I have heard the river talk. But to me it is not a living being."

"Then who is talking?" asked the Gunsmith.

William did not have an answer.

"It is Long Man who talks," said the Gunsmith, "and not just in Keowee. Long Man is everywhere. His head is in high country and his body stretches out across all lands. His feet touch against sea. He talks to everyone. If you can listen to him as Old Fox knows how to listen, he will tell you about hidden causes. You will see."

The divining pool was located in a bend of the river upstream from the men's swimming pool. It was shallow, just downstream from a notable shoal. As they approached it in the half-light of early morning, William could hear the murmuring of the water as it coursed over and around the rocks that laced the shoal. Old Fox and Otter Queen stood at the edge of the water, while William and the Gunsmith stood a little behind them and to one side. As they all looked across the water toward the east, they could see the first blush of dawn, the sun just edging up to the horizon. They waited quietly while the sun's rays came creeping down the bank toward the river. At the moment the light reached the water, Old Fox motioned to Otter Queen, and she stepped forward into the river until she was standing ankle deep. Old Fox followed and used his white staff to inscribe a circle in the water around her. As the sun's light illumined the area where he had drawn this circle, he began to intone an incantation, his voice rising and falling with earnestness, his eyes fixed on the area within the imaginary circle.

William watched it too, not knowing what they were looking for. Then a tiny object floated into the circle, and Old Fox reached over and picked it out of the water. William had not been able to make out what it was. Old Fox appeared to be puzzled as he and Otter Queen came back onto the bank and spoke together with the Gunsmith, who had walked over to join them.

This concluded their visit with the Long Man. On their way back to the house the Gunsmith explained to William that Old Fox was sure that Long Man had spoken, but he was unsure about what was said. The object he had picked up was a feather. It was not a wing or tail feather, but a bit of down, and because of this, he did not know the identity of the bird from which it had come. He told Otter Queen that she was to continue fasting, and the next morning they would try again.

"So the river speaks no more clearly to Old Fox than it does to me," said William.

The Gunsmith glanced at William and shook his head hopelessly. "Long Man speaks more clearly to Old Fox than to you. But even for Old Fox, Long Man can be hard to understand."

When they reached Otter Queen's house, Old Fox spoke briefly with her, and then he and the Gunsmith departed. Otter Queen knelt by the hearth and poked up the fire. "He says he does not know whether it is a conjurer or a *tchki:li* that is causing me to feel so bad," she said.

"Is there a difference?"

"There is all the difference in the world." Otter Queen sounded tired, as if she were weary of having to explain things to him. "It is like this," she said, summoning up her patience. "A conjurer works in known ways. He utters black words. He sends evil tobacco smoke your way. He collects a bit of your spittle and conjures it. If he conjures against you, you can hire a different conjurer to work against him. Your conjurer can block the other, and that will cure you. But a *tchki:li* is much more serious. It is not what a *tchki:li* does on the outside that matters—it is what he is inside. I have talked to you about this. Because it is what he is that is hurting you, not what he is doing. You can't very well take measures against him. He is not doing anything that you can block. You have to discover who he is. If you can do that, he will die. But a *tchki:li* is hard to smoke out. He fears nothing more than being discovered, so he hides his true self very well. And if you cannot discover him, you cannot stop him."

William tried to take in what she was saying. He could not quite grasp the full implications of it, but he had heard something in it that he had never understood before but now almost could. He could almost comprehend the reason she was so oppressed by the Birds' relentless accusations against her. It had to do with the fact that they were maligning the very core of her, discrediting her deepest being. Though why she would let this accusation penetrate her to such depths, he still did not understand. What did it matter, in the end, what they said or what they thought? Why wasn't it enough that she knew herself to be innocent? That he knew her to be innocent? That her mothers and brothers and uncles knew her to be innocent?

Then suddenly an idea came to him, a ray of hope, a thread of logic. "The Birds have already said that you are a *tchki:li*," he said hopefully, "and yet you have not died. Doesn't that mean that you are not a *tchki:li*? By their own logic it should mean they are wrong about you."

"No, that is not what it means," Otter Queen said flatly. "It just means they have not yet found their proof."

William shook his head. "Then this is as far as I can go in thinking about this. It defeats my reasoning. From now on I will not try to think about it. I will just go along with whatever you say." He reached out and touched his hand to her cheek. "Are you feeling better? Is Old Fox helping you?"

"I am a little better," she said and smiled at him a little, a faint flicker of the Otter Queen he used to know.

"I have to go to the store now," he said, "but I will try to come home early. Perhaps tomorrow Old Fox can learn more from Long Man." She smiled to hear him talk that way. He kissed her and headed for the door.

As he stepped outside into the full light of morning, he saw something out of the corner of his eye that he had not seen before when it was dark—a small object pinned to the side of the house. He stopped to inspect it. It was a baby bird skewered with a fat lighter splinter that had been pressed through its body and into a crack in the daub.

William pulled the splinter, with the dead bird on it, out of the crack and took it back inside to show to Otter Queen.

"Did Old Fox put this on the house?" he asked, imagining that it might be some kind of magic protection. Perhaps she would want it to stay there.

She took the skewered bird from him and looked at it closely. Then the color went out of her face. She staggered backward and sat down heavily on her bed. Then she threw the bird across the room and began to weep.

William's heart sank. Why had he showed it to her? He was a fool. "It's just a dead bird," he said lamely, unsure what else it was but knowing it must be more.

"It is not just a bird. It is an owl. And not just any owl: it is a *tchki:li*. And it is not just a *tchki:li*, it is a baby *tchki:li*. And it is not just dead, it was stabbed through the heart. Don't you see? The Birds put it on our house. Now they are threatening my baby, too! They are saying they will treat my baby the way they have treated me. My baby, who is not even born, is already a *tchki:li* to them. I cannot go on like this, Willy. I cannot go on."

"It is only talk," he said. "It is mean and vicious, but it is only talk. And how can you be sure it was not put there as a prank by some child who did not know what he was doing?"

"You don't understand anything," she snapped. "Go on to the store and leave me alone."

"Otter Queen . . ."

"Go on! Please!" Tears were streaming down her face.

All morning William tried to keep his mind focused on the hunters who were still coming into the store from the winter's hunt. The Gunsmith came in around noon and stood about for a while, passing the time. William thought of telling him about the dead owl, but decided against it, not knowing what else it might stir up. Both of them were surprised when Otter Queen came walking into the store carrying her digging stick and a small basket. She had cleaned herself up and had dressed her hair with bear oil as neatly as she used to do. She was wearing the earbobs she had bought on the day William first met her. Both he and the Gunsmith broke into smiles. It was as if she were back from a long absence.

"I am not going to mope about any longer," she said. "I am hungry for vegetables. It has been a long winter without them. Last fall I saw a stand of Jerusalem artichokes in an out-of-the-way place, and I doubt that anyone else has found them. I am going to go dig some up for supper."

William could not stop grinning. It seemed that Old Fox and Long Man had done their work on her, despite the incident of the dead bird. "I would love some Jerusalem artichokes," he said, "with lots of bear fat."

"The way you like them," she smiled. She walked over and embraced the Gunsmith. "No sister could have a better brother. Do not worry so much about me. You have helped me feel better." The Gunsmith was clearly relieved, but also a little embarrassed at the display of affection.

"I'll ask Sam if I can get off and go with you," said William. "He's back in his house. Maybe he'll come take my place and let me go."

"No, you have already asked so much of him, Willy. I will be all right. We don't have Bloody Mouth to worry about around here, and I'm not going far." She smiled at him and shook her head. "We have had a time, haven't we, Willy? After you left the house this morning, I thought about the story you told me of Romeo and Juliet. That has been like our story, yours and mine, two lovers playing together like otters and rabbits. Someone should write the Willy and Otter Queen story." She laughed, and it was music to his ears. She embraced him tenderly. "I am going now," she said. She touched his face. Then she turned away and walked out of the store.

"I cannot believe the change," William said to the Gunsmith. "Only this morning I thought that she would never be happy again."

"This is the work of Old Fox," said the Gunsmith, nodding with satisfaction.

William turned back to the business of the store, and as the day went on, he would stop now and then and let Otter Queen's laughter rise again in his memory. But after a time it became harder to bring it back, and eventually he could not remember it at all. And then he began to wonder about some things. Why had she talked to him about their lovemaking? Why had she embraced her brother that way? It had all felt good when it was happening, but now it was beginning to make him feel uneasy.

Just before it was time to close the store, a wail went up from the Wolf side of the town yard. "That is my mother!" said the Gunsmith from the bench outside the store, and he took out running across the town yard. William, leaden with dread, ran after him. They headed toward Pretty Baskets's house but then stopped short when they saw that it was at Otter Queen's house where people were gathering.

They wheeled and ran toward the crowd, William's heart pounding as they plunged through it and ducked inside the house. Pretty Baskets was there, as were several of Otter Queen's sisters. The younger women were weeping and tearing at their hair. Otter Queen lay on her bed and William hurried to her. She was wet, her clothing drenched. She was not breathing. It was her own sweat and saliva that soaked her.

William gasped for air, but he could not get enough into his lungs. His legs felt wobbly, and he thought he might fall. Was she dead? He knew she was. How could that be?

"Who has done this to you, Otter Queen?" William sank down to sit on the bed beside her. The bedclothes were drenched.

"She did it to herself," Pretty Baskets said grimly. "This was found beside her on the bed." She held out what looked like a half-eaten parsnip, wrapped in a small piece of deerskin. William leaned forward and sniffed it. It smelled somewhat like a turnip—something he had smelled before.

"What is it?" he asked, reaching for it. Pretty Basket pulled it back.

"It is *kanesála*—water hemlock—the same plant that killed Little Wren. Except this is the root. If you touch it, you will have to wash your fingers before you put them in your mouth."

Jim-Bird came into the house and stood for a moment beside the bed. He put his hand on William's shoulder. "I am so sorry to see this," he said grimly. "This is very hard." He stood silent for another long moment. Then he said, "The Wolves will want to claim her now and prepare her body for burial. You will have to leave. We will take your things back to Sam's winter house."

The new reality began to sink in on William. Otter Queen was gone. She was no longer his. And this was not in his house. Their life together was sinking into a morass, and the water was closing over it. Tears streaming, he leaned over and kissed Otter Queen's forehead. Then he and Jim-Bird gathered up his belongings and carried them away to Sam's winter house.

March 3. The light has gone out of my days. My Otter Queen has taken her life. Why did she do it? How can I begin to answer this question? She left me in an instant, and completely. Even her dead body was taken from me by the Wolves.

Do Witches Exist?

The Wolves buried Otter Queen's body beneath the bed she and William had shared in her house, just as she had once told him it was their custom to do. But though she was dead and buried, the matter of her death was not at an end. The town swirled with the question of why she had killed herself and her unborn child. Had she done it by her own will or had something or someone driven her to it? A few days after her death, the Gunsmith and Old Fox came into the store to talk with William, asking him to come outside and speak privately. The Gunsmith explained that Old Fox thought there was something hidden in the whole affair and that everyone was missing it. He wanted to know what William had concluded about Otter Queen's death.

"I have thought of nothing else day or night," said William. "I do not fully understand it, but I will tell you what I am thinking. Ever since Otter Queen was a young girl the Birds have accused her of being a *tchki:li*. I think it had gone on for so long that at times she feared it might be true. Then when someone impaled a baby owl with a fat lighter splinter and pinned it to the side of our house, she took that to mean that the accusation would also fall on her unborn child. I believe that was the final blow. That was what killed her. When she saw that her child would suffer her same fate, she could not bear to go on any longer."

The Gunsmith explained all this to Old Fox, who responded at length. The Gunsmith translated to William. "Old Fox says Otter Queen proved by killing herself that she was no *tchki:li*. Above all, *tchki:li* hates to die. This is why *tchki:li* steals livers of others—to prolong his own life. *Tchki:li* takes lives of others, but never his own."

Old Fox stepped closer to William to make sure he had his undivided attention. The Gunsmith translated. "Otter Queen proved she was no *tchki:li*," said

Old Fox, "but I fear a powerful *tchki:li* does dwell in Keowee. I have talked to King Crow. At sunset we gather in town house to discuss it. Will you come?"

"Yes, of course," William said, though he did not feel easy about the prospect. Did this mean that someone else would now have to suffer the false accusations that Otter Queen had to endure?

At the appointed time, the clans of Keowee assembled in the town house. King Crow was wearing the white deerskin matchcoat that he wore on occasions like this. The townhouse was illumined by a small bright fire in the central hearth.

"Two lives have been taken from us," King Crow said to the gathering. "Two lives: Otter Queen and her unborn child. We know that Otter Queen died by her own hand. She ate the same poison that killed Little Wren. But why did she choose death in this way? What did she mean to say to us by dying as Little Wren died? This question has been raised before us today by Old Fox. He believes that by taking her own life, Otter Queen meant to prove to us that she was no *tchki:li*. And she succeeded in proving that. But that is not the end of the story. Old Fox believes that there is a *tchki:li* among us—one none of us has suspected, not even Otter Queen. Listen now to what Old Fox has to say."

Old Fox hobbled to the fire with his white staff. He looked about at the people, who had fallen utterly silent. Jim-Bird translated quietly for William.

"On the day she died, I went to water with Otter Queen," said Old Fox. "Before we went to the divining pool, we divined in her house with fire. I heaped up the coals in her hearth and sprinkled them with old tobacco. A small spark popped on the coals, showing that something bad was on the far side of the town yard. The Deer, Wild Potato, and Bird clans are on that side. It was not a large spark, and I thought little of it. Then when we went to water, a feather floated into Otter Queen's circle. It was a down feather, and I could not tell from what bird it had come. Yesterday I showed this feather to King Crow, who knows birds better than I do." There was some small, nervous laughter in the assembly. "He thinks it may be a down feather from a hawk. But let us see what the fire says to us today."

Old Fox raked up the coals in the fireplace into a sizeable mound, which he then sprinkled with finely ground tobacco. Instantly there was a loud pop and a flash of bright light right at the top of the mound. Some of people nearby flinched. A murmur went through the crowd.

"You all know what this means," Old Fox said. "You saw it with your own eyes. A *tchki:li* is here among us in this town house." People shifted in their seats, looking about the room.

"We have the feather, and we have a spark that grows brighter each time we consult the fire. Could it be that the *tchki:li* is a Bird? Could the *tchki:li* be hiding among the very ones who were Otter Queen's accusers?"

"That cannot be true," said a man of the Bird clan. "We would know of it."

"Would you?" asked Old Fox. "A *tchki:li* is hard to find. But I have brought something with me today to help us see clearly. It comes from the forehead of an *uktena*. I seldom bring it out but while it is resting I keep it well fed with deers' blood."

As Old Fox reached into a pouch that hung from his belt, William expected to see him pull out a horn of some sort. But the object he brought out was so small that at first William could not see what it was. Old Fox walked around the room, holding it out in the palm of his hand so that everyone could see it. But even when he got a good look at it, William could not recognize it. Jim-Bird explained that it was a crystal, partially sheathed in deerskin. Old Fox returned to the hearth and held his hand close to the fire, the crystal in his fingers illuminated by the flames. As William watched, the crystal actually seemed to move of its own accord.

"My *ulunsuti* is awake. He smells something." The old man looked closely into the crystal. "I see a form. A streak of blood. No—it fades, it fades. Now it is a hawk. It flaps its wings slowly—an old hawk. No, it spins, it spins. The hawk has changed. It is an owl—a *tchki:li*. No—it turns, it turns. Now it is something else again—an old woman."

All eyes in the room had moved to Hawk's Mother. She looked about frantically. "Why are you looking at me? Do you believe him? He is an addled old man! This is nonsense! He is making this up!"

William stood up, and Jim-Bird, looking surprised, stood up beside him to translate. "I have something to say," said William.

"Listen now," said King Crow. "The husband of Otter Queen has something to say."

Hawk's Mother folded her arms and looked away, still showing her disdain for Otter Queen even after her death.

"On the day Otter Queen died," said William, "she was frightened and distressed by a baby horned owl that was pierced by a splinter and stuck to the outside of our house. Does this tell us anything? Where would someone get a baby owl? Does anyone here know where there is an owl's nest? Otter Queen once told me that there are eyes and ears everywhere in Keowee, even in the woods."

A long uncomfortable silence ensued. Old Fox and King Crow remained still. They waited. Then a young man of the Deer clan stood up, hardly more than a boy. "I know where there is an owl's nest," he said. "Not long ago several of us were out in the woods near dusk and we happened to see a horned owl sitting on the top of a hollow tree. It dropped down inside when it saw us, but we climbed up and the owl flew out. Inside we found a nest with three baby owls. We took them out and threw them to the ground to kill them. We didn't want them to grow up to be witches. But when we came down from the tree, Hawk's Mother was there and she scolded us. We were deep in the woods, and we were surprised to see her so far from the town. But even so, we thought she would be pleased with what we had done. Instead she was very angry. She said that to kill such birds was to invite bad fortune. And she told us to leave the woods and go home. We did as we were told. That is all I know."

"We have only to ask the right questions," said William. "Nothing happens in Keowee that someone doesn't know. Perhaps we are learning the truth here. This has reminded me that on the day Otter Queen died, she told me that she met Hawk's Mother on the path to the river, and Hawk's Mother asked Otter Queen if she had a baby *tchki:li* in her belly. What kind of question is that for a clan matron to ask of a young woman of her own town? Now let us see what more we can learn. Was anyone seen near Otter Queen's house during the night before she died? Someone came there and left the baby owl pinned to the wall. We know that nothing happens in Keowee without somebody seeing it."

Sam Long stood up. "I hate to say it," he said, "but I was in the trading house early that morning, in the very earliest, faintest light. I saw Hawk's Mother crossing the town yard, trying to catch up with that old dog of hers. I didn't pay it much attention, but I have to say that she was on the Wolf side of the yard."

"This means nothing, Sanee," the old woman spat. She fairly hissed the words with a viciousness that must have been like what Otter Queen had heard on the trail in the woods that day. "I am always chasing after that crazy dog." Her tone was frantic, rising almost to a scream. "Don't any of you listen to them! These are lies!" She looked around at the Birds for support, but none was forthcoming. Her own people were moving away from her. The case was made. The *tchki:li* had been discovered. King Crow and Old Fox stood up and walked out, and everyone else followed, leaving Hawk's Mother standing alone, still sputtering, but weakened and dazed.

In the days that followed, Hawk's Mother was shunned by her own clan as well as by the other clans of Keowee. Her fate was sealed, and no one took mercy upon her. She closed herself in her house and stopped eating. It did not take long for death to come. And even then her clansmen refused to give her a proper burial.

March 15. Hawk's Mother is dead. In a single day she fell from being the most admired clan mother in Keowee to the most despised, just like the Goodwife of Glen Gyle. The Book Maggots used to debate whether the Red Indians of America have natures as simple and transparent as those of the creatures of the American woods. The answer has come in on that particular question. The Red Indians of America are human beings through and through, as capable of concealed motives and duplicity as any Scotsman in Glasgow.

They say Hawk's Mother was a witch, and they would not even bury her when she died. Her own family took her body deep into the woods and left it there to be devoured by wolves and vultures. I am ashamed to say that I was not sorry to see her treated so. I cannot forget that her unrelenting cruelty drove my wife to her death.

Otter Queen's death remained a bad dream from which William could not awaken. Each day he got up and tried to get back to work, but often Sam would send him away by midmorning, worried that William's distracted state was costing him money. "Take some time to get things sorted out inside yourself," Sam told him.

William took long walks in the woods, watching the earth as it turned towards spring. The tree buds were swelling and beginning to show color here and there, like swatches of pale lace. He searched for his Otter Queen there and everywhere, knowing he would not see her in any of the places where he looked. At night he would wake up and reach for her, as if she were still beside him. He had the strongest feeling that a part of his corporeal existence was missing, amputated. And he missed her keen understanding of things, of the country and its resources, its seasons, the twists and turns of its mountains and valleys, its rivers, creeks, and rivulets. He missed her knowledge of the birds and the creatures of the forest and streams, and he missed the countless stories she could tell about them. He missed her knowledge of Cherokee philosophy. He missed her wry and sometimes bawdy sense of humor. He missed her beauty, and most of all he missed her grace.

And why had she left him while she was still such an impenetrable mystery to him? He would never understand Otter Queen. How could it be that she was so transparent and easy to understand in some ways, and so opaque, enigmatic, and even beyond reason in others? Why had she taken such an extreme and ir-revocable solution to her dilemma?

How could he ever sort this out? Could his philosophy stand on its own two legs in Keowee? Could he reconcile what he had found here with what he hoped for the enlightenment of mankind? Would reason ever make its way into this dark corner of the world? Or was reason here already? Did another kind of reason exist that did not depend on the strength of empirical knowledge, or on the force of argument and logic? None of the reason that he himself champi-oned was able to have the least effect on the Birds' insistence that Otter Queen was the worst kind of witch. But using their own reason she had driven her ar-gument home.

March 20. It comes down to this: Would Francis Hutcheson and all the philosophers in Glasgow be able to help me understand what I have seen with my own eyes in Keowee? Not only do I doubt my understanding of what I have witnessed, I doubt its very substance. And yet not only did I witness—I participated. I stood before their assembly and asked questions about dead baby owls and helped them uncover a witch. Were Shakespeare yet alive, he could write me a part in Macbeth.

In recent memory, witches have been hanged in Scotland with Pres-byterian clergymen presiding at the gallows. But just last year Scotland abolished the death penalty for witchcraft. The law exonerates the people who carried out past executions, but are these same people now exoner-ated by God? Am I?

For some time, enlightened people in Europe have denied that witches exist or have ever existed. Yet ignorant people in Scotland to this day are still persuaded that witches do exist. Witches, they say, are people who have joined league with the Devil.

The Cherokees do not believe this. The Devil is of no account to them, for they are not Christians and have no place in their pantheon for the Devil. And yet they too believe that witches exist.

I, William MacGregor, do not believe in the existence of witches of any sort, whether they be the progeny of the Devil or of some other dark source. Witches are figments of our imaginations, terrors of our minds. Though I helped to expose her, I cannot believe that Hawk's Mother was a witch. But I do believe that she bore an unnatural, baseless, and per-nicious hatred for Otter Queen, and that she poisoned the thinking of many of the people in Keowee against my darling wife.

I have also seen that in the wake of Hawk's Mother's death, the Birds and the Wolves have begun to reconcile. They no longer insult and shun each other when they come into the trading house. Otter Queen once said that the true moral of the story of Romeo and Juliet was that their suicides reconciled the Capulets and Montagues. The thought that most clouds my mind in the dark of night is that I am the one who told her that story, which she interpreted in her own way, and that this may have played a role in her decision to take her own life. She even said, on the day she was going to her death, that our own story was like that of Romeo and Juliet. These dark clouds will not soon lift from my mind. But even in this gloom, there is a bit of light. I take some consolation that in her death she did succeed in bringing to her family the peace she so greatly desired.

I have found that it is no simple matter to enter into another way of life with understanding. One cannot simply jettison one's own philosophy and take up another, nor cling to one's own and reject the other. The only course is to hold onto one's own beliefs, but keep them in abeyance, while grasping the beliefs of that other way of life in their own terms. There is little comfort to be had in such a predicament, but I can never go back to the simpler world I once knew.

23   Just Sing

In late March the weather began to warm. The nights were still cool, but during the day Sam's crew seldom wore their hunting coats over their linen shirts. The water in the river was too cold for swimming, but the men could tolerate it for quick baths to wash off the grime of winter. As work in the store turned toward packing for the spring journey to Charles Town, William's spirits began to rally. He was ready to put some distance between himself and Keowee, though for how long he did not know.

In bringing the season to a close, the first task of the traders was to go to the storehouse and shake out all the skins. They untied every bundle and inspected each hide for fly-deposited weevils, and then, for good measure, they beat each hide vigorously. They repacked the skins into equally weighted bundles. As they moved the bundles around, Wesa, the cat, was on high alert for the occasional mouse that lost its safe haven and went scurrying to find another.

William was in the middle of this job of shaking out and repacking skins when Five-Killer came into the storehouse one day and entered into earnest conversation with Sam. William paid little attention until he heard Sam say, "I'm staying out of this. It's between you and William."

William motioned to Jim-Bird to come with him to translate, and they walked over to where Sam and Five-Killer were standing.

Sam said to William, "Five-Killer here says he gets credit for Otter Queen's skins."

"I am her mother's brother," said Five-Killer. "They are mine."

"Otter Queen told me to put her skins with mine in Sam's book," William replied. "I helped kill and skin every one of those deer."

"Otter Queen is gone now," said Five-Killer. "She cannot collect on her skins. They are Wolf skins, not yours. You are only the husband."

William's anger rose, but it was not a hot anger. He felt strong and clear, and he knew where he stood. He stood on the freezing days in the woods with Jim-Bird, on the lying for hours against the cold ground, barely breathing, waiting, waiting for the deer. He stood on the confrontation with Bloody Mouth, on his endurance of the loss of his beloved Otter Queen. Five-Killer was nothing to him compared to any of that. "The skins are mine," he said. "I was her husband, yes, but I was not a Cherokee husband. I was a Scottish husband—a Carolina husband—and the skins were ours together. Now they are mine."

As Jim-Bird translated, Five-Killer looked at William cooly, measuring the resolve he had heard in his voice. He nodded ever so slightly, giving way. "I loaned you two deer decoys," he said.

"Jim-Bird and I killed six deer with those decoys," said William. "For that I will give you three skins."

"I want all six," said Five-Killer.

"Nothing doing," said William. "Jim-Bird shot all six of them; I was only a driver." He looked at Sam and said, "Transfer three of my skins to Five-Killer's account."

"I will take the three skins," said Five-Killer, "but I will not forget about the rest." And then he turned and walked out of the store.

William shook his head. "So now I'm on the outs with the Wolves."

"Welcome to Keowee," said Sam.

"It never ends," added Jim-Bird.

"Five-Killer can't afford to fall out very far with you," said Sam. "You're a trader, and that puts him at a disadvantage. But don't expect any favors from him in the future."

When everything in the store was packed and ready to go, they went out to the horse-pen to prepare the packing gear. Thomas had repaired the pack-saddles through the course of the winter, and he had crafted five new ones. There was not much left for the men to do. They examined all of the rope rigging and cut and spliced where necessary. William said nothing as he spliced the cut rope he still had in his packsaddle from the summer before. Now it was so much water under the bridge.

They got their horses together and saddled them for a little while to get them used to being rigged out again. Most of the horses had spent the winter without being saddled even once. When they were finished with all of this, there was nothing more to do but wait for John Coleman to come in from Tugalo.

They spent two days sitting idly beneath the corncrib. During this time

King Crow and some of the other Cherokee men came to the crib, joining them for periods of conversation. At one point the talk turned to the trouble between the Birds and the Wolves. "It clears," said King Crow, "like mud settles to bottom of a pool. It pained me, pained me and all the Birds, but Otter Queen and Old Fox unmasked the true *tshki:li*. All the clans agree."

Sam nodded. "Every one of the Birds are saying it now. They admit it must have been Hawk's Mother all along. They are remembering how she treated her sister. Funny how that had fallen right out of their memories. Now they are saying there was bitter jealousy between them."

"What does that have to do with it?" asked Thomas.

"It was when Hawk's Mother's clan sister died that she accused Otter Queen's grandmother of eating her sister's liver," Sam said. "Now they are saying it was Hawk's Mother who was the liver-eater."

"She killed her own sister?" asked Thomas.

Sam shrugged. "What does it mean to say that she ate her sister's liver? I can't answer that question."

The sun was near to setting when Jim-Bird shushed them and cocked his ear. They all listened and heard the faint sound of a lilting tune played on a recorder. Getting up, they walked around to the front of the store and saw John Coleman coming alongside the town yard with a short packtrain loaded with deerskins.

"It's about time, you laggard!" Thomas called loudly.

John waved his recorder at them and then stuck it in the sheath hanging from his belt. They watched as he closed the distance to the trading house. "I'm so glad to see you darlings I could kiss every one of you," he said as he slid off his horse. Then he looked at Thomas and laughed. "Though I might make an exception of you. What in God's name happened to your nose?"

Thomas had an ugly red scar across his nose. It still had stitches in it.

"I got tangled up with a man's wife," said Thomas, reaching up to feel the wound.

"She did that to you?"

"Not her," laughed Thomas. "It was that husband of hers. He was tougher and a damn sight meaner than me. There weren't hardly any stopping him. I tried to explain that I had no mind to keep her, I just wanted to borrow her for the afternoon. But it didn't do no good. That's when he jumped me with his knife and tried to relieve me of my nose. Before it was over, I had to give him my best horse to calm him down."

John clapped Thomas merrily on the shoulder. "You're lucky to still have a nose on your face." Then he looked at William and sobered. He walked over and held out a hand, taking the hand William offered into both of his own and shaking it slowly. Then he did the same to Sam. "I was sorry to hear about your losses," he said. "It's a cruel world." They both nodded wordlessly, and everyone shifted around uncomfortably.

Then Sam clapped his hands together. "All right, you crackers, let's give John a hand unloading these horses."

They all went to work helping John carry his skins into the storehouse, which was already so full of bundles it was difficult to walk from one end to the other. When they had finished unpacking, they returned to the corncrib, where Rose had set out some food for them. After eating, Sam brought out a bottle of rum.

"So, we're heading out tomorrow," he said, lifting the bottle in a toast. He took a long pull from the bottle and handed it off to William to start it around. "This has been a God-awful year. I lost Little Wren, William lost Otter Queen, John lost several friends at Tugalo, and Thomas came close to losing his nose. But as bad as it was, I'll have to thank the good Lord that at least we made some money this year. We're going back with more than we came with. Even William made a little, once you add in what he got for Bloody Mouth's musket."

"That calls for a tune," said John, reaching for his fiddle case. He took out the fiddle and tuned it and played a gay jig. Thomas and Jim-Bird got to their feet and danced a little. They tried to get William to join them, but he shook his head, feeling no heart for it.

When John set down his fiddle, Sam asked him about Tugalo, and John re-told the grim tale of that dying town. "The best thing that happened all season," said John, "were the two visits we got from Jim-Bird and William." He looked over at William. "That Otter Queen was a rare jewel, William. She lit up the place on that first visit." William nodded, smiling a little. John shook his head sadly. "But there was a cloud covering her on that second visit. Even I could see it. There just seemed to be tragedy hanging all around her."

He picked up his fiddle again. "I've been practicing a song to sing for you, William. It came to my mind the minute I heard the news. I don't want to make you all too sad here, but this is a fine old song. It goes with times like this. If you don't mind."

John played a few bars and William recognized "Fair Margaret and Sweet William." He nodded his approval. John played the tune through and then dropped the fiddle from under his chin to sing. "Listen close," he said, "and you'll hear how love, once it blooms, is stronger than death."

"Just sing," said Thomas.

And John sang out in that high, tragic voice of his.

Fair Margaret at her bedroom window,
A-combing down her long, yellow hair,
She saw Sweet William and his new bride,
Unto the church repair.

Down she cast her iv'ry comb,
And up she tossed her hair,
She went out from her bedroom alive,
But never more so to come there.

William listened to the song's long, tangled story. Though Sweet William had a new bride, the woman he truly loved was Fair Margaret. Their love had been thwarted, and Sweet William did not know that she also loved him. When Fair Margaret learned that Sweet William had married another, she was so distraught she killed herself. The news of her death did not reach Sweet William, but on that very night he dreamed that she stood at the foot of his bed, and he confessed his love to her, though in his dream his bride-bed was full of blood. The next day, with a sense of dread, he rode to her house and asked for her. William looked out into the night as John sang the fateful words.

He called up his serving men all,
By one, by two, by three,
'We will go to Fair Margaret's hall,
With the leave of my wedded lady.'

When he came to Fair Margaret's hall,
He knocked at the ring,
And who were so ready as her brethren,
To rise and let him in.

'Oh is she in the parlor,' he said,
'Or is she in the hall?
Or is she in the long chamber,
Amongst her many maids all?'

'She's not in the parlor,' they said,
'Nor is she in the hall;
'But she is in the long chamber,
'Laid out against the wall.'

'Open the winding sheet,' he cried,
'That I may kiss the dead;
'That I may kiss her pale and wan,
Whose lips used to be so red.'

Fair Margaret died yesterday,
Sweet William died on the morrow;
Fair Margaret died for pure, pure love,
Sweet William died for sorrow.

Fair Margaret was buried in the old churchyard,
Sweet William lay close beside her,
And out of her grave sprang a red, red rose,
And out of his a brier.

Rose and brier twined up the old church roof,
Until they couldn't twine no higher;
They looped and tied in a true lovers' knot
The red rose round the briar.

When John finished the song the men remained silent. William's eyes had filled with tears, and he wiped them quickly with his sleeve.

"Ah, William," said John. "Tears ain't nothing to be ashamed of. We all know what you're a-feeling."

"Well," said William, "I *have* heard a song darker than that one. Back in Glasgow, when my Aunt Callie would grow melancholy thinking about her dead husband, she would sing "In the Dark Dismal Dungeon of Despair.""

John smiled, and Sam reached for the bottle of rum. "One more round to help us sleep. Then off to bed. We take the trail at first light,"

William left without the last drink. By the light of the fire in the winter house he finished packing his gear. The one memento he had of Otter Queen was the small, black-and-red, double-wove hamper that she had fashioned so proudly. Pretty Baskets had brought it to the store after William's falling out with Five Killer. She handed it to him without a word and then turned around and went out again. Inside it he found Otter Queen's earbobs. Now he packed his two little Shakespeare volumes into the hamper, along with his journal and pen and ink. Then he put it into his bag with his clothing and gear.

Early the next morning, Thomas, John, and William brought the train of packhorses to the storehouse and went to work carrying out the bundles and rigging them onto the packsaddles. This time around, William packed as neatly and as quickly as the others.

The sun was well up by the time they were ready to set out. Tazzie and Binkie knew what was in the offing and were running around, now and then springing up in front of Jim-Bird with their front legs outstretched, bouncing off of him. A third terrier was coming with them on this trip, too little yet to keep up with his elders, though he tried. Jim-Bird had given William one of Binkie's puppies. White with brown and black markings on his head, he had a large black spot in the center of his back and a cropped tail. The other puppies had gone to people in Keowee, who were anxious to have them because they were sired by the famous dog who changed a Creek marauder's name from "Bloody Mouth" to "Bloody Balls." William scooped up his new charge and put him into one of his saddle bags, strapping it shut to keep him in. The puppy yelped and complained.

"Are we ready to go to Charles Town?" shouted Sam.

"More than ready," shouted John.

Sam yelled at the top of his lungs and cracked his whip, and the horses set in motion, heading down to the ford across the Keowee River.

Tazzie and Binkie swam across the river. In the saddlebag the puppy was still crying. Once on the other side, William took him out and put him on the ground, where he ran along after Binkie. Only when he began to tire and lag behind did William retrieve him and put him back into the saddle bag. This time the puppy settled down to take a nap, though he kept his little black nose sticking out of the bag to sniff the new smells along the way. Every now and then William reached back to pat the saddlebag, making sure its small passenger was still in it. He did not intend to keep the pup—his life was too unsettled to take him on—but he had a new owner in mind for him.

The packhorsemen made good time, stopping at the same campgrounds they had visited on their journey into the country. They crossed the mile-marker creeks in the high hills that led away from Keowee and pressed on hard and camped for the night at Three-and-Twenty-Mile Creek. Then they crossed the upper courses of the creeks leading down to the Savannah River and camped the second night at Barber's Creek. Then came the headwaters of the creeks and rivers emptying into the Saluda River: Coronaca, Buffalo Swamp, Western Branch Saluda River, and then the mile-marker creeks leading to Congaree. William stopped noting the camp sites. Just before reaching Congaree, they crossed the fall line, where the piedmont hills gave way to the upper coastal plain. At Congaree they saw that more people had moved in than had been there the previous summer. Some were immigrants from Europe, and others had come down from the colonies to the north. The Carolina backcountry was beginning to fill up.

Beyond Congaree they traversed the sandy hills and piney woods and crossed the headwaters of creeks emptying into the Congaree River. They camped at Beaver Creek and then at Captain Russell's, where they relished the good hospitality of his wife even more than they had when coming from Charles Town. The next day they set out early, determined to make it all the way to MacDonald's cowpen.

Laying eyes on that cowpen was the most comforting thing that William had experienced in months. The little cluster of house, barn, and outbuildings was just as he remembered from that July day when they had ridden away with all the MacDonalds waving good-bye. He wondered how it would be to see Rosemary again. After all that had happened to him, he was surprised to find himself feeling unexpectedly uneasy, as if he had somehow been unfaithful to her. He almost hoped she had been taken up by another man, just to save him from the prospect of conflicted feelings.

As they pulled up and halted the horses, John MacDonald came out to greet them. The men got down and stretched their legs. Sam and John exchanged pleasantries for a while, but they let the serious gossip wait until dinner.

The packhorsemen cooled down the exhausted horses and stored their packs in the barn. As they headed for the house, William excused himself, saying that he would rejoin them directly. Then he turned away and made for the cowpen.

As he neared the pen, he saw the milkmaids at work. Rosemary sat on a milking stool with her head resting against the cow's flank, concentrating on squirting the milk into a wooden bucket and taking care that the cow not kick it over. William slipped into the pen and came up behind her.

She started when he called her name and turning her head she wiped a lock of flame-golden hair from her green eyes. "Why, William MacGregor, I never expected to see you."

"I'm back," he said. "Go ahead with your milking. I have something for ye when ye finish."

She looked at his hands but saw nothing there.

"I'll wait," he said and leaned against the fence.

She finished the cow and then picked up the pail and came over to where he stood.

"Set it down," he said, "and I'll show ye."

As she put down the pail, he reached into the bosom of his hunting shirt and pulled out the squirming puppy, who fairly leapt out of his hands, eager to get down to explore the cow-pen with its strange new smells. Once on the ground he ran over to Rosemary, who picked him up.

"What a sweet little feist," she said. The puppy nipped at her fingers. "Och, he has the sharpest little teeth."

"You can train him out of that nipping after a while," said William. "Once grown, he will keep your cow-pen clear of snakes and rats and most any other pest smaller than a bear."

"Are you giving him to me? Why, William, he is pretty as can be. Does he have a name?"

"Not yet. He's yours to name."

She looked at her nipped finger. "I think I will call him Butcher Bob, after my uncle Bob, who's a butcher in Charles Town."

William laughed. "That's too long a name for a dog. You will want something shorter, handier."

"But that is his name. I might call him Bob or Butch for short. I don't know yet. But I love him, and I thank you for giving him to me." She looked up at William and smiled, and he remembered again how that tilt of her head had once made him feel. Like it or not, he was starting to feel it again.

As they walked back to the creamery, William carried the bucket of milk and Rosemary carried the puppy.

"I'll feed him a saucer of cow's milk," she said.

"He's only drunk milk from his mother till now," said William.

"Then he needs to get used to the saucer. After you leave, he's not going to have his mama to tug on."

William stood with Rosemary and watched and laughed as Butcher Bob became acquainted with a saucer of milk. First the puppy stepped his foot into it, and then he breathed it in and sneezed it out, and finally he tried lapping it and found the new pleasure.

"He'll do fine," said Rosemary. With the evening milking over, she began tidying up the creamery. "You go on up and get your supper," she said. "I'll be up directly."

William left her and returned to the house, where the men were taking their places around the dining table. As they ate, John MacDonald caught them up on the news from the low country. The greatest object of gossip in Amelia Township was Christian Gottlieb Priber, who had migrated from Saxony but had failed to find the Congaree River a fruitful place for his learning and philosophical ambitions. He talked to anyone who would hear him about how a Christian utopia might be founded. He was beginning to talk of going among the Cherokees to try his experiment at creating a human paradise.

"Good luck to him with that," William said skeptically.

Their talk turned to their season at Keowee. "It was a decent year as far as the trade went," said Sam. "The deer are scarce as can be around Keowee, but the hunting is still right strong in the Broad River country. William and Jim-Bird can tell you more about that. They did some hunting there."

"Even there the hunt gave out a little sooner than we had hoped," said Jim-Bird. "But there was enough for us to come out ahead at the end of the season."

Nothing was said about the human losses they had suffered during the past year. This was not the time to revisit their grief nor to impose it upon their hosts. The night began to fill with stories and songs. Rosemary and her sister Betsy came in and joined them, and they were still going strong when William took his leave and went out to sleep in the hayloft of the barn. He was getting better at being light-hearted, but he still could not keep it up for long.

Through the veil of sleep, William sensed that something was crawling on his face. He brushed his hand across it but felt nothing. A minute or so later he felt it again, and he opened his eyes to see a human form leaning over him in the darkness, and a hand passing over his head. He reached up and grabbed the wrist and found it small and dainty. He felt the hand and found the fingers clutching a straw.

"It's Rosemary," she whispered. "I'm out to tend to a sick calf. Do you want to come with me and see Butcher Bob? You'll be leaving out with the light and you'll not get to see him again."

It felt good to be talking to a woman in the dark. He remembered what Otter Queen had said about Juliet, that she was foolish to end her life just because she thought that Romeo was dead. New lovers were easy to come by, Otter Queen had said. While William still could not agree with that, he could nonetheless feel within him a newly rising sense that she was not altogether wrong. But he was not yet ready for new love.

"I think I had better get my last hour of sleep," he said. "We have a long day ahead." He still held Rosemary's hand and he put it to his face for a moment. Her fingers stroked him ever so slightly. Then he released it and she slowly pulled it away.

"Just you remember that you are always welcome in our house," Rosemary said. "And remember that you have someone here who cares about you. His name is Bob, or Butch, or whatever. And he's not the only one." She slipped something into his hand, a band of some kind made of leather.

"What is this?" he asked.

"Something to remember me by." She leaned over and kissed him on the forehead, and then she quickly moved away and disappeared down the ladder, going off to her morning chores.

William was not able to sleep that last hour, though he tried mightily, tossing and turning until the first light of dawn. When he got up, it was still too dark in the barn to make out what the keepsake was, but outside he saw that it was a hatband, plaited out of cowhide, with a slip knot cleverly fashioned in the form of a heart. He slipped it around his hat and tightened it.

When they departed that morning, John MacDonald was there to see them off. Rosemary was still in the dairy. MacDonald came over to William as he was about to mount his horse. "I'm telling you this, William MacGregor, if ever you want to give up the life of a packhorseman and take up the life of a cow hunter, we will always have work for you here. I would not say that to anyone, but I'm saying it to you. And I am remembering your father as I speak. I hope there is a way I am standing in for him. He never knew you, but I almost feel that I am looking at you through his eyes. So there's a place for you here, and don't you forget it."

William felt tears welling up, which embarrassed him. His heart was too tender these days. He shook MacDonald's hand gratefully. "Thank you, sir. I will remember it."

As they rode away, William looked back and saw John MacDonald and some of his family standing in front of their house—Rosemary was not among them. He turned away, trying not to feel disappointed. Then he looked back again, and this time he saw her standing behind the house, off to one side, out of sight of the others. In one hand she held up a squirming Butcher Bob, and with her other hand she blew William a kiss. He waved to her in return.

They pushed on to Eutaw Springs and Nelson's plantation. The following day they stretched their travel out and reached James Kinloch's plantation just as the sun was setting. The next day it rained, and they sat it out at Kinloch's. After another day's travel they reached Goose Creek and their old camping place at Izard's. They were almost back to Charles Town.

Their supper that night used up most of what remained of their rations. As they sat around the fire, feeling light in spirit, John played a few notes on his recorder. "Here's a song about a famous philosopher," he said. "A fellow by the name of Tom o' Lynn."

William smiled. He had heard a version of this song back in Scotland.

Tom o' Lynn was in Scotland born,
His head was bald, his beard forlorn,
His cap was made of a jackass skin.

John paused, looked playfully at William and in a gruff voice he said, more than sang, the last line of the stanza:

I'm bull and alligator, says Tom o' Lynn.

William laughed heartily. John sang his way into the remaining verses, making each of the last lines more speech than song.

The weather got cold and Tom needed a coat,
He borrowed the skin from a neighbors's goat,
The horns on his forehead he set with a grin,
'I wish they was mine,' says Tom o' Lynn.

Tom went up to the rich man's hall,
Went hipping and skipping amongst them all.
They asked why he came so boldly in,
'I've come a-courtin',' says Tom o' Lynn.

Tom o' Lynn went to church to be wed,
The bride followed after, she hung down her head,
She hung down her cheeks, she hung down her chin.
'Her beauty is rare,' says Tom o' Lynn.

Tom o' Lynn's house had no door,
With the sky for a roof and a bog for a floor.
'They's a way to jump in and a way to swim out,
'Oh, very convenient' says Tom o' Lynn.

Tom drove his sheep into a manger,
Went home and his wife was abed with a stranger.
The night was chilly, the quilt was thin.
'Make room in the middle,' says Tom o' Lynn.

Tom, his wife, and his wife's mother,
They all fell into the fire together.
Them that lay neathmost got a hot skin.
'We are warm enough now,' says Tom o' Lynn.

John picked up his recorder and played through the tune one more time. Then he put the recorder in his lap and looked at William. "I love that old song," he said. "I can't decide whether Tom is no philosopher at all, or the best philosopher of the pack. Tom doesn't let the world wear him down. For him, the glass is not only half full, its full to the brim. Tom takes the world as he finds it—through thick and thin."

"That's about enough of that," said Thomas. "You're wearing me out, John."

They all chuckled and sat quietly for a while, and then they bedded down for the night.

The next morning, as Jim-Bird made ready to take his leave, William walked over to say good-bye.

"I saved a treat for your dogs," William said. He held a small strip of jerked venison over Binkie's head. She instantly knew what was in his hand and jumped up as high as William's waist and snapped the morsel out of his fingers. Then Tazzie, a stickler for fair play, saw a treat of his own in the offing and ran over and jumped into the air just as high and snapped up his own piece of jerky.

William reached down to pet them, but they were concentrating on chewing their tough pieces of meat and wanted nothing to do with him.

"Well, my friend," William said to Jim-Bird, "we've had quite a time this season. I will miss your company."

"Carolina is a small world," said Jim-Bird. "We'll meet again. If you are ever in Four Hole Swamp, ask around for me in the Indian camp. If I'm not there, they can tell you where to find me."

"And if you're in Charles Town," William said, "come to the Packsaddle Tavern and ask for me." He laughed. "If I'm not there, they can tell you where to find me."

The two men shook hands, and Jim-Bird mounted his horse. He waved to the others, and then rode off, with Tazzie and Binkie taking the lead.

"This is what he's been waiting for," said Sam. "To get back to that Natchez girl in Four Hole Swamp."

The rest of them rounded up the packtrain and rode on to Charles Town, arriving there in the middle of the afternoon. They had been just over two weeks on the trail and were glad to have reached the comforts of town. They were in high spirits as they offloaded their bundles of skins at Crockatt's warehouse. Sam remained behind to see that all was accounted for, while John, William, and Thomas took the horses back out King Street to the horse-pen.

At the pen William attended to his packhorses, and then he stood back and looked all around. There was nothing more to do. His work was done. He stood a moment longer and then turned away and went over and mounted Viola to head on over to the Packsaddle Tavern.

"We'll see you there for supper, Billy," John called out.

"Don't start without us," said Thomas.

"Maybe Delilah will cook us up some turtle soup," said William. He waved at his friends, prodded Viola with his heels, and set off up the broad, sandy street. It felt like home.

Notes

The map of William MacGregor's travels is closely based on George Hunter's manuscript map of the Cherokee Nation and the Traders' Path from Charles Town via Congaree, 1730. (Library of Congress, Faden Collection, No. 6). The map in the front of this present volume was designed and drawn by John Chamblee.

Chapter 2. "If the Heart of a Man Is Depressed with Cares" is from John Gay, *The Beggar's Opera,* Brian Loughrey and T. O. Treadwell, eds. (London: Penguin Books, 1986), 72. The best recording is the Hyperion CD by The Broadside Band, Jeremy Barlow, director.

John Coleman's poem about Charles Town is quoted from Walter Edgar's *South Carolina: A History* (Columbia: University of South Carolina Press, 1998), 155. The poem is dated 1769 but it applies as well for 1735.

"Barbados fever" is an early term for yellow fever.

Chapter 4. For the use of whips to drive livestock, see the movie *The Man from Snowy River.*

Chapter 5. For William MacGregor's edition of Shakespeare's works, see Andrew Murphy, *Shakespeare in Print: A History and Chronology of Shakespeare Publishing* (Cambridge: Cambridge University Press, 2003), 64–69.

A recording of "Green Stockings" may be heard on the CD *The Musitians of Grope Lane,* The City Waites, Musica Oscura.

"A Lusty Young Smith at his Vice Stood a Filing" is from Thomas D'Urfey's *Pills to Purge Melancholy, 1719–1720,* vol. 4, 195. A recording may be heard on the CD *The Musitians of Grope Lane.*

Chapter 6. It must be observed that in the late seventeenth and early eighteenth centuries, pineland savannahs (treeless areas for grazing cattle) occurred on both sides of the Savannah River. "Savannah" in this sense is a word brought in from the Spanish Caribbean much earlier than the earliest appearance of the Shawnee Indians in South Carolina.

At the time of earliest European exploration, longleaf pine forest covered about 60 million acres in the lower South, and it was mixed in with other trees in about an additional 30 million acres. Today, longleaf pines grow in the South on less than 3 million acres, and only about 12,000 acres of old growth longleaf forest remains. This dwarfs current deforestation figures for Amazonia.

Chapter 7. A hog "crawl" is thought to be an Anglicization of "corral," perhaps a borrowed word from Jamaica.

Chapter 10. "Man Is for the Woman Made" is from *Pills*, vol. 3, 223.

Chapters 12 and 13. The sexual riddles are from Annikki Kaivola-Bregenhøj, "Sexual Riddles: The Test of the Listener," *Elektroloristi*, 1/1997, vol. 4, 1, 8.

In the eighteenth century, "cony" rhymed with "honey," and more to the point, with "cunny," i.e., a slang word for vagina. Hence, as pronounced, "cony" and "cunny" sounded the same. "Cunny" is a diminutive of "cunt," which derives from ancient Indo-European root words. Rabbits are not native to Britain and are not mentioned earlier than the Norman conquest, at which time they were perhaps introduced to Britain. Hence, English speakers evidently borrowed an ancestral form of "cony" from French invaders.

In the eighteenth century English speakers began pronouncing "cony" to rhyme with "boney." Today "cony" has given way to "rabbit," and "cony" is now rarely used by English speakers.

Chapter 13. "The Witch of Glen Gyle" is closely based on the story "The Witch of Laggan" in Sir George Douglas (ed.), *Scottish Folk and Fairy Tales* (New York: A. L. Burt Co., n.d.), Dover offprint, 2000, 221–227.

"Stone Dress" is closely based on James Mooney, *Myths of the Cherokee*, Nineteenth Annual Report of the Bureau of American Ethnology (Washington, D.C.: GPO, 1900), 316–319.

Chapter 14. William's telling the story of Romeo and Juliet to Otter Queen was inspired by Laura Bohannon's essay "Shakespeare in the Bush," much read by students in introductory anthropology courses taught by college teachers of my generation.

Chapter 16. John Coleman's riddle song is based on Child ballad number 1, "Riddles Wisely Expounded." Francis James Child (ed.), *The English and Scottish Popular Ballads* (New York: Houghton, Mifflin, 1884), vol. 1, 1–6.

Chapter 21. Old Fox's divinatory diagnosis is based on James Mooney, "The Cherokee River Cult," *The Journal of American Folk-Lore* 13 (1900):1–10, and Frans M. Olbrechts, "Some Cherokee Methods of Divination," *Proceedings of the 23rd International Congress of Americanists* (1930), 547–552.

Chapter 22. "Fair Margaret and Sweet William" closely follows a version of Child ballad number 74. Child (ed.), *The English and Scottish Popular Ballads*, vol. 2, 199–203. A beautiful version of this song can be heard on the CD *Jean Ritchie Ballads from her Appalachian Family Tradition*, Smithsonian Folkway Recordings.

Versions of "Tom o' Lynn" go back to the sixteenth century. This version is loosely based on "Tommy Linn" in Joseph Ritson, *The North Country Chorister*, 1810. This song has seldom been recorded, though Oscar Brand recorded a version of it as "Tom Bolynn" on his album *Bawdy Songs and Backroom Ballads* in 1957.

Selected References

Bartram, William. *The Travels of William Bartram.* Francis Harper, ed. New Haven: Yale University Press, 1958.

Boniface, J. J. *The Cavalry Horse and His Pack.* Kansas City: Hudson-Kimberly Publishing, 1903.

Bowne, Eric E. *The Westo Indians: Slave Traders of the Early Colonial South.* Tuscaloosa: The University of Alabama Press, 2005.

Braund, Kathryn E. Holland. *Deerskins and Duffels: The Creek Indian Trade with Anglo-America, 1685–1815.* Lincoln: University of Nebraska Press, 1993.

Crane, Verner W. *The Southern Frontier, 1670–1732.* Durham: Duke University Press, 1928.

Devine, T. M. *The Scottish Nation, 1700–2000.* New York, London: Penguin Books, 1999.

Early, Lawrence S. *Looking for Longleaf: The Fall and Rise of an American Forest.* Chapel Hill: The University of North Carolina Press, 2004.

Edgar, Walter. *South Carolina: A History.* Columbia: University of South Carolina Press, 1998.

Harper, Jared Vincent. "The Adoption and Use of the Horse among the Southeastern Indians." *Tennessee Anthropologist* 5 (1980):26–32.

Hill, Sarah H. *Weaving New Worlds: Southeastern Cherokee Women and Their Basketry.* Chapel Hill: The University of North Carolina Press, 1997.

Hoose, Phillip. *The Race to Save the Lord God Bird.* New York: Farrar, Straus, and Giroux, 2004.

Hudson, Charles. *The Southeastern Indians.* Knoxville: University of Tennessee Press, 1976.

———. *Conversations with the High Priest of Coosa.* Chapel Hill: University of North Carolina Press, 2003.

Jordan, Terry G. *North American Cattle-Ranching Frontiers: Origins, Diffusion, and Differentiation.* Albuquerque: University of New Mexico Press, 1993.

Murray, W. H. *Rob Roy MacGregor: His Life and Times.* Edinburgh: Canongate, 1982.

Oatis, Stephen J. *A Colonial Complex: South Carolina's Frontiers in the Era of the Yamasee War.* Lincoln: University of Nebraska Press, 2004.

Perdue, Theda. *Cherokee Women: Gender and Culture Change, 1700–1835*. Lincoln: University of Nebraska Press, 1998.

Post, Charles Johnson. *Horse Packing: A Manual of Horse Transportation*. Reprint, New York: Skyhorse Publishing, 2007. First published 1914.

Reid, John Phillip. *A Law of Blood: The Primitive Law of the Cherokee Nation*. New York: New York University Press, 1970.

Richards, Matt. *Deerskins into Buckskins: How to Tan with Natural Materials*. Cave Junction, Oregon: Backcountry Publishing, 2002.

Rogers, George C. *Charleston in the Age of the Pinckneys*. Columbia: University of South Carolina Press, 1969.